CW00847975

Books by Derek Power

*Filthy Henry Novels*

Filthy Henry: The Fairy Detective
The Impossible Victim
Accidental Legend
Stolen Stories

Derek Power

# Stolen Stories

A Filthy Henry Novel

ISBN-13: 978-1987608502
ISBN-10:198760850X

For O, the real life Elivin,
for T, quickly following in his sister's footsteps
and for K, who makes all the magic happen for real.

## *Foreword:*

Another Filthy Henry novel, another foreword. They are starting to become a habit.

As I mentioned at the start of 'Accidental Legend' there were a few side characters in the story that came about as suggestions from attendees at Dublin Comic Con 2015.

When I returned a year later to the convention I figured why not run the same little contest again. Three people and their little made up quirks were selected as the winners, at random, to be turned into some little side characters for 'Stolen Stories'.

A big thanks to **Carolyn Griffin, Andrew Kerins** and **Bosco Burns.** While the characters are only small I like to think they add a touch of 'real' to the story.

Now if it only didn't take me so long to write the story...

# Chapters

# Chapter One

Becky watched rain rivulets running down the outside of the coffee shop window, each droplet moving like a drunken toddler, as she pondered things. Like how the weather could be perfectly in sync with a person's crappy mood. An external reflection of her heart-wrenchingly awful internal feelings. Becky, however, did not mind that it had started raining the minute her boyfriend broke up with her. As she left the office where they both worked, the rain splashing on her face helped mask the tears.

Every cloud had a depressing lining. All you had to do was look hard enough.

She had wandered through Dublin city aimlessly for nearly half an hour, the rain doing its very best to work into her bones, and let the tears flow. After her fifth sneeze, Becky figured getting out of the rain would be a healthy move. The warm, inviting, coffee shop had beckoned her like a grumpy moth to a caffeinated flame. It was completely empty, with the exception of a man sitting by himself at a table and two members of staff. Becky stepped inside and traipsed over to a corner booth by the window, dripping rain water down onto the brown tiles. As the young waitress came over to take her order, Becky smiled apologetically and looked down at the puddle of water forming by her feet.

"Bad day?" the girl asked.

"The sort they make movies about," Becky replied, taking some napkins from the dispenser on the table and dabbing at her eyes. "Can I just get a coffee, please? Maybe a tea towel, if you have one to spare. I'm sure I've got Panda Eyes."

The girl smiled, politely nodded her head, and walked back towards the order counter. If there was one thing all women understood, it was how nobody deserved to have Panda Eyes. Why make-up companies could not create a mascara that just stayed in place until the wearer desired it to be removed was one of Life's Great Mysteries. The company that came out with that product would, in Becky's view, be raking the cash in. Basically printing money! It was true that some companies claimed they had already cracked the secret, but it was easy disprove such claims. All you had to do was find a heartbroken woman at three a.m. in any night club toilet, then you would have all the proof required to refute the big companies.

Becky turned and stared out the window, left alone with her thoughts and heartache.

It would not have been so bad if Barry had at least given her a valid reason. For the past three years they had been referred to as 'B&B', because when it came to couple names you could always count on your friends to come up with dreadful ones. Everything had been great. Fantastic even. Then, suddenly, out of the blue, Barry decided that he wanted to go and count snowflakes in Antarctica. Unless Antarctica was the name of the new Spanish exchange student that had moved into the apartment two floors down, Becky found it to be a horrible excuse. Not that Antarctica from Spain was a more acceptable excuse, but it was slightly more believable. But Barry, apparently, had made his mind up, and nothing she said seemed likely to make him change it. After two hours of tears, battling with the desire to take up the coffee pot and smash it into his face, Becky had figured leaving the kitchen at the office was the only way forward.

She was annoyed, both at Barry and herself. Him, for being a stereotypical male that did nothing but think about himself and his selfish needs. Her, for letting emotions get in the way of logical thinking and airing their private matters at work for all to hear and see.

Also for not smashing the coffee pot into his lame, stupid, handsome face. She was really annoyed at that.

Becky had been in a better position at the company than Barry for years. If he wanted to break up with her, with somebody who had a blossoming career, well that was his own idiotic mistake to make.

But now, alone with her thoughts, Becky had nothing to distract her. There was only so much staring at the rain on a pane of glass a person could do. After that, your mind kicked back in and started to do what it did best: think. Think about all the reasons that not having Barry in her life was going to be bad. Trying to figure out what she could change about herself to win him back.

Even though there was absolutely nothing wrong with her to begin with! This was all Barry's fault, making her question … everything.

From the corner of her eye, Becky saw a mug of coffee placed down on the table. Followed by another and two plates with some apple tart on each. The other chair in the booth suddenly gained an occupant, an occupant who put some forks and napkins down beside the mugs of coffee. Becky turned back in her seat and looked at the new arrival.

"Sorry," she said, dabbing at her eyes again to dry up the tears. "I think you have the wrong booth."

"Oh, not at all," the new arrival said. "When a man sees a pretty lady like yourself crying all alone in a coffee shop, well the least he can do is bring over some cake."

Becky frowned at this rather random, albeit nice, statement and smiled at the man seated across from her. He reached out and pulled one of the slices of tart towards him, Becky noticing that he had on those blue medical gloves usually worn by doctors during examinations with patients.

"What's with the gloves?" she asked, looking back over her shoulder quickly to make sure the waitress was still able to see her.

17

The girl was standing behind the cashier counter, reading something on her phone. She glanced up at Becky, smiled, then returned to whatever was on the device's screen. At least she was still there, which was good. Becky may have grown up in Dublin but that did not mean she fully trusted randomly kind strangers. You always had to keep your wits about you when out in the city, even your home city. Even when dealing with the elderly sort, or the middle-aged sort.

It was very hard to guess the man's age.

"Oh, these," the man said. "They are just because I have a really bad cold at the minute. I'm trying this new thing were I don't go out in public without these gloves. Read it online, it is meant to help your immune system because you are touching less things with new germs."

Becky picked up her mug of coffee in both hands and slowly sipped it. What the man had said was not the dumbest idea in the world. It was, however, a slightly creepy looking one. After all, who walked around in public wearing surgical gloves? Except maybe a surgeon running to get something on their way to the operating theatre. She eyed the cake with a little suspicion.

"If you wouldn't mind," she said. "I'd rather be on my own."

"Oh?" the man said, his expression one of confusion. "Why is that? You look upset. Surely being on your own isn't the best idea right now."

She lowered the coffee cup and turned to look out the window again.

"It is for me," Becky said. "I just want to be alone for a bit. Probably longer, once I settle my thoughts and stop imagining Barry's stupid face being smashed into a wall."

The man put his fork down on the plate, placed his hands on top of each other, and stared at Becky. She could feel his stare, like he was trying to see through to her brain. After a few seconds, Becky looked back and met his gaze with silence. Wanting to make it perfectly clear that his company was no longer needed.

She matched his stare and saw two jet-black eyes looking back at her. Two eyes that seemed to have little sparks of red light flickering in them. In the actual eyeballs themselves, rather than reflected light from some external source. Eyes which gave the impression they had seen things, lots of things, over many years.

It was hypnotic looking into them.

"My name is Séan," he said.

"Becky," Becky said, although she was not entirely sure why. It just seemed right to volunteer the information, polite even.

"Have you ever heard that a problem shared is a problem halved?" Séan asked, his voice slightly changed so it sounded deeper somehow. Almost like it was coming from far away. "Tell me your problem, Becky. Tell me your story."

#

Linda Faul sat down on the ancient swivel chair at the nurses' station and let out a huge sigh, closing her eyes in the process and leaning her head against the wall. From the chair a matching, if somewhat unsettling, sigh came as air wheezed through a gap in the material. It was a chair long overdue an introduction to a rubbish tip, but budgetary constraints ensured its continued survival. Much to the chagrin of the nursing staff.

It had been a long shift and the horrible clock on the wall, with its round face and black numbers, told her there was still one whole hour to go. Which could not possibly be right because the shift already felt like it had been a double. The clock had to be lying, it was the only thing that made sense. She checked the pocket watch attached to her nurses uniform by a little pin and saw it agreed with the clock on the wall.

There really was still an hour to go.

"Bloody things are in cahoots," she said to nobody in particular.

The shift had started off quietly enough, or as quiet as things could get in St. Patrick's Hospital. Thankfully the Hollywood depiction of mental hospitals was just the stuff of fiction. Here, helping the patient was the top priority for all the medical staff, doctors and nurses alike, in order to get them back out into the world happy and healthy. St. Patrick's offered the creature comforts of any hospital in modern day Ireland. Large white common area rooms with the smell of antiseptic heavy in the air, clean pyjamas, fresh bed linens and enough hospital grade food to make everyone want to get better faster purely for an improved diet. The patients were allowed to spend their days in the common room doing whatever kept them happy, provided it was safe and did not harm anybody, or they could go out into the garden area and enjoy some confined nature.

Even still, you got into a certain routine about things after a while. The patients were part of that routine, their little quirks becoming something you just accepted. Like how drinking on a school-night was a bad idea.

Such as Carolyn Griffin with her love of geocaching, that outdoor activity that involved hiding things for other geocachers to find. Not that geocaching was a bad thing, after all any hobby that got people out walking more was viewed as a good one by all in the medical profession. It was just that Carolyn was slightly obsessed with the activity. To the point that she spent nearly every waking moment at it. Each morning Linda would have to wait while Carolyn completed the geocaching of her bedroom. An act that included the geocaching of previously geocached things. There was no harm in it, it just was part of the ritual to get Carolyn to come down for breakfast with the other patients.

Patients who would have had their breakfasts geocached if Carolyn had anything to do with it.

Then there was Andrew Kerins. Andrew had been in the

hospital for well over a year and, to Linda at least, really should not have been in St. Patrick's. As near as anyone who dealt with him could tell, he had self-admitted. Even all the paperwork said that Andrew had just walked in off the street one day and filled out the forms on his own. The reason for his admittance: claiming he was from Cork and should be locked up as a result. A strange reason to demand a room in a mental health hospital, Linda figured. She had been to Cork a few times on holidays. It was a wonderful county in the southernmost part of Ireland. Hailing from it hardly seemed like a reason to be concerned for one's mental state.

Although Corkonians, people who hailed from county Cork, did have that whole "The People's Republic of Cork" thing going on. Anyone who subscribed to this concept fully believed that Cork, not Dublin, was the true capital of Ireland. Maybe that was something Andrew wanted to get treated for. Two competing geographical capitals not being something a human mind could accept.

But St. Patrick's was a not-for-profit hospital that would treat anyone and everybody who needed treating, regardless of the symptoms they presented with. Although Andrew and Carolyn were on the easier end of the spectrum when it came to dealing with patients. Dreams for any nurse to work with. It was the other sort that gave Linda the chills. The ones who were seen to by Dr. Brendan Milton.

The Blank Slates.

They started to show up roughly one month before Dr. Milton had joined the staff at St. Patrick's. Patients were brought in by family members most of the time, random members of the public on rare occasions. People who were physically healthy, not injured in any way or showing signs of external trauma or damage. Yet they were, for want of a better term, blank.

It was like a strange amnesia. The person could speak, move, knew how to feed themselves and use the bathroom, but they had

21

no personal memories at all. Nothing. Zero. Zilch. If they were a mobile phone it was like they had been reset to factory conditions. Everything still worked as expected, just you had to redo all the settings and information contained within.

Medically speaking this was possible. Long-term memory could be broken down into three basic groups, any of which could be hit with amnesia. There was semantic memory, which was all about association and meaning. You knew an apple was food because you had a memory associating it with food. Then you had procedural, or muscle, memory. Basically, the reason why it seemed like a person's fingers knew their password without having to first think about the password. Finally you had episodic memory, memories created based on a person's experience in life. Essentially the memories that made a person who they were.

This type of long-term memory, the episodic stuff, was what each of the Blank Slates mysteriously lacked. All the semantic and procedural stuff remained intact, but memories about who they were were completely missing.

All the staff at St. Patrick's could do was put The Blank Slates into the same ward and see about helping them recover their memories. The problem was they kept showing up. One or two cases was nothing too concerning, strange, true, but not the sign of a countrywide problem. But the last count of patients had nearly twenty of them in the hospital. Twenty people with absolutely no memory of anything they had done for their entire life. Twenty people ranging in various ages.

Twenty Blank Slates.

A name the nursing staff had started to call patients with the strange condition.

There was not a lot of work involved caring for them. How could there be? The Blank Slates had no preferences for anything at all. They did not know what food they liked or disliked. If they enjoyed watching movies or reading books. Being too hot or too cold was not a thing they even spoke about. They just sat in the common room, at the tables and chairs, watching everyone around them with interest.

All except for Quinn.

Quinn arrived at the hospital five weeks ago, brought in by an ambulance crew who had found him wandering around St. Stephen's Green dazed and confused. It had taken three of the grounds-keepers for Stephen's Green nearly half an hour to corner him, eventually resorting to a technique usually reserved for capturing stray dogs. They fanned out and showed him tasty treats while calling to him in a soothing voice. When he had arrived at the hospital, Quinn was like all of the other Blank Slates. Except he could remember his first name. Since there was no form of identification on him, such as a passport or driver's license, the nurses had just taken it at face value and admitted him under the name 'Quinn'. Another Blank Slate to be assigned to Dr. Milton's care.

The other patients all had their proper names associated with them through a combination of identification they arrived with, or family and friends coming to the hospital to identify them. But Quinn was just Quinn, no last name needed. Nobody even came looking for him.

He was an oddity in a sea of curiosity.

Linda straightened up in her seat, rolled it over on four broken wheels to some papers at the far end of the desk, and began completing the daily logs. Two knuckle taps on the counter-top got her attention. She looked up and saw Quinn smiling down at her.

When Quinn had been admitted to the hospital the staff made some best guesses at his information, such as his age. He looked like a healthy individual in his mid-thirties, but with a shocking amount of grey hair amongst the ginger. That was not an indicator of how old he was, though, because ginger hair tended to go grey quicker than most other colours. Shaving was something that had not happened since coming to the hospital, so now he sported a lovely beard. At least it was the attempt at a lovely beard. Quinn seemed to be one of those men afflicted with facial bald spots, making his beard look more like a hamster graveyard glued to his face.

"Howdy," he said.

Nurse Faul smiled and stood up, leaning forward so that she could rest her folded arms on the counter-top.

"I was just thinking about you," Linda said.

"I bet you were," Quinn replied. "Writing me into your dirty novel again are you?"

Linda laughed and shook her head.

That was another strange thing about Quinn. He had no personal memories, but could be funny when the situation presented itself. Almost as if the personality reset had only partially worked on him. It was the strangest of the strange cases they had to deal with when it came to The Blank Slates.

"Would you behave," she said. "Besides, you know me. I hate reading books, boring collections of dead tree parts is all they are. Why in God's name would I spend my limited spare time writing one of the bloody things? What can I do for you? You know you aren't meant to be down here unless one of us brings you along."

Quinn nodded his head, then looked up and down the hallway to see if anybody was paying the nurses station any attention. He leaned closer and gave her a conspiratorial wink.

"Any chance of an extra jelly pot?"

Since arriving at St. Patrick's, Quinn had fast become their biggest eater. He packed away food like a hungry child and never seemed to put on any weight at all. If anything, Linda thought he had started to lose weight somehow. The problem was Quinn clearly knew which of the nurses were the easy marks. The ones who would fall for his charms.

On the desk the intercom buzzed. Linda held up a finger in front of Quinn's face, indicating she needed him to be silent for a minute, then pressed the button down on the speaker.

"Nurse Faul," she spoke into the intercom mic.

"Hi, yes, thank you," Dr. Milton's voice said from the speaker. "I was wondering if you could, you know, do your job and bring me my next patient."

Linda slowly counted to ten. It was the age-old problem of working in the medical profession. Some doctors seemed to think that nurses were just educated gophers. Go for this, go for that. Not all of them, but then the ones who did hold this view of the world seemed dead set on making up for the ones who treated nurses with respect. Plus, Linda was not entirely sure how she felt about Dr. Milton. Fluid, as the other members of the nursing staff had nicknamed him. A joke based on the cleaning product with which he shared a name.

She let out a low breath, calming herself.

"Who were you meant to see next?"

"The one who has a name," he said, his voice crackling on the speaker. "Quinn. I'm running a little late, just back into the office. No time to be doing the collecting part of the job."

"I'll bring him right down, doctor," Linda said.

The line disconnected with Fluid not saying another word.

"Did you know you had an appointment with him now?" she asked Quinn.

"Dunno," he said. "I have a bad memory, remember? So...about that extra jelly pot?"

Linda walked around the counter of the desk and cupped

Quinn's right elbow in her hand. She gently started to guide him down the hallway, in the direction of Fluid's office.

"Check under your pillow after this consultation," she said. "Least I can do to help you out after dealing with that jerk."

#

According to somebody, presumably a customer, the customer is always right. This is something that leans heavily in favour of the customer when it comes to goods and services. A customer can feel they have the right to complain that the sky-blue jeans they bought are the wrong shade of sky-blue. They had not desired the clear-sky-blue sky-blue jeans but wanted the April-sky-blue sky-blue ones. Maybe the customer would take umbrage with the tepidness of a glass of tap water or the shape of an ice-cube.

Being right is a slightly subjective thing. Everyone thinks they are right but only one side of an argument can really be the correct side. Meaning the other side, eventually, had to accept they might be wrong.

Either that or continue to live in a world of disagreement.

Leo was wondering which side of the 'the customer is always right' argument he currently sat on at that moment.

While true the coffee shop was hardly busy, the woman in the booth had not ordered anything for the better part of two hours. In fact, she had not done much of anything in the last two hours. In front of her sat a freshly poured cup of coffee, courtesy of Claire topping up the woman's empty mug. Even when the fresh coffee had been poured there had been very little reaction. She simply looked up at Claire, smiled, then turned and stared down at the coffee as if it was the first time ever seeing such a beverage.

"Do I like this?" she had asked Claire.

"I think so," Claire replied, confused. "You ordered it when you came in. Don't get many people coming in here and ordering

26

something they don't like. Is your friend going to come back later? I can freshen up his cup too."

The woman had just stared up at Claire blankly, smiled again, then turned and looked out the window. An hour later, no change.

"She hasn't said or done anything else since?" Leo asked Claire.

The waitress shook her head.

"Nothing at all. The guy who had been over talking with her got up and left after finishing his tart..."

"He paid first, right?" Leo said, glancing at the cash register.

"Yes, he paid first, God in heaven," Claire said. "Anyway, it was only after he left, maybe an hour or so, that I noticed your one hadn't moved. That's the third mug of coffee I've put in front of her. The other two just went cold."

Leo looked over at the glass coffee jugs on the hot plates.

"You sure she didn't touch the previous two? 'Cause we could just..."

"Leo! I'm not tipping cold coffee back into the jugs to reheat it. That's disgusting!"

"Fine, fine," he said, waving his arms in the air. "Just, coffee doesn't grow on trees. You know?"

Claire pulled out her phone from its temporary home in her apron pocket and started to tap on the screen. After a second she turned the device around so that Leo could read the screen.

"Yes, it does," she said, tapping at a search result. "You are so cheap it isn't even funny."

"Whatever," Leo said, waving his hand at her dismissively. He pulled out his phone, ran a figure over the cracked screen to unlock it, and started to tap on it himself. "You can find any old answer on the internet if you look hard enough."

"You're not even opening an app to browse the web," Claire said, looking at his phone. "Also didn't you just get that phone?"

"I don't have a lot of luck with them," Leo said, holding the phone out at arms length so he could read the text.

Why they made the font so small he could never figure out. Big screens, small letters.

"As in you just got it yesterday," Claire said. "How did you break a phone in less than twenty-four hours?"

Leo pressed a button on the side of the phone, secretly delighted that he knew it locked the screen again, and put the phone back in his rear pocket. The same pocket it had been in when Leo sat down, cracking the screen in the process.

He looked over at the woman in the booth and pondered.

Technically she had been a paying customer, so sitting in the booth was one of her customer-based rights. The issue Leo had was based on how long that purchase entitled her to sit in the booth. Surely there had to be a 'Stature of Limitations' when it came to things like loitering in a coffee shop.

Particularly after milking them for all the free refills you could get.

"Is she okay, do you reckon?"

Claire glanced up from her mobile phone.

"Dunno. Been crying, definitely. Face is all make-up smudged and what not. I reckon she got the shove. Hasn't cried in the last while though. Must be all cried out."

Leo sighed and slowly shook his head.

"I'm going over to her."

He took a cup down from the shelf over the brewing

machines, poured himself a cup of coffee, then walked around the counter and over to the booth. Without speaking to the woman, he slid into the seat opposite her and sat down.

She did not even register his arrival. It was like she was in her own little world.

Leo decided to break the ice by doing the one thing that annoyed most people. He took a loud, bubbling, slurp from his drink and slapped his lips a few times before putting the mug down on the table.

The woman turned and stared at him. It was a strange sort of stare; one which Leo had never seen before. Her eyes focused on him, taking in all the details, but not doing anything with the information. As if the lights were on in her mental home but it was devoid of all occupants.

"Everything alright?" he asked her. "Just, you've been sitting here for a while and haven't done a whole bunch of anything. Miss…?"

"I don't know," she said.

"Don't know what? Don't know if everything is alright?"

The woman shook her head slowly.

"No, not that. Although I suppose I don't know the answer to that as well. You were going to ask me my name. I don't know my name."

Leo raised an eyebrow at this statement.

"You don't know your…name? Did you hit your head after coming in here or something? Because that's on you if you did. I'm not libel for injuries on the premises before you make a purchase."

She pursed her lips and tilted her head to the left, a thoughtful look on her face.

"I don't know," the woman said. "Honestly I don't know a whole lot of anything up until that lovely girl brought me over some coffee. Did I order coffee? Do I like coffee? The girl who brought it along didn't seem to know."

"I think we need to get you some help," Leo said, frowning. "Something obviously isn't right here."

The woman nodded at that statement.

"I agree. Except...where are we exactly? Plus, how come you think something isn't right?"

Leo never proclaimed to be a great business man, but he was sure when it came to customer service you were obligated to get medical help in situations like this.

He pulled out his battered phone from his jeans pocket, unlocked it with a swipe of his finger on the shattered screen and dialled the emergency services.

#

Dr. Brendan Milton watched the pendulum swing back and forth beneath the wall clock and smiled.

It was amazing how the human mind found the repetitive motion of something swinging back and forth a short distance calming. Put a person in a quiet room with nothing but a pendulum clock to entertain them and the result was always the same. The person would watch the clock, letting their eyes move left and right, while their mind emptied of all thought.

This was one of the main reasons Dr. Milton had gotten a pendulum clock installed in his office. It hung on the wall, just inside the door, positioned in such a way that whoever lay on the examination sofa had full view of it. His own desk was angled away from the clock, so that he could observe the patient. Most of his sessions with a patient began exactly the same, by saying nothing. The nurse would bring in the patient, Milton would wave towards the sofa, the patient would sit down on the edge and lean back. When the nurse left the room the patient usually watched the door close behind them, then stare at the clock.

Such a simple setup and it practically hypnotised the person. All with no effort from Milton.

It gave him time to read over the case notes and formulate how the session would go. A lot of other psychologists would usually prepare their sessions well in advance, or at least have a rough idea of how the conversation would begin. Dr. Flynn, the other attending psychologist at the hospital, frequently boasted about all the preparation work he did at home. Milton, however, saw each session as an opportunity to study the mental afflictions of his patient in the here and now. The notes were more for his benefit than the person needing help. If, at the end of the day, he somehow had improved things for the patient that was just a bonus in Milton's eyes. The primary purpose of these sessions was to enrich his own understanding of the human psyche, to further his place in the world.

Quinn, the current patient dropped off by Nurse Whatshername, lay on the sofa staring at the clock. His hands rested on his chest, fingers interlaced. The man could have easily just been at home watching television, he seemed so at ease. As a Blank Slate he was definitely one of the more interesting, for multiple reasons.

Dr. Brendan Milton had been dealing with the Blank Slates for a couple of months now and they all shared a common, fascinating, trait. They lacked any proper memories of their own. Surprisingly they seemed to retain all their education through life. Whatever language they commonly spoke in they still had full mastery of, some of them even slipping into other languages they had learned on rare occasions. Survival instincts remained intact as none of them had yet tried to put their hand in a boiling cup of water or lick an electrical socket. They just, en masse, had no personal memories. No names. No history.

Except for Quinn.

He had presented with very similar symptoms to the others, except Quinn could recall his name. At least when the nurse on handling admissions had asked for one Quinn did not hesitate in answering. Although it seemed that he only remembered his first name. Jokingly, the nurse had filled in the surname slot with the old 'Doe' adage, making him Quinn Doe. Aside from the Blank Slates who were brought in by a family member, or arrived with a valid form of identification on them, Blank Slates were assigned names at random.

Dr. Milton tided up the papers on his desk, opened his notepad to a new page, and smiled at Quinn.

"Shall we begin?" he asked.

"What's up, doc?" Quinn replied, miming a cigar in front of his lips that he wiggled in the air.

"Do you remember who I am? Have we met before?"

Quinn considered the question.

"Yes," he answered. "I've been coming here for a couple of weeks. In fact you ask the same question each time."

Milton smiled at the answer and jotted down some notes. Keeping track of what the Blank Slates said was important, it allowed him to gauge if their memories were returning. Any sort of improvements were important and had to be dealt with accordingly.

"So, you don't remember me from any other place? From a time before you arrived at the hospital?"

Quinn slowly shook his head.

"Nope. But then I don't remember anything else either, so if we ever had met outside the hospital I couldn't tell you."

Milton wrote down some more notes in his notepad.

"Nurse Faul promised to sneak me an extra jelly pot later,"

Quinn said. "She is nice. The other day she said she could see the fairy creatures Bosco was babbling on about. Something about a man turning into a duck on the front lawn. Although I'm fairly certain she was just playing along to keep him happy. She does see things that I see though, sometimes. At least when I talk to her about them she doesn't seem to just be playing along with me."

Dr. Milton frowned at this. Sometimes gossip came to him from the patients, because they overheard things the nurses said. Topics that the nurses probably did not think would be remembered by people with memory issues. This was how Milton learned about the nickname given to him by the nursing staff. A stupid play on words because of his surname.

Fluid, because his surname was Milton. Making him Milton Fluid, just like the brand of sterilising products. Hilarious stuff.

The intelligence of others, or lack thereof, amazed him sometimes.

Still, getting such information from the patients during a session was always useful. It never hurt to understand what the people you worked with talked about when a person was not around.

"Does she now?" Milton said. "How often has Nurse Faul said she has seen your fairy creatures?"

Sitting up a little on the sofa, Quinn looked over at Milton confused.

"No, she never says she sees the fairy folk with me," he said. "She sees things. Things that I see as well, but I can't figure out."

This was new.

"Such as?"

Quinn tugged on his bottom lip and settled back down on the sofa.

"Just things. Like people having improvements and then

suddenly they go back to square one. Things like that. I said to her I remembered something that might help, but she doesn't think it will. At least I think I said it to her..."

Milton adjusted the tie around his neck slightly, loosening it.

"What did you think would be needed to help with...whatever it is Nurse Faul is also seeing?"

"Not a 'what', more of a 'who',' Quinn said, making air quotes as he spoke.

"A who?"

"Or maybe a 'whom'? I never like that word though. Whom. You say it and it makes you sound like an owl with a blocked beak."

Milton pinched the bridge of his nose.

"Who do you think would help?"

"The fairy detective," Quinn said.

Dropping his pen on the tabletop, Dr. Milton sat upright in his seat.

"Is this another of your fairy creature things?" he asked.

Quinn shook his head from side to side.

"Nope. Just somebody that I reckon will be able to help me recover my memories. I need to get in touch with the fairy detective."

# Chapter Two

During his time serving in the *Garda* Síochána, Ireland's peacekeeping police force, Garda Bob Downy had seen some strange things. Preventing or investigating crimes was never going to be a boring job, everyone knew that. If the daily activities did not involve patrolling the streets, to let the public know they were being protected, then you could be guaranteed of at least one surprise cardio workout. The 'surprise' part being because shoplifters never had the courtesy to let people know in advance when they might steal something. Other crimes occurred as well, of course. Ranging from break-ins to, thankfully infrequent, suspicious deaths. These were all events covered during a new recruit's training, which went a long way to preparing a Garda for when they encountered such crimes out in the field. But in Ireland, in fact anywhere in world, there was always going to be an edge-case that all the years of training never prepared a member of the police force for.

Luckily, depending on how you viewed such things, Bob Downy was well versed in edge-cases when it came to strange things the Guards had to work on. This was, primarily, down to the fact that Downy was not a typical Garda. He was a Leerling. A race of fairy creatures who could change between human form and that of a swan. For years they had operated as magical couriers to the fairy people. Then, as humans formed services such as the police force or the healthcare system, Leerlings saw a niche in the market for their shape-shifting skills. They signed up, trained hard, then kept an eye out for anything that happened which had a hint of the magical about it. This allowed the fairy folk to stop normal people from finding out too much about a world they had no right being involved in.

It also meant that certain calls could, usually, be intercepted by a fairy and the necessary actions taken.

So, as Downy looked at the young lady sitting in the booth of a coffee shop on Henry Street, he knew the fairy who intercepted calls to the emergency services had done the right thing. With a glance to the front door Downy saw his recruit, Trent O'Shea, talking on his mobile phone. He looked back at Downy, giving the Leerling a nod of his head, then hung up the call. Putting the phone into a pouch on his belt, Trent returned his attention to staring at the street in front of the coffee shop. As people approached the door Trent shook his head, held up his hand, then directed them on their merry way.

The owner of the coffee shop, a man with a mobile phone held together using gaffer tape, walked over to Downy and frowned.

"What's the plan here exactly? Put me out of business by having the tall string of misery turn away all my customers?" Leo asked.

Downy groaned inwardly and put on his professional face to deal with the owner. It never ceased to amaze the Leerling just how insensitive humans could be to others of their own race. They behaved even worse when figures of authority were involved.

Here was a woman, clearly in some sort of trouble, and all Leo cared about was when he could get back to selling bad coffee. Very bad, cheap, coffee, if the smell of it was anything to go by. What Downy wanted to do in such situations was slap some basic manners into people who acted this way, but the uniform prevented him from passing out these much needed slaps.

Not that the uniform was enchanted and stopped Downy with some sort of preventative magic. Although technically, as a plain clothes detective, he did not actually wear a uniform. Just a nice suit. But the principal of the uniform, what it stood for, was the same. The thing that actually stopped Downy from doing as he pleased was the Garda higher-ups. They did not take too kindly when members of the force went around slapping people just to put manners on them. It had something to do with being sued, paying out compensation, and bad publicity.

The sort of PR crap which ruined things for everyone.

"Ten," Downy said out loud, having counted mentally up to nine. "Well, sir, we have to wait until our medical expert shows up to examine the lady here. She seems to be in some sort of semi-catatonic state. We don't know if we can move her or not."

Leo, his frown deepening, looked from Downy to the lady and back again.

"Isn't catatonic when they are in a coma or something?"

Downy rubbed some imaginary dirt out from his left eye and stared at Leo.

"Semi-catatonic, I did say semi-catatonic. Besides, I wasn't aware that running a coffee shop required a medical background qualifying you in field diagnoses," he said, putting as much sarcasm into his tone as was Leerlingly possible. "Do tell me, tell me, how you juggle it all and still run a coffee shop that clearly needs a mop ran over the floor."

Before Leo could respond Trent walked over, joining them. He looked at Leo, gave him a dismissive wave of his hand, then turned to Downy. Leo, clearly not happy about anything that was happening in his world at that moment, walked back over to the serving counter and sat down on a stool.

"Nice," Downy said to Trent. "Although you probably shouldn't wave at somebody like that. People tend to get ratty when they are treated like children."

"Who cares, we have the uniforms. They don't. Anyway, your specialist has shown up. Although they are being far too familiar with me for my liking."

"The fairy detective is here?"

Trent nodded.

"Yep, but they keep going on like we've already met. I know you're my superior officer and all, but I don't buy into this whole fairy detective lark. More so when they show up at our crime scene and start talking to me like we've worked a case before. Anyway, I didn't want to let just any old nutter walk by the tape before checking with you first."

Downy nodded his head, to give the impression that he fully approved of what Trent had just said.

What the young Guard did not know was that he had in fact met the fairy detective before. They all, Downy included, had worked on a case involving a murdered Celtic god. It had happened two years ago, shortly after Trent joined the force and was assigned to work with Downy. As events transpired it turned out that Trent was working against the good guys for most of the case. Thankfully this had been due to the fact that the villainous types in the tale had threatened Trent, not because he was a bad guy at heart. But, after solving the case, Filthy Henry did not want to let the young Garda off easy. He convinced Dagda, Chief of the Celtic Gods, to punish Trent by having him float above Ireland for a few months, before wiping his memory of the entire affair. The wipe had removed all traces of magic from Trent's memories, but left behind a crippling fear of heights.

For Trent to not remember the fairy detective made perfect sense. It just meant that Downy could not explain why the fairy detective was being overly familiar with Trent.

At least not without sounding completely crazy.

"I'm sure it's the right person," Downy said. "There is only one idiot who will show up when called to things like this. Let them in."

"You're funeral," Trent said, shrugging his shoulders. "We

should have called a medical type I reckon."

He walked back to the front door and waved at the person standing outside before pointing towards Downy.

"I swear if his dad wasn't the super," the Leerling mumbled to himself as he sat down in the booth opposite the silent lady.

She had not spoken the entire time they had been there. Just stared out the window. It was not bordering on creepy, it had moved past that a long time ago and went straight into weird.

"I'm sorry, miss," Downy said. "I had to call in some outside help, a specialist if you will, because I think this is a magical case. I'm not apologising for that, because I want to make sure you get the help you need. I'm apologising because the help I've called in is a bit of an irritating prat."

The woman blinked, a bit slower than Downy typically saw people blink, and turned to look at him.

"That's fine," she said, before returning to gaze out the window.

"Somebody called for a fairy detective?"

Downy turned away from the lady in the booth and looked up at the fairy detective. They were standing beside the table and staring down at the women.

The Leerling was instantly confused.

There were a few problems with Filthy Henry, Ireland's first and foremost fairy detective. He was rude. Tended to be very sarcastic. Had a nasty habit of stealing food from people and making no apology about it. Then there was his actual existence in the world. The fairy detective was not just a human who worked on fairy related cases, he was himself half-fairy. A human with fairy blood in his veins, blood which allowed him to perform magic. Not just street magic either, actual magic. Limited in some regards, not as powerful as a full-blood fairy could cast, but still magic. If Filthy Henry did not try to cast a fireball at least once during a case something was very wrong.

His existence was something that irked everyone in the Fairy World. Every fairy viewed half-breeds like Filthy Henry as abominations. Generally, the fairy folk were good at cleaning up these little accidents of nature. Possibly using solutions that would not be the most humane. But once a half-breed survived their first year they were safe from the fairy folk trying to fix things. So far only one half-breed had ever lived long enough to see their first birthday, winning the right to exist according to The Rules.

Downy, reluctantly, had to admit that while Filthy Henry was a wrongness, he was also a useful one. Sometimes the lines between the fairy and human worlds were blurred and you needed a person with a foot in each to get involved. Over the years of working with him Downy had, begrudgingly, grown to like the fairy detective. As the local fairy spy in Pearse Street Garda Station, Downy had to interact with Filthy Henry on several magic related cases. Even if your entire race did not like a person for being a half-breed that did not mean you could not like them, especially after they proved themselves to be a good guy. Well maybe good was being too nice, but decent.

Decent was a slight stretch as well, but right then Downy did not want to spend any more time coming up with the right word to nicely describe Filthy Henry.

It had been a few months since their paths last crossed, but Downy was sure there was something different about the fairy detective. You did not have to be a crime solver to see that.

It was not the new hair style, although that was a nice change from the normal mess of hair. The different type of coat was a pleasant alteration as well, the stereotypical trench-coat of the private investigator had just been a fashion eyesore for years. Hell, the new shampoo made the usual assault on the nostrils a joyful experience. Still, these were mere cosmetic changes that anybody could have overlooked. After all, if it was months between seeing a person changes would occur on their own, time waited for nobody. But sometimes changes could be drastic as well, so huge that you had to notice.

"Em," Downy said, slightly confused at who he was looking at. "Trent did call for the fairy detective to come down, right?"

"He sure did."

"And you're the number that he dialled?"

The fairy detective nodded.

"There hasn't been any sort of magical accident? You didn't try to change form and get stuck?" Downy asked.

"Nope."

"This isn't a body swap thing? Like those dreadful movies? Freaky Friday starring Freaky Filthy Henry?"

"Not that I know of."

"We're not on some practical joke show? I'm not being set up for a cheap laugh?"

"Why would this be funny?"

"So, then you're..."

"Shelly," the fairy detective said, smiling. "I'm Shelly, the fairy detective."

#

Quinn knew something strange was going on at the hospital. If you asked him how he knew something was up he would have found it hard to explain. It was a gut feeling and if there was one thing Quinn knew it was you trusted your gut.

In so far as he knew anything for certain.

When all your memories, your entire personal history, were

no longer floating around in your skull it became hard to be sure what you did and did not know. But that could be considered a blessing as well, if you were a silver lining sort of person. Which Quinn liked to think he was.

At least, he thought he was a silver lining kind of guy. Double guessing had become second nature when it came to his thought process these days.

With a mind free of anything else to occupy it, Quinn found that he had started to pay attention to the happenings of the other patients. This resulted with him noticing changes in them from one day to the next, because there was nothing else to get in the way of his recall. Quinn had, after all, only a few weeks of experiences built up.

He noticed that things were not all as they seemed after Nicky, one of his fellow Blank Slates, came back from her treatment session that day. Only last week she had been playing cards with Quinn in the common room. They had made up a game, because neither of them could remember any real ones. The nurses had encouraged it, rather than explain the rules of an actual game to them. They said it would be good for the patients, maybe trigger memories to come back by accident because the creative juices were flowing. Quinn and Nicky had written down the rules, played the game for most of the day, then went to bed after dinner. The following afternoon Nicky had dealt out the cards and they played once more, a pattern they continued throughout the week.

It had been brilliant fun, a break from the semi-monotony of St. Patrick's.

Then Nicky had returned from her session, looking slightly dazed and confused. She walked into the common room and just stood by the door. Nurse Faul had suggested she come and sit down at the table where Quinn was shuffling cards.

"Want to play Nonsense?" he had asked her.

Nicky looked at him blankly.

"Nonsense?"

"The game we made up last week," Quinn had said.

She shrugged her shoulders, then turned and stared out the window.

"Sure," Nicky had said. "But you will have to teach me the rules."

That had been the first big indicator for Quinn. True none of the Blank Slates were exactly brainboxes, but they had at least started to form new memories during their stay in the hospital. For Nicky to not remember the card game she co-invented was a little strange. Something had happened to her, causing those memories to vanish just like her original ones.

"Nicky," Quinn had said, an almost pleading tone to his voice.

She never looked at him, just continued to stare into thin air.

"Nicky," she said. "That's my name?"

Deep down, almost in his bones, something told Quinn he had to figure this out. He did not know why, but it felt like something he would normally do. Look into a situation and help set things right again. To help Nicky though he needed something. If Nicky's memories could suddenly vanish then the same could happen to him. At least if he wrote some stuff down Quinn figured he could read it later, avoiding the risk of losing his memories completely.

He needed to get his hands on some paper and a pen, to keep track of his findings.

Quinn had stood up from the table, leaving Nicky alone with the cards and her vacant mind, and gone to a seat over by the window. There was no need to sit apart from the rest of the Blank Slates, nobody was actively annoying anyone else, but the simple act of sitting alone helped him to think.

43

Thirty minutes past by, with Quinn left alone and only his thoughts for company.

A plan was needed, something that made sense and could be used to figure out what exactly was going on. Doctors would no doubt just say he was being paranoid, a symptom of his condition. But then doctors would say that. It was easier to diagnose a person with paranoia than listen to their wild theories. That meant the nurses were an obvious choice to seek help from. The question now was which nurse?

"You not playing today?"

Quinn looked over his shoulder and saw that Nurse Faul had entered the common room from one of the other doors, the one which led back down to the bedroom wing. He looked back over at Nicky, then at Nurse Faul.

"Not today," he said. "She doesn't seem to be right in the head."

Nurse Faul smiled.

"Do you try to be a wise guy in here or does it just come naturally? This is a hospital that specialises in people not exactly 'right in the head'. They come here for help."

He shrugged.

"It must be natural, since I can't remember enough about my life outside to be sarcastic in here," Quinn said, grinning. "I need a favour."

"You trying to get some poor nurse on the desk to get you more secret snacks?"

"No," he said, shaking his head. "Well, yes. But I was also wondering if I could get a notepad off you actually. Maybe a pen as well."

Nurse Faul gave him a quizzical look.

"Well, no," she said. "You're not allowed to have anything in the rooms that you could use to hurt yourself. That's why I never leave a spoon with your jelly pots."

Quinn slowly stood up from his chair, to appear not threatening, and took a couple of steps closer to Nurse Faul. He looked around, but none of the Blank Slates nearby were paying any attention to them.

"I think something is going on," he whispered. "I know that sounds crazy, coming from a crazy person, but Nicky isn't the same after her treatment today. She isn't the first person I've noticed a change in either. But I can't be sure if I am remembering things or not. I was going to write it all down, keep a record of it all. That way if I think I have lost my memories again there is something to go back over."

Nurse Faul pursed her lips and thought for a moment.

"We've talked about this before," she said.

"We have?" Quinn asked, genuinely shocked.

It had already happened, he had forgotten.

"Yep," Nurse Faul said. "Two weeks ago, you said you thought something was happening to the other patients. The new memories they were making. Then last week you made the same claim, right after declaring that there was a man turning into a swan outside your bedroom window."

"Then you've got to help me," he said, keeping his voice low. "I need to start recording things or else I'm going to be forever spotting something is up and forgetting about it it."

"Okay, look," she said. "I can't give you a pen and pad. It is against the rules. But how about this. You come with me to the station and we write all this down in a pad for you. Then, every day, just before lights out in the rooms, we go over what's in the pad and add anything new to it. Sound like a deal?"

Quinn could see sense behind what she said. They could not risk giving anything to the patients which might be turned into a weapon. Unless the patient definitely posed no risk to themselves or others. Her deal was the best that was on the table at the minute.

He nodded.

"Okay, deal," Quinn said. "But in that case can I ask two more small favours from you?"

Nurse Faul let out a short laugh.

"You're some chancer aren't you? Go on then."

"I can't explain how I know, but I need to talk to somebody about this stuff. A non-hospital person, before we bring it higher up the food-chain in here. I want to talk to the fairy detective."

"Okay, that all you have to go on?"

Quinn nodded his head.

"Can't remember any other details, like a name or number. But can you try find them for me?"

"I'll see what can be done there. Although you know Milton won't like that. He will say it is feeding into your delusions of being able to see fairy creatures."

"Yea, but what the doc doesn't know won't hurt him," Quinn said, winking. "Besides, I'm sure that this fairy detective person can help me."

Nurse Faul rolled her eyes.

"You're going to be the one that gets me fired from here, I just know it," she said. "Right, what's the second favour?"

"Any chance of a sneaky tub of jelly before dinner?"

#

"Let me get this straight. I tell Trent to call Filthy Henry and the half-breed sends you along instead?"

Shelly looked at Downy and shook her head.

"On the phone Trent said he was looking for 'the fairy detective', not Filthy Henry. If you wanted Filthy you should have called him directly."

Downy rubbed at his eye. It was bad enough having to work cases with Filthy Henry when you did not want to. For him to decide that Shelly was now a valid substitute just indicated how annoying the fairy detective could be remotely.

Without even being in the room, Filthy Henry was getting on Downy's nerves.

"Look," he said, smiling up at Shelly. "I need Filthy down here, not his understudy. No offence."

"Some taken," Shelly said, leaning forward and examining the lady in the booth. "For starters, I'm not his understudy."

She reached into her coat pocket and pulled out a business card. With a flick of the wrist, Shelly threw the card towards Downy. The Leerling caught it, flipping it around so he could read it.

"Pagan Investigations," he read out loud. "Ireland's First Polite Fairy Detective."

"In the flesh," Shelly said, grinning at him.

"You've got to be kidding me. You branched out on your own? What about Celtic Investigations with Filthy?"

"We had a disagreement," Shelly said, closing her eyes briefly. "He withheld something from me that he had no right to. So, myself and Filthy went our separate ways. I haven't seen or spoken to him in almost six months."

Downy tapped the business card on the table top and watched

as Shelly flicked to her fairy vision, the second sight that allowed her to see the magical spectrum. She continued her visual inspection of the lady in the booth.

Downy had noticed that Shelly referred to the half-breed as 'Filthy'. This was an indication of just how big their disagreement had been. As long as Downy had known Shelly she never once called the fairy detective by his full name, always preferring to just call him 'Henry'. The fairy detective had taken on the moniker of 'Filthy Henry' when he learned that the Fairy World thought of him as a filthy abomination. In typical Filthy Henry style, he figured why pass up a good opportunity to annoy people even more by showing them how little their insults hurt him. But if Shelly had started to use 'Filthy' instead of just 'Henry' then the great and powerful ginger-haired detective must have done something pretty amazing to get under her skin.

Shelly was one of the few people who, having spent more than five minutes with Filthy Henry, still volunteered to be in his presence. Sometimes she even defended him to others in the Fairy World. Saints had less patience than Shelly when it came to dealing with Filthy Henry.

Downy thought about a rumour he had heard roughly a year ago, concerning something that caused a sudden cessation of life for Shelly. Now, any sane person would clearly discount this rumour as just that: a rumour. Considering the fact that Shelly was obviously very much alive and standing in front of him indicated just how much of a rumour it was. But when you came from a world of magic, when you were yourself a creature who could perform magic, it made it difficult to completely rule out everything you heard.

"Is it true?" Downy asked, figuring there was no point in beating around the bush.

"Yea," Shelly said, glancing at him. "I am assuming you are referring to the fact that I died and Filthy used a wish to bring me back to life?"

Downy nodded his head slowly.

"It is one hundred percent true," she said, staring at the cups on the table. "How many coffees have you had since getting here?"

"Huh?" Downy said, his mind not shifting gears quick enough to follow the change of topic. "Oh, em, none. It smells rotten. Why?"

Shelly pointed at the mug sitting in front of the silent woman.

"She has a mug sitting there, looks like it has been topped up a few times. But there are rings on the table surface from another cup, on your side of the table."

Downy leaned back in his seat and stared down at the table. He could not see anything to indicate another cup had been there.

"How can you tell that?"

"Because the table hasn't been wiped down yet," Shelly said, looking around the coffee shop. "They don't usually do that unless there is a spill, or the customer has left. That the owner?"

"Yea, Leo. But hang on a minute," Downy said, sliding out of the booth and standing up. "What are you doing?"

Shelly turned on the spot and looked at Downy, her eyes glowing a shade of light blue as the fairy sight remained in effect.

"I'm doing my job," she said. "This case involves magic. You requested the services of a fairy detective. Now, shut up and sit down so I can work."

#

Shelly walked across the coffee shop floor towards the owner, who was perched on the stool like a caffeinated parrot. She started to channel her inner Filthy Henry. Then immediately stopped thinking like that because it sounded extremely weird and nobody wanted to be like Filthy Henry. Most of the time she was

49

not even sure if Filthy Henry wanted to be like Filthy Henry.

There was a new fairy detective in town and she was going to start making a name for herself. A nice name at that, one that was never used in conjunction with insults and subtle digs.

Since starting her own agency Shelly had followed one rule: Do Not Take Advantage.

Filthy Henry, for all his actual magical abilities and knowledge of the Fairy World, had a nasty habit of taking advantage of normal people when they came to him for help. It was not unheard of for him to take on a case, figure out that nothing magical or fairy related was going on at all, then charge for 'solving' such a case. It was very unprofessional, at least in Shelly's view. But Filthy Henry seemed to sleep soundly at night. Conning old dears out of their pension money did not seem to faze him one bit.

Shelly, on the other hand, had decided that Pagan Investigations would only charge for cases with definite magical aspects to them. Which meant that she had, so far, worked around twenty cases for dear-old-granny types that had resulted in no payment at the end. The other cases had all been relatively easy to solve as well, complete with moderate payments. This case, though, would be her first big one. Not just making a Red-man stop playing pranks on people or convincing a Cat Síth that talking around mortals was a bad idea. This was going to be the case that put Pagan Investigations on the map, even if it did involve work with a slightly corrupt Garda.

When Trent had called her, Shelly was not sure known how the call was going to go. The last time she had seen Trent, Dagda, Chief of the Celtic Gods, had made him no longer require food or water then turned him invisible and sent him sailing into the sky. Which was where Trent remained for six months, floating over Ireland, as punishment for helping some evil gods try and rewrite Time itself. Upon his return Trent was meant to have been mind-wiped, with the exception of having a respectful fear of being in the air without an airplane. So, hearing his voice on the other end of the line had made Shelly wonder if, somehow, Trent had remembered everything. As it turned out he was just following the orders of his superior. Which explained why, when she had shown up, Trent had not immediately wondered why Filthy Henry was not there.

Trent had no idea what the fairy detective Downy requested looked like.

A win-win situation for her, even if it was because of mistaken identity.

She stopped a few feet from the coffee shop owner, took out her notepad and pen, then cleared her throat with a little cough.

This was it, time to show everyone she was ready for the Big Show.

"Excuse me, sir," Shelly said.

He turned around in his seat and looked her up and down.

"And you are?"

One bit of advice that Filthy Henry had given Shelly on their first case together came back to her. When at a crime scene you should always act like you belonged to the investigation, assuming an air of superior authority. It confused people while at the same time giving them the impression you were not to be messed with.

"That would be my opening question for you, sir," Shelly said sharply, tapping the nib of her pen on the open page of the notepad. "Generally, I don't go around telling people my name when I am investigating a crime."

This clearly rattled the owner a little.

"Excuse me? What crime? Your lads just showed up, kept people out of my shop, then started to watch that oddball in my booth."

"Yes," Shelly snapped. "A woman who has clearly been drugged. I'm not sure if you're aware, but generally if a person is drugged without their consent then that is considered a crime. Not just in some parts of the world. Everywhere!"

The owner spun his stool around fully and stared at her, his eyes opening slightly wider.

"Wait, what? She was drugged?"

Shelly let out an exasperated sigh.

Pretend you knew more than the person being questioned and it put them on edge. That trick she had learned on her own.

"This entire process will go so much faster for the pair of us if you leave the questioning to me. Sound like a plan? Now, tell me everything that took place from the moment that woman entered your fine establishment."

Leo took a deep breath and started to recount what had happened prior to the authority types showing up. Shelly could tell he was repeating a lot of what he said, not for the first time, but that did not matter to her. As far as Leo was concerned she needed to know everything, she jotted down notes on all that was said.

"The guy," Shelly said, cutting Leo off mid-sentence. "Where did he come from?"

Leo shrugged.

"I dunno, he was here before the lady showed up. Just sitting at the counter, in the corner there, sipping at a coffee. When she sat down in the booth he ordered two pieces of cake and went over to chat with her."

"Anything unusual about this guy? Description?"

Leo shook his head.

"I'm not the best at remembering people like that. He was

average, in all aspects. There was something about his hands, though. They were blue, but not from cold or nothing like that. Didn't get a good look at them, if I'm being honest. You never know if people have a condition these days and will get easily offended because you ask a simple question."

Shelly looked up at the ceiling, checking the corners of the room. Over the cash register she spotted a small black dome security camera. The sort favoured by casinos because of the three hundred and sixty degree viewing angle they offered. She pointed towards it with her pen.

"But you got a shot of him coming in," she said, pointing at the camera with her pen. "We can get that footage and make some pictures from it."

Glancing up at the camera Leo went slightly red in the face and leaned closer to Shelly.

"Between you and me," he said in scarce more than a whisper. "That's a fake. Can't afford a proper one so I bought the casing online and put it up. Mainly use it as a deterrent for staff taking money out of the cash register."

"Brilliant," Shelly said, rolling her eyes.

She looked at the case notes she had taken. They looked lonely as no clues wanted to hang out with them. All in all, things were off to a bad start.

"Is she alright?" Leo asked, nodding towards the lady in the booth.

Shelly looked over at the woman and watched her for a moment.

It was hard to say what exactly was going on, but it was certainly magic related. There were no injuries on the lady, at least none that Shelly could see, and the woman did not appear to be hurt in any way. She could talk, was breathing, responsive. If anything, she appeared to be just another person out for a quiet moment in Dublin city. Yet something had definitely been done to her. Wisps of magic clung to her ears and tiny specks floated in front of her mouth. Not that Leo would have seen these, because you needed fairy vision to see the magical spectrum.

Whoever this mystery man had been, he was a fairy creature of some description. Aside from Filthy Henry, no humans were able to cast magical spells. Druids could, to a certain degree, perform limited magic but it required them to channel the powers of a fairy creature in order to do it. That did not rule out the suspect being a druid, but the fairy detective had once explained the limits of Druidic magic even when channelled from a powerful fairy creature.

Meaning the suspect list definitely was populated with just fairies, making this a case for a fairy detective.

A case Shelly was adamant she would solve before the other fairy detective got wind of it. As much to rub it in his smug face that she was up to the job as to show the world that they had a new fairy detective to work with.

"She appears to be fine, physically at least," Shelly said to Leo. "But we will need to get an ambulance to bring her to hospital so we can have a doctor look her over. Is there anything else you can remember from earlier? Maybe any other staff members I can talk to?"

"There is the waitress who was on shift," Leo said. "The Garda let her go after answering some questions, seeing as the pair of us were here they figured I could just hang around. I have her contact details somewhere, let me go get them for you."

"Thanks," Shelly said, pocketing her notepad again and walking over to Downy.

The Leerling was standing beside the booth, staring down at the silent woman and frowning.

"I've never seen anything like this before," Downy said.

"Really?" Shelly said, looking over at Trent. "Isn't your recruit sort of a living example of this?"

"Nah," Downy said, shaking his head. "Trent had a small block put in place by a Celtic God. Most fairy creatures can do the same trick, but only wiping out a few hours. A day at the most, but that takes a lot of power. You can target a specific memory that took place over a long period of time, but you're only making them forget one thing in that case. Like making them think they have no idea what tea is. But this, this looks like the woman has had everything blocked. A factory reset."

"Something going on out here, boss," Trent shouted over at Downy as he looked down the street.

"Let one of the lads on patrol handle it," Downy said. "We've a crime-scene to run."

Outside people started shouting. Trent straightened up and tried to fill as much of the doorway as was humanly possible while keeping his attention on whatever was happening. Leo came over to join Shelly and Downy, a folded piece of paper in his hand.

"Here you go," he said, handing the paper to Shelly.

The shouting grew louder and was closer to the coffee shop now.

"Thanks," Shelly said to Leo, taking the paper from him and putting into her inside jacket pocket.

"I'll let her know that Detective…"

"Shelly," Shelly said. "Just tell her Shelly…"

Right then the main window of the coffee shop exploded inwards, showering everyone inside with shards of glass. Downy dove forward and landed on top of the lady in the booth, using his body to shield her from the glass. The lady screamed, covering her head with her arms as the Leerling landed on her. Trent

55

ducked to the ground and pulled out his telescoping night-stick, extending it with a flick of the hand. Leo and Shelly, who had been standing more or less dead centre in front of the window, both turned around as fast they could to shield their faces with their hands.

Something sailed through the air and slammed into Leo, knocking him to the ground. He fell like a sack of potatoes, hitting his head off a table leg as he went down. Shelly leaned right and tried to see what had come through the window.

A table to her left suddenly turned over on its own, followed by two chairs being pushed across the floor by an invisible force. Shelly mentally flicked on her fairy vision and checked the area to see what could be seen.

On the floor, its face being firmly mashed into the ground, was a Red-man.

Red-men were a strange, lowly, fairy creature with no real magical abilities at all other than being able to turn invisible when humans were around. They were renowned for being mischievous individuals who liked nothing better than to play pranks on people. A lot of the quick cases that Filthy Henry took generally involved Red-men playing pranks on mortals for their own amusement. The Red-man, in itself, was not the most interesting thing on the floor though. That honour belonged to the fairy who was keeping the Red-man's face mashed into the ground while pinning one of his arms behind his back.

The fairy was wearing, for want of a better term, S.W.A.T. body armour. It was a dark green colour, but looked like something a vigilante dressed up similar to a flying rodent would wear. The arms had pads, the chest had pads, the pads had pads. A small backpack, also padded, was strapped to the back of the suit. Shelly could not see the fairy's face because they wore a green biker helmet with a reflective visor pulled down.

"Stop squirming dirt-bag," the armour wearing fairy said in a feminine voice. The mirrored visor turned and looked up at Shelly. "You can see me?"

Shelly nodded once.

"Crap. Guess we need to have a chat then."

# Chapter Three

Nurse Faul remained true to her word and found an A4 refill pad for Quinn to use in order to jot down his notes. It was the sort with a gummy binding along the top. No metallic spiral coil for him to pull out and injure himself, or others, with. She had remained steadfast on him not having a writing implement while unsupervised though. Any scribblings had to be done at her desk, so she could keep an eye on him. No pens in the bedrooms without proper supervision. There was 'breaking the rules' for small things, topics that were really only guidelines, and then flat out snapping the rules in two.

Quinn sat opposite Nurse Faul at the nurses station and wrote down his notes, information pertaining to his 'investigation'.

All the textbooks said that this was not the worst sort of treatment to give a patient suffering from memory loss. But, secretly, Nurse Faul wanted to know what was so suspicious to Quinn that he felt it needed to be looked into. If there was something going on in the hospital, something that none of the staff were noticing, then they should treat it seriously. She watched him finish off another page of notes, turn it over, and continue his writing on a fresh page.

"Can I read these later?" she asked him.

Quinn nodded his head and kept writing.

"No problem," he said. "Maybe you can help me figure out if I am being crazy or not. Current accommodation notwithstanding, of course."

Linda laughed.

"Fair enough. But what do you think is going on?"

He put the pencil down and looked at her.

"People are recovering. Slightly, or at least they are forming new memories. Then suddenly a Blank Slate is blank again. Except for me. While I did forget that we've spoken about this a few times already, I am remembering my name."

"That's true. But you can't know that for sure," Linda said. "I mean they could be getting worse as well. Maybe the treatments just knock them out for a bit."

"Possibly," Quinn said, picking up the pencil again. "But that could be what they want you to think. Did you get the fairy detective for me yet?"

Initially, Linda had decided not to go looking for Quinn's fairy detective. One thing you were definitely not meant to do was feed into a patient's delusions. Plus who had ever even heard about a fairy detective? Then, on a mad whim during her lunch, Linda looked up the fairy detective online and found one operating in Dublin. However, every time she rang the number listed it went straight to voicemail. After a few attempts, she decided it must be a wind-up number and stopped trying.

"I did try to get them for you," she said. "But they don't answer the phone. Must be busy."

"Keep trying, please," Quinn said as he handed over the stationary to her. "I remember them being a real thing, at least I think I do. Narky fellow, but the real deal. If I am remembering things from before my...whatever scrambled my mind, then we need to look into them. Maybe you could drop around to them on your way home?"

He smiled briefly at her then turned and walked down the corridor, back towards the common room. Once she was sure that he had gone inside, Linda opened the notepad. For somebody with memory lost, Quinn was certainly able to write a lot of stuff in a short space of time. She started to read.

Downy instructed Trent to remain outside the coffee shop and keep any pedestrians from entering at all. If they asked what happened to the window Trent was to make something up about youths partaking in random acts of vandalism. But, above all else, he was to prevent people from looking into the shop. Himself included.

Between them, with a small amount of effort, Downy and Shelly shifted Leo upright and leaned his back against the table. He looked fine, the bump to the head just knocking him out. While they had manoeuvred the coffee shop owner, the armoured fairy had cast a spell over the Red-man who crashed through the window. A dark purple bubble enveloped the Red-man and he now floated two feet above the ground.

Shelly looked over at them.

"Care to explain a few things?"

Removing the helmet, the fairy placed it on top of the bubble. Inside, the Red-man started to thump beneath the helmet to try and knock it off. He was shouting, but no sounds made it out from his magical prison. Now that the armoured fairy was upright Shelly could get a better look at them.

The fairy stood at a little over three foot, roughly the height of a leprechaun. More padding covered the front of the body armour, some of these held in place by little green rivets. Hanging around their waist was, for want of a better term, a utility belt. Shelly could not tell what was in the pouches as each was closed, but they seemed to be packed to the brim. Now that the helmet was off she could see that the fairy was indeed female. Her red hair was short and wavy, two little curls popping out from behind her ears gave her a slight 'mad scientist' look. Two bright, brilliant, green eyes twinkled out from a cherub like face. The fairy reached up and scratched underneath her adorable button nose.

"Em," Shelly said.

"Let's just get the basics out of the way first, alright?" the fairy said. "Leerling, what the hell is going on here?"

Downy, looking a little taken aback, just stood there with his mouth open.

"Okay," the fairy said. "You're next to useless. So, human. Half-breed?"

Shelly shook her head.

"Right, so we still just have the one. Great. Which means you can see fairy folk because..."

The fairy twirled her left index finger around in the air, motioning towards Shelly to start talking.

"Oh, em, I know the half-breed," she said. "He unlocked my latent ability to see the Fairy World. Then I died and was brought back using a leprechaun's wish. Now I can see the Fairy World without being around Filthy Henry."

"Huh," the fairy said. "That makes sense, I guess. Dead and brought back with a wish, why not? Latent ability? Meaning you're a creative sort, right? You're not a bloody writer, are you?"

"No," Shelly said, shaking her head. "I'm an artist, painter mainly. At least I was."

"OK, I can work with that. Don't have much time for writers. Artists paint something and move on. Writers spend pages describing a meal nobody ever ate so you can picture it in your mind. Why bother? Anyway, back to the introductions. I'm a leprechaun, in case you were wondering."

"Oh," Shelly said, somewhat surprised.

She had been part of the Fairy World for a little over two years at this stage and knew that there were many races of fairy she was yet to meet. The few that had crossed paths with Dublin's newest fairy detective had definitely shown up in both genders at one point or another. All except for leprechauns. It had gotten to the point that Shelly was convinced leprechauns were like dwarfs in an epic saga based in the Middle of the Earth. She assumed both males and females had beards and the only way to tell them apart was to watch how they went to the toilet.

Now she had just received a little education in the difference of leprechaun sexes. It turned out the females did not have beards and looked like chubby, cute, little children. Very similar to Changelings, but with less of the crazy talking baby aspect.

Maybe saying Elivin looked like a toddler was a more accurate a comparison.

"Yea," the leprechaun said. "I get that a lot. Name's Elivin."

"Eleven?" Downy said, cupping his hand around his ear and leaning forward.

It happened so fast Shelly was just about able to keep up. One second Elivin was standing beside the captured Red-man, the next she was jumping up onto a table and squaring off at Downy, her tiny fist clenched and held beneath his nose. Her eyes so wide Shelly felt certain it should be possible to see into the leprchaun's skull.

"Don't call me 'Eleven' again! Got it?!"

Downy swallowed and slowly nodded his head.

"That ... sort of escalated quickly," he said. "I just didn't hear your name correctly."

"It's Elivin," she said through gritted teeth. "Elivin, with two 'I's."

The leprechaun jumped from the table, landing on a chair, and sat down. She crossed her legs and looked around the coffee shop.

"Okay, go," she said, nodding at Shelly.

Shelly pointed at the Red-man.

"What's the story with him? Also, why are you causing a scene out in public with so many people around?"

Elivin kicked the floating orb with the toe of her military style boot and caused it to float backwards into a table. This caused the Red-man inside to bounce around, like a ping-pong ball pumped up on caffeine.

"This waste of space," Elivin said, indicating her captive. "Has been on the run for a few months now. I got the job of bringing him in. The only thing he did that was useful at least was keep his Veil up so that the humans didn't see what was going on."

"But...who are you?"

"I'm a bounty hunter," Elivin said. "A fairy bounty hunter, if we're being specific."

"That's a job?" Downy asked Shelly.

"I dunno," she said. "I'm a fairy detective not a fairy tour guide. Shouldn't you know if that's a job in your world? Why would there even be a need for a fairy bounty hunter?"

"Simple," Elivin said. "Not everybody goes to the fairy detective for their problems. Sometimes a rich and powerful fairy might put a bounty on another fairy's head. Other times a fairy could go on the run from the magical authorities and need capturing. Don't forget fairies are just like humans. Some of them love to steal crap from other fairy folk. Such unsavoury sorts need to be brought to justice. Enter me."

It made sense, Shelly had to admit. If the world could have a fairy detective solving crimes that involved the magical races doing things in the mortal world, why not a fairy bounty hunter?

"But you're a leprechaun, you said. Right?" she asked Elivin.

The bounty hunter nodded her head, the movement causing the protective padding around her neck to make that stretched sound rubber makes when it is being twisted and bent. Elivin crossed her arms and looked at Shelly.

"Biologically I am, yes," she said. "But does that mean I have to do the job of a female leprechaun? Is there a rule that says a bounty hunter can't be a woman?"

Shelly waved her hands up in front of her, a gesture of peace.

"I'm not saying that at all," she said. "In fact, that's why I am out on my own too, as a fairy detective."

Elivin chewed thoughtful on her bottom lip, then seemed to notice the woman in the booth. She was still lying down on the seat, watching the conversation unfold before her. Slowly the bounty hunter climbed down from her chair and walked over to the booth. Downy and Shelly just watched her without saying anything. When the bounty hunter was standing beside the booth she turned and stared at them both.

"You've got to be kidding me," Elivin said.

Downy took a small step backwards, moving behind Shelly.

"I'm spitting feathers over here," he whispered in her ear.

"That means you are angry not scared," Shelly said.

"Potato, tomato," Downy hissed in reply. "I'm making a pillow in my pants from all the feathers I am losing. She is scary. I thought you were bad, she is worse at half the size."

"If bird boy has finished chatting you up," Elivin said, pointing at the lady in the booth. "What's the story with this one?"

"That's why I am here," Shelly said. "Downy got wind of some strange goings on and called in a fairy detective to figure out if it was magical or not."

"Oh, it's magical alright," Elivin said. "I've been tracking this guy for centuries. The trail had gone cold, until right now." She looked directly at Shelly. "Say hello to your new partner. A partner who gets to keep the full bounty."

#

Quinn found the common room uncommonly quiet for the time of day. Not that it was lacking in people, very much the opposite. Situated on the various plastic chairs, the two threadbare sofas and, in one case, a pile of books, were the patients of St. Patrick's. Most of the Blank Slates had gathered together, forming an odd little clique in the corner of the room. But nobody, at all, was speaking.

At this time of day, it was normal to see some of the guests, because Quinn had started to dislike using the term 'patient' to describe himself and the others in the ward, to be playing board games. They would chat, play cards, maybe go for a stroll around the room because it was Ireland and generally rained when you decided to do anything outside. Anyone would be forgiven for thinking that the common room, at such times, was actually just a social club were everybody happened to have the same taste in fashion. After all, who would not want to spend all day in white cotton pyjamas?

But today there was no such illusion as everyone stared vacantly about the room. Even the other guests, the non-Blank Slates, were subdued.

Quinn sat on a stool in the farthest corner of the room and watched everyone doing nothing.

Yesterday there had been some energy to the guests as they carried on with their daily activities. True some of the guests were a bit more energetic than others, but that just meant they balanced each other out. Now they all were doing nothing.

Clearly something had caused the change, he just had no idea what.

"Oh, surprised to see you here."

66

Quinn turned his head and saw Dr. Milton standing in the nearest doorway, the one which led back down to the doctors' offices. He smiled at the doctor.

"You know me," Quinn said. "I had big plans to sit on the floor and do nothing but then figured sitting on a chair would be better for my back."

Dr. Milton frowned at the statement.

"Indeed," was all he said. "Everyone else seems to be tickety boo."

"Really?" Quinn asked. "You call sitting around drooling into your hands 'tickety boo'?"

Fluid slowly looked around the room at everybody.

"Nobody is drooling, young man," he said. "Certainly not into their hands."

"You know what I mean," Quinn said, gesturing towards the assembled guests. "They were all chatty yesterday and now they aren't. Even the ones who are in here for something other than being a Blank Slate. What gives?"

"The mind is a strange thing," Dr. Milton said, staring out the window thoughtfully. "One second it can be an impenetrable fortress, the next a cloud blown away on the wind. Who is to say what does and doesn't cause it to change from one state to the next. Now, as everyone else is more or less subdued, how about we have another session? My room in ten minutes?"

Quinn shrugged.

"Sure," he said. "Not like I am getting any stimulating conversation out of this lot."

"Excellent," the doctor said, turning and walking out of the room. "Ah...hello...nurse...somethingorother..."

The door did not swing shut behind him as Nurse Faul

entered.

"I swear to God he is the rudest man alive. How hard can it be to learn some names? Quiet in here today, isn't it?"

"I know," Quinn said. "I'm telling you, something is up."

Nurse Faul pulled over a chair and placed it beside Quinn's stool. She sat down, crossed her legs, and folded her arms.

"Look," she said, her voice low. "I'm starting to think you're right."

"You believe me then?"

"I didn't say that."

"You didn't not say it either," Quinn countered. "Which I know is a double negative, but still."

Nurse Faul sighed and watched Nicky as she stared blankly at the wall in front of her.

"It just doesn't add up is all," she said to Quinn. "When you pointed out the change in Nicky I started to talk with the other nurses on staff. They've noticed it as well, but always brushed it off as being just the dosage of pills we're giving the patients. How else could you explain it?"

"Magic?" Quinn said, raising an eyebrow and looking at her.

Nurse Faul shook her head.

"There's no such thing," she said. "But I've been reading your notes, which is hugely boring for me because I hate reading anything that isn't part of the job or the plays I am in, and I am adult enough to admit that something does seem...off."

"You are in plays?"

"Yeah," Nurse Faul said. "It's good to have a hobby outside of work. Not that I get to do nearly as much of them as I would like, thanks to this place, but still. Anyway, if you promise, swear even, not to make a big deal about this, I will drop into the detective's office like you asked."

"You will?" Quinn asked. He could feel the smile spreading across his face. "So, you do believe me."

"I still haven't said that," Nurse Faul replied. "But maybe an outside agency is needed to look at this from a purely subjective manner. Before we take it further up the food-chain it can't hurt to have a third party look into things. If I remember, I will call into your detective friend on the way home, since they still don't seem to be answering the phone or returning calls."

"Ah, ah, ah," he said, waggling his right index finger in the air. "You have to say the magic words."

Nurse Faul rolled her eyes.

"Fine! I'm going to drop into the fairy detective."

#

"Hold on. Why is this my responsibility?"

Shelly looked at Downy, then pointed towards Trent standing at attention in his Garda uniform.

"You're the law and order around here," she said, smiling. "Meaning you get to make sure the lady is seen to and this whole mess is covered up from mortals."

"While you…?"

"Go solve the case, of course," Shelly said. "Look, Elivin has handled the window repair and a short memory realignment on Trent. She even patched up Leo and altered his memories of events. Can't you do something for a change?"

Downy let out a long, exasperated, sigh and stared at her.

"You're more like Filthy than you think," he said. "Fine, but don't expect this to become standard operating practise between

69

us. Even the half-breed doesn't get free run of a crime scene."

"Just make sure...what's her name?" Shelly asked the Leerling.

Downy looked at her for a couple of seconds, then turned to the lady in the booth.

"Um..." was the best answer he could apparently come up with.

"You've got to be kidding me," Shelly said. "Isn't checking for identification sort of Garda training day one?"

"Don't mind me," Elivin said to the lady in the booth. "Just looking for...here we are. Name on this work idea says her name is Becky Jones."

"Is that right?" Shelly asked the lady. "Is your name Becky?"

She stared blankly back at them all.

"I don't know. I do like the sound of the name though. Sort of musical...I think."

Shelly was not entirely sure what to make from that statement. She smiled at Becky, then turned her attention back to Downy.

"Right," she said. "Since Elivin just did your job for you that settles the whole 'Why is it my responsibility?' question I think."

The Leerling groaned.

"Fine," he said. "But just because I am part of the emergency services doesn't mean I have to cover all aspects of it. We will look after Becky, just this once. Now, get out of here the pair of you. If you find out anything let me know."

Shelly nodded.

"No problem at all. Elivin, you ready to explain what you think happened to her?"

"Not here, in case it is hanging around. Don't want to give it any sort of advantage. Plus I need to make a stop first," the leprechaun said, collecting her helmet from the bubble prison. "Downy, I'm going to bring this Red-idiot with me if that's all the same to you."

The Leerling went to say something, then ran his hand over his face and waved for the pair of them to leave. Elivin made a slight gesture with her hand and the bubble containing the Red-man started to float directly behind her, two feet above her head. She fell into step with Shelly and the pair of them walked towards the coffee shop entrance.

Trent glanced over his shoulder at them as they approached, then shook his head and blinked rapidly.

"Everything alright?" Shelly asked him, mentally flicking on her fairy vision.

"Thought there was somebody walking behind you with something on their head," Trent said, stepping aside so they could pass. "Guess I need a cup of coffee, because there's nothing there now."

Shelly stepped out onto the street and saw Elivin quickly follow suit. Giving Trent a curt nod, Shelly turned and started walking amongst the people on the street.

There was something strange and wonderful about Dublin City in the middle of autumn. For whatever reason, the city and its citizens seemed in a good mood. It was as if everyone was in tune with the changing of the seasons from summer to winter. They knew, deep down, that winter could be horrible and full of cold, misery and maybe even some snow. That summer was fast becoming a distant memory and, given it was Ireland, had probably been a complete wash out as it did nothing but rain every bank-holiday weekend. But during autumn, that strange middle season that never really had anything going for it, everyone shifted gears and became more pleasant.

You could see it on the faces of the people in the crowd. As

Shelly walked down Moore Street, casually glancing at the wares for sale on the various vendors carts and stalls, nobody around her was in a rush. Sure, people had places to go, things to do and all that. But nobody was grumpy about it. The weather was the perfect temperature between overbearing heat and nose freezing cold. A Goldilocks situation if ever there was one when it came to the weather. Everyone seemed to adjust nicely and nobody complained. With no foul moods caused by things beyond their control, people just got along better.

Shelly enjoyed walking through the city on days like this. It reminded her that, sometimes, everybody in the world could relax a little. Then again, not everyone in the world could see the magical side of Dublin City either.

The actual magical side of it, not just the 'Isn't it a magical place to be?' side.

With her fairy vision Shelly could see through The Veil that kept normal folk from going crazy at the sight of fairy people living among them. Her first stroll down Moore Street with Filthy Henry had been a literal eye-opener. Moore Street always had market stalls on it, operating for more years than anybody could remember. But there were always some stalls with large empty spaces between them. Once Filthy Henry had unlocked her fairy vision Shelly had seen why this prime retail space had been left alone.

It was because some fairy folk ran stalls on Moore Street as well.

The human mind filtered out this information completely and simply presented empty spaces that could not be used to setup a stall. It made Moore Street all the more interesting, at least to Shelly. Now she could see an elderly, true blood, Dubliner selling apples from their cart while right beside them a fairy was hawking some magical potions or unguents to any fairy folk passing by.

"I do love this street," Elivin said as they strolled along, the bubble prison floating overhead like a disturbing sort of balloon. The visor on her helmet was flipped up, allowing Shelly to see her face.

"Are you going to just carry that guy around with you all day or something?"

"Not exactly," the leprechaun said. "There is a drop off point down here. The humans built their shopping centre and then decided that the décor out the back was some sort of landmark, unlikely to change. Naturally enough the fairy folk took advantage of that."

Shelly instantly knew what Elivin was talking about.

The Ilac Centre opened its doors in 1981 and was one of Dublin City's first shopping centres. It was home to a number of stores ranging from fashion boutiques to cosmetic shops. It also had a number of gadget shops frequented by husbands dragged out to visit fashion boutiques and cosmetic shops. When it was built the designer took full advantage of the fact that the building would touch three streets simultaneously, resulting in entrances built on Parnell Street, Henry Street and Moore Street. For some reason, the Moore Street entrance had large, brightly coloured, pyramids installed over each of the store windows. They were gaudy looking, modern art-eqsue, things roughly the size of a Mini Cooper. Over the years the Henry Street and Parnell Street fronts of the building had been refurbished and brought kicking and screaming into the modern era. All glass walls and polished metal frames. However, the Moore Street side was left alone. Untouched.

There were a few theories as to why this was the case, but most people all agreed it was because of Moore Street itself. The stalls of Moore Street brought some character to Dublin City that other cities in the world could not replicate, no matter how hard they tried. Those same stalls came from a time when people cared more about what they could afford to buy and not if they should

73

be seen entering a fancy and expensive shop to purchase something. As such, the pyramids, with all their brightly coloured madness, made up a part of that Moore Street charm. When people mentioned getting rid of the colourful eyesores the stall folk of Moore Street rallied, shooting down such crazy ideas quickly and loudly.

Elivin moved through the crowd of fairy and human shoppers, walking up towards the nearest of the pyramids. It was bright red and had fallen victim to a number of well-placed bird droppings in the last few days. She stood directly beneath it and turned around to face the imprisoned Red-man. With a quick gesture of her right hand the bubble floated so that it was beneath the pyramid. Another hand movement and the bubble began to drift up, towards an opening in the base of the pyramid. Inside the bubble the Red-man started to bang on the purple surface, a panicked look on his face. Like a child's helium balloon released in a shopping centre, which Shelly felt was an oddly appropriate analogy to have given where they were, the bubble floated up into the pyramid and bounced around the metal frame inside. Elivin watched it for a minute, then clicked her fingers twice. A red, metal, sheet slid into place, closing the base of the pyramid completely.

"Done," she said, turning back to smile at Shelly.

"What's that about? Some sort of portal to fairy land that you drop your bounty off at?"

Elivin frowned and shook her head.

"No," the leprechaun said. "That has to be the dumbest thing I've ever heard. It's the collection point for this particular bounty. That pyramid is magically sealed and hidden from detection. In an hour, a Leerling will come by and collect the Red-man. Then I get paid. Job done."

"Huh," Shelly said, slightly disappointed. "Sometimes I think you fairy folk don't do things with a magical twist just to try and be boring."

"Could be," Elivin said. "Could be that you've read too many fantasy novels and when faced with reality you disappoint yourself. Anyway, we need to talk about that woman back in the coffee shop."

Shelly nodded in agreement. She spotted an empty bench near the shopping centre door and headed towards it. Dropping down onto the metal frame, clearly designed for short periods of rest based on how uncomfortable it was, Shelly waited for Elivin to come and join her. The leprechaun came over, examined the spare spot on the bench, then shrugged and jumped up onto it. She wiggled in her spot twice, her padded armour rubbing noisily in the process.

"Why humans can't have nice benches out in public I will never know. It isn't like they are expensive."

"Well maybe not for a bunch of people who can conjure whatever the hell they want out of thin air," Shelly said.

"True," Elivin said. "Anyway. Let's talk."

"Right," Shelly said. "You've seen a person with no memories like that woman before?"

The leprechaun reached into a pocket on her utility belt and pulled out a little cloth pouch. She took a small crystal sphere from the pouch and held it in front of her face, resting it on the palm of her hand.

"I've been tracking the thing that causes that to happen for nearly fifteen hundred years," Elivin said, her voice sounding cold.

Shelly looked over at the leprechaun, amazed at what she had just heard. It never occurred to her that the fairy folk could live so long. Filthy Henry, despite looking like a man in his mid-thirties, had once told Shelly he was closer to ninety than he was eighty. It was something to do with the magic in his blood, coursing through his veins and slowing the ageing process greatly. That was what happened with a half-breed. Presumably for a full-blood fairy the effect was even more pronounced. To look at Elivin, ignoring the fact she was a leprechaun, you would not have put her past twenty.

"Fifteen hundred years!" Shelly said. "You're looking well."

"Thanks," Elivin said. "When I got into the bounty hunting business the main thing I wanted people to say to me was that I looked good for my age."

"How did you get into the business?" Shelly asked, ignoring the sarcasm. "I mean you're a leprechaun, why no crock of gold and granting wishes and all that stuff?"

Elivin looked away from the sphere in her hand, down the street at some school children clearly trying to avoid being seen outside when they should be attending class. Shelly could tell, without any magical powers or fantastic detective skills, that the leprechaun did not want to answer her question.

"I just decided to try something different," the leprechaun said.

"Are there many fairy bounty hunters?" Shelly asked, deciding to give Elivin an out and not press further on the topic of her career choice. "I mean I've only been involved in the Fairy World for two years, give or take, and I know they all generally can't stand dealing with Filthy Henry. If there were a bunch of fairies working as bounty hunters wouldn't that sort of do away with the need for a fairy detective? Particularly one that nobody likes."

"It's because of The Rules," Elivin said, turning back and looking at the little crystal sphere. "Plus, not every fairy that steps out of line gets a bounty put on their head. The half-breed serves a purpose that both worlds, fairy and human, need. Even if nobody wants to admit it. Humans probably couldn't care less about Filthy Henry, really. Fairy bounty hunters basically just

76

focus on fairies that are running rampant and don't leave a lot of time to get a detective involved. Either that or they are cases that have a huge reward offered."

"Like this?" Shelly said, pointing at the crystal sphere.

"Exactly," Elivin said. "This piece of crap has been running around Ireland for centuries and nobody can find him or get next to him. We've tried magic and everything to track this thing down, nothing has worked. Anytime I've gotten close he has given me the slip."

She handed the crystal to Shelly, indicating with a slight nod of her head that it was safe to pick up.

"If I wake up with no clothes on, you're in trouble," Shelly said, reaching over and taking the little sphere from the leprechaun's hand.

Shelly felt the magical effects of the sphere as it did some hocus pocus on her mind. A golden coloured map of Ireland appeared before her, floating in the air. As a young teenage couple walked past they strolled through the image, causing it to ripple slightly, oblivious to it being there at all. This was just for Shelly to see.

Little red stick figures began to appear on the map, popping up slowly at first before picking up a decent pace. In a matter of seconds, they covered most of Ireland. Some were clustered in the same area, others out on their own. One or two spots were devoid of the little figures completely. Then, slowly, the map started to pivot on its southern most point and flipped over, revealing an empty map of Ireland on the other side. The stick figures began to reappear, but this time in different places.

"What am I looking at?" Shelly asked.

"Each flip is a century, starting from the first recorded appearance of people like Becky back in the coffee shop. Around five hundred A.D. The little figures are where people with no personal memories popped up in Ireland."

"But, there must be dozens each century."

"Yep," Elivin said. "With nobody having a bloody idea why, what or how it is happening."

The map spun once more, although Shelly had lost count as each representation displayed the figures faster than the previous one. She guessed they were in the Middle Ages, but still the number of people appearing continued. Except as the map changed every few seconds Shelly noticed that the fifth or sixth spin would have less of the little figures. Sometimes it spun and there were no figures on it at all.

"Whatever is doing it stops every few centuries?"

"Either that or goes into hiding," Elivin said.

"Why do you say that?"

"It isn't a phenomenon. If it was there would a pattern to it. You can see that is purely random. Meaning that we have rational thought behind this, whatever this is. The people are being selected for a reason, just not one that anybody has figured out yet. That's why I reckon every so often the thing goes into hiding, only to resurface a century later."

"Why?" Shelly asked, watching the map continue to display its information.

"At a guess? To prevent whoever is chasing them finding them. It's what I would do. A few of those blank maps coincide with when I was close to catching it."

Shelly slowly nodded her head in agreement.

It made sense. If there was a creature of some sort running around and stealing something from humans then maybe it was like a strange magical bear. Storing up for a long hibernation period before starting all over again. That was a chilling thought. Shelly was not extremely familiar with everything that came from the Fairy World, but magical soul eating bears was something she felt Filthy Henry would have mentioned.

Which made Elivin's thinking the easier pill to swallow. If there was rational thought behind the people turning up with no memories that meant this was a person, a fairy of some description. One who was up to no good.

"Huh," she said as the map finished its last display and then faded away.

Shelly blinked a couple of times to refocus her eyes on the world around her and passed the sphere back to Elivin.

"Noticed, right?" the leprechaun asked as she took the crystal sphere and returned it to the pouch.

"There haven't been as many in recent years."

Elivin nodded her head slowly.

"Exactly," she said. "Becky is the first one I've stumbled across in a while. I think whatever is doing this has come back out of their little hiding spot. Plus, they've gotten better at covering their tracks."

#

It was dark, or possibly pitch black. There was a definite lack of light, on that nobody could disagree. Without light, it was very hard to see. Especially given the limitations of how the human eye worked. Whatever higher power had decided eyeballs required light in order to process things visually had clearly not thought about all scenarios a human might be in. But the fact remained that light was not something in an abundant supply at that moment, making it difficult for Filthy Henry to see things.

A person could not look around and figure out their surroundings if they could not see.

At first, he had thought there was a blindfold in play, but that was quickly ruled out. If something had been covering his eyes

Filthy Henry would have felt it against his skin. There was nothing to feel on his face. In fact, there was nothing to feel anywhere on his body, but the fairy detective decided not to dwell on that right now. The trick to keeping a level head in any situation was a simple one: you focused on one problem at a time. People who tried to figure out everything in one go overloaded their brain and panicked.

Right then, the main problem was trying to figure out where he was.

Since having a look around was out of the question, Filthy Henry decided to try his other senses. He concentrated on listening. The muffled sounds of a city came to him, as if somebody had their hands over his ears. It was impossible to pick out any distinct noises.

*Well that's just brilliant,* Filthy Henry thought.

Trying to call out for somebody was met with resounding failure. No sound came out of his mouth at all. It was almost like he suddenly had no mouth.

The fairy detective stopped trying anything and took a minute to think about his current predicament.

His hearing was muffled, eyesight reduced to nothing and he could not to call out for help. On any other day of the week this would have been a nice vacation from the chaos of the world, but not today. Today, Filthy Henry wanted to work on his case and that meant being able to see and speak. Not to mention have his hearing work at pre-muffled levels.

Wherever he was, Filthy Henry felt cold. But it was a strange sort of cold, with an almost…plastic feel to it. Even as the fairy detective had that thought he knew it made no sense. Cold was cold, just like hot was hot. You did not have such a thing as a plastic feeling of cold. Yet, if somebody held a gun to his head right then and asked him to describe the cold feeling, that was how he would describe it.

A plastic cold feeling. No sight, limited hearing and no speech. The list of problems grew.

*Move,* Filthy Henry thought.

He tried to move his arms. They did not play ball, nor did his legs or head. It was as if his entire body had decided to go on strike.

Filthy Henry stared into the darkness, listening to the muffled sounds of the world outside wherever he was, and silently swore.

*Guess I just wait for some to rescue me,* the fairy detective thought to himself. *That's just super annoying.*

# Chapter Four

Sudden, debilitating, headaches can occur for a number of reasons. As a doctor, Milton knew this.

One second a person could be happily sitting on the bus reading their book then, in an instant, they are curled up in pain while their brain tries to punch through their skull. Some people got headaches after not eating when they were hungry, others because they were ate something that triggered the brain pain. Technically headaches caused from a food related trigger could be classed as migraines, but you had to be very precise in diagnosing them. Otherwise you opened the door for people who got headaches after drinking too many beverages of the alcoholic variety seeking sympathy for their 'migraine'.

No matter how you tried to present it, a hangover was just a self-inflicted form of mental torture. Self-inflicted, from the ancient Latin phrase which meant you should suffer them in silence. Anybody daft enough to listen to a hungover person bemoan their current condition deserved to be slapped in the face with a fish. At least that was Milton's professional, personal and medical views on such matters.

But never had Milton seen a person get a headache so intense as the one he was currently witnessing, particularly after a simple conversation involving a basic question. It was truly astonishing.

Quinn had shown up as requested, sat down on the sofa, and started talking. He complained about being hungry, but Milton always made sure his sessions with Quinn were scheduled for directly after mealtime. Mind over matter may have been a mantra that most of the world subscribed to, but it was a weak mantra when faced with stomach over mind. All it took was one hungry burble from the belly and a patient's level of concentration crashed straight into the floor. That was why the way to a man's heart was through his stomach. Well, anatomically speaking the way to a man's heart was through his ribcage with enough force. The more romantic version served to reinforce the stomach over mind hypothesis. A full belly made a man much easier to deal with. So, when Quinn started moaning he wanted food, Dr. Milton simply ignored the request.

Nobody could be so instantly hungry directly after lunch. Especially given the amount Quinn was able to eat.

Their session proceeded as normal, then the headache struck.

It totally knocked Quinn for six. He clutched his head so tightly that Milton was sure he had to be causing more pain from pressure alone. There was only one course of action in a situation like this.

Milton reached over and pressed the buzzer on his desk phone, connecting with the intercom at the nurses' station. After three short beeps, somebody picked up on the other end.

"Yes, doctor?"

"Em, nurse…," Milton said into the speaker, then paused.

One of these days he might learn the name of a single nurse. Then just call them all by it and only be correct some of the time.

"It appears that Quinn has taken a bad migraine attack," he said. "Can you come and bring him back to his room? Maybe give him something to ease the pain, make him sleep?"

"Of course," the nurse said. "But can't you do it? Being his doctor and all?"

Milton rolled his eyes.

People sometimes forgot to show a person the proper respect. It was definitely a problem that had been going on for generations, getting worse as people started to see each other as equals. Milton did not like it at all. If folk on the lower rungs of society did not see those above as better, then what was the point of it all? He checked the time and decided that he had more important things to do. Plus, he was feeling peckish. A hunger that was definitely more mind over stomach in his world.

"I have another engagement," Milton said. "I'll bring him down to the station on my way out."

With that he released the button and sat back in his chair.

"Doc I need some help," Quinn said, gritting his teeth as he rocked back and forth on the sofa. "Codeine or something."

"Yes, yes," the doctor said, staring at the forlorn man on his sofa.

Quinn intrigued Milton for a number of reasons. After today's session that list had grown slightly. A knock on the office door distracted him from his thoughts.

"Come in," he said, loudly.

The door opened and a nurse, the one who seemed to be very friendly with Quinn, entered. She held two small plastic cups in her left hand. One with tablets in it, the other half filled with water. She did not even look at Milton as she walked across the floor, towards the sofa, and bent down close to Quinn's head. The patient opened his mouth at her gentle prodding with the cup. She tipped in the tablets, then poured some water in.

"I'll take him back to his room," the nurse said, giving Milton what he felt was meant to be an 'evil' glare.

She carefully helped Quinn to his feet and guided him towards the office door. As they left, turning to walk down the hall, the nurse did not close the door behind her.

Milton ignored the obvious attempt at showing even less regard for him, gathered up his wallet and keys and got ready to leave. Along the way he would try and sort out the peckish feeling.

85

#

Nurse Faul gently lowered Quinn down onto his bed, turning him onto his side just to be safe, and propped up his back with an extra pillow.

He looked dreadful and that was not something she generally liked to think about anybody. You never knew what circumstances caused a person to outwardly look bad, so as a rule Linda avoided judging a book by its cover. Quinn had been fine before going into the session with Fluid though. That fact was ringing an alarm bell in her head.

"No smoke...," Linda said quietly to herself.

But what could she do about it all? If she went to senior levels to raise her concerns they would look for evidence. No, before going any higher with it Linda knew she needed to find something concrete to back up her concerns. The scribblings of one patient would not be enough.

She pulled over the battered plastic chair from the desk, a common piece of furniture in all the bedrooms, and sat down on it beside the bed.

"OUCH!" Linda shouted.

Reaching underneath her left butt cheek, she felt around for the source of her discomfort. Her fingers found a small plastic soldier on the chair, a little scrap of paper held in place with some tape. Written on the paper in tiny, delicate, handwriting were some map co-ordinates.

"God dammit, Carolyn," Linda said. "Geocaching is all well and good so long as it doesn't try to poke a hole in my posterior!"

She placed the little solider down on the ground and looked at Quinn.

He had uncurled slightly and was not trying to crush his skull with his bare hands. One half of his face was buried into the pillow, like a cotton sandpit swallowing him slowly. His right eye was half opened and focused on her.

"Believe me now?" Quinn whispered.

"What?" Linda asked. "This is a migraine that's all. You think Milton did this?"

The barest of movements suggested that he tried to shrug a shoulder.

"Seems to be a bit of a co-inky dink," he whispered, weakly. "Any jelly pots?"

"You sure you aren't meant to be checked in here as a patient with an unhealthy addiction to tubs of jelly?"

The part of his mouth not obscured by pillow moved into a slight smile.

"Man's got to have some sort of vice, otherwise what's the point in living," he said.

Linda sighed and watched Quinn as he lay on the bed. He looked like he had just done ten rounds with a championship boxer. Ten rounds condensed into a few seconds.

Maybe Quinn was right and there really was something nefarious happening at the hospital. The way Fluid went around with his secretive sessions had always been a red flag to Nurse Faul. She had made a promise to Quinn earlier, one she intended to keep it now. If nothing else, the health of a patient in her care was at stake. Medical professionals took an oath. One that they took very, very, seriously. Regardless of the colour of scrubs worn.

If this fairy detective Quinn so badly wanted to speak to was a decent detective maybe they could help Linda find some evidence as well. Sure it meant bringing in a third party to the hospital, but the nurse knew doing any sort of investigating herself would only end badly. A detective could be more discreet, plus they might actually know who Quinn really was.

She reached over and gently placed her hand on-top of his.

"Need anything before I go?"

"The jelly, woman?"

"There is no jelly-woman," Linda said, grinning at him. "But I'll tell Katherine that something happened and you need a few extra tubs dropped off. Fair deal?"

Quinn slowly nodded, wincing as the movement clearly caused some pain, then settled back into his pillow and closed his eye.

Linda rose from the chair and went to get her belongings from the locker room. On her way home she would keep her promise and hire a fairy detective.

It was that sort of sentence that made Linda wonder if she did not deserve to be a patient in the ward herself.

#

Middle Abbey Street had, for many years, been one of the central city streets in Dublin. Not that it was central in a geographical sense, more because life seemed to rotate around it. For years it had acted as a terminus to a number of the routes serviced by Dublin Bus. Throngs of people would crowd onto the pavement, in varying sorts of typical Irish weather, and wait for their double-decker people carrier to come and take them onwards. Back in the good old days this wait could be anything from five minutes to fifty, depending on how many of the infamous 'Out Of Service' buses passed by. People always wondered why that route was so popular. Especially when said buses were always devoid of any passengers and the drivers seemed to be singing a happy tune as they drove by a bus-stop full of waiting customers.

Then the times changed and Dublin built a lightweight urban

tram system called the Luas. It was installed only a few decades after the previous tram system's rails had been ripped up from the city streets, because trams were not the way of the future. If anything, the Luas was proof that even idiots in governmental power can tell when something is suddenly back in vogue. The bus terminus was moved from Middle Abbey Street and the Luas lines laid so the large, silver, carriages could trundle through the city at a plodding pace.

Shelly and Elivin stood outside Filthy Henry's building on Middle Abbey Street as a Luas tram slowly went by. They both were looking up the steps at the front door, while around them the people of Dublin walked past. Nobody paid any attention to Elivin on account of her using The Veil to prevent mortals from seeing her. Anybody that came close to bumping into the bounty hunter simply altered their path, their mind subconsciously handling any messy business that involved a leprechaun standing in the middle of the road. Very few people paid attention to Shelly either, but there was nothing magical about that. Dubliners, as a rule, tended to avoid paying attention to things that did no concern them. It made life so much less interesting if you did not go getting involved in things that were none of your concern. Less interesting and less likely to suddenly become dangerous.

A survival mechanism stretching back to the dawn of time.

Elivin looked from Shelly to the front door of the fairy detective's building and back again.

"Do we have to wait for something to happen here or are we going inside?"

"Just a minute," Shelly said, gesturing to the leprechaun to wait. "I haven't been inside in a while."

"So?"

"So, I need to work up the courage again."

"Just how long has it been since the pair of you talked?"

Elivin asked.

"Did you hear about that thing that happened outside of Carlingford about six months ago?"

"Vaguely," the bounty hunter said with a dismissive wave of her hand. "Something about a legendary hero returning from the dead and killing an evil queen or something. Why?"

"Well it was about two minutes before the hero saved the day. That is the last time I spoke to Filthy Henry. Even that isn't one hundred percent accurate, because he ran off to do his thing about five minutes before. Let's call it ten minutes before."

Elivin crossed her arms and stared up at the door, thoughtfully. After a couple of seconds she coughed twice in the most pantomime of ways to clear one's throat Shelly had ever heard.

"Are you hoping the door will open by magic if we just stare at it long enough? Trust me, that's not likely to happen. That's coming from somebody who actually has a door in her home that opens magically."

Shelly groaned and reached into her jacket pocket, pulling out a single door key.

"Alright, fine! But if he is in here you're talking to him."

"Yeah, that ain't happening," the bounty hunter said.

Shelly climbed up the three giant stone steps to the front door, put the key into the lock and turned it. The locking mechanism clicked loudly on the other side of the door. With a twist of the old bronze door-handle, Shelly opened the door and stepped into the hallway. Elivin stepped in behind her and shut the door once through.

The building Filthy Henry had set up shop in was an old three storey structure. On the ground floor were rooms that he used just for general storage and clutter. Some boxes were even stacked up in the hallway itself, with no obvious rhyme or reason behind them. The fairy detective's idea of a filing system. If there were rooms on this floor, Shelly had never seen them.

Just inside the front door, on the threadbare welcome mat, was a mound of mail. Mostly leaflets from nearby shops judging by the looks of it, along with some utility bills. There were enough gathered that when Shelly opened the door the leaflets had been pushed across the mat. Either Filthy Henry had stopped bothering to leave the building via the front door or he had not been around for the last few weeks.

"Strange," Shelly said, pushing some more of the mail off the mat with her foot.

Leading up to the next level was a rickety wooden stairs, one which Shelly felt sure had to be held together by hopes and dreams. It looked like something that was just waiting to fall down. They both climbed the stairs, Elivin letting Shelly keep two steps ahead so that the weight was spread out, and reached the first floor landing.

More boxes and clutter occupied this floor, creating a strange winding trail from the top of the stairs to the only visible door on the floor. Shelly looked around the landing but did not see any sign of Filthy Henry. His office door was open slightly, enough that they could easily see inside the room. Nobody was seated at the desk and nothing moved within the office either. She looked down at Elivin.

"He might be upstairs."

The bounty hunter looked around at their current surroundings.

"What's upstairs? More of this collected detritus?"

"He lives on the top floor. It's like a small apartment," Shelly said. "You wait here and I'll go check. He has magical wards setup around his home, to protect the place he sleeps in from fairies. Don't want to risk you setting them off."

Elivin shrugged and walked over to the office door, leaning against the frame. Shelly strolled down the landing and took the second flight of stairs up to the top level. At the apartment door, at the very top of the stairs, she stopped and pressed her ear against the surface, listening for any sounds on the other side.

It was as still as a house full of children late at night on Christmas Eve.

Shelly knocked twice, lightly. She knew that knocking lightly was cowardly, but when you wanted to avoid talking to somebody the last thing you did was announce yourself at their front door. On her second tap the door opened a little, seemingly of its own accord. Shelly pushed it with her foot, the door swinging inwards.

The apartment was a tip.

Had this been some sort of movie or TV show, the apartment in its current state would have been cause for alarm to anybody seeing it. Empty pizza boxes were stacked all over the place, clothes strewn around the floor. What looked like a bottle of milk sat on the small coffee table beside the sofa. The reason it 'looked' like a bottle of milk was because its contents were not white, rather they were a sickly green colour.

It seemed like the apartment had been ransacked.

Shelly knew that this was not the case. Filthy Henry was just one of the dirtiest people she had ever known. He took the bachelor lifestyle to a new art form. Having magic made him one of the slovenliest folk around.

Why wash the dishes when you could click your fingers and have a month's load of them cleaned at once?

Despite his known magical cleaning abilities though, Shelly was concerned. While cleaning up after himself was not a daily habit for the fairy detective, he very rarely left food and drink lying around long enough that it went bad. Given that his fairy side converted food into magical energy, it was rare that Filthy Henry even left food behind after a meal. He either ate everything in sight or ran the risk of his own body fat being converted into magical juice. Which gave Filthy Henry the annoying ability to eat whatever the hell he wanted and not gain any weight.

She slowly walked through the living-room area and went down the small hallway that led to Filthy Henry's bedroom and kitchen. Both rooms were empty. The bed looked like it had not been slept in for weeks, the blinds on the window still drawn closed. In the kitchen stood the now customary stack of dirty dishes by the sink. But no sign of the fairy detective. She walked over to the dishes and saw that the food had literally dried onto the surface of the plates and cutlery. These had definitely been here longer than was normal, even by Filthy Henry's standards.

"Stranger and stranger," Shelly said to the empty apartment, looking around the kitchen.

Closing her eyes Shelly mentally flicked on her fairy vision and started to examine the apartment again.

Nothing immediately jumped out at her in the kitchen in an 'obvious clue' sort of way. She slowly walked out of the kitchen, back down the hallway, carefully looking at everything along the way. When she reached the bedroom door Shelly stopped and peered inside. Whatever about being brave enough to walk around Filthy Henry's dirty apartment, there was not enough money in the world to make her step into his bedroom voluntarily.

Even with that steadfast resolve, Shelly could see nothing revealing itself as being strange or out of place. No trails of magic to indicate a spell had been cast and whisked the fairy detective off somewhere. She continued back down the hallway into the living room and stood in the centre of the pizza box graveyard. A graveyard devoid of any useful information while containing an overpowering smell of cheese. Shelly turned off her fairy vision and dropped down onto the sofa.

"What in the hell is going on?"

A knock on the apartment door drew her attention. She looked over the back of the sofa and saw Elivin standing out on the landing. There was a shimmering orange light around the door-frame, bright along the wood and flickering slightly before Elivin. One of Filthy Henry's anti-fairy apartment protection spells in effect, Shelly guessed. She had never actually seen any of the alarm-spells working, let alone one so powerful enough that she did not need her fairy vision on in order to see the magic.

"What's keeping you?" the leprechaun asked, eyeing the orange light suspiciously and taking a step back from the door-frame.

The protection spell faded slightly, the light only visibly along the door-frame now.

"He isn't here," Shelly said, waving her hand around the empty apartment. "It looks like he hasn't been here for a month, maybe longer."

"He hasn't," Elivin said. "His office downstairs has dust all over it. Even if he was as dirty as this, just being in the place would stop the dust building up in some areas. Does he go on vacation much?"

Shelly shook her head. She got up from the sofa, walked out of the apartment, closing the door behind her, and went back down to the floor below, heading into Filthy Henry's office.

The bounty hunter was right; dust lay over nearly every surface. Not the general 'it needs a bit of a clean' dust, but a layer of the stuff. Nobody had been in the office for a while. Either that or they had been so careful that they never disturbed any of the dust, which was highly unlikely. That is what made dust so useful in detective work: once moved it was impossible to put back in place.

Unless you lived in a world where the crimes being

investigated involved magic.

"Maybe..." Shelly said to herself, only half entertaining the thought of a fairy magically moving all the dust back to where it had been.

Filthy Henry's office followed a similar state of disorganized madness to the rest of the building.

Along the right-hand side wall, if you were facing into the office from the hallway, stood three filing cabinets. On top of these were cardboard boxes, bags and a couple of jars. In the very middle of the office there was a large wooden desk, its surface home to a number of files and loose papers along with a desk lamp and telephone. Behind the desk, positioned in front of the window, was a large, red, leather armchair on wheels. Shelly knew that the chair was similar to one conjured by Lé Precon, the current King of the Leprechauns, when he had hired the fairy detective to recover his missing crock of gold. It had been a wasteful display of magic; one the King of the Leprechauns had used to remind Filthy Henry about the magical limitations a half-breed had. If the fairy detective tried creating chairs like that they would have faded away within a few hours. For Lé Precon the chair would remain in place forever, a constant torn in Filthy Henry's side.

All it had really done was made the fairy detective redecorate his workplace slightly. He threw out his old chair, along with any chairs clients may feel inclined to sit in, and bought a new chair that looked identical to Lé Precon's.

Then Filthy Henry had brought the magically conjured chair up to the roof and burnt it to ash. A petty act of defiance from somebody who should know better.

Shelly walked around the desk, pulled out the chair, and sat down. She looked at the files on the desk. It was rare that Filthy Henry actually had files when working a case. Most of the time he left the boring work of note taking and clue recording to

Shelly. It was only if the case required some research at a deeper level that files got pulled out from various sources and poured over in the office. If the problem did not resolve itself in twenty-four hours, or after a bunch of fireballs were thrown at it, then the fairy detective usually became irked. For him to research a case meant he was seriously irked.

She reached over and lifted up the nearest folder, opening it so that she could read its contents. As Shelly scanned over the pages there was a soft thump as something landed on the desk. Bending the folder over slightly, she looked for the source of the noise.

A small toy figure lay, face down, on the wooden surface. Shelly picked the toy up and examined it.

It was a toy detective, shaped from a single, solid, piece of plastic. The design was similar to the old gum-shoe stories of the 1960's. A wide brimmed fedora, long trench-coat, and a grizzled chin. No part of the toy moved, making it more of a statue Shelly figured. It, strangely, lacked a face. Only a nose and ears were on the head, but that seemed to be by design rather than wear and tear. From the looks of it, Filthy Henry had been using it as a paperweight. She placed it back on top of the nearest pile of sheets, standing on its flat feet, and returned her attention to the file in her hands.

"Anything?" Elivin asked, walking into the office. "Why do you reckon the half-breed puts magical wards around his apartment but not his office?"

"He doesn't care about what is kept in here, I guess," Shelly said. "Wouldn't you protect the place you sleep in more than the place you work in?"

The bounty hunter shrugged, coming around to stand beside Shelly. As she drew up alongside Shelly the toy fell over again, dropping to the floor.

"He collects toys?" Elivin asked, bending down to pick up the figure. "Oh, it's the Faceless Detective. I used to read that comic.

This is probably a collectors piece or something."

"I didn't know he collected anything to be honest," Shelly said. "That's new, or at least I haven't seen it around here before. Look at this. I think he was working on your case as well."

She pulled out a sheet of paper from the file and passed it to the bounty hunter.

"See there, it lists some of the locations that your crystal sphere had in it. There are a few sheets with information like that, all detailing a person showing up with no memories at all but able to talk."

"Interesting," Elivin said, reading over the pages. "Doesn't seem to have made any headway with it though."

Shelly closed the file and dropped it back onto the desk.

"Come on," she said. "He usually stocks up before going out into the field if he has made a discovery. There are only two places that will deal with him in Dublin. If we hurry we can make one of them before they close for the day."

"Think he'd mind if I kept this?" Elivin asked, holding up the toy detective.

"Don't see why he'd have a problem," Shelly said, dropping the file onto the desk and pushing back the chair so she could stand up. "Why do you want it?"

The leprechaun smiled.

"Bragging rights. Not many fairy folk get to say they stole something from inside Filthy Henry's home."

"But you didn't, it's from his office because you can't get into his apartment."

Elivin dropped the toy into a pouch on her utility belt and closed the lid, clipping the button in place.

"Yea, but nobody else will know that. Our little secret," the bounty hunter said, winking.

#

Public transport in a modern city has any number of pros and cons that the average commuter will experience at least once in their commuting life. They can range from the mundane to the mad. Anyone who has taken the bus or train to get from their abode to their place of employment, or back again, will have at least one story that involves a "crazy person" doing something a bit strange. Sometimes it may be nothing more than a lady singing a song on the morning trip into the city. Other times it could fall into the realm of a story with the opening line being "So, your man wasn't wearing any pants!".

People aware that time is a precious commodity, that life is short in the grand scheme of the universe, use commutes to the best of their abilities. Rather than sit and stare out the window, watching the world go by, such enterprising individuals will convert this "dead time" into something productive. Some will read a book, others will watch a show on their smartphone. Really brazen people try to write cheap fantasy novels on tiny laptops balanced precariously on their knees, fully sure it is the greatest piece of writing to ever happen.

Then you get the commuters who understand what this travel time really is meant for. They are battled-hardened veterans of the working world. People who have made the same journey countless times. Folks with young children or people coming home from working the night-shift.

They are the sleepers.

Look around any bus or train carriage during rush hour and you will generally see at least a quarter of the people on it asleep. Heads pressed up against windows or swaying around, following the movements of the vehicle as it turns. Some will lean forward, their heads hanging limply, others will have covered themselves

98

in a coat. The true stalwarts of the sleeper commute community will have travel pillows to rest their head against. The only problem with this skill-set, this ability to sleep anywhere for short periods of time, is that it requires a seat in order to achieve true commuting restful slumber.

Unless you had just pulled a double shift. Then all you needed was a handrail and some determination to catch a bit of shut-eye. The only drawback to this standing approach was that if the bus driver suddenly jammed on the brakes there was a very real possibility of injuring yourself.

Not to mention the rudest awakening from a power nap an individual could ever receive.

Linda had just managed to settle into the sway of things, sleeping with both hands firmly gripping a safety rail, when the bus stopped suddenly. If that was not bad enough, the driver had to blow the horn a few times. It was possible to ignore the sudden stop, but a bus horn blaring was harder to dismiss. Groggily, Linda looked around and peered out the bus window to get her bearings.

They had stopped at the intersection of O'Connell Street and Middle Abbey Street. The bus driver was leaning out his window and shouting at a taxi driver who was letting a passenger get out in the middle of the road.

Buses and taxis were like two competing gangs in a Broadway Musical when it came to the streets of Dublin. Both driving on the same tarmac, certain that they had complete and utter right of way over everyone else. Other road users were meant to just pay heed to them and where they were headed. The problem was when a bus and taxi wanted to occupy the same spot on the road and both were sure the other driver was completely in the wrong.

Linda moved down the aisle of the bus and tapped on the protective glass of the driver's door.

"Can you let me out here?" she asked politely.

"YOU'RE ONLY A BLOODY, sure thing love, WANNABE BUS DRIVER YA BLEEDING..."

The hiss of hydraulics was followed by the doors sliding open. Linda, checking nothing was coming up the inside lane of the bus, climbed down the steps.

"Thanks," she said back to the driver as the doors closed behind her.

She stepped up onto the pavement and started to walk along with the crowd.

According to the Internet, Quinn's fairy detective had an office on Middle Abbey Street. As Linda arrived at the address listed her confidence levels did not change at all. Quinn obviously wanted to see somebody who was nothing more than a con artist, preying on easily led people. It was an old building, standing out like a sore thumb amongst the other, modern, edifices that lined the street. Just as she started to climb the steps the front door opened and a woman in her late twenties with dark hair stepped out.

"I don't know why they don't get on, they just don't," she was saying to somebody behind her.

The woman stepped outside and pulled the door closed. Nobody else was with her. Linda stayed on the bottom step and looked up.

"Em, are you the fairy detective?"

The woman's cheeks went red as she saw Linda. She looked down to her left.

"Be quiet," she said.

"Sorry," Linda said.

"Not you," the woman said, coming down the rest of the steps to stand beside Linda. "Hi, I'm the fairy detective."

She offered Linda her hand.

"You go by the name 'Filthy Henry'?" Linda asked, shaking hands with her.

"Oh, him. No, that's the other guy. I'm the newer, more friendly, version of fairy detectives. Name's Shelly."

Linda looked back up at the building's front door.

"Was that who you were talking to when you came out? Filthy Henry?"

"No. That was somebody else," Shelly said, glancing down at the ground to her right. "On the phone..."

"Do you go by 'Clean Shelly' or is the other guy's name some sort of joke?"

Shelly shrugged.

"You know, I don't...why waste time talking about him? You wanted a fairy detective and here I am. How can I help?"

Linda looked at Shelly with her medically trained eye. Nothing about the woman screamed 'crazy', but then she was professing to be a fairy detective. If nothing else, bringing Shelly into the hospital may help to calm Quinn down on the whole topic. Then again Shelly could make him worse, it was all a flip of the coin really. Linda shrugged her shoulders.

"This might sound a little crazy..." the nurse began.

#

There was no more joyous a sound to a store owner then when their cash register clanged shut after a sale. In the old days tills used to have a small bell mechanism inside. You would pop out the drawer, put in the money, give back as little change as possible, then slam the drawer shut. All with a satisfying 'ding' at the end. Some people argued that the bell was more for the shop owner than the person working the till. It announced that the drawer had moved and if you did not trust your person handling the cash it might be time to check all the receipts added up.

For the small business owner, however, the little ding sound as a cash register closed was music. Like popping bubble wrap or managing to find that really hard itch to scratch. It was an immensely satisfying sound.

As Dru the Druid, Dublin's main retailer for things mystic and magical, handed over one cent change to his customer he smiled at the ding the cash register made. His modern model originally lacked the little bell inside, as most tills did these days. To fix it, Dru went and installed one. Money well spent as far as the druid was concerned.

"And you're sure this will do the job?" the old lady asked as she took her shopping bag off the store counter.

"But of course, my dear lady," Dru said. "Have a look around this store. Do you see any of the wild Antarctic Hunting Foxes around here?"

The little old lady looked around the shop then back at Dru and shook her head.

"Of course not. Nor are tere any of the little critters living nearby," he said. "Because that rock keeps them away. Once you put it in the southerly most spot of your garden the entire property will be protected."

Over the shop door hung a little bronze bell on a curved piece of metal. It was positioned to jingle whenever the door opened and did just that as some more patrons of the purchasing arts entered Dru's store. He looked up, a big smile on his face. A smile which instantly vanished at the sight of the new arrival.

"Shelly" the druid said.

"Dru," Shelly responded. "Do I need to check everything is above board?"

The druid gritted his teeth.

"You're not the sheriff of magic in these here parts, missy," he said. "How I conduct my business is of no concern to you. Unless I cross the line."

"True," she said. "But you have crossed that line before, haven't you. If this was above board then I'll not interfere."

Dru gulped involuntarily and regretted it instantly. Shelly had an almost magical ability to spot when he was guilty of something. Ever since she had started working as a fairy detective on her own she visited The Druid Stone at least once a fortnight. Any normal person would have assumed that helping out on a few of Filthy Henry's cases warranted a little leeway on some things. Shelly, however, saw it as part of her job to keep tabs on the druid.

"What brings you to this fine establishment today, young lady?" Shelly asked the old woman.

The little old lady had stood grinning as Shelly and Dru spoke. When Shellly called her a 'young lady' the grin transformed into a smile.

"Oh you," she said, visibly blushing. "I have just purchased a statue that will keep away some critters from my garden."

Shelly looked over at Dru with mock surprise on her face.

"Really," she said. "Pray tell, did you come here today to make that very specific of purchases?"

The little old lady shook her head slowly.

"Why no, dear. I actually came in to get directions to the train station on Tara Street. This kind young man just happened to mention how the statue he had for sale was exactly what I needed. Still don't know the way to the station, mind you."

Dru closed his eyes and felt his shoulders sag. He did not even bother waiting for Shelly to say it. With his left hand, the druid popped open the cash register, reached inside, and took back out the lady's twenty Euro. Without saying a word he handed it over to her.

"It's on the house," Shelly said as the old lady, looking very confused, took the money from Dru. "Now if you step out here, turned right at the quays and keep walking you will stumble upon Tara Street station in about twenty minutes."

"Thank you," the lady said as Shelly held open the shop door.

"Don't mention it. Also, tell all your friends about The Druid Stone."

Dru watched as the old woman walked past his shop window, smiling and waving at them both.

"What the hell, Shelly," he said. "I thought we were friends."

Shelly turned and walked over to the counter.

"We're friends so long as you don't con old women on fixed incomes out of money. I don't mind you selling that crap to hipsters that have more money than sense, but not pensioners. Got it?"

The druid waved his hand in the air.

"Fine, fine," he said. "No need to get on your high horse about it. Just trying to make a living is all."

"You actually have stuff worth selling in here," a voice from beneath the counter said.

Dru leaned over and looked down at the leprechaun in dark green body armour standing beside Shelly.

"Whose that?" he asked. "I'm guessing she came into the shop with you while invisible so as to not spook the little old lady?"

"How very astute of you, Dru. Her name is Elivin," Shelly said. "We're working a case together."

104

"Ha, is that really her name? Is she quick to anger? Goes straight to eleven in any given situa...."

A lot can happen in the blink of an eye, something that most people do not realise. Dru was not entirely sure how events transpired as they did. One second the leprechaun was on the other side of the shop counter. The next he was flat on his back with a very angry, riot gear wearing, midget standing on his chest. She was firmly holding onto the collar of his grey druid robe. With a handful of material, Elivin pulled his head up close so that his hooked nose touched the tip of her cute little button nose.

A nose that looked less cute when paired with the murderous glare accompanying it.

"Say it again, smart guy," Elivin snarled. "I'll make your eyeballs boil inside that bald, egg-shaped, head of yours and then spread them over some toast."

"No offence meant," Dru said, remaining as still as possible.

Having annoyed Shelly more than once, the druid knew that not moving was always a good way to avoid being struck with a fist. He was hoping the same applied to homicidal fairy types

"Whatever," Elivin said, sneering at him.

She released her grip and jumped down from his chest. Dru waited for the leprechaun to walk back around to the other side of the counter, then slowly got to his feet. He was greeted by the grinning face of Shelly, leaning against the counter and watching his assault by fairy.

"Did you enjoy that?" Dru asked.

"Little bit," Shelly said, smiling. "She's my new partner, did I mention that?"

"What do you bloody want?"

"Filthy, seen him lately?"

Dru rolled his eyes.

"You know bribes generally don't involve being beaten up in one's own store. How about you purchase something, like that geode over there that keeps elephants from trampling your garden?"

Elivin held up her left hand in its very padded glove. She wiggled each finger in turn, then slowly made a fist. A slight popping sound came from each knuckle. The druid stared at the fist for a moment.

"Should you be able to hear knuckles crack through a glove that padded?"

"Dunno," the leprechaun said. "But we could punch you in the face a few times to see if either of us can come up with an answer."

"No thanks," Dru said.

Shelly was smiling even more.

"Isn't she the best partner a fledgling fairy detective could ask for?"

"She's delightful," the druid said. "I haven't seen him in weeks."

"Really?" Shelly asked, frowning. "Like, how long?"

Dru started to tidy up the leaflets on his counter, the ones detailing local Wiccan meet-ups and Pagan ritual parties. The former being an interesting collective of people involved in modern day mysticism, the latter just a bunch of college students trying to get funding for parties on campus.

"I dunno, maybe six or seven. He usually drops in at least once a fortnight for supply top ups and the likes, not to mention the barbed insult thrown my way. But he hasn't been by at all. Last I heard, he was working on some case."

"What case?"

"Something about people losing their voices or memories or something. I dunno, I don't listen all the time."

Elivin put down a toadstool statue she had been examining, carefully placing it back on then shelf, and walked over to stand beside Shelly. She closed over one of the pouches on her belt and looked up at Shelly.

"He was definitely working our case."

"Looks like it," Shelly said. She turned back to Dru. "You haven't seen him in weeks. How do you know what case he is working on?"

"I talk to my customers. Some of my customers frequent the same places that Filthy does. Word gets around, you know how it works. Now get the hell out of here if you aren't going to buy anything. One annoying fairy detective is bad enough without you becoming another one that is just as bad. You might even be more annoying because of your little helper there."

Elivin glared up at the druid.

"That better not have been a dig at my height," she said, pointing at him.

Dru took a small step back from the counter.

"Fine," Shelly said. "I'll have another of those protection charms before I go."

"Of course," the druid said, reaching to a nearby hook and taking a small packet down. Inside there was a small, flat, stone shaped like a disc.

He handed the charm over to Shelly.

"Last one worked perfectly," she said, taking the packet from him. "You can put it onto my tab."

"I should have bloody seen that coming," Dru said.

# Chapter Five

There had been voices, of that Filthy Henry was certain. Somebody was nearby, or at least in the vicinity. Close enough to be drowning out the sounds of the city he could just about hear.

The voices were muffled, like all the other noises he had been hearing recently, but Filthy Henry knew they were voices. They had to be. One second they were close, the next moving away from him. Voices were good because voices meant people. Maybe not people he wanted to deal with, but people nonetheless. As they moved away from his current location the fairy detective started to worry.

What if they did not come back?

He tried to call out, get the attention of whoever was speaking, but once again no sounds were made. His prison, whatever was containing him, was absolute and complete. Nothing out and very little in.

Filthy Henry could feel his frustration levels rise and tried to hit something. No limbs moved, but something strange did happen. There was a very definite sensation of movement. Not enough to fall over, but it had definitely moved. The fairy detective felt things rock back into place.

*Interesting,* he thought.

Time passed, how much exactly was hard to tell when nothing could be seen. But, eventually, the voices returned. Louder this time, still muffled but closer. Filthy Henry listened as best he could, trying to make out any words. It was impossible to tell but he was certain that the speakers were beside him, in the very next room at a stretch. Close enough that they could possibly see whatever was holding him. With all his concentration behind it, the fairy detective struck out at his prison again. Stronger this time, with greater force. He felt it topple forward, or possibly backwards.

The voices stopped.

*Dagda above!* he thought. *I am in here! Help! Get me out!*

Whoever was outside began to speak again. With even more anger thrown into it, Filthy Henry struck out at his prison once more. It caused the container to fall to the ground with a loud thump. Whoever was outside might not want to talk to him, but the fairy detective was not going to let them ignore him.

That was for damn sure.

#

It had just been 'one of those' days. The sort when you woke up and the first thing you realised was your alarm clock had not gone off. Followed by the toast you hurriedly made as a quick breakfast burning because the toaster was set slightly too high. Burnt toast that was still eaten on the mad dash to the bus, since time was not on your side. Only to discover that the slice of bread had mould growing in the middle of it. Then, at the bus stop, a taxi decided that today was the day to drive through the large puddle and spray the sole occupant waiting for the bus. A bus which, according to the digital display at the stop, was running thirty minutes behind schedule.

It was a day were everything that could possibly go wrong went wrong, then had little babies of further wrongness who grew up quickly into adulthood so they could continue the run of bad luck.

Pat had watched the clock slowly change on his office desk, rolling forward towards lunchtime, and bolted out the door the second it was one o'clock. A day which had started out badly could sometimes be salvaged by a good lunch, he found.

Not only had his morning been a complete disaster, the run of bad luck continued once he arrived at work.

A report that had taken the better part of a month to complete suddenly no longer opened, the file corrupted. The I.T. guy, some fat man who rarely left his rightful place in the basement of the building, made a complete mess of recovering the file. Rather than restore it from a backup, one Pat had purposely made to ensure the report was not lost, the I.T. troll destroyed the backup and Pat's desktop computer as well.

Mr. Smith had not liked it when Pat informed him of the mishap, because the report was due to be presented to the American board members that afternoon. The I.T. troll had said he could probably recover some of the file, but that process would take a couple of hours. In the meantime, Mr. Smith told Pat to get the hell out of his sight and return with either the finished report or a valid death certificate to justify no longer working at the company.

Apparently either one would suffice.

This collection of unfortunate events resulted in Pat deciding he would turn his fortunes around, erase the bad luck factor, and have a cheat-day lunch. He had been good all week up to this point and the universe clearly did not care about all that effort. Meaning the universal scales had to be levelled once more. As he sat down on an empty park bench in St. Stephen's Green, unwrapping his double cheeseburger, Pat's mood slowly started to improve.

"One of those days?" a voice asked.

Pat looked over at the second occupant on the bench. The man who had not been there a moment before. He looked around at the four other benches in the area, each of them clearly devoid of people, then back at his newly acquired neighbour. The new arrival looked like the sort of person who would stick around if a conversation was started. Pat decided to say nothing and hope the hint was taken. Pulling back some of the wrapper from his burger, he brought it up to his mouth, a mouth that filled with saliva as the anticipation of the fatty goodness grew, and went to take a bite.

"I hear ya," the man said, leaning back against the wooden seat.

He had on a pair of those rubber gloves that dentist's used. Pat shuddered at the sight of them. If there was one thing he hated more than visiting the dentist, forking out insane money for something Pat felt his taxes should pay for, it was the feel of those gloves as the fingers they covered poked around his mouth.

Pat bit into his burger and started chewing slowly. His park bench buddy remained. Eventually there was no chewing left to be done and Pat swallowed the mouthful of burger.

"Do you work around here?" the man asked, as if he had been waiting for Pat to swallow the mouthful of food.

Rolling his eyes, Pat took another bite from his burger and started the slow chewing process once more. He hoped that his lunchtime intruder, not getting any conversation at all, would just leave.

The man did not.

Pat decided to alter his tactics. If he answered a question, engaged in general chit-chat, the man might be satisfied and go on his merry way. Since, clearly, he had no problem being ignored.

"Work in the offices over there," Pat answered curtly, nodding his head in the direction of his workplace.

The man turned and looked around the little park area. Nobody had come into it for the past few minutes. It was one of Dublin's little hidden secret spots, slightly off all the beaten paths. This was why Pat loved it so much.

"Nice little spot this," the man said to Pat. "You come here every lunchtime?"

Pat shrugged.

"Mostly just when I need a little alone time," he said, putting emphasis on the last two words. "Some downtime for good old Pat."

The lunch time intruder was still not getting it. He started to rub his left thumb and forefinger together, the rubber making a nerve-hitting squeaking sound.

"What's with the gloves?" Pat asked, glaring at the noise producing source.

"Oh these? Nothing really. I just am very conscious about germs is all. You know what I mean?"

"Not really," Pat said, taking another bite from his burger. "Don't get sick all that often."

The man turned on the bench and faced Pat directly, tilting his head slightly to the left.

"Really?" he asked, a slight echo entering his voice. "Pat, tell me your story."

#

No one fairy race ruled over all of Ireland, that would have taken far too much planning and power than any single race had to spare. But some races did have grudges that stretched back millennia. When humans in different countries did not get along it sometimes erupted into a war, one that involved bullets and carnage. When fairies did not get along the same sort of escalation happened, but instead of bullets magic was involved.

For the casual observer, it made things much more entertaining to watch.

As such, there were places dotted around Ireland designated

113

as neutral ground. Locations that any fairy could enter, safe in the knowledge that no violence could occur within the neutral ground for fear of reprisals from a third party. One such spot, the most famous of them, was Bunty Doolay's Bar in Dublin. An establishment that had existed for hundreds of years, allowing the city to grow up around it while the bar never changed itself. This was because Bunty Doolay, a powerful *Sidhe*, owned the bar and ensured the mortal world had no idea it even existed. To their non-magical seeing eyes, Bunty's was just a derelict building sitting amongst some finer examples of architecture. A pimple on the complex complexion that was the face of Dublin City.

Elivin smiled as she approached the building.

"I'm still impressed, I have to say. Not every day you meet a human that knows about this place," she said. "Morning, by the way."

After their most entertaining chat with Dru the Druid the previous evening, Shelly had decided to call it a day and head home. Before leaving Elivin for the night they both agreed to meet up the following day and continue working their case. The bounty hunter said Shelly could pick the time and place, using a stupid quip about 'mortal's choice'. Shelly decided to surprise the leprechaun, naming Bunty Doolay's Bar as their meeting spot.

Secretly, Shelly was delighted when she saw the shocked look on Elivin's face. Once in a while the fairy folk needed reminding that not all mortals were clueless.

"Good morning to you too," she said. "I've been inside the bar a few times as well, just so you know. You can't be part of the Fairy World and not know about this place. That's like a rule or something."

"Probably is now that you mention it," the leprechaun said. "But how does Bunty feel about you?"

Instead of answering, Shelly stepped up to the front door and pulled it open using the ornate brass handle.

114

Bunty and Shelly had not gotten off to a great start when they first met. The *Sídhe* had decided that Shelly was a bad influence on Filthy Henry. Apparently the world needed a half-breed detective with an abundance of sarcasm and few friends. Shelly had changed that by making Filthy Henry care what happened to her, particularly as she muddled her way through the Fairy World. Not in any sort of misguided romantic way, that had been something they both resolved quickly after finishing their first case together. More in the 'older brother looking out for his little sister' style. For whatever reason this rubbed Bunty the wrong way, because it meant Filthy Henry would do things to protect Shelly which he would never have done for anyone before.

However, after their last case together, Shelly learned that Filthy Henry had been hiding something big from her. The minor fact, according to the fairy detective, that Bram Stoker, the famous author who had been living in modern Dublin due to the fact he was a vampire, had killed Shelly.

Killed.

Dead.

No longer of the living.

Filthy Henry had used magical means to bring Shelly back to life. Then he had proceeded to lie about this little hiccup in her existence for the following year.

Shelly had not taken too kindly to this, despite the fairy detective trying to explain how his actions were done out of kindness. When she returned to Dublin, sans the lying sack of crap known as Filthy Henry, it had been nearly a month before Shelly once again stepped out into the Fairy World. At a loose end one day she had walked into Bunty's and sparked up a conversation with the powerful *Sídhe*, who seemed only too happy that Filthy Henry and Shelly had dissolved their friendship. Bunty Doolay even agreed to help Shelly as she started working as the newest fairy detective in the country.

Inside, the bar was empty. Given that it was just after breakfast, a mealtime shared by both humans and fairies, this was not surprising. Behind the bar-counter, resting against the shelves, stood Bunty Doolay, reading a book in her right hand while making idle gestures with her left. Around the bar dirty plates and cups were floating into the air and drifting slowly towards her. She looked up from her book and smiled.

"Didn't think you'd be in..." Bunty said before she stopped mid-sentence and stared at Elivin.

Shelly knew enough about the art of conversation to see that something was not right.

"You two know each other?"

Bunty narrowed her eyes to slits. The eyes of a *Sidhe* lacked pupils, being one solid colour instead. Right then Bunty Doolay's blue eyes flashed briefly.

"Sort of," the leprechaun bounty hunter said, raising her hands up slowly into the air. "I'm on neutral ground."

The *Sidhe's* upper lip curled slightly, her teeth showing.

"You're barred," she snarled.

"Technically my father is barred," Elivin replied. "I am a different person."

"It's a family barring," Bunty said, closing her book by slamming the covers together.

Shelly figured getting involved before the fireballs started was the best way to keep the peace. Not to mention avoid losing an eyebrow to flaming balls of death.

"She's working a case with me," Shelly said to Bunty, walking over to take a seat by the bar. "Can't you deal with your beef after that? You know I could use the magical assist."

Elivin shrugged and gave the *Sidhe* a smile.

"I don't have any problems with Bunty."

"It's Ms. Doolay to you," Bunty Doolay said. "Fine. Seventy-two hours grace until you get the case sorted. After that I'm going to get a bit more magical. Fire and brimstone style."

"We have an accord," the leprechaun said, coming over to the bar-counter and climbing up onto one of the stools.

Bunty gave her one final glare for good measure, then reached under the counter and brought up three glasses.

"What's the case?" she asked, turning to look at Shelly.

Shelly told Bunty everything she knew about the people showing up with no personal memories. Rather than risk Elivin aggravating the situation she relayed all the leprechaun's information as well, including the fact that these people had been showing up for a few centuries. When Shelly was done, Bunty raised her perfectly shaped eyebrows.

"Like some sort of serial...what?"

"Memory thief?" Elivin suggested.

Bunty did not acknowledge that the leprechaun had spoken.

"You talked about this with Filthy?" the *Sidhe* asked Shelly.

"I haven't seen Filthy in weeks," she said. "In fact, it looks like nobody has. We were over at Dru's last night and he hasn't had any visits either. I even dropped into his office, before you ask. Elivin was with me. Doesn't look like he has been home in a while."

"Now that you mention it, he hasn't been in here at all lately."

"Maybe he was barred for something that wasn't his fault?" Elivin said in that 'under the breath but loud enough to hear' way loved by moody teenagers the world over.

"No, he generally gets barred for a valid reason," Bunty said, reaching behind her and taking a bottle of white wine off the rack.

"But usually he tries to sneak back in early or, at the very least, mopes about outside in the hope that I change my mind."

This bothered Shelly. While it was not unusual for the fairy detective to go to ground when working one of his cases, he rarely vanished completely off the map. Annoying Dru was one of Filthy Henry's favourite hobbies. Shelly would have even said the ginger haired detective had raised it to an art-form. Bunty Doolay was on the very short list of fairy folk who tolerated Filthy Henry. Her bar was one of the few places that served a form of alcohol which the fairy detective could drink and feel the effects of. True it was fairy alcohol, but then he was half fairy so that made some sense in the grand scheme of things.

If neither Bunty Doolay nor Dru the Druid had seen the fairy detective for a few weeks and his apartment showed no sign of him living in it then, logically, that could only mean one thing.

"I think Filthy Henry is missing," Shelly said out loud.

#

Quinn opened one eye as slowly as he could and looked around the room. He was secretly happy to discover it was his room.

The movement of his eyelids and eyeball did not cause any pain, which Quinn took as a very good sign. While the migraine-level headache had been underway merely thinking about opening his eyes hurt. Now all the pain had subsided. Quinn uncurled from the foetal position and slowly sat up on the bed, swinging his legs over the side and placing his feet on the cool tiles of the floor.

With an immensely satisfying crack of his neck, Quinn looked around the room.

The single plastic chair had been moved, pulled up right beside his bed. On the little desk, the one bolted to the floor, were two tubs of jelly. He had no memories of the chair being moved or when the jelly arrived. In fact, without taxing his brain too much, Quinn found he could not recall why he had woken up in his room. His last clear memory was of lying on the sofa in Dr. Milton's office. After that there was a gaping hole in his recollection of events, punctuated by the pain caused by the migraine.

Quinn reached over and grabbed a jelly tub, peeling back the lid and scooping some out with his finger. He rose, a little unsteadily, to his feet, making sure to keep his grip on the precious gelatinous treat, and shuffled out the door of his room. With a wobble to his steps, Quinn headed in the direction of the common room. Right now all he wanted to do was have a chat with somebody to try and figure out why he had been in his room. In the back of his mind there was a niggling thought that something with the nurses had to be retrieved as well. Something that would have helped clear up the missing memories. But for the life of him, Quinn had no idea what that something was.

Entering the common room he spotted Bosco Burns, one of the few patients to frequent the room who was not a Blank Slate, sitting over by the window. Everyone else in the room had gathered in their little groups. Some playing games, others watching T.V., the vast majority of them sitting on the floor and watching everyone else blankly. Bosco had settled onto the window sill and was staring out, casting a furtive glance at his fellow guests every few seconds. As Quinn approached, Bosco looked at the tub of jelly goodness.

"Where'd you get the jelly?"

"Dunno," Quinn said. "Want some?"

He offered the tub to Bosco, who took it and smiled.

"Thanks," he said, dipping a finger into the green goo.

"No problem," Quinn said, leaning against the window and folding his arms. "What you at?"

Bosco pointed out the window with a jab of his thumb.

"Pixies," he said through a mouthful of jelly. "Just watching them fly around. Keeping me occupied while everyone else is away."

Quinn leaned forward and looked out the window. It showed an area of the hospital grounds that had been converted into a little relaxing garden of sorts. Under a large oak tree, whose branches spread out far enough that they cast a lot of shade, were a number of wooden benches. Flowerbeds with seriously neglected plants were spaced out in rows. Any sign of pixies, however, Quinn could not see.

"Gotcha" he said to Bosco. "But why aren't you yapping with anyone else. Not like you to be out on your own."

Bosco tipped the tub upside down, tapping on the bottom, and got the last clump of jelly out. He smiled and handed the empty tub back to Quinn.

"They are doing something," he said in a whisper. "I dunno what, but they are. You sure you can't see the pixies outside?"

Bosco Burns was harmless, even if he did go on and on about seeing fairy creatures outside. Apparently he had been brought into the hospital after standing outside a derelict building on Pearse Street for hours, claiming it was actually a fairy pub. Then, on the ambulance ride in, he kept ranting and raving about how Moore Street had stalls between the stalls. Invisible stalls, magical ones. That the streets of Dublin were actually packed with things nobody else could see.

"Listen," Quinn said, pinching the bridge of his nose. "You didn't happen to see who brought me back to my..."

The scene outside the window stopped Quinn from finishing his question.

Flying around like Christmas lights were a number of pixies. Little brightly coloured balls of light darting back and forth. All the colours of the rainbow, dancing in the air. They spiralled around some of the dead plants in the nearest flower-box and then, as one, shot up into the sky.

"Holy crap!"

"Pretty, right?" Bosco asked.

The top door of the common room opened and a nurse's head appeared.

"Bosco, you free?" she said. "Dr. Flynn is ready now for your weekly session."

He nodded and jumped down from the window sill.

"I guess," Bosco said. He looked over his shoulder at Quinn as he walked to the nurse. "Remind me about them later, yeah?"

"Sure," Quinn said, looking back out the window. All the lights had vanished. "I mean…what the hell! You're not crazy, there really are fairies in the world."

#

One thing that always amazed Shelly was how the fairy folk would use magic to do any simple, mundane, task. Almost as if they could not help themselves from showing off, even though the people they were showing off to were other fairies. Like Elivin's little sphere that had contained all the information on her bounty. What exactly was wrong with a few sheets of paper with some scribbles on them containing the same details? True it would have been a bit bulkier to carry around and not look nearly as interesting when another person used it, but still. Showing off for the sake of showing off seemed to be a big part of the Fairy World.

Right then Bunty displayed this trait, minus the glowing little sparks that would have made it look cool. After Shelly declared that Filthy Henry must be missing everyone remained silent. The *Sidhe* had stood still for a heartbeat or two then raised her right hand and pointed it towards the doors of the bar. Closing her fingers slowly caused all the locks on the door, a good twenty feet away from her, to slide and click into place. She then snapped her fingers twice before turning to stare directly into Shelly's eyes.

It was slightly unsettling how intense Bunty Doolay was looking at Shelly, making her want to avoid eye contact with the fairy at all costs. Suddenly looking down at the varnished wood of the bar-counter was the most appealing thing in the world.

"What do you mean by 'missing'?" Bunty asked.

"Well I'm fairly sure the word is the same in the human world as it is in the fairy one," Elivin said, pulling out the little toy detective figure from her belt pouch and placing it on the bar-counter.

The *Sídhe* did not find this remark funny.

"I've just locked the bar and made it completely invisible from everything outside for the foreseeable future. Even Ogma himself won't know what is going on in here. Keep up the lip, see where it gets you. Mortal, spill."

Shelly understood just how serious that statement about Ogma was.

Roughly a year ago she had worked with Filthy Henry on a case which involved the old Celtic Gods. Gods who turned out to be very much real, walking around in the clouds like it was the most normal thing in the world. One of them, Ogma, was the god tasked with writing down everything and anything that happened in or above Ireland. For Bunty Doolay to have completely hidden the bar from even his ever watchful eyes meant that things were after stepping up a gear in the seriousness factor.

She looked at the two fairies. If Filthy Henry was definitely missing then it was up to them to find him. Which meant that, right then, Dublin's newest fairy detective had just stumbled across her second big case without even meaning to.

"I think," she said, looking up into Bunty's completely blue eyes. "That Filthy Henry is missing, actually missing, and has been for some time."

"Based on what?"

"Well you and Dru are the only two people in the world that would see him on a somewhat regular basis. Dru, because even the fairy detective needs to get his magical supplies from somewhere, along with throwing insults at the druid. You, because this is the only fairy bar in Dublin that will serve Filthy Henry and not spit in his drink. Also, I think you're the only fairy bar in Dublin. Right?"

"Wrong," Elivin said. "She's just the safest one for a mix of races to drink in. The other bars all play the 'Management reserves the right to refuse admission' card fairly freely."

"Something I'm thinking of starting myself," Bunty said, eyeing the leprechaun.

"Not for seventy-two hours you aren't," the bounty hunter replied, smirking.

"Anyway," Shelly interjected before the fairies kicked off again. "We stopped by his office to see if we could...borrow...some files for our case. But it looks like he hasn't been there for a while either."

Bunty stood up straight and frowned.

"He could just be on holiday."

"Have you ever known Filthy Henry to take a vacation? He hates leaving Dublin most of the time. Hell it took The Moirai to threaten she would reveal how and when he was going to die before the ginger idiot agreed to go to Carlingford."

The *Sídhe* smiled, showing a mouthful of perfectly straight, white, teeth.

"Threaten to tell him his time of death, oh that's a good one," she said, almost to herself. "I might use that on him the next time he decides to step out of line with me."

Shelly clicked her fingers in front of the fairy bar-woman's nose.

"Focus! I think we have a problem if Filthy Henry is genuinely missing."

"Maybe he is just laying low for some reason," Elivin said, playing with the toy detective by walking it along the bar-counter.

"What are you doing with that?" Bunty asked.

The leprechaun looked up sheepishly at both Shelly and Bunty, then slowly returned the toy to its pouch on her belt.

"Nothing. At least not any more," she replied.

"Follow me," Bunty said to them both.

She walked down the length of the bar, flipping up the swinging top at the end of the counter, and headed towards a door at the back of the main room. Shelly and Elivin did as instructed and followed after the *Sídhe*, navigating the randomly set tables and chairs with the ease of sobriety. Not for the first time, Shelly wondered if Bunty purposely laid out the floor of her bar in such a chaotic pattern on purpose. It seemed that the more drunk one got the harder it would be to traverse the floor without crashing into something or, worse, someone.

Maybe it was all part of a grand design, one which ensured that people could not get violent in a collective manner. An obstacle course that required clarity of thought and control of ones motor-skills, neither of which would happen during a session of drinking.

At the back wall of the bar Bunty stopped, placing her hand on the door handle, and turned to look at them.

"You're entering my inner sanctum here," she said, giving them both a stern look. "I don't want to hear anything about the décor and likewise no mention of how you suddenly can't use your magic."

"Why wouldn't I be able to use my magic?" Elivin asked, looking at the *Sídhe* with suspicion.

"Oh, I know this one," Shelly said, feeling very proud of herself. "It is because the back rooms of Bunty's are warded to prevent anyone and anything from seeing into them. It also nullifies magic in the room so that Bunty can run back-room poker games without anybody cheating."

Both the leprechaun and Bunty stared at Shelly.

"How do you know about the poker games?" the *Sídhe* asked. "I never told you about that."

"Em...Filthy might have mentioned it after that time you healed me in there. I think."

Bunty's eyes narrowed.

"I'm going to have to have a word with that fairy detective when he resurfaces," she said. "Need to teach him not to run his mouth so much. Anyway, once inside only my magic is going to work. If you have anything that is keeping you alive, like a magical pacemaker, you may want to stay out here."

This rang a little alarm bell in Shelly's head. Her untimely death at the hands of Bram Stoker had been undone by a wish, one granted by the King of the Leprechauns. In essence, magic had resurrected her. She had never sat down and given this little fact much thought, beyond the point of getting annoyed at Filthy Henry for keeping such important information from her.

The fairy detective had explained that the power of a wish altered reality, rather than conjure things out of thin air. Wishes were powerful magic, bending the universe around the wisher so that they existed in a world where their wish had, literally, been granted. Since the number of instances of a human getting a leprechaun to grant them a wish were rare, the documented cases were small in number. But humans, by and large, were simple creatures. Those lucky few who had been granted a wish sought wealth and power, with only one or two seeking happiness and health. Such requests were minor in scale when compared with what a wish could grant a person.

After all, if you could bend reality why not wish for super powers?

The power of a wish was only limited by the strength of the leprechaun granting it. Thus making any wish given by the King of the Leprechauns one of the 'all powerful' variety. What a lowly commoner garden leprechaun may find hard, if not outright impossible, to grant, Lé Precon, the current King, would be able to do with ease.

But when all was said and done a wish was still magic. Shelly was currently sucking down oxygen because of reality bending magic and now Bunty was telling her that only the magic of the *Sidhe* would work beyond the doorway.

Gingerly, she raised up her hand to ask the question.

"No," Bunty said, shaking her head. "Use your brains, Shelly."

"I didn't ask my question yet," Shelly said.

"You're going to ask if stepping over this threshold is going to cause the wish that brought you back from the dead to stop working. Right?"

Shelly nodded.

"Wishes don't work like that," Elivin chimed in. "Wishes alter reality, they aren't a spell that keeps going. Reality was doing one thing, then a wish is granted, and reality is doing something completely different. Of course reality doesn't know this, because as far as it is concerned the events pre-wish were such that those post-wish make perfect sense."

"Reality is...aware?"

"No," Elivin said. "What gave you that idea?"

Sometimes Shelly hated dealing with the Fairy World. Before meeting Filthy Henry her only encounter with any of the magical races had been Kitty Purry, Shelly's deceased cat. It turned out that because Shelly was an artist her creative side had kept a toe in the mental doorway, allowing her to see glimpses of the Fairy World even though she was an adult. This was something that young children all could do, giving adults the idea that they were seeing imaginary friends. The truth was children were seeing the fairy people all around them, an ability they lost as they grew older. However because some adults, the creative kind, still believed in magic on some level they would get glimpses. The feeling that somebody brushed against them in an empty room or the sight of a person who was there one minute and gone the next. Kitty Purry, a Cat Síth, had technically kept within The Rules and used Shelly's latent ability to set herself up a nice kitty retirement pad.

She had never gone out of her way to make Shelly feel stupid. All Kitty Purry ever wanted was to be rubbed on her head and a bowl of cream with breakfast. Although she had been vocally critical of some of Shelly's paintings, but always insisted it was constructive criticism.

Not unlike a normal cat, it had to be said. Just more articulate in her critiques.

"I was just asking," Shelly sullenly said to the *Sidhe*.

"Think about it for a second," Bunty said. "You woke up in one of these rooms after a magical healing session. That was before you knew that a wish had brought you back to life. Why would you now consider the wish no longer working as a possibility if it didn't just stop back then?"

Shelly felt a little foolish.

"Carry on," she said, stuffing her hands into her pockets and hoping neither fairy noticed how red her cheeks had gotten.

Bunty made a series of intricate hand gestures and the door opened inwards. She stepped into the room and held the door open so that Shelly and Elivin could get inside, then closed it after them. There was a sudden sense of something missing, like when you wake from a dream filled with activity into an utterly silent night. Shelly felt that she had just put on some noise cancelling headphones. Elivin seemed undisturbed as she walked down the hallway and examined the walls.

"These are impressive," the bounty hunter said, reaching out and touching a design on the wall.

Shelly knew without asking what the leprechaun was talking about. Bunty Doolay had cast wards all over the walls of her back-rooms, it was how they remained completely hidden from all sources. Filthy Henry had said that the wards not only obscured what went on in the rooms but also protected them. In theory, which was how a lot of the fairy detective's knowledge on magic seemed to come about, the wards would protect against damaging magic as well. Bunty had, in essence, built herself a magical bunker. One capable of withstanding any assaults on the bar.

The wards glowed faintly blue, giving the room a cold light.

"Thanks," Bunty said. "That means so much to me that I managed to impress you. I can't wait to call my parents tonight and let them know that, finally, all my dreams have come through. Come on, the room I want to use is this way."

The *Sídhe* walked to the back wall of the room where there were three doors and opened the middle one, stepping inside and leaving the door open behind her. Elivin looked up at Shelly.

"I think that was sarcasm. Was that sarcasm?"

"Yea, it was sarcasm," Shelly said, following in Bunty Doolay's footsteps. "I find that most of your magical world is made up of sarcasm and very little magic."

The bounty hunter fell into step beside her.

"Maybe if queen Bunty didn't have such a stick up her backside we'd get along better," she said.

When they walked into the room they found Bunty Doolay sitting in the lotus position, in the very centre of the floor. Around her were four candles, all made from a red wax that seemed to pulse with an inner light.

Shelly ushered Elivin into the room and closed the door behind them.

"Do you need us to do anything?" Shelly asked Bunty Doolay.

The *Sídhe* shook her head.

"I'm going to cast the spell, all you need to do is pay attention. Once we lock onto where he is you two can go and get him."

Bunty closed her eyes and each of the candles flicked into life, small blue flames burning on their wicks.

"Because scrying is just so last century," Elivin whispered to Shelly.

"Ssshhh," Shelly hissed back.

"Silence in the audience," Bunty Doolay said, eyes still closed. "This isn't going to be a magic trick like your pint-sized practitioner performs. This is proper magic."

Shelly placed a restraining hand on Elivin's padded shoulder as the leprechaun went to take a step towards Bunty. The bounty hunter looked up at Shelly and nodded her head slightly, then pulled out the toy detective from her belt pouch and started to examine it. Shelly did not mind what the leprechaun did so long as it avoided a magical throw down between her and the *Sídhe*.

Not for the first time Shelly thought about how it would have really helped if her resurrection had not only put magic in her blood but also given her some abilities as well. As it stood she was less than a Red-man in terms of magical skills. At least Red-men could still use magic to hide themselves from humans. All Shelly could do was see the magical side of the world without assistance.

"How are you going to track him?" she asked Bunty. "Don't these things usually require a lock of hair or a fingernail or something?"

"There are other things that can be used," Bunty said, opening her left eye and staring directly at Shelly.

She looked annoyed at the disturbance, but Shelly had learned from Filthy Henry that when you were asking questions people got annoyed. The only solution was to continue asking your questions and hope that the person's annoyance made them reveal more than they intended to.

"Like what? Shelly asked.

The *Sidhe* shook her hands loose and flexed her fingers.

"You can track a person by their magical essence if they are a fairy. One of the useful things about Filthy Henry is that he is a half-breed so he has this very unique essence for us to track."

"Sorta like a soul," Elivin added.

"But then why can't you find the guy that has been running around Ireland for centuries if you know how to track a person by their essence?"

"Doesn't work like that," the bounty hunter explained. "You need to be very, very, familiar with the person's essence in order to track them. Otherwise you don't get a good lock when casting the spell. That's where the hair and fingernails thing comes in. They have a link back to their owner for a few hours, so you can use them for all sorts of magic. After that they are useless for tracking spells. The essence burns off them, so to speak."

Shelly looked at Bunty again. The *Sidhe* had tilted her head to the left and was still just looking at Shelly.

"Go on," she said. "Ask the next question so we can get it out in the air and finally start working some magic."

This caught Shelly a little off-guard. She had no further questions lined up after Elivin's explanation about the fingernails bit, but clearly Bunty figured there was one final bit of information worth sharing. She thought about it for a minute. The way the *Sidhe* had phrased her last sentence suggested that whatever the answer to the unknown question was it would be...embarrassing maybe?

Then the slow light of realisation dawned on Shelly.

For a person to know another's essence well enough that they could track them using magic a level of trust had to be in place. Trust that the person would not use this knowledge for nefarious ends. There were a lot of Rules in the Fairy World, but having power over another fairy creature was one that each race knew how to avoid as much as possible. Which meant that for Bunty to know Filthy Henry's essence they must have gotten very intimate at some point in the past. If that was true, it went a long way to explain why she put up with his crap so much and not just bar him from the pub forever.

"I think I understand how you'd know his essence so well," Shelly said, feeling her cheeks go hot for the second time in the same hour.

"Really?" Bunty asked, settling her hands back onto her knees. "I could draw you a picture if you wanted. Now if we are all done with today's magical biology lesson, let's begin."

Shelly watched as little streams of light rose up out of the candles, like threads. They swirled around the *Sidhe* on unfelt winds before gathering over her head in a beautiful display of light. The collection continued to grow, fed by the flames of the candles, flames which started to cycle through the full spectrum of colour. Then, at some silent instruction, the threads over Bunty's head shot outwards in the four directions of the compass. They passed through the walls without any hindrance at all.

"Alright," Elivin said, sounding hard done by. "Her way is definitely nicer to look at than our way. Stupid *Sidhe*."

A hint of a smile touched Bunty's lips as around her the threads of light continued on their way.

# Chapter Six

It was the perfect prison. Isolation coupled with complete and utter sensory removal. Left alone with nothing but the thoughts in his head.

What was worse; Filthy Henry had no memories of ending up in this place. None at all. For an indeterminable amount of time, the fairy detective tried to work out how he had arrived in this most special of prisons. But there was a gap in his memories. The last thing he remembered was chasing somebody down an alleyway, then he woke up in this place. Filthy Henry was not even sure if the waking up had taken place, because that would require being unconscious and the memory gap obviously covered that event.

If falling unconscious had actually happened, of course.

Filthy Henry did not care for his current situation at all. The only positive thing about it all was he seemed to not get hungry. Since arriving wherever he was, the fairy detective had not felt hungry once. Being hungry was annoying at the best of times. While you could not physically move and get food would have made it a thousand times worse.

He tried to work the problem with his limited amount of data and grew frustrated almost instantly. Filthy Henry was not just out of his comfort zone, he was out of an entire country's comfort zone. Agitated to the point of throwing fireballs around the place.

Just as soon as he figured out how to cast them.

#

Nurse Linda Faul stared into her cup of coffee and wondered if there was anything else in the world that could give her an injection of energy.

It was always worse changing shifts from night to day when you did not have a weekend in between to adjust. The lucky few nurses who had a weekend in between their shift change used the two days off to get into another rhythm. They got out of bed later if going into a night-shift, or made sure to be up by nine in the morning if moving into a day-shift. Sadly, due to the insane number of cutbacks in staffing levels and total lack of proper funding from a government more interested in lining their own pockets, not many nurses had the luxury of a weekend in between the shift changes. In fact, many of them considered themselves lucky if they could go home and get some rest in between the changes. Most of the time you simply went to the canteen, grabbed a bite to eat, and rolled into your new shift. Sometimes the truly lucky got a quick nap and a shower in the staff changing rooms.

Linda had been somewhat lucky. Changing from the night shift to her daily rotation had been broken up by a quick visit home. One that had included talking to the fairy detective, a person nothing like the nurse expected.

When you heard about private detectives you rarely considered that they were not scruffy looking individuals, very gruff and grumpy. Add the word 'fairy' in front of that job title and the mental image any sane person would have conjured up involved a hermit, living in the woods, with dirt all over his face and a fedora on his head. Possibly mumbling about some pixie crime boss who he had to get incriminating photos of. At the very least there was an expectation of some 'crazy' element to them.

Linda's short meeting with Shelly had shattered all these preconceived notions, except for the crazy element. After all, not many people go around talking to themselves in a way that suggested they were actually having a full-on conversation. But, babbling away to herself notwithstanding, Shelly the fairy detective had seemed completely normal, despite her career choice. She treated Linda with professional courtesy and listened to her, even taking on the case there and then. What is more, Shelly had noticed that Linda was clearly exhausted and told her to go and get some rest, insisting they could meet up the following day to talk further.

Ask any nurse coming off a double-shift, they do not need to be told twice to go and get some sleep. Linda had thanked Shelly, exchanged details for the follow-up, and headed straight home for a two-hour nap.

It had been a nap about twelve hours too short.

A bubble popped on the surface of her black coffee. She simply stared at it, too tired to even lift the mug up. Thankfully, the day shift had more staff on the floor for a change. If Linda played her cards right she could stay at the nurses station all day and just do paperwork.

That selfish thought made her think about Quinn's little project. She looked around, saw nobody was watching, then unlocked the pedestal under the desk and pulled out his folder. With the skills of one who has avoided work while looking busy many times before, Linda positioned her seat so nobody could see over her shoulder. Then she propped the folder on her knees, opened it, and began to read its contents. Anyone coming towards her would just see a nurse reading a file.

The perfect crime.

Quinn had added some notes after Linda's shift ended the previous day, the last line being that he was about to go for a session with Fluid. As if reading his name somehow called out to him, Dr. Milton appeared on the other side of the station. He rapped the wooden surface with his knuckles and looked down at Linda. Seeing his face made Nurse Faul groan inwardly. But, being the professional she was, the nurse smiled at the good doctor.

"Hi, how are you today?"

Dr. Milton frowned.

"I'm not here for ideal chit-chat. I was wondering if we had any new admissions."

Linda rolled her eyes and closed Quinn's journal, placing it back into the pedestal drawer. She pushed the chair over closer to the computer and started searching through the system for any new admissions. It was only when the search started working that Nurse Faul stopped to think about how odd it had been for Fluid to come looking for new patients. Generally the doctors only found out about new arrivals when a nurse told them. For one to come looking was strange, more so when it looked like there had been a new admission only an hour ago.

"Almost like you knew," Linda said under her breath.

"What was that?"

"Nothing," she said. "Yeah, seems we had a new person brought in earlier today. Another of the Blank Slates. Are they to go on your roster?"

Fluid grinned.

"But of course," he said. "Blank Slates need to be seen by the best in the business. Please find the woman and bring her to my office in twenty minutes."

Without saying anything else, he turned and walked down the hallway towards his office in typical ignorant Fluid fashion.

"Hang on," Linda said to herself, reading over the new admittance file. "I never said it was a woman."

#

More threads of white light had gathered over Bunty's head, swirling in the air. It looked like a cotton candy machine had made a baby with a lightning storm, resulting in a brilliant display in the back room of the bar. Something truly mesmerizing to watch. Which was a good thing, otherwise Shelly and Elivin would have had very little to do for the past hour.

"Doesn't usually take this long," Elivin said.

She had taken a seat on the floor, her back resting against the wall, the little toy detective placed standing on the ground beside her.

"Really?" Shelly asked. "It isn't like searching for something on the Internet though, right? I mean, we are talking about tracking a moving target. You'd expect it to take some time."

"Just saying," the leprechaun said, smiling. "If Bunty has access to his essence like she claims, she should have found him by now."

At her feet, the toy fell over. Elivin picked it up, examined it carefully, then placed it upright once more.

A few more threads of light passed through the walls, returning from their search beyond the room and moving towards the swirling collective blob above Bunty Doolay's head. These new threads merged with the floating cloud of light, going into formation like some jazzed up electric eels. It all spiralled around for a minute before, without any indication, the cloud of light dispersed. Bunty Doolay opened her eyes and stared directly at Shelly and Elivin.

The *Sidhe* looked annoyed.

"Are you two messing with me?" she asked, her tone cold. "I mean it. Are you both here just to screw up my day for some reason? From the leprechaun I expect this, but mortal if you're in on it I will bar you for your short little life."

Shelly looked at Elivin, who was staring at Bunty with a blank expression on her face.

"What do you mean?" Shelly said. "Nobody has seen Filthy Henry in weeks. You suggested that you could find him using this spell. How could I have done anything to mess that up?"

137

The *Sidhe* stood up with a grace that Shelly had never seen in a living creature before. It was like watching water suddenly rise from a river and flow vertically into the air. Bunty Doolay walked over to them, her eyes narrowed to slits.

"I've spent the last hour sending my magic all over Ireland, even into parts of the fairy realm, looking for one fairy detective," Bunty Doolay said, alternating her glare from one to the other. "But I couldn't find a trace of his essence. At all. Except, for whatever reason, in one place. A location that couldn't possibly make sense. Which would have me thinking that you pair are up to something and want to just waste my bloody time."

"I blame the human," Elivin mumbled.

"Hey!" Shelly snapped back.

The leprechaun stood up, jutted out her chin and stared directly into Bunty's blue eyes.

"More importantly, if you don't back on out of my personal space things in here are about to get really interesting."

There was a coolness to her words, one that Shelly was sure Bunty Doolay would pick up on. Pick up on and not, in any way, appreciate. The *Sidhe* grinned and slowly brought her left hand up, in between herself and the leprechaun. Opening her long, elegant, fingers revealed a tiny fireball floating above the palm of her hand.

"Oh, are we going to go to eleven? With no magic?"

Elivin's body armour creaked as she stood on her tippy-toes, leaning towards Bunty.

"Did you just call me 'eleven'?" the bounty hunter said, clenching her fists.

Shelly put her right hand in her jacket pocket and wrapped her fingers around her recently accquired protection charm. When she had decided to go into the fairy detective business some serious

138

considerations were made. One such charm had saved her life after Filthy Henry stole it from Dru's store and hid it in Shelly's coat pocket. The way the fairy detective had explained it such charms could protect a person from three minor destruction spells or a single major one.

Shortly after starting her detective business, Shelly had had a conversation with Dru. He had gifted her with ten of these charms, all real. It had only taken a small slap to the back of the head to remind him of his manners. So far, she had not needed to use them, so every charm was still fully loaded.

Clutching the one in her pocket tightly, Shelly figured now was as good a time as any to test them out.

"Alright you two," she said, pushing the fairies apart with her free hand and stepping between them. "Let's find Filthy Henry first, blow each other up over name calling second."

"Find Henry?" Bunty said, turning her glare to Shelly and keeping the fireball in her hand. "You're being funny?"

Shelly was not a fan of rhetorical questions when asked by somebody other than herself. Mainly because it meant she had to try and work out just what the other person expected the answer to be. Either you gave an answer and looked like an idiot because the question was itself the answer, or you said nothing and looked rude because the question required some form of response.

When the asker could cast magic, it made your answer even more important.

She thought about the path that would lead to the least amount of death and destruction, took a deep breath, and spoke.

"Bunty, I came here because I don't have magic. Elivin came here because she is my partner. But right now, neither of us has a bloody clue where Filthy Henry is and that is the honest truth. If I could have called down Ogma and checked his Big Book of Everything I would. But I can't, so I didn't."

139

"Ogma?" Elivin asked, sounding genuinely impressed.

"Worked a case with him last year. Nice guy, you should see his tower."

"I bet," the leprechaun said, snickering. "Can't beat the tower of a god."

Shelly rolled her eyes.

"It must be a fairy trait to be a wise-ass," she said. "Bunty, honestly. If I knew where Filthy was I wouldn't be wasting your time. I don't even want to talk to the jackass. But we all agree that he seems to have gone missing while working the very case myself and Elivin are on. So, sadly, we need him."

Bunty Doolay took three steps back from them and seemed to loosen up, her shoulders relaxing slightly.

"You genuinely aren't messing with me?" she asked, a confused facial expression replacing her annoyed one.

Both Shelly and Elivin shook their heads.

"Okay," the *Sidhe* said. "Then this doesn't add up. At all. Every thread came back from outside the bar with no results at all. Filthy Henry isn't anywhere to be found. When the spell first started, I got an instant result. But I just brushed it off as false positive. Since it was just the three of us in here..."

"I'm not following," Shelly said.

Bunty shrugged her shoulders then started to run her fingers through her raven black hair.

"The only trace of Filthy's essence that I could find was in this room," she said. "A room which he clearly is not currently in. Filthy Henry is definitely missing."

#

Quinn stared out the window at the world, watching the

140

clouds go by. Since Bosco had gone off for his session with Dr. Flynn there had been nobody to chat with in the common room. Not a single person seemed inclined to do anything other than sit down and stare at the four walls. Which made it very hard to try and spark up a conversation. The only difference between talking to a wall and conversing with a silent partner was the wall did less blinking.

Unless it was Jessica talking to the wall, then all bets were off. She had a tendency to see eyes everywhere.

Quinn had pulled over a chair, positioned it directly in front of the window with the best view of the flowerbeds, and sat down to stare at the Mother Nature show. Not that anything particularly interesting was happening beyond the window, but it was more entertaining than the highbrow conversations currently not taking place around him.

He had tried for the past hour to get the pixies to reappear in his field of vision, but it seemed that that little bit of insanity required proximity to the source. Without Bosco beside him, Quinn was not entirely sure if the little specks of coloured light would return. Then again, he was not completely sure if he had seen them to begin with. It could easily have been some sort of shared psychosis brought on by the energy of Bosco's personality.

That theory made more sense than seeing genuine fairy creatures flying around the hospital grounds.

Of course, such a line of thinking made certain requests of Quinn's seem contradictory when properly examined. Why would a person who doubted they could see pixies require the services of a fairy detective?

Quinn mulled that over and was pleasantly surprised to come up with a logical answer in a couple of seconds.

A person who was in a hospital with no memories of anything other than how to communicate, that was the sort of person that asked for a specialized detective. If you had a missing puppy you got onto a pet detective. Wanted to prove that your wife was having an affair, you hired a standard detective. Needed somebody to help figure out how you had no memories you had only one option. Regardless of whether or not the request made you look like a hypocrite.

Well, technically, Quinn figured you might try and hire a memory detective. But if the one thing you could recall was somebody who worked as a fairy detective, then that was the detective you needed to get in touch with.

It only took a few minutes with his inner monologue to align every life choice on the side of logic. Then again, 'inner monologue' was just a fancy way of saying 'the voices in your head'. It all depended on how you acted when listening to those voices that meant society could determine if you were crazy or not.

How you acted, plus the amount of money in your bank account. Money could make all sorts of problems easier for society to accept, or at least pass off as a harmless 'quirk'.

"Now how would I know something like that," Quinn said to himself.

"We need to talk."

He looked over his shoulder and saw Nurse Faul standing behind his chair, her arms folded so that her hands were tucked under her armpits.

"What's up, doc," Quinn said.

"That's not funny," Nurse Faul said. "Mainly because you know I'm a nurse. How come you never updated your file after last night's session?"

Quinn frowned.

"What file?"

She uncrossed her arms, handing him a brown paper folder.

"This file," Nurse Faul said. "You playing with me?"

He took the offered folder and shifted his chair around so that it faced her.

"What the hell is this?" Quinn asked as he opened the folder and placed it on his lap.

The hand writing looked familiar and he felt sure that it was his very own, but for the life of him he could not remember the last time pen had been put to paper to jot down his thoughts. Quinn started to read the scribbles. It was as if he was seeing his handwriting for the very first time, including how appallingly bad said handwriting was.

It looked like an epileptic chicken had just ran across the page with a pen it its beak.

After reading the last entry in the file Quinn looked up at Nurse Faul.

"What is this about?" he asked her.

Nurse Faul let out a long sigh and slowly shook her head from side to side.

"This doesn't add up," she said. "You don't recognise anything in that folder?"

Quinn shook his head.

"Should I? You don't have any extra jelly by any chance, do you?"

"How come you remember who can get you extra jelly pots but you can't remember something in your own handwriting?"

Quinn smiled up at her and closed the folder.

"Always remember where your next meal is coming from," he said, tapping his fingers on the cover of the folder. "How else are you going to enjoy it?"

"You don't remember anything you just read?" Nurse Faul asked, sounding concerned.

"Nope," he said. "But it sounds like something has been happening here for a while now. Any sign of the fairy detective yet?"

"You remember that and not what you wrote down in the notes?"

"I had a lot of time to think about stuff," Quinn said. "One telly showing nothing but the weather report, coupled with a bunch of people who spend most of their time staring into space, gives a person a lot of 'me time'."

Nurse Faul nodded.

"Yes, I found her. She said she would come out sometime this afternoon, to have a chat with you and see about the case. Said that it sounded like something she should at least look into."

This information caused Quinn to frown. While nobody was going to deny that he was not in possession of a complete set of memories, the ones that did flitter across his mind all indicated that the fairy detective was not female. In fact, each one suggested that the fairy detective was six foot three with ginger hair, although greying slightly, and a penchant for wearing trench coats. The only thing Quinn's fragmented memories could not give him, however, was a clear picture of the guy's face. Nor could he recall the man's name, just his job description.

Which begged the question; just who had Nurse Faul spoken to? Maybe Quinn's memories of the fairy detective were not to be trusted on their own.

"You sure it was a woman you spoke with?"

"I passed enough of the medical exams to be able to tell male from female," Nurse Faul replied, her tone dripping with sarcasm. "Hang onto that folder, read up on everything you wrote down. Can't have you wasting this woman's time when she gets out here.

144

Her name is Shelly, I'll bring her into the visiting room so that you can have some privacy. I've to go. We've a new Blank Slate just arrived. Mention that to Shelly when you see her."

She turned around and headed back out the door that led to the nurse's station, leaving Quinn alone with the folder and his thoughts.

Something was not adding up. One thing that kept ringing as false was that the fairy detective was a woman. Not that there was anything sexist about this line of thinking, Quinn knew enough about himself to be sure that every human had the right to be and do what they wanted with their life. It was just there were no memories, fragmented or otherwise, floating around in his head that suggested the fairy detective was anything other than a man.

"Shelly," Quinn said to himself, opening the folder and reading from page one of, apparently, his notes. "Name doesn't even sound familiar."

#

They had left the back-rooms and moved their little meeting into one of the corner booths of the bar. Bunty Doolay, with a wave of her hand, magically brought over some clean glasses and a bottle of wine. As she poured, the *Sidhe* looked across at Shelly.

"It's a very weak vintage," Bunty said. "But I'm still only giving you a quarter glass. Can't risk making you go blind because you drank some fairy wine."

Shelly smiled and took the barely filled glass Bunty Doolay offered her.

"Thanks," she said, sniffing at the contents.

Instantly she started to feel light-headed, the sensation similar to what happened after sniffing a whiteboard marker for too long. Only this was much more pleasant an experience, with less risk of ending up with a big blue dot on the end of a nostril. As the initial effects wore off Shelly thought about Christmas morning, when she was six years old.

It had snowed during the night, making for a picture-perfect Christmas. Frost had formed in the corners of her bedroom window. Young Shelly tottered down the stairs at half five in the morning, wrapped up in her fleecy dressing gown, making sure to avoid the third last step so that it would not creak. As she pushed open the living room door the Christmas tree caught her eyes immediately.

Every night, before going to bed, the lights on the tree were turned off. Except on Christmas Eve. For on that one night of the year Santa Claus needed to use the lights as a beacon, guiding him to all the good little boys and girls. As the multi-coloured lights twinkled in the morning darkness they gave a magical aura to the room. Not enough light to read by, but enough to make out shapes on the ground. Shapes that had not been there the night before. In place of the plate of cookies and glass of milk there now stood dirty dishes, resting just in front of a large cardboard box. Along the side of the box Shelly could just about make out little holes punched into the cardboard. Even more interesting than that, however, was what the box itself was doing.

It was moving, ever so slightly, and making little yipping sounds.

Shelly slowly walked over to the box, knelt on the carpet beside it, then opened the battered lid flaps and peered inside. Two tiny, black, eyes stared up at her, nestled amongst a mop of snow white fur.

"Awww," young Shelly said to herself. "Santa listened."

The box's occupant let out a little bark that would have barely scared a new-born baby. Shelly reached in and carefully lifted the puppy out from the box, nestling the small white ball of fur in the crook of her arm.

"I'm going to call you 'Snowy'," she said, tickling the puppy under its chin.

146

"Little girls should still be in bed."

Shelly looked back to see her father standing in the doorway, framed by the light coming from the top of stairs on the landing. He was smiling, watching her cradle her present from Santa Claus.

"Look, daddy," Shelly said. "Look what I got."

"You must have been a very good girl this year," her father said, his smile growing wider.

"I must have been because that's not all I got."

She reached into the box and scooped out her second present, rising a little unsteadily to her feet and walking over to show her father.

"See?" Shelly asked, stretching out her right hand with the second present while keeping a firm grip on Snowy with her left. "What is it? A surprise do you think?"

"Oh, for God sake...MARY," her father shouted up the stairs. "WILL YOU COME DOWN AND WASH HER HANDS. SHE'S ONLY GONE AND PICKED UP A BIG LUMP OF..."

"Whoa," Shelly said, shaking her head and returning to the present.

She looked around the bar, then at her fairy drinking partners, and finally down at the glass of wine in her hand.

"That had to have been the most vivid memory I ever recall having," she said. "What the hell is this stuff?"

Bunty Doolay reached over and slowly pulled the glass back to her side of the table.

"Maybe you shouldn't have any of what we drink," she said to Shelly. "Just to be on the safe side."

Elivin nodded, then took a huge mouthful from her drink and

147

slapped her lips together, clearly satisfied with the taste.

"So, Bunty, what happened with your big impressive magical search back there?" the leprechaun asked, placing the toy detective down on the table beside her glass.

"What is your fascination with that thing?" Shelly said. "I mean seriously, it's a little concerning for somebody who looks like..."

"Looks like what, hairless monkey?" Elivin asked, leaning in towards Shelly.

"Like you could take on a tiger and win," Shelly quickly said, sliding along the booth away from the leprechaun. "It's just strange, is all. You don't seem the sort to get so attached to a toy. Particularly a human toy."

Elivin took a deep breath.

"Sorry," she said. "Nearly lost my temper there."

"Nearly?" Bunty Doolay said under her breath. "I'd hate to ask what actually 'about to lose it' looks like."

"Keep yammering and you might find out," the leprechaun snarled.

"For Pete's sake, will you two lower the magical testosterone levels a little. You're giving women in both worlds a bad name."

"Fine," Elivin said sullenly. "And the reason I like the toy is...I dunno why. I just seen it in Filthy Henry's office and it looked so...great. That's all."

Shelly and Bunty exchanged a glance but said nothing.

"Sooooo," Shelly said, deliberately drawing the word out to defuse any residual tension in the room. "Back to that whole search spell not working..."

Bunty Doolay settled back into her seat and crossed her arms in front of her chest.

"My spell worked," she said, coolly. "Let's just put that one to bed right now."

"Sure, sure," Shelly said.

"But something clearly isn't making sense because the spell just kept saying he is here."

"Which he clearly isn't. Unless you have him tucked away upstairs, maybe," Elivin said, a cheeky grin on her face.

Bunty did not reply.

Shelly sometimes rued the day she went to Filthy Henry, all just to hire him to find her talking cat. If not for that eventful day she would never have gotten dragged into the world of magic and fairies. The butterfly-effect ripples to that would have meant Shelly never met Bunty Doolay, or Elivin, and by extension would not be sitting at this table right now. Stuck in the middle of a school-yard tiff between two people who could conjure fireballs without any fire-starting implements.

"If you two ladies could stop bickering for five minutes," Shelly said, not looking at either of them directly. "How about we discuss the case of the missing fairy detective first, figure out why the magic didn't work second. Sound like a good plan?"

Neither fairy acknowledged Shelly had spoken. This was not the first occurrence of fairies pretending she had not said a word, but it was the first time since becoming a solo operating fairy detective. Old Shelly would have just let the slight pass and allowed the pair of fairies to continue as they were, but that was not the persona of Shelly the Fairy Detective.

She slammed her hand down so hard on the table that the glasses rattled. It had the desired effect as both Bunty Doolay and Elivin turned to look at her.

"Well you've a bit of a temper on you, don't ya?" the

149

leprechaun said, pointing towards Shelly with the toy detective in her hand.

Shelly bit back the response that immediately came to mind.

"When was the last time you saw Filthy?" she asked Bunty Doolay instead, looking away from Elivin.

The *Sídhe* looked at Shelly and began swirling the contents of her wine glass around slowly with her finger. Not by sticking her finger into the fluid itself, rather by twirling it just above the glass and moving the contents magically.

"He came in a month and a half ago looking for some information, actually," Bunty Doolay said. "Filthy wanted some help working out how to create a *coimeádán spiorad*. But he wanted to do a modified version, one that would work for him."

"A comedian spore?" Shelly asked, regretting that she had never paid attention during Irish class in school.

It was hard to tell, due to the lack of identifiable pupils, but Bunty seemed to roll her eyes. There was definite movement in an upwards direction, at least Shelly thought there had been.

"They seriously need to start teaching Irish better in schools. You mortals can't pronounce half of the words or even try to figure out the contents of a conversation," the *Sídhe* said. "Who learns a language for twelve years and still isn't fluent in it afterwards?"

"Yep, not going to disagree with you at all," Shelly said. "When I was in school the teachers used to speak to each other in Irish because none of the students understood. A somewhat strange idea for encoded speech, considering it relied on the teachers being bad educators. But I still have no idea what the hell you just said. Is that a spell or something?"

"Its literal translation into English would be 'Spirit Container'," Elivin said. "Does exactly what it says on the tin, or urn, or anything really. Whatever you decide to use to contain a spirit in."

"So it's for catching ghosts?" Shelly asked, confused as to how anything at all could be used to contain a spirit. Surely it would have to be an object that would contain things normally.

"Not exactly," Bunty Doolay said. "Ghosts are creatures of pure energy, created after a person dies and involving some degree of magic. Wisps are your most typical spirits, I suppose. They are everything that made up a person, left behind when the body is gone. They just don't have a whole lot of energy to maintain that form. Typically they float around for a few decades, unless something causes them to exert compact bursts of energy."

"Seem to know a lot about wisps," Elivin said, taking a sip from her drink.

"I've had some experience working with them, thanks to Filthy," Bunty said. "He needed me to create one from a suspect so a few questions could be answered."

"Then what are Spirit Containers for?" Shelly asked. "If they aren't to catch a ghost?"

"Are you afraid of ghosts or something?" the bounty hunter said.

"I ain't afraid of no...NO! We are not doing that!" Shelly said.

Elivin gave her a sly little smirk and returned her attention to the toy detective figure in her hands.

"Spill already!" Shelly snapped at Bunty Doolay, forgetting for a brief instant who she was speaking to. "I get enough of this 'round about' explaining from Filthy Henry."

"Well now, the little mortal has some fire in her belly," Bunty said, grinning. "OK. A *coimeádán spiorad* is more like a safe house for a person's spirit, or soul if you prefer. Should anything happen to cause the spirit to come under attack or stress, maybe even risk being removed from the body, the *coimeádán spiorad*

151

pulls the spirit into it. Then keeps it safe until such time as the body is brought back in contact with the spirit container."

Which sounded highly implausible, if Shelly was being completely honest with herself. Bunty Doolay had just described a construct that could be used as a backup location for a person's soul. In the age of computing, where everything and sundry was being stored 'in the cloud', it seemed like the fairy folk had just latched onto another idea and made it magical. Although in what situation would a person, fairy or otherwise, need to have some sort of backup storage location for their spirit?

Not that this explained what Filthy Henry had been up to when Bunty last saw him. It just sounded like he was working on one of his little magical projects that came up from time to time.

"Okay, let's just take it that he was making one of those things. Why come to you?" Shelly asked.

"He's a half-breed," Bunty said. "He doesn't have access to the same information a normal fairy would. Plus he needed to make it a bit different to how they normally would be created."

"Why?" Elivin asked, walking the toy detective around her glass on the table.

"Well they need to be powered continuously. Which for you or me is not going to be a problem because we have a vast well of magic to draw from. But Filthy Henry doesn't have that in his favour, so he had to make it require less power to work."

"I still don't get what that would be used for in terms of a case," Shelly said.

They sat at the table in silence for a couple of minutes, each of them just looking off into space. Elivin placed the toy detective standing up beside her glass. Something about it caught Shelly's attention and for the first time since seeing the statue she decided to look at it using her fairy vision. She closed her eyes, mentally flicked the switch, and opened them to see the world of magic.

As everything moved into the magical spectrum, Shelly watched the toy detective light up bright and shiny. From somewhere within the plastic statue energy pulsed, enveloping the figure with a soft blue light. All colour was stripped away from the statue as the blue hue shone.

Then, without anything to cause it to happen, the toy detective fell forward onto its face.

# Chapter Seven

Quinn lay stretched out on the sofa in the common room, reading a book he had found amongst the board games. It was some old science-fiction novel, the sort that read like an epic space opera, or at least that was the blurb on the back. This did not really matter to him, because it was just a way to escape the mind-numbing boredom of the ward. Nobody was talking, or doing much of anything. Even the new arrival had just slotted into the routine of staring into space, doing nothing, and only interacting when people spoke to her.

Not that this bothered Quinn. He had decided to stop trying to make any friends in the ward. It was an immensely pointless exercise given his current situation. With each of the Blank Slates basically resetting every couple of days, any memories of a budding friendship vanished. So why bother? Better to just sit down, read as many books as a person could and hope that whatever wires went wrong in your mind fixed themselves sharpish.

A jelly pot dropped down onto his stomach.

"Thank you jelly angels," Quinn said, picking up the pot. "Although I am more partial to strawberry over purple."

"Purple isn't a flavour," Nurse Faul said, moving into view. "Also, how many of the other patients do you see getting extra snacks?"

He ripped open the container's lid and started to dig a finger into the purple goo.

"But sure, I'm your favourite," Quinn said, smiling up at the nurse. "Plus, I am sure if they could remember to ask for extras they would."

She rolled her eyes at him and looked around the room at the other Blank Slates.

"Did you get a chance to talk with the new girl yet?"

Quinn shook his head.

"Not yet," he said, shifting around on the sofa so that he was sitting upright. "She went straight down to a session with Fluid. I might wait until dinner, sit beside her and spark up a conversation then."

Nurse Faul sat down on the sofa beside him and leaned in, giving them an element of privacy to the chat. Not that she needed to do this, Quinn thought. Everyone was in such a dopey stupor it was highly unlikely they would have paid the slightest bit of attention to anything interesting going on around them.

"Did you remember anything after reading your journal?" she asked in a whisper.

"Not really," he said, digging out another finger full of jelly. "Although it was an interesting read, because I had been thinking something was up. Have I been investigating for long?"

"Seriously, with notes and everything? A few days," Nurse Faul said. "Maybe if we got everyone to start keeping journals that they read each day. Might stop them losing any newly formed memories."

Quinn shrugged his shoulders and nodded his head once. He reached behind the cushion at his back and pulled out the folder. Without saying anything, he plucked a pen out from the shirt pocket of Nurse Faul's uniform, flipped open the file, and scribbled down onto the last page a note to himself about getting others to start journals.

"Couldn't hurt. Where is my visitor?"

"Dunno," Nurse Faul said. "But she did have another case she was working on, maybe that one is taking up more of her time than she figured."

"I'm still not convinced about this whole 'she' aspect," Quinn said. "I don't know how, but I am nearly positive the fairy detective is meant to be a guy."

"Doesn't matter," Nurse Faul said, talking back her pen and picking up the folder. "I kept up my end of the bargain, so that is that. Now, Fluid wanted another session with you today. Says that yesterday's one didn't count properly due to your sudden migraine attack."

Quinn tipped the last of the jelly pot into his mouth, stood up, and handed the empty pot back to Nurse Faul.

"The doctor will see me now," he said, with a dramatic flourish of his arms.

"Are you sure you're not completely insane?" Nurse Faul asked him.

#

Everyone sat and stared at the toy detective standing in the middle of the table, not entirely sure what to do with the new information they had just stumbled across. Shelly turned off her fairy vision, removing the blue hue from the figure before her, and was looking from Elivin to Bunty and back again for guidance on what to do next. Not only had they answered the question of why Bunty Doolay's spell had not worked as expected, they had also found the spirit container that Filthy Henry had been working on.

"That's it, right?" Shelly asked Bunty. "That's the container?"

Bunty Doolay slowly nodded her head. She reached out with her long, delicate, fingers to touch the toy. A couple of centimetres short of physically placing her finger tips on it, the small detective fell over.

157

"That's him alright," the *Sidhe* said, righting the toy on the table once again.

"You mean I've been carrying around the spirit of the bloody half-breed in my belt for the better part of a day?" Elivin asked.

"Less of the half-breed," Shelly said.

"I went to the bathroom with that thing in my pocket," the leprechaun mumbled, staring at the toy.

"How come there isn't some sort of trail floating off it? You know, back to whatever is powering it?"

Bunty Doolay leaned forward and spread her hands out wide above the toy's head. Little tendrils of white light fell from her fingers and gathered around it, pulsing ever so slightly as they doubled up on themselves. With some gentle movements of her fingers the tendrils began to swirl around the toy.

"Hey, hang on a second," Shelly said. "I can see that spell but I've my fairy vision turned off. What gives?"

"You've had the second sight for so long now that you don't have to actively turn it on for most things. When your mind detects magic is taking place it will show you just enough of the Fairy World to see the spells. Plus, you're gaining a degree of control over your fairy vision, as you call it. Impressive, for a mortal. Being able to turn it up a notch and see the spell around the toy is no small feat."

Shelly felt her cheeks flush red and focused on the spell being woven around the toy detective. She never took praise well.

Bunty wiggled her fingers and the tendrils fell away, falling to the table like wool. The toy stood nestled amongst them, doing nothing worthy of note. After a few seconds each of the lights started to fade away, the tendrils dissolving into thin air, until none were left. This made the *Sidhe* frown, clearly annoyed by the outcome of her spell.

"I sometimes hate that fairy detective, you know that," she said.

"Why?" Elivin and Shelly asked at the same time.

"He has somehow managed to do the one thing he shouldn't be able to do. This *coimeádán spiorad* is completely custom, like Filthy said he was going to make it. Seems to have some sort of defensive spells cast around it, preventing a person from tracking it to the power source."

"I'm right in assuming the power source is the person whose spirit essence is inside, right?" Shelly said, picking up the toy detective and examining it closely.

"Not really, although in most cases it is. The power source just has to be the person who cast the spell, creating the *coimeádán spiorad*. After that anyone can be inside them," Bunty Doolay explained. "Some fairies might create an external power source, ensuring that even if their body is destroyed they will be safe in the container. But you generally can track the source."

"Then why don't we just, you know, open the container?" Shelly asked.

"Not how they work," Elivin said. "Only the person that created the container knows how to open it and release the spirit contained inside. Plus, if you don't have their body really close there is a big chance that their spirit never returns to the body."

This was just what Shelly had wanted in the case of the missing annoying ginger man. A clue. A big, stinking, slap you in the face like a wet fish, clue. The sort of clue that, had this been a movie, would blow the case wide open. Except this clue was one of the least useful clues in the history of detective work. It basically told the three women exactly what they already knew. That Filthy Henry was in some sort of trouble. Trouble that they had to get him out of, somehow using the worst clue in the world.

As she twirled the toy around in her hand, Shelly had a

sudden notion.

"Elivin," Shelly said, focusing on the toy detective. "Your bounty hunting would have specialized spells, right? For tracking purposes?"

The leprechaun nodded her head.

"Sure, not that I get to use them all that much. It generally requires something from the person that I am trying to find. Like we said earlier you'd need hair, blood, teeth..."

"Or their spirit?" Shelly asked, waving the toy at Elivin. "Right? Just like what Bunty Doolay was able to track down earlier in the back rooms."

The bounty hunter stared at her and slowly began to nod her head.

"Yes," she said. "Yes, possibly. But we'd just be tracking the toy, which we already know is here."

"Exactly," Shelly said. "Which is why we use the essence inside the toy detective to track it back to Filthy's body."

"Not a bad idea that," Elivin said. "Yeah, yeah I should be able to come up with something."

"Really," Bunty said. "You think your little tracking spell will work after figuring out you were carrying around his spirit container? Where my magic failed, your pint sized spells will succeed?"

The leprechaun stood up on her seat, reached over, and plucked the toy detective out of Shelly's hand. She stared directly into Bunty Doolay's blue eyes the entire time.

"Just because you and my father don't get along, don't for one second think that my magic isn't every bit as good as yours. Besides, you were looking for the half-breed as a whole and found his spirit. My magic will be looking for the body. We didn't know they would be separated earlier."

"Every bit as powerful as mine? That's not what I heard about your abilities, given your current profession," Bunty said.

Shelly groaned. This was starting to give her a serious sensation of déjà vu.

Elivin sat back down on her seat, dropping into it like a stroppy child would, and positioned the toy detective directly in front of her. She removed her big, padded, gloves, tugging them off one finger at a time. With the most theatrical of gestures she bundled the gloves together, slapping them down hard onto the table surface. The toy wobbled slightly, but remained upright.

Interlocking her fingers, Elivin stretched her hands out before her with the knuckles pointed to her chest. Grinning, she cracked them all, the bone popping sound clearly audible in the empty bar. Taking a deep breath, the leprechaun bounty hunter exhaled slowly and closed her eyes. She parted her hands, twirling the index fingers on either side of the toy. Little sparks of green light started to appear, spreading out from the tips of her fingers. They spiralled above the toy briefly before forming a bright cocoon around the little detective Elivin stopped casting her spell, the sparks no longer coming from her fingertips, and settled back into her seat.

Bunty Doolay and Shelly watched the green energy cocoon. It formed tightly around the figure on the table, pulsed twice with a bright light, then faded from sight.

"Well that," Bunty Doolay said, looking over at Elivin. "Was a great, yet expected, disappointment."

The leprechaun glared at Bunty.

"If you ever left your precious bar, *Sidhe*, you'd know that not all tracking spells send out pretty little ribbons into the air. More importantly, you'd know that a spell should constantly update you on your targets location. When you are out in the field you don't want to go to the last place your target was, you want to get to where they currently are."

161

"Meaning?" Bunty Doolay asked, clearly not impressed.

Shelly slid out of the booth, walked over to Elivin's side of the table, and picked up the toy detective. It looked completely normal, even under her fairy vision. There was no obvious change to the object at all. But, for some reason, she was feeling an overpowering urge to turn to her right. She carefully put the toy back down and the desire went away, as if it had never been a thought at all. Picking the little figure up once more caused the urge to return.

"Meaning that it's a compass, with true north being wherever Filthy Henry is right now," Shelly said.

"See," the bounty hunter said, nudging Shelly in the knee with her elbow and smiling from ear to ear. "The human figured it out. You're slipping in your extremely old age."

"Let's go," Shelly said, putting the toy into her coat pocket and pulling Elivin's chair back from the table. "I'm fairly sure I know where this is going."

Bunty's upper lip curled, showing her teeth. She pointed at Elivin.

"Get out of my bar you pint-sized pain in the arse before I do something you'll regret."

It happened in the blink of Shelly's eye. One second Bunty Doolay was pointing her finger at Elivin and the air was devoid of anything in the death and destruction realm of things. The next the *Sidhe* had conjured up a shield made from bright, white, light while Elivin lobbed fireball after fireball at her. They shattered harmlessly against Bunty's shield, disappearing in puffs of purple smoke and causing no damage at all to the surrounding area. Bunty Doolay did not even appear to be under pressure from the assault. As each fireball was thrown, Elivin took a step closer to her target. Tiny beads of sweat glistened on her forehead as she continued with her attack. It seemed like the destructive magic was tiring her, something Shelly had never seen when dealing with full blood fairies.

Shelly pulled over a nearby chair and kept it between her body and the fairy creatures, for no real reason other than it made sense to have something she could duck behind if a fireball headed her way.

Bunty Doolay brought up her right hand, since her left one was conjuring the shield, and curled her fingers into a claw shape. Every wineglass on the table became very animated for inanimate objects. Each of them started to visibly vibrate, their contents bubbling up and shooting out through the mouth of each glass. Rather than spilling over, however, the wine spiralled up into the air like tentacles. Each one seemed to be created by more wine than there had been in the glass, but Shelly learned early on never to question things when conjured by magic. It just made your brain hurt if you tried to figure out how something was happening in the realm of the fantastic.

Each of the wine-tentacles grew to be slightly taller than Elivin. They hung in the air, seemingly unnoticed by the leprechaun, swaying back and forth like crimson snakes. Meanwhile, Bunty kept her shield up while the bounty hunter threw another volley of fireballs.

Shelly reached into her coat pocket and once again confirmed that one of the protection charms was in there.

The two fairies continued there little stalemate, until Bunty Doolay moved the fingers on her free hand and stopped holding her wine-tentacles back. Each one lashed forward, two of them headed straight for Elivin's hands while the third zeroed in on her head. As the first of them wrapped around her wrist the leprechaun saw them, but it was too late. They looped around both wrists in a second and tugged her hands upwards, while the last tentacle wrapped itself around her eyes like a blindfold.

Bunty Doolay lowered her shield and looked at the captive leprechaun.

"You have no idea just how much you screwed up, Eleven!" the *Sídhe* said. "In here I am as powerful as Dagda himself. You're not the only fairy who has a temper that goes straight to ten plus one!"

"Yeah? Well let me get a look at you, you lanky string of porcelain misery, and we will see who has the most power," the bounty hunter snarled in response.

"Oh, that's why you covered her eyes," Shelly said, straightening up from behind her protective chair. "It isn't just being able to use your hands, you need your sight as well. See, Filthy never explains this stuff to me."

Neither fairy spoke for a moment. Bunty Doolay slowly turned her head and looked at Shelly with those amazingly blue eyes.

"Get your pint-sized partner out of my bar. The truce is still in effect, despite her going straight to eleven. As always. But when you come back it better be with Filthy Henry so that I don't have to keep the truce in place indefinitely. Now leave!"

There was no sense of movement. No swirling of the landscape or blur of motion. One second they were inside Bunty Doolay's Bar, the next Shelly and Elivin were standing on the street outside. Of the wine-tentacles, there was no sign. Elivin's bounty hunter gear was at her feet, the helmet resting on top of her gloves. Shelly looked behind her but saw only the derelict facade that mortals all saw when they looked at Bunty Doolay's Bar.

"She upped the illusion," Elivin said, pulling on her gloves and picking her helmet up. "It's how all her kind deal with being rude. They hide behind magic. Nobody is going to find that bar now, unless she lowers the spell again. Bloody *Sídhe*."

Shelly spotted a taxi further down the street, waiting at a pedestrian crossing for the lights to change green in favour of traffic.

"You know, she has impressed Dagda. I'm pretty sure what went down in there could have gone much, much, worse."

Elivin shrugged her shoulders and put on her helmet, popping the visor up so her face could be seen.

"She started it," the leprechaun said.

"I'm not so sure about that. Come on, let's go and find wherever Filthy Henry is. But, can you cast an illusion over yourself or something so that you look human? I don't want people to think I am crazy person walking around the city talking to myself."

"Yea, sure, whatever," Elivin said.

The lights changed, the taxi started driving towards them. Shelly held out her hand to flag it down and then hoped that this was not going to be a long journey. After all, she was a fairy detective without the ability to conjure fake money out of thin air. Bills had to be paid somehow and taxi fares in Dublin usually required a loan from the bank in order to pay them.

#

People often spoke about how they 'went for lunch with some friends from work'. It sounded like a lovely idea, but one which Tim never could wrap his head around. Friends, in general, always seemed to fade from his life, no matter what he did. Over the years he had made some firm, fast, friends. But after a while or so they just stopped bothering with him.

At the start Tim had thought it must be something he was doing. After the third time the 'friend ship' had sailed, leaving him behind on the pier of loneliness, he started to analyse things. His behaviour, how he helped his friends out when they needed it. Giving people space, lending them things. Being supportive. After much self-examination, Tim came to the conclusion that he had acted like a good friend. So, the next time people came into his life, ones he would have regarded as pals, he changed his personality slightly. He was sarcastic, a bit mean, rarely helped and skipped one in three social events.

The results were the same, solitude with no real reason as to the trigger.

Once he found a new job, one that challenged him mentally and helped to pay the bills nicely, Tim figured maybe things would change. After all, your school friends might get bored of you talking about work stuff all the time. But your work friends surely could not. They would, at the very least, have the work stuff in common.

Again the cycle started. Idle chats around the coffee machine became conversations about movies or weekend events. These evolved into lunches together in a group, sometimes just Tim and one other person. Life was good. Then it all stopped again. No warning, no explanation.

Tim had started to ponder if maybe his body odour was the issue. He had never noticed a pong coming from himself, but then a person could easily become nose blind to their own musk. This had led to a period of extreme showering, cleaning himself on a level that should have been classed as a sport in its own right. Not just a daily barrel wash, as his father would refer to the sink scrub after a hard day in the workshop, but an out and out full on body wash. The removal of dirt and quite possible a layer of skin as well, to ensure that what was left behind would be considered clean. Tim even invested in some products from the local pharmacy. Things with the phrase 'skin peel' or 'deep pore cleanse' became part of his daily scrubbing routine. Afterwards came the lotions and balms, not just for the lovely smell but the skin healing effects they offered. Scrubbing oneself to within an inch of your life left a very red, nearly raw, skin to display to the world.

Still this had no effect on his friend situation. The metaphorical leaky holes in his friend ship remained, leading Tim to believe that maybe, just maybe, he was the sort of person other people did not want to hang out with.

It had been a sad fact of life to stumble upon, but Tim did what anyone would do in such a situation. He grinned and powered onwards, because you never knew what was waiting around the corner. The next week or month could be the one were you met your best friend, that buddy who wound up in the same nursing home helping you shout at kids to get off the grass.

Although if that person decided to show up during lunch, Tim always thought to himself, it would have been just peachy.

Thankfully, the intelligent folk in government had decided that Grand Canal Dock, a busy and popular spot in Dublin at the best of times, needed a bit of a facelift a few years ago. They had a number of fancy, metal, benches put in around the edge of the water. A spot for people to come, eat, and stare out into the canal. Somewhere for folk like Tim to go, enjoy the world around, and see all the people.

Just not with anybody to talk with.

"I'm sorry, is this seat taken?"

Tim looked up from his sandwich at a gentleman standing near the end of the bench. A gentleman in every sense of the word, Tim noticed. The man wore a very expensive looking suit, had a newspaper tucked under his left arm and his lunch held in front of him. In fact the only un-gentleman-like thing about him were the blue, rubber, gloves on his hands.

But friendships could be struck up with stranger quirks than having surgical gloves on.

"No, no, of course not," Tim mumbled through a mouthful of sandwich. He scooped up his work stuff and dumped it on the ground by his feet. "Please, sit."

"Thank you," the gentleman said, with a slight incline of his head.

They sat in silence and ate their food. Tim slowly chewed on another bite of his sandwich and mulled over his next move.

This was the tricky stage. Depending on how the conversation went they could either start up a lunchtime-friendship or part ways and never see each other again. Key to the entire affair, however, was to not come across as too desperate. It had to appear natural, like nothing was being planned five or six moves in the future.

A delicate game of conversational chess.

"Lovely day," Tim said, leaning slightly towards the gentleman.

He felt happy with that opening gambit. It was just perfect, in every way. There was enough room to start yapping about other things, while being generic enough for the man beside him to answer politely and proceed no further with the conversation. He tilted back over to his side of the bench, took another bite of his lunch, and waited.

"It is indeed," the man said. "Figured I would get out, have lunch outside for a change."

Tim smiled. The gambit had worked.

"Oh, I couldn't agree more. I hate sitting in the office all day, then having my lunch either at my desk or in the kitchen area. Sure why would you do that?"

"Very true," the man said. "People need to enjoy work and life. Balance is important."

"Absolutely," Tim said, hiding a smile.

This was going well, he felt. With any luck they could meet here again during the week and create a solid foundation upon which to build a friendship. He worked through the next possible topics of conversation in his mind and decided that a gentle probe would not be the worst move.

"What is it you do yourself?" he asked.

"Oh, me? My job is very boring. I suppose you could say that I help people. Although a more accurate description would be that I collect things, stories. Histories. That sort of thing. What about you...sorry I never even asked your name before imposing myself on your bench."

Tim felt elated. Without having to prompt first, names were about to be exchanged.

"I'm Tim," he said, leaning across the bench to shake the man's hand.

The gentleman took Tim's hand firmly, the rubbery feel of the gloves bringing back a recurring nightmare of dentists to Tim, and looked at him. Tim noticed that the man's eyes were an amazingly bright shade of blue. As he looked at them Tim guessed there was a reflection of sunlight hitting them from the water of the canal. He could have sworn that the iris of each eye started to glow, a slight red tinge forming.

"Well now, Tim," the gentleman said, his voice echoing strangely. "Tell me your story."

#

So far every visit to this room had been the same. Lie down on the sofa, stare up at the ceiling, get asked some daft question about how he felt. Rinse and repeat for about an hour. Although, somewhere in the back of his Swiss-cheese addled mind, Quinn could not shake the feeling that something else happened in the room. Something greatly out of the norm when it came to seeing a head doctor.

This trip, however, differed from the previous ones due to the simple fact that Dr. Milton was nowhere to be seen.

Nurse Faul had told Quinn to go for his appointment with the good doctor and being the dutiful patient, one filled with stolen jelly, he had gone. But after repeated knocks on the office door had not resulted in Fluid calling him in, Quinn tried the door handle. It pulled down easily and the door opened, the office completely unlocked. A normal person may have considered this strange and returned to their life of quiet contemplation in a room filled with silent comrades, but Quinn's mind clearly worked differently. Instead, he felt the best course of action was to go into the empty office.

Once inside, Quinn had no idea what to do with himself. The little voice that had told him to enter seemed to run out of ideas after that. It was entirely possible that Dr. Milton had just stepped out for a minute and would return shortly. Plus, having a little lie down on a sofa while waiting for somebody would hardly be detrimental to one's health.

That had been twenty, long, non-napping, minutes ago and still no doctor. Quinn wondered what the protocol was in situations like this. Presumably you waited for a certain amount of time and then politely left, maybe after writing a little note to explain that life was too short. But surely it behoved the person who was missing to provide entertainment for their guest while the waiting took place.

Quinn sighed and turned onto his side, staring at the vacant desk of Dr. Milton.

It looked like most of the desks he had seen in the hospital. Mounds of paperwork, folders, pens, a collection of coffee cups in varying degrees of Goldilocks temperatures. Fluid had his computer positioned on the left, pushed as close to the edge as possible without actually knocking the machine to the floor. Resting on the keyboard was an open folder, the cover slightly dog-eared and bent back just enough for Quinn to read the patient's name.

It was his own name.

Curiosity got the better of him, as Quinn felt sure it would with anybody in a similar situation. Your medical records ripe for the reading and no responsible adult in the room to prevent you from looking at them. What else would a person do? It was possibly a moral dilemma, but then when you had no memories how could you know what your morals were usually like in such a situation.

He rolled off the sofa, landing upright, and walked over to the desk. Quickly glancing at the door to make sure the doctor was not about to enter, Quinn reached over and picked up his file. The sheets inside were loose, not attached to the actual folder itself. There was also a small, skinny, notebook tucked in between some of the pages. Taking them all out from the brown cover, Quinn pulled another file from the stack on the other end of the table and took some pages out from it. He stuffed these into his folder, closed it, then stuck it half way down the stack of files. Quickly, without much precision, he folded the pages from his own file and stuffed them, along with the little notebook, down the back of his trousers so they were held in place at the waist.

"Some light reading for later," Quinn said to himself. "Assuming I remember I have them back there after this session."

As he straightened the pens and pages on the desk so it looked like nothing had been disturbed, Quinn spotted a leaflet tucked under the keyboard. He pulled it out, unfolded it, and read it. It was about some writer gathering that was happening in a few days. A collection of aspiring and successful writers meeting up and shooting the breeze, headlined by some woman called Tracey Fitzgerald. Quinn folded the leaflet and put it back under the keyboard again.

The clock on the wall continued to do what all clocks with a working battery did; it told the time. Each second passed by and was followed by the next, with no sign of Fluid returning to the office. Most people would have considered such behaviour to be the height of ignorance. As the seconds turned into minutes, Quinn found himself agreeing with that assessment. He decided to wait around for one more minute and then, failing an appearance by the doctor, head back to his room. Which, sixty seconds later, was exactly what Quinn did.

He hopped off the sofa, checked the pages and notebook were secure, then walked over to the office door. Just as Quinn reached for the handle the door opened and Fluid entered the room.

"Oh," the doctor said, seeing Quinn. "Em, right. Yes. Good. You're here. I was looking for something...to do with you. Your...file."

Quinn frowned and quickly looked around the walls of the office for a security camera.

"Em," he said, taking a step back from the door so that Fluid could fully open it. "Is it over there? You've a big stack of files there."

Dr. Milton eyed Quinn with suspicion, then walked over to his desk and pulled back the chair. He started to search through the stack of files, sliding them like giant cards to better read the names written on their covers. Once Quinn's folder appeared the doctor stopped and slid the other ones back into place.

"Yes, it is here. Listen, I've had a busy morning and my previous engagement ran a little longer than I intended. I was meant to go over your file before you arrived for today's session. How about I just catch up with you tomorrow instead? Same time? You don't look like any improvements have been made..."

The stolen pages felt like a weight around his waist. Quinn took the suggestion from Fluid, nodded his head in agreement, and left the office. Pulling the door closed behind him, Quinn could have sworn, just as the gap closed, that Dr. Milton was staring after him. It may have been nothing more than a mild case of paranoia, but Quinn was not going to wait around in order to find out while he had a medical record to hide back in his room.

He turned and power-walked down the corridor.

#

It had been an entertaining taxi ride, although Shelly figured the driver enjoyed the entire experience more than anyone. Generally when a person gets into the back of a cab or taxi, regardless of where they are in the world, that person will have an idea of their final destination. Maybe they wanted to head to the airport, or just needed a lift down-town. Possibly the hotel did not provide a pick up service or there were two pubs, with the same name, on opposite sides of the city and the party was in the other one. In a movie, the passenger could even be the sort of person whose destination involved following 'that car'. Regardless, it was a rare thing, in the private transportation world, for a fare to get in, sit in the back seat, and instruct the driver to 'head up that way and I will tell you when to turn or stop'.

But that was all Shelly had been able to her driver, a gentleman called Jim judging by the medallion all taxi drivers displayed on their dashboard. As Elivin and Shelly climbed into the back seat neither of them had any real idea what direction to head in. Thankfully the leprechaun had heeded Shelly's request, conjuring an illusion around herself so that mortals saw a ten-year-old girl sitting in the back-seat with Shelly.

"So, we just drive around?" Shelly asked the bounty hunter beside her.

"Well, sadly they don't blink with a big arrow saying 'Target is here', on account of always updating to their latest location. But we could get lucky and Filthy Henry might be in same spot for a while. Just hold the toy up and listen to the directional urge. We just have to drive around until we work out where the fairy detective is now."

Shelly held the toy up, ignoring the curious look the taxi driver gave her, and decided that the back of the figure was going to be 'north' for the duration of the journey. By keeping it and the front of the car in alignment they would be able to head straight for wherever the fairy detective was. It was such a simplistic plan that she felt sure something would have to go wrong fairly quickly.

The taxi pulled out in that way that most taxi drivers do in Dublin; without any indication at all. This move was met with a horn toot from the car behind and an expletive phrase shouted out the window by their taxi driver. He drove to the end of Pearse Street, slipping into the bus lane that allowed traffic to go by the front of Pearse Street Garda Station and one of the side entrances to Trinity College. They merged onto College Street and headed towards College Green. Shelly held the little toy detective up and felt no urge to turn or change direction, meaning that wherever Filthy Henry was lay directly ahead. Due Back-of-Toy, for want of a directional term.

College Green was busy, as it generally was during the day. In late 2009 the government of Ireland had come up with a brainwave to make the area a 'public transport only' zone. Buses, taxis and cyclists had free reign during peak hours. The idea behind this move was to encourage more people to use public transport over private. 'Leave the car at home' had been the mantra uttered by those in control of traffic flow, all in order to reduce the amount of private vehicles in the city. It would probably have worked as well, if the buses had not both increased fares and reduced the number of buses due to 'falling passenger numbers'.

Shelly never professed to be an economics whiz, but she always figured that if you wanted to increase the amount of people using or buying something surely dropping the cost was the better option. Raising fares on a reduced services seemed like an oxymoron of an idea.

Taxis moved through the area like a herd, taking up the two lanes in great numbers. She stared at the traffic through the window, watching the age old battle between cyclists and cars. Both certain they were more entitled to the road, neither wanting to share with the other.

"You people really need to come up with a better way to get

around the place," Elivin said, gazing out her window. "This is just chaos."

"Well not everyone can shape shift or teleport," Shelly said.

"That's...true, I guess," the bounty hunter said, her tone oddly sad.

"We going the right way, love?" the taxi driver asked, before Shelly had a chance to check what Elivin meant.

"Yea, just keep heading...that way," Shelly said, eyeing the metre.

She could feel her wallet cringe at the fare already, after only five minutes in the car.

As they drove down College Green, onto Dame Street, no desire to turn appeared.

The taxi drove on, down Dame Street and onto Lord Edward Street, which brought them around by Christchurch Cathedral. Even Elivin was impressed by the Gothic looking building, standing with defiance among the more modern buildings of the city. Shelly instructed the driver to go down High Street, judging it was the correct route by holding the toy detective up and seeing which of the multiple street options best lined up with her need to change direction. They went down Bow Lane West.

"Turn up here," Shelly said.

The driver nodded his head and turned onto James' Street. The walls of the local hospital came into view. As the taxi drove paste them Shelly suddenly felt the need to turn completely around.

"Guess he is in there," Elivin said.

"Anywhere here is fine," Shelly told the driver.

He flicked on his hazard lights, a method used in Ireland to stop randomly wherever a person wanted, and pulled into the bus lane. With a few button presses the final tally for the fare rang up, bright red digits displayed on the unit.

"I've got this," the leprechaun said as Shelly felt her heart skip a beat at the cost.

Elivin handed over a fresh, crisp, fifty Euro note.

"Keep the change," she said to the taxi driver.

"Ta," he replied.

She opened her door and got out, Shelly sliding across the back-seat and joining her on the pavement. With a firm push, Shelly closed the back door and the taxi pulled out into traffic, the hazard lights still going. The result of this being another car blowing the horn loudly.

"Fairy money?" Shelly asked.

Elivin smiled.

"Of course! That was insanely overpriced. It will turn into a fiver at the end of the day, which is much more realistic for a trip that short." She turned and looked at the hospital walls. "Wonder what Filthy is doing in there."

"Who knows," Shelly said, holding up the toy detective. "Come on, let's go wandering in the hospital grounds and see if we can't find the missing annoying detective."

# Chapter Eight

Quinn made it back to the common room faster than ever, his stolen medical report safely tucked into the back of his trousers. Rather than go inside, he ran by the room. While the Blank Slates were hardly going to be asking him questions, since most of them had no idea what questions people asked anyway, he did not need people questioning what the stolen report was. Best case scenario it just made the reading awkward, worst case a crowd would draw the attention of the medical staff. As friendly as Linda was, Quinn did not think she would turn a blind eye to such a blatant disregard for the rules.

At the end of the corridor Quinn swung left, heading for the garden area. He pushed open the door, glad to see the weather had not turned miserable, and stepped outside. Nobody was in the area, for whatever reason, so that made things a lot easier. He checked the enclosed space quickly and figured the northern corner offered him the best protection from prying eyes. It had no windows in the nearby walls and a small tree to hide behind. Without wasting another second, Quinn headed over to the spot and dropped down to the ground. He leaned against the trunk of the tree, brought his legs in close, and sat still for a minute.

He waited to see if anything happened.

Nobody appeared to have followed him out and the silence suggested no one was banging on windows for his attention. Carefully, Quinn reached behind and pulled out the file. The pages had slightly dog-eared, but otherwise were undamaged. He gripped them in his left hand, tight enough to ensure that the pages did not separate, and started to read.

A lot of the first page was just a description of Quinn. Hair colour, height, age. Boring information, stuff he had figured out by looking in the mirror. Although for some reason his age had a question mark beside it, which he found odd. Then again, since none of the Blank Slates could remember anything about themselves maybe all their ages were guesstimates at best. It hardly seemed important enough to occupy space in his brain. He continued reading through the file but it was mainly just short notes about sessions with Dr. Milton, followed by medical jargon and useless information. He decided to skip reading anymore of the medical file, instead tugging free the small, skinny, notebook that had been nestled among the pages. Opening the cover, Quinn began to read the first page.

Which was when things got very interesting.

The passage read:

> Quinn has displayed no memories of our previous encounter. It seems to be purely chance that has brought him to this hospital. Regardless, this is good for me. It allows me to continue working on him, trying to figure out what exactly happened. Any memories that are formed now can be addressed accordingly. Somehow a personality has manifested itself after our last meeting. A meeting that I am sure went successfully as I can hear him, even now.

Quinn stared at the words in silence, blinked a few times, then read them once again. On his third reading he started to frown.

"What the hell is he talking about?" Quinn asked the page.

Considering the notebook was in no way sentient, it did not respond to his question.

178

He flicked through a few more pages. It seemed some of the entries in the notebook matched back to pages in the medical report, coinciding with Quinn and Fluid's sessions. Other pages had no dates on them, just more odd passages about Quinn and how his time at the hospital had been going.

Quinn was surprised to find he had been in the hospital for a lot longer then he realised. This was information that gave him mixed feelings. On one hand, it made some sort of sense given the whole missing memories situation. Then again, the other hand suggested that even without your memories you should still be able to note the passage of time. Unless the stay at the hospital involved further memories disappearing from your head.

Meaning that something was definitely going on, something which fell under the title of 'bad stuff'.

The question now was simple: what could be removing newly created memories? Sure, some of the people when they visited Fluid came back slightly dopey but that was not concrete evidence against him. Had the doctor a device hidden in the office, one used during sessions? Something that could remove memories? Without being able to clearly remember anything, Quinn was stumbling around in the dark. He could recall some of his sessions with Fluid, but had no idea how many had taken place. Presumably that was why he started the journal which Linda kept safe for him.

He continued flicking through the notebook.

Another page detailing one of his sessions caught Quinn's attention. He ran his finger over the words, slowly reading them to absorb the details. The passage mentioned his migraine attack and how it had been somehow triggered in the session with Fluid. There was mention of magic, something about it filtering through and energising the doctor as he spoke with Quinn. Then a note about it possibly being some sort of defence mechanism, one not present in other people.

"The lunatics have taken over the madhouse," Quinn said, flicking through the pages further.

He continued to read the notebook and medical report, certain in the belief that something in one of them was going to just make everything click into place.

#

After searching roughly half of the hospital grounds, Shelly wished she had invested in one of those step-counting watches. At least then the somewhat aimless walk around the buildings, car-parks and green areas would have been useful. She could have updated her social networks and bragged to the world about all the steps taken in a single day. More steps than usually happened in a week. After all, if you could not rub it in people's faces about how healthy you were being what was the point in doing exercise at all?

The problem with Elivin's tracking spell was that it involved a lot of back tracking to triangulate where they had to go. After nearly forty minutes they had narrowed it down to one place through a combination of the toy detective and Shelly getting tired of walking around. The building, though, did not exactly inspire confidence in it being the correct spot to find Filthy Henry.

They stopped outside the door and stared at it.

"You think this is it?" Shelly asked.

"Has to be," Elivin said. "My tracking spells always work once they have something fresh from the person to track. A person's spirit is about as fresh as you can get. So, unless that spirit container isn't holding the soul of Filthy Henry, the fairy detective has to be in there."

Shelly frowned and read the sign over the door.

"Saint Patrick's University Hospital," she read out loud. "This place is for people with mental issues and geriatrics. It doesn't make sense for Filthy Henry to be in there. Why would he be in there? Sure, he is eighty odd years old, but you wouldn't know it to look at him."

"Fairy side slows the ageing process?" Elivin asked.

"Yea," Shelly said. "I thought everyone knew that."

The leprechaun shook her head.

"There are a lot of unknowns when it comes to half-breeds," she said to Shelly. "None ever survived their first birthday, so Filthy Henry is a big bucket of 'nobody has a clue'. He could, in theory, turn out to be the most powerful of us all someday. If he unlocked his powers fully. Either that or he will just be around forever annoying humans and fairies alike, casting nothing more impressive than a fireball. We just don't know for sure."

That was a disturbing thought. An immortal wise-ass forever prowling around the streets of Dublin, causing problems for people while solving magical crime. Shelly wondered if Filthy Henry had ever considered that was in his future. He rarely spoke about himself, other than little snippets of information that fell out from time to time, so chances were the fairy detective had never considered he might live forever.

But that still did not explain why the tracking spell had brought them to this hospital. Shelly handed the toy to Elivin, then unbuttoned her coat.

"Make yourself invisible," she said. "I might need you to..."

It was then that Shelly spotted a nurse walking through the foyer, holding a mug close to her chest like it contained the Elixir of the Gods. The very same nurse who was currently a client of Dublin's newest fairy detective.

"God dammit," Shelly said. "He is in there."

"How come you're so sure?"

Shelly pointed at Linda as the nurse went behind a large desk and sat down.

"That's the nurse who hired me about coming to speak with one of her patients. Said he kept asking for the fairy detective."

Elivin craned her neck slightly and peered in the window at the nurse.

"Oh, yeah," she said. "Right. Well then, I guess that's a coincidence worth investigating for sure. Still want me to go invisible?"

Shelly nodded.

"She already thinks I am mad, so if I start talking to myself but really give you instructions it won't seem so crazy."

"I'm sure that makes some sort of sense," Elivin's voice said, her body fading from sight.

"I really need to figure out how to cast some magic," Shelly said, mostly to herself, as she walked up to the hospital automatic doors and waited for them to open.

Nurse Faul looked up from her desk at the sound of the doors sliding open. She took a mouthful from her drink, her eyes opening wide at the taste, and waved at Shelly.

"Hey," Nurse Faul said. "I honestly didn't think you'd show up after mad story I told you yesterday."

"Yea, sorry I didn't get around sooner. Other case I was working sort of took more of my time than I thought it would," Shelly said, lying with ease. It was only a partial lie, really. "Figured I should come and look into your case."

Shelly walked up to the desk, leaned against it, and slowly looked around the foyer.

It was a standard hospital foyer. White painted walls with a few pillars dotted around. Some potted ferns randomly placed in the corners to bring a bit of colour to an otherwise bland and sterile place. One painting of what could have been the sea, Shelly assumed, hung on the wall over an old sofa. At least she really hoped it was the sea, but painted by a painter who had never actually seen the sea. All in, there was nothing remarkable about the place.

The desk behind which Nurse Faul sat took up some floor space and was positioned right beside a set of double doors, ones that led further into the hospital. A security panel to the right of the doors indicated that only authorised personal would be able to get through them. The air was filled with the smell of cleaning products, that ammonia scent which made you feel like your nostrils were being cleaned with fire every time you inhaled through them.

Shelly activated her fairy vision and looked around the foyer once again, but nothing jumped out at her in the magical spectrum. For all intents and purposes this was just a hospital. She was not entirely sure if that was to be expected or not. While it was true that the Fairy World existed right beside the human one, hidden behind magic and spells, veils and invisibility, Shelly had gotten used to fairy folk being everywhere. If leprechauns were involved in the banking world it would not have been too crazy to assume some race of fairy healers could be found at a hospital.

Then again, it would probably go against The Rules if humans suddenly recovered from fatal injuries and illnesses. If that did not scream "magical assistance from beings that you thought only existed in stories" nothing would.

"Quick one," Shelly said, switching off her fairy vision with a blink of her eyes. "You don't happen to have an extremely sarcastic and annoying ginger in here, do you?"

"Go again?" Linda asked.

"See, I'm looking for my friend," Shelly said. "I think he is here, for reasons I won't get into right now. Maybe I could have a look around?"

Linda pursed her lips and gave Shelly a quizzical look.

"I can't exactly do that," she said. "I know I asked you along to help me with one of my patients, but that was more from the point of view that he wouldn't stop asking for you. Also, I think he may have stumbled onto something that is happening here. Something strange."

That caught Shelly's internal curiosity cat by the metaphorical whiskers. She looked down at Elivin, or at least where she thought the leprechaun was standing while invisible.

"If only I could have a quick look around the wards without being escorted," she said, hoping the bounty hunter would take the hint. "Maybe I'd stumble upon whatever it was your patient apparently found."

"Yea, I just told you that can't happen," Linda said, taking another sip from her coffee. "But I was going to bring you into one of our Visitor Rooms and let you talk with Quinn. Show you the notes he has been keeping."

One of the double doors beside the desk opened suddenly, slamming against the wall, startling both Linda and Shelly. Nurse Faul dropped her coffee cup on the desk, spilling the black liquid all over some sheets, and stood up quickly from her seat. She ran around the desk, passing Shelly, and closed the door. It clicked shut. A few tugs on the large, metal, handlebar showed it was locked in place again.

"What the hell caused that?" Linda said, coming back around and picking up a box of tissues from the corner of the desk. She pulled out a few and started to mop up the spilled coffee.

"Ghosts maybe?" Shelly suggested, smiling. "Okay, I guess I will work on your case first and then maybe you can bring me around to see if my friend is here?"

Dropping some dark brown, wet, tissues into the small desk

bin, Linda eyed Shelly.

"No," she said, flatly. "The only ginger you're going to get talking to today is the one I brought you here to help. I can't have every Tom, Dick and Harry just wandering around the wards because they think somebody they know is here. There are procedures to follow, plus I have a duty of care to the patients in here."

"Henry," Shelly said. "The person I am looking for goes by the name Henry. Not Tom, Dick or Harry. Henry"

"Still not happening," Linda said, righting her cup on the desk and giving the surface one final wipe with a bundle of clean tissues. "Now, let's get you setup in one of the rooms. I've a file somewhere here for you to read."

#

Quinn was honestly more confused after reading his medical report and the secret notebook than he had been before reading them. He folded the file in half, stood up from his secluded reading spot in the garden, and walked over to an empty bench beside the flower beds. Quinn sat down on the end of the bench, placed the file and notebook on the armrest beside him, and sighed.

Nothing in the notebook made sense. Maybe the good doctor's mind itself had snapped after years of working with those suffering from mental problems.

"You are a hard guy to find," somebody said from the other end of the bench. "I mean you should take that as a compliment, really. Finding people is what I do. Although it would be a much easier task if I had my full magical abilities, but that's a different topic entirely."

Quinn slowly turned to his left and looked at the person speaking. Rather, to the clear figment of his imagination dressed up in a child's riot squad uniform. A uniform coloured in varying shades of green, for some strange reason. They stared at each other for a minute, then Quinn closed his eyes and shook his head.

"Clearly I was reading too much from that notebook if I'm seeing pint-sized police."

"Hey! Who are you calling pint-sized?"

This question made Quinn open his eyes and look at the figure again. The tiny imaginary person held up her small fists and squared her shoulders. Both fists suddenly burst into flame as she glared at Quinn. It was impressive what the mind could conjure up without any real concentration. As she slowly stepped towards him, Quinn could feel heat coming from the flames around her hands.

"I'll talk with Linda and get my meds upped," he said, turning away from the little woman. "Your imaginary friends shouldn't go straight to eleven when they get called out for being imaginary."

"Oh, you did not just call me 'eleven' when I'm here on a bloody rescue mission to save your sorry ass," the little woman said.

She threw a punch, swiping at thin air, and launched a little fireball towards Quinn. The sensation of heat increasing caused him to lean back on the bench. The fireball sailed past his face, so close that he could smell the smoke trail in its wake. It flew over the folded sheets from his medical report, a spark falling from the fireball on-top of the pages. The spark lit the top sheet and started a small flame. Quinn realised that, in general, figments of one's imagination did not cause things to catch fire. He swatted at the sheet, patting at the flame before it spread further along the page, and jumped to his feet. The little lady had stopped midway across the bench, the second flame still burning brightly in her left hand. She glared at Quinn.

"You wanna dance, tallboy?" she asked.

Even though his memories had decided to take a little vacation at that moment, Quinn's gut feeling about how he would respond in a situation like this seemed to made a great deal of sense.

He grabbed the damaged file and notebook, made a feint to the left, then ran to the right and headed straight for the door that led back inside. Without looking to see what the tiny lady was doing, Quinn pulled open the door and ran through. The slam of the door behind him seemed to have taken the correct amount of time, which at least suggested that the fire throwing woman was not following too closely. Then again, the woman had appeared in the garden without making a sound.

"Midget ninja of death," Quinn said to himself as he raced down the hallway.

None of the other Blank Slates were in the hallway as Quinn ran by. He needed to find a responsible adult to whom he could turn to for help. All the offices used by the doctors were closed and the nurses station was devoid of a single nurse. Then Quinn spotted Nurse Faul on the other side of some double doors, the ones which led back to the foyer. He knew, however, that those doors could not be opened by the guests. There was a security scanner on the wall to the left of the door, requiring a swipe from a staff card to unlock the doors.

Leaving only one course of action to take.

Quinn ran up to the door, pressed his face against the small pane of glass set in the top of the left door, and started to bang his fist furiously on the corresponding pane in the other door. Then, to fully get her attention, Quinn started to scream at the top of his voice.

"HELP! THERE IS A LITTLE MIDGET NINJA OF DEATH TRYING TO KILL ME! OPEN THE DOOR! OPEN THE DOOR FOR THE LOVE OF ALL THAT IS HOLY!"

"Who you are calling a midget?"

Quinn leaned back from the door and looked down the corridor, spotting the little woman walking towards him with a purposeful stride.

"SWEET MERCIFUL CRAP OPEN THE DAMN DOOR!" Quinn shouted, banging even harder.

An electric buzzer sounded and the doors jolted slightly beneath him, indicating the locks had been released. Quinn pulled the handle of the left door so hard he was sure it should have come away in his hand, then ran through into the foyer. With all the grace of a wounded gazelle, he ran around the woman standing in his path as she looked at him very confused, and towards the far side of the big reception desk. Nurse Faul was already coming around to meet him.

"Quinn, take it easy," she said, holding out her hands and making a calming gesture with them. "I was just coming to get you. This is the fairy detective you asked to see."

He stopped running, his feet sliding a little on the polished tiles of the foyer floor, and held up the crumpled medical report with both hands.

"There is a person of restricted growth, a genuine porg, throwing fireballs at me back there," Quinn said, ducking down slightly so that he was obscured from view. "A midget ninja of death and destruction. I'm not crazy, don't say that it is just my condition! I'm telling you I just ran here from the garden to avoid being incinerated."

Nurse Faul gave him that concerned look she generally used when one of the other Blank Slates started to spout some crazy nonsense. It was followed up with her using a tone that let you know whatever you were saying she was hearing, but not fully believing. The other woman in the foyer just stared at him, saying nothing at all.

"Quinn," Linda said, hunkering down and placing both her hands gently on his shoulders. "Have you been at Bosco's medication again? I told you that what we give one patient isn't something you can all share with each other. Now, I'm going to go and check you don't have somebody chasing you, just to be sure, and when I get back we are going to have a chat with your guest here. Just like you wanted. But you need to calm down first, otherwise it is back to your room."

"Calm down? Calm down! You try having a tiny person running after you with balls of flaming death. See how calm you'll be then. Also, why is your one just staring at me?"

"Sorry, Shelly," Linda said to the other woman in the foyer. "He isn't usually this excited."

Quinn looked at the other woman.

"Filthy Henry if this is your bloody idea of a joke I am going to burst you!" Shelly said, her eyes narrowing as she seemingly tried to make Quinn's head explode with her mind.

The double doors opened of their own accord and a little girl walked out. She came around the desk and stopped a few feet away from Nurse Faul and Quinn, smirking.

"So, I found him," the girl said to the woman, her voice identical to the midget ninja of death's voice. "I should have made you hire me, least I would have been paid."

Nurse Faul stared at the kid for a second, then looked over at the woman by the desk.

"Okay," she said. "Something is going on here and I think we should find somewhere a little more private to figure it all out before I decide if security needs to be called."

"I couldn't agree more," the woman, Shelly, responded. "But keep that ginger muppet on the other side of the desk to me, because I reckon I will end up taking a swing at him before we finish having our little chat."

#

189

In the interest of speed, coupled with a desire to avoid anybody stumbling upon them and asking questions, Linda did not waste time trying to figure out where the little girl had come from. Instead she ushered everyone, little freaky girl included, into one of the Visitor Rooms just off the foyer so they could continue their conversation in private. It would have been easier to herd cats.

Shelly and the little mysterious girl had no problems doing as they were asked. Both walked on ahead, checking with Nurse Faul before entering the room that it was the right place. Quinn, on the other hand, had decided that there was no way in hell he wanted to voluntarily be in the same place as the 'Porg of Death'.

"You wanted to talk with her!" Linda said, exasperated. "Now that she's here you don't want to talk with her? You shouldn't even be out of the ward like this without approval from a doctor. If we're caught you are in big trouble, not to mention me. Also, what the hell is a Porg?"

He looked at her, slowly stood up from his crouched position by the reception desk, and started to mess with the bundle of sheets in his hands.

"Person of restricted growth. Porg. This one can throw fireballs," Quinn said, looking over at the open door which Shelly and the little girl had gone through. "Fireballs, nurse. Not just balls that are flaming, she just conjures them out of thin air like..."

Linda waited for him to finish the sentence, but instead Quinn stared down at the sheets in his hands and stared at a small notebook nestled between them.

"Like magic," he said after the brief pause.

"What is that you have there?" Nurse Faul asked, reaching out to take the sheets from him.

Like an ugly little creature holding onto a powerful golden

trinket, Quinn snatched the pages out of her reach and held them close to his chest. He shook his head from side to side.

"You don't want to know what I've been up to," he said. "More so if you think me just being out here will get you into trouble."

She grabbed him by the shoulder and started to half-guide, half-drag, him towards the room on the other side of the foyer.

"In that case," Nurse Faul said. "Maybe it is better if we get out of sight. I'll make sure your 'porg' isn't anywhere near you the whole time we are inside, okay?"

Quinn nodded, only barely resisting her gentle push.

"Also, drop that 'porg' stuff. It isn't nice and in general anyone over six foot, like yourself, is going to see others as short," Linda said before pushing him through the doorway and following quickly behind.

The interior of the Visitor Room was a simple enough affair. Such rooms existed in the hospital so that family members could meet their loved ones, who were currently in the hospital for treatment, in a safe and private place. Nobody really wanted to bring young children into the wards to visit a sick patient on the road to recovery, just in case the other patients acted up. Not that it ever happened, of course, but there was a first time for everything. The bean counters over in the HSE, Ireland's centralised body which governed the health care system and did a fairly bad job at paying those on the front-line correctly, had figured the private rooms were a sure-fire way to avoid any problems.

Problems that would no doubt lead to a lawsuit and money being paid out.

Each room was painted white, for the calming effect, with some beige sofas and chairs to sit on. There were no tables, because a bright spark had read that tables made a room look 'official' and it ruined the comforting feel. This particular room even lacked a window, giving the people inside complete and utter privacy. It was also the Visitor Room favoured by the nursing staff when they wanted to sneak off for a quick power nap. This little napping ritual had led to an unwritten rule amongst all the staff: if the door was closed tightly do not even think about knocking on it.

Those who did knock on the door when it was firmly closed generally thanked their lucky stars they were in a hospital already.

Linda closed the door, firmly, behind her, while Quinn walked over and sat down on the sofa by the back wall. Shelly and the girl had taken up seats on the chairs nearest the door.

"Right," Nurse Faul said, walking down to sit beside Quinn. "Let's get started, shall we? First of all, who is she?"

"She's with me," Shelly said. "Look, Linda. I'm not sure you want to be in here for this. The conversation is going to be a little crazy and I'm fairly certain you'll want to keep him here and lock us both up to boot."

"She can try," the little girl said. "Won't be much fun for her though."

"This is my friend, Elivin," Shelly said, gesturing towards the little girl. "Just don't do or say anything that might tick her off. Not that she has a short temper, but people tend to...rub her up the wrong way."

"How elegantly put," Elivin said, crossing her arms and settling back into the sofa. "If I didn't know any better I would say you were trying to keep the air free from flaming spheres of death."

Linda shook her head at that last statement. Generally, children did not speak in such a strange, adult-like, manner. Plus, not many of them mentioned being little arsonists in front of grown-ups. That sort of speech always ended up with a trip to a shrink, primarily in order to figure out just why little Johnny enjoyed setting the curtains on fire so frequently.

"OK, Elivin," Nurse Faul said. "Lovely to meet you. So, next, what's with the stink eye of Quinn? I wouldn't have asked you to come and speak with him, to help him, if I'd known this was your bedside manner."

"Quinn...Quinn?" Shelly asked, pointing towards the man who responded to that name daily since arriving at the hospital. She threw her arms up in the air and slowly stared up at the ceiling lights. "You've got to be kidding me. This is just another one of his bloody pranks. His jokes. That man there is not called 'Quinn'."

"That's a bit insensitive," Quinn said. "Do you know my current medical history and why I'm in here?"

Shelly jutted out her chin and stared directly at him.

"Do you think I care? After the stunt you pulled you're lucky I even bothered showing up. In fact, I probably should have asked your nurse buddy here to describe you and saved myself the trip. I don't know what you're playing at, Filthy, but I'm done."

She rose from the sofa and only Elivin reaching out and tugging the hem of her jacket sleeve stopped her from walking away.

"Hold on there for a second," the little girl said. "Maybe there is something going on here that we don't know about. I mean he hasn't really acknowledged you."

Shelly turned back and looked at Elivin, then slowly gazed over at Quinn.

"That is true," she said, almost as if speaking to herself.

She sat back down on the edge of the sofa, leaning forward so that her elbows rested on her knees.

"Filthy," Shelly said, her tone noticeably softer. "Do you

193

know who I am?"

"Not a clue," Quinn said. "Also, why do you keep calling me that? All I know is that Nurse Faul said she would get me a meeting with the fairy detective so that I could ask him some questions."

"Him?" Elivin said. "You mean you weren't expecting Shelly to show up?"

"No," Quinn said, shaking his head. "Although I can't tell you why, I just knew that the fairy detective was meant to be a guy. Not this name caller over here."

"You've got to be kidding me," Shelly said, looking up at Nurse Faul. "Okay, what's going on here?"

Nobody spoke. Elivin eyed up Linda. Shelly glared at Quinn. Quinn looked at everyone in the room in turn. All that was missing, Linda felt, were a few guns and they could have turned this into a very interesting Mexican Stand-off.

"OK, OK, OK," she said, finally breaking the silence. "I think we need to get everything out in the open first and then, maybe, we will move on from this odd situation."

Shelly gave a curt nod of her head. Elivin shrugged. Quinn hugged the sheets of paper closer to his chest and kept his eyes focused on Shelly.

"I'll take the silence as a group agreement," Linda said. "Right, this is Quinn. He thinks something is going on here at the hospital that is causing people to lose their memories. Now, we do have patients here that are currently missing, well, all their memories. Quinn is one of them, but he at least was able to recall his name when he arrived. But he seems to think that..."

Elivin jumped off the sofa, waving her hands in the air.

"Whoa, whoa, whoa," she said. "Just hold on there for a second. What do you mean that there are people here missing

194

their memories?"

Nurse Faul frowned at the little outburst from the girl. What sort of child would pick up on a detail like that, let alone show so much interest in it?

"We have a lot of patients that have shown up in the past few months with no memories of who they are. None at all."

"But they remember how to speak?" Elivin asked, looking genuinely curious. "They can still dress and feed themselves? Are able to read and write? It just seems like the bits that made them a person are missing?"

They had moved past the curious and into the outright strange.

"Yes," Linda said, looking at the odd child before her. "That's exactly it. How did you..."

"We're working a case like that already," Shelly said. "People showing up without memories of their past but seemingly still have all the normal stuff like language and the such in their heads. It's been happening for...a while. Somebody has been going around the country, taking memories."

That statement made very little sense to Linda. How could something be going around taking memories out of a person's head? True, the world had moved into a digital age, a place where you could store pictures and videos in clouds and then access them wherever you wanted. Not that Linda fully understood how any of that worked. The clouds, apparently, were not actual clouds in the sky but some other guys computer in a big warehouse somewhere. Which, she had to admit, sounded very less cool and surely meant that you just were relying on somebody to be smarter than you at backing things up. But memories were not stored in big computers dotted around the world. They were in a person's head and you simply could not go in, pick and choose the ones you wanted, then pull them out and leave everything else behind.

195

Brains did not operate like that. If they did surely somebody would have started a memory related service by now. One that allowed you to go in and get the memories of your choice, both good and bad, removed. Who would not turn down the chance to read their favourite book again as if for the very first time or forget the heartache of a loved one passing?

Shelly and Elivin were clearly mentally unstable and needed to get some medical help. The trick now was getting them to see that point of view. Clearly playing into Quinn's delusions had not been a clever move on her part. Linda sighed and carefully thought about what she would say next. None of the others in the room with her could be allowed to just walk out the hospital's front door. If they did who knew what would happen.

"So," she said to Shelly. "You think that somebody is running around and stealing memories? That's the most sane theory you could come up with?"

Shelly nodded.

"Look," she said to Linda. "I know what you're thinking. That we are both obviously off-the-wall mad for making such a crazy statement. But, bear this in mind. You contacted me, a bona-fide fairy detective, to come and talk with your patient. Which means, on some level, you must know that there are things that just can't be explained without a little magic being involved."

Quinn perked up at the mention of the word 'magic'. He lowered the sheets of paper from his chest and spread them out on his lap. Picking up the small notebook he slowly flicked through the pages, opening one and handing the notebook over to Linda without saying a word. She took it from him and read the words written on the page.

"What the hell does this mean?" Nurse Faul asked him.

"I'm not entirely sure," he replied. "But I think these ladies are on the up and up. Magic must be an actual thing and somehow it is connected to the Blank Slates."

196

She read over the page one more time, then looked back up at Shelly.

"Say, for a moment, I believe you," Linda said. "What's the next step here, exactly?"

Elivin reached into a pocket, somehow hidden in her dress because Linda could see where the parting in the material was, and pulled out a small toy figure. She held it before her and slowly walked over to Quinn.

"First off," Elivin said. "We return this to its rightful owner."

Linda watched as Quinn gingerly reached out to take the toy from the little girl.

# Chapter Nine

Shelly was not completely sure what she had expected to happen when Filthy Henry touched the toy detective. Possibly an explosion of power as the container released his spirit. Maybe even the pair of them glowing brightly as the magic of the container did its thing. A dimming of the lights in the room while the fairy detective's soul returned to its rightful place, maybe.

What she had not expected to happen was absolutely nothing. Zilch. Nada. Zippo.

Filthy Henry, or Quinn as he was going by, took the toy from Elivin and examined it carefully. He turned it over a few times, looked at the little figure's blank face, then grinned at the leprechaun before him, still under her illusion spell, and shrugged.

"Thanks, I think," he said.

Linda watched the scene play out, but the confused expression on her face told Shelly that even the nurse had no idea what was meant to be going on.

"Okay, that was fantastic and everything, but it doesn't really clear things up," Nurse Faul said. "About Quinn or the mental health of you two."

"Yea," Shelly said, staring at Filthy Henry as he held the toy detective still. "I was sort of expecting something different myself. It would have made explaining things to you a whole lot easier."

"Such as?"

That particular question caused a problem for Shelly.

The human and Fairy Worlds were kept apart by powerful magic, something that only fairies could work around so that mortals could see them. However, to ensure that the fairy folk did not run amok in the mortal world, there were The Rules. Something Filthy Henry had never fully explained to Shelly, as they seemed to just be things that everyone born on the magical side of the street knew instinctively. While working with the fairy detective she had heard a half dozen different examples of The Rules, but they always were ones pertinent to their current case. With each new one explained, Shelly had done what any human trying to navigate the Fairy World would have done.

She jotted them down in her notebook.

It quickly became a pet project for her. New entries were examined in as much detail as allowed, which was not always a lot considering Filthy Henry's love of being vague to maintain an air of mystery. Shelly had even applied a very loose ranking system to them. Sometimes the rankings changed, as one of The Rules clearly seemed more important than others.

One Rule, however, clearly stood head and shoulders above the rest. The one about not revealing the Fairy World to a human who was not already, on some level, aware of it. Shelly had been slightly clued in before ever meeting Filthy Henry, which was the main reason the Fairy World had allowed her to continue living with the knowledge of all things magical. Linda, on the other hand, was obviously a mortal without any exposure to the fairy folk. Just because the nurse had come looking to hire a fairy detective did not necessarily mean her life was filled with magic. Which meant that for Shelly to answer Linda's question required some thinking and careful planning so that nothing was said which might break The Rules.

Then Shelly had a thought.

Standing in the room with them, albeit under a very clever disguise, was a leprechaun. A bona-fide, pot of gold, able to cast magic and grant wishes, leprechaun. As near as Shelly could figure out, the leprechaun race sat very near the top of the fairy society ladder. They acted as serious enforcers of The Rules and were one of the few races who had open and direct relationships with the human world, at least the banking part of it. If any fairy race had the authority to decide whether a human could be let in on the big secret surely it had to be a leprechaun.

"Elivin," Shelly said. "Can you do some of your tricks so that Linda over here can be temporarily let in on things?"

The little girl looked, for want of a better term, embarrassed. She turned around and stared directly at Shelly.

"Em," Elivin said. "I haven't fully explained to you about my magic and me being a bounty hunter. But I was planning on doing it."

"Your magic?" Linda asked.

"Great," Shelly said, ignoring yet another question while she tried to figure things out. "My second partner in the detecting world and they lie to me about magical stuff as well."

"Not a lie, as such. Just an omission. Sort of."

Shelly rolled her eyes.

"Whatever, just give me some options. Can we let Linda in on the secret or not?"

"What secret!" Nurse Faul demanded, clearly getting annoyed.

"Actually, I'd like to know about this as well," Filthy Henry added, leaning forward in his seat and looking at Shelly with great interest.

"Show them," Shelly said to Elivin. "I'll figure out how to smooth things over later with whoever looks after The Rules."

Elivin nodded her head, then raised her right hand into the air. She clicked her fingers twice, causing the illusion spell to cease.

Her outline shimmered, like a heat mirage, and started to fade inwards. The little girl disappeared from sight, replaced by the green body armour wearing leprechaun. As the illusion fully stopped, revealing her entirely, Elivin took a bow and smiled.

"Any questions?" the bounty hunter asked Linda.

Nurse Faul simply stared down at the leprechaun bounty hunter, her mouth opened wide in disbelief. Filthy Henry was doing likewise, which Shelly found very unsettling. Considering he was Ireland's first fairy detective Filthy Henry cast magic on a regular basis. Now he was as amazed as anybody else when they saw magic for the first time. Real magic, not just the usual birthday party stuff.

A knock at the door of the room drew everyone's attention. Elivin vanished from sight in the blink of an eye. When Nurse Faul did not say anything, Shelly took it upon herself to answer.

"Come in," she called out loud.

The door to the room open and a man half-entered, keeping the door between himself and those inside. He wore a pair of half-moon glasses, perched on the end of his nose, and looked like a lost college professor. Without even acknowledging anyone in the room, the man addressed Nurse Faul.

"I do believe that you were meant to bring along my next..." he began.

He spotted Filthy Henry and stopped talking. Without saying a word, the man extended his right hand towards the fairy detective.

"I was looking for those," he said to Filthy Henry, pointing at the medical report. "Please give it back, right now. Patients are not meant to have their medical files."

In as uncharacteristic a move as Shelly had ever seen him make, the fairy detective handed over the sheets of paper to the man without saying a word. Then, clutching the toy detective in his left hand, he moved down along the sofa a little. The man in the doorway took the sheets, gripping them firmly, and turned back to stare at Nurse Faul.

"We shall be having words about this later," he said, curtly. "Do not think that you will be allowed to continue working here when you allow such blatant disregard for the rules to take place."

He stepped back out of the room, slamming the door closed in the process. The nurse just stared at the closed door without saying a word. Elivin reappeared, walking over to Linda and placing a hand on her knee. Linda looked down at Elivin, still speechless. The leprechaun looked back over her shoulder pads at Shelly.

"We can't do this here. I think we should go back Bunty's, get her to help us figure out whatever the hell is wrong with the tall ginger one there. Plus, we've sorta gotten this mortal in trouble. Least we can do is take her with us and come up with a plan to help her out. Permission to cast a calming spell? Since you're sort of advising that I break The Rules at the minute and I want a scape goat."

Shelly grimaced at that statement. Elivin was right. The Rules had just been broken and all on Shelly's say so, not the leprechaun bounty hunter's. Once they got Filthy Henry back into his normal state of mind she would have to ask the fairy detective just what happened when people broke The Rules. Particularly mortals. Last year, during the case in Carlingford, Filthy had explained that magic itself would get involved. But that had been when they were meant to follow very strict, precise, rules in order to save the day. The Rules, it seemed, were more like guidelines than actual rules which had to be followed to the letter. Unless it was a Rule with very serious letters to be followed.

Regardless, they needed to bring Linda into the fold. At least until Filthy Henry was fixed. That meant helping the nurse's mind accept what was happening.

"Nothing crazy," Shelly said to Elivin. "Calm her down, help her mind process all this. Short-term sort of thing. Then let's get the hell out of here before somebody else just happens to walk by."

Elivin crossed her heart, then raised her hands and aimed her palms at Nurse Faul's head.

"*Scaoill stad leathcheann*," the leprechaun said, purple sparks forming around the tips of her fingers and flowing through the air towards Linda's head.

Filthy Henry stared at the spell like a slack-jawed idiot as it floated by. Something clearly had broken in the fairy detective's head if such things amazed him, Shelly was sure of it. She wondered if she had reacted in a similar fashion when first stepping into the magical world? Hopefully there had been less wide-eyed, jaw dropped, expressions on her face. It was still unsettling though, to see the man who had introduced her to the Fairy World behaving like he was completely unaware of it.

The leprechaun's magic drifted above Linda's head for a moment, like a sparkling mist, then faded away. Nurse Faul blinked twice, before slowly shaking her head. She looked like somebody who had just taken some very strong pain killers, ones which not only helped get rid of a headache but gave the patient a slight euphoric high as well. The sort that generally came with a warning about not operating heavy machinery.

"Right," Linda said, looking at everyone in the room one by one. "Quinn might not be Quinn. Leprechauns are a real thing and you're a fairy detective in the actual fairy sense of the word. Plus, one of the doctors has seen me with a patient's file outside of his office and I might lose my job."

Shelly mulled over the summation of their current situation for a minute, then nodded her head once.

"About the height of it," she said to Linda. "Now, we need to go and visit a specialist. Coming?"

204

Nurse Faul shrugged her shoulders.

"Sure, why not," she said. "Today probably can't much weirder. Why not follow two strangers."

"You might regret saying that later," Elivin said.

#

The taxi trip had been entertaining, in an oddly surreal way. Quinn just followed Shelly's instructions, climbing into the back seat of the car without question, and sat there in silence. He clutched the toy detective tightly, not wanting to let it go for some reason, in his right hand and the notebook he had conveniently forgotten to give back to Fluid in his left. He simply stared out the window as the car drove through the city. Linda sat next to him, sitting in the middle of the back seat. Shelly sat in the passenger seat, up front with the taxi driver, while Elivin, wearing her disguise again, had taken up the last spot in the back of the car.

Nobody spoke for the entire taxi journey, although Quinn caught the driver giving him funny looks in the rear-view mirror from time to time. Particularly eyeing Quinn's current attire. Something he was beginning to wonder about himself. Everyone else in the car at least looked like they belonged out in the world. Whereas Quinn was wearing his hospital issued leisure suit, his medicinal pyjamas. It was fairly obvious from the colour of the clothes, not to mention the material they were made from, that he was not wearing the latest in Parisian fashion.

The taxi turned off the quays, crossing over the river Liffey which divided the city, via O'Connell Bridge and drove up D'Olier Street. At the top of the street some roadworks were underway, causing the taxi to make a wide turn in order to go up Townsend Street. All the traffic lights seemed to be in their favour, remaining green as they approached, and the driver was able to go down Shaw Street before turning onto Pearse Street without needing to stop.

"Hang on," Quinn said, looking over his shoulder out the back window. "Have we just gone in a loop instead of the most direct way?"

"A lot of the city is one way," Nurse Faul said.

She had been calling out the names of the streets for Quinn as the taxi took them to their destination.

"But it's one way in a manner that doesn't make sense," Quinn said. "I mean I'm apparently crazy and even I can see that. Like, every second street should alternate with the direction you can go. No?"

Linda smiled.

"You're not the first person to think that."

"No, you are not," the taxi driver chimed in. "But sure, if the lads that came up with the stupid systems had to use them you'd soon see things done a lot better. The hotel here, is it?"

This last bit he asked to Shelly. She shook her head and pointed at a derelict building on the corner of the street opposite the lovely looking hotel.

"No, that's us there. On the left," Shelly said. "Elivin, can you pay?"

Elivin nodded.

"Just like last time," the leprechaun said.

"God that is hardcore, getting the little one to pay," the taxi driver said smiling.

He pulled the taxi up to the kerb, turned on his hazard lights to act as a poor apology for stopping where he should not, and parked.

"She got a birthday card from her granny the other day," Shelly said, opening the car door and stepping out onto the pavement. "She'd only spend it on sweets otherwise."

Nurse Faul nudged Quinn gently in the ribs with her elbow, nodding towards the door near him. He opened it and climbed out, Linda and Elivin following close behind. Once everyone had gotten out, closing the doors, the taxi driver pulled back out into traffic and drove off. Everyone turned and looked at Shelly.

Shelly looked back at each of them.

"Right," she said. "This might be a little tricky to explain, so I'm not even going to try."

She closed her eyes for a moment and opened them once again. Quinn stared, amazed at the blue light that suddenly appeared around each of her eyes. He looked across at Nurse Faul, who seemed to not have noticed the glow that Shelly was now sporting. Elivin was paying none of them any attention, looking at the derelict building they had all been dropped off outside. When he looked back at Shelly the blue glow had vanished. It was like the little pixies outside the window all over again.

"She's still in a moody," the little girl who was not really a little girl said to Shelly.

"I can see that," Shelly responded, frowning at the building.

"Sorry," Quinn said, holding the toy detective up in the air. "What exactly is going on here? Is this just part of the oddest day trip ever or am I the butt of some insane practical joke."

Elivin chuckled and walked over to a low wall that ran outside the derelict building. She climbed up onto it, wiggling her butt in a comedic way during the movement, and sat down.

"I'm not sure what's going on either," Nurse Faul said, leaning in to talk quietly to Quinn. "But you said you wanted to talk with the fairy detective and after that girl turned into a leprechaun back in the hospital I think, maybe, they might be the real deal. As crazy as that sounds."

"Sure," Quinn said. "But the problem is we never even got to talk about what I wanted to discuss. She just kept calling me 'Filthy Henry' or just 'Filthy', as if that name is meant to mean something to me."

"It's your name, idiot. You just are up to something," Shelly said, walking up to the door of the rundown building. "Bunty! Bunty Doolay! Open! Up!"

Shelly started thumping on the wooden door with her fist, shouting each word over and over. Nurse Faul and Quinn exchanged a glance, one he felt meant they both knew something was not adding up in the current situation. Some old paint chips fell away from the door with each fist bump it received.

"Would you mind stopping?"

Quinn nearly jumped out of his hospital blues as the new arrival suddenly appeared beside him. Linda let out a startled yelp.

"You have no idea how annoying it is having to repaint an illusion so that other humans don't look too closely at the place."

Shelly ceased her one sided battle with the old door and turned to face the woman beside Quinn.

At least he hoped she was a woman. Whoever they were there was a definite female quality to them, but unlike any lady he had seen around the hospital. She was simply beautiful to look at, with pale skin that perfectly complimented her long, raven black, hair. Two completely blue eyes stared at Shelly, a hint of anger to them. Quinn knew he was a little over six foot tall and this mystically attractive lady was easily matching him in height. As a slight breeze blew it gently moved back some of her hair, revealing pointed ears.

Quinn looked over his shoulder at Nurse Faul.

"You see her, right?" he asked.

Linda nodded once.

"Good, so it was just the blue eyes on Shelly you couldn't see."

"That's because I've extended my spell past the kerb for a minute," the new arrival said. "Anyone looking here will see some torn up section of pavement and a little path made from cones to walk around. Nobody will see us, but everyone inside can see everything that's going on. Mortals included. Nice to see you found the idiot detective as well."

"About that," Shelly said, walking over. "We need your help."

"I told you to not come back any time soon after the midget anger machine over there decided to throw down with me."

"Bunty," Elivin said. "If I'd thrown down with you properly you would know about it."

Bunty gave the little girl a dismissive wave of her hand.

"Wouldn't we need to be at full strength in order to do that?" she said to Elivin, smirking. "What exactly do you want, Shelly?"

"I already told you, we need your help," Shelly said to the tall and beautiful woman. "I'm a lot out of my depth on this one. Saying a 'little out of my depth' would have made my nose do the best Pinocchio impression ever. Elivin isn't exactly an expert in all things magical. The other option I would have used is suffering from an annoying case of amnesia."

"She talking about me?" Quinn asked Linda.

"I think she just might be."

"Besides," Shelly continued. "You said we could come back, grudge match ignored, when we found Filthy. Well, we found him."

The tall, beautiful, new arrival turned to stare at Quinn and Linda as they stood by the low wall. A group of college students came walking down the street towards them. Right on the edge of the building, were the wall of the derelict faced onto Lane Street,

209

the students abruptly turned left and stepped out onto the road. They formed a single line, continuing their conversation about upcoming exams and post exam drinking sessions, then they stepped back onto the pavement and spread out once more. As they went on their way Quinn stared after them, amazed.

Not once had any of the students even acknowledged the group of people standing no more than five feet from them, nor the strangeness of the one called Bunty.

As if everyone actually was invisible.

Nurse Faul slowly raised her hand into the air.

"I'm sorry," she said. "You're a fairy as well, is it?"

Bunty frowned at the question, shook her head dismissively and looked directly at Quinn.

"No idea about his identity at all? Really?"

Quinn looked from Bunty to Linda, over to Shelly, then back again. After a minute he shrugged his shoulders and smiled at Bunty Doolay.

"That's what they tell me," Quinn said to her.

Bunty looked back at Shelly.

"You sure he is completely not in there? Nobody else in the world can do a sarcastic shoulder shrug like that when asked a simple question."

Shelly nodded.

"He has no idea about anything. Elivin did some fairly small spells back in the hospital and he nearly freaked out on me. Doesn't seem to have any idea who I am either. Although he did know that there was a male fairy detective, because when we met he said as much."

The tall woman walked over and crouched down in front of

Quinn, balancing her hands on her knees. This close, he could see that her skin was perfect, flawless even. Without a trace of a wrinkle or hint of a blemish to be found. Nurse Faul was even staring at her, a strange look on her face.

Bunty obviously noticed the attentions of Linda and turned her head slightly to look at the nurse.

"Don't worry about it," Bunty Doolay said, her Northern lit like music. "It happens to every mortal the first time they meet me. Shelly over there nearly spilled her drink all over the place."

"Did not!" Shelly said, a shocked look on her face. "OK, well almost not. But come on...have you seen you?"

Bunty smiled, reaching over to gently pat Linda on the thigh.

"Should pass in a few minutes and then you will be back in control of your urges," Bunty Doolay said, giving Linda a little wink. "Now, back to this sorry excuse before me. He has the *coimeádán spiorad*, I see. Chances are that something was left behind, a breadcrumb memory if you will, that would let him figure out his identity. Maybe that's how he knew about his previous job."

Quinn shook his head from side to side, reached into his left trouser pocket, and pulled out a battered business card. He handed this to Bunty without saying a word. She took it from him and examined it, turning it over in her elegant hands.

"What is it?" Elivin and Shelly asked in unison.

"His business card. Filthy Henry's," Bunty said, holding it up in the air for all to see. "The wise ass was smart enough to keep it on him as a clue of some sort. That's how he knew to expect a male fairy detective. His name is printed on the card."

"That would have been handy when I went looking for your fairy detective," Linda said to Quinn.

"I know, right. Carolyn had hidden it on me, part of her stupid

211

geocaching. I found it stuffed down between the sofa cushions this morning."

Shelly rubbed her forehead, massaging the skin just above her eyebrows.

"Look," she said, closing her eyes firmly. "Can we all just get inside and figure this thing out? I know that most of us are barred or will be or you're holding a grudge against us. I don't care. What I care about right now is getting that idiot over there sorted. I, not wanting to say this out loud, need him to help me solve a case."

Bunty Doolay let out a long sigh and pinched the bridge of her nose.

"Fine," she said, looking at Shelly. "Everyone inside until we sort this mess out. Mortal...just don't say anything stupid?"

Linda frowned at the statement and looked up at Bunty.

"Like what?" the nurse asked.

"That's a bad start," Elivin said.

"Besides," Shelly added. "She meant me."

#

Bunty Doolay did not even bother bringing people in through the front door of her illusion. Without saying a word or moving a muscle, the *Sidhé* teleported everyone from the street into the pub. There were no warning sparks of a spell taking place, nor suggestion that magic was even afoot. One second everyone was outside, the next they were all inside and still in the same relative positions they had been. Linda and Quinn were sitting at a table with only two seats, Elivin and Shelly stood side by side near the bar and Bunty was placed directly before the front door. She gestured with her hands towards a wooden, circular, table surrounded by chairs in the middle of the floor, then walked towards it and sat down.

Everyone in the room followed her lead.

Shelly decided to sit close to Linda, just in case the nurse needed the reassurance of another mortal when magic started flying around. In hindsight she could have done this back at the hospital, but at that stage Shelly had been convinced Filthy Henry was up to one of his nasty pranks.

Filthy Henry sat down beside Linda, on her left-hand side, allowing Shelly to take the other seat near her. Elivin climbed up onto a chair, lined up directly across from Bunty, and slowly tugged off her padded green gloves. These were dropped onto the table, one over the other, as she leaned casually back in the chair and looked across the table at *Sidhé*. Shelly rapped her knuckles on the wooden surface to get the leprechaun's attention, pointing her finger directly at the bounty hunter.

"There is to be no repeat of last time," Shelly said to Elivin. "We get the ginger one sorted. You just behave yourself until that happens."

Elivin shrugged her shoulders, the armour squeaking from the movement, and rolled her eyes.

"Right," Bunty Doolay said. "If everyone is settled, let's begin. Filthy, pass over that toy figure if you please."

Filthy Henry remained seated, his eyes opened wide as he stared around the room. At this point Shelly was starting to believe that he genuinely possessed no memories of who he was. The expression on his face right now was that of a person who had never before experienced a teleportation spell.

"Fil...Quinn," Shelly said. "She means you. Can you put that toy detective into the middle of the table?"

"Huh? Oh...right...sure," he said, leaning across and putting the figure in the centre of the table. "There you go."

As he withdrew his hand everyone stared at toy, then looked up at Bunty. Her utterly blue eyes remained focused on the toy detective.

"Well?" Shelly asked.

Bunty Doolay looked up at her.

"Well what?"

"What do we do now? Is there some spell to cast or magic incantation to say?"

"Why are you asking me?" Bunty Doolay said. "I just know the theories behind these things, I've never actually had to use one."

"I'm sorry," Linda said, leaning forward on her seat slightly. "What are you all talking about?"

"Can I take this?" Elivin asked, going so far as to raise her hand in the air like they were all sitting in a classroom.

Shelly nodded her head.

"Excellent," the leprechaun said. "Well, mortal, here's the thing. That toy detective there is really a magical container holding the essence of the man sitting beside you. The original, not whatever moron is currently there."

Linda slowly nodded her head in agreement while Elivin spoke. As soon as the leprechaun stopped speaking the nurse shook her head in the negative.

"Nope, don't follow that at all. Quinn is sitting right beside me. Are you saying that somehow he is inside that toy? How is that possible?"

"The man sitting beside you is actually Filthy Henry, the fairy detective," Bunty Doolay said, reaching over and picking up the toy. "He deals with crimes of a magical nature and, for whatever reason, created a spirit container. Using this little figure here. We believe that his spirit, or soul if you are one of those people, is inside the container. Quinn is, sadly, a left over remnant of who

Filthy Henry really is. He isn't a real person, just a very faint echo of the man. A copy of sorts, but a corrupted one."

At this statement Quinn forcibly pushed back his chair from the table and stood up, hands clenched into fists by his sides with the knuckles going white.

"Hold the bloody phone one second," he snarled at Bunty. "You can't just go around telling people they aren't real. I am real, I know I am real! I have feelings and I know what I like and I have memories. Okay the last two are very recent things but they still count towards me being a person. Now you're telling me, what? That I am just a bad copy of the guy you all think I am? That really, I am not here and there is something in that toy that belongs in this body? I'm not going to lie, the last few hours I have seen some crazy things happening but this is where I am drawing the line. From the sounds of it you all don't even like Filthy Henry!"

He kicked his chair out of the way and stormed off, marching down the floor of the pub towards the stools at the farthest end of the bar. Everyone sat in silence, looking down the room at him. Filthy Henry, or Quinn, pulled out the last stool, climbed onto it, and turned his back to the rest of the pub.

"That could have gone better," Linda said, shifting around in her seat.

"Agreed," Bunty Doolay said. "I never factored in that whatever is currently the consciousness in Filthy Henry's body would be self-aware."

"I eat jelly, therefore I am," Linda said.

"I'm going to guess that is hospital humour," Elivin said.

The nurse nodded once.

"He was always asking for an extra pot of jelly. Even caught him stealing them one time. I swear I have no idea how he managed to eat so much and never get full."

"You get used to that," Shelly said.

She reached over and took the toy detective out of Bunty Doolay's hand.

"I'm going to talk to him," Shelly said to everyone at the table. "At the end of the day he brought me in this world of magic and madness. Seems only fitting that I am the one to bring him back."

#

Quinn was sure there had to be guidelines in polite society, rules even, which this group must have completely broke in the last thirty minutes.

People did not sit around a table and then kindly inform somebody they, technically, did not exist. It definitely had to be considered, at the very least, rude. Who gave whom the right to tell a person that, while they did have a body and a mind, it was not their body or mind. Rather it was not their body, the mind was up for debate and apparently just an optional issue that would be addressed at a later date.

For the first time since 'waking up' in the hospital, Quinn wished more than ever that his memories were not completely A.W.O.L. Whatever had happened to make him a Blank Slate was seriously handicapping him right now. It made it hard to argue your case when said case was only a few weeks old and, in the grand scheme of things, you had no ancillary stories or topics to bring up which would back up your statements. The only similarities Quinn could draw were how it would be mean to ask a totally colour-blind person to finish a paint-by-numbers in under an hour, with no help. Even then, the only reason he knew about colour-blind people and paint-by-numbers was because he read some articles in the newspaper a week ago on both topics.

What made the entire situation worse was that Nurse Faul had not jumped to his defence immediately after the crazy statement. Sure, they were currently sitting in a magical pub, owned by a beautiful fairy creature, with a leprechaun and her best friend. But

216

that did not excuse bad manners. If somebody you were meant to be looking after, in a medical capacity, is told they are not real you defend them. Otherwise who would?

Behind him, Quinn heard a stool being pulled back from the bar and the groan of leather as somebody sat down. He looked over his left shoulder and saw the toy detective being placed on the bar counter.

"Can we talk?"

"I've nothing to say," Quinn said, turning his head back to stare at the far wall.

"Sure you do," Shelly said. "You've loads to say, that's your biggest problem. The only thing is you can't say them, because you don't remember how annoying you can be."

Quinn shifted around on the stool and rested his arms on the bar counter in front of his seat. He looked at the little toy detective, feeling the urge to pick it up and hold it the second he laid eyes on it. It was just one more strange thing happening in a day of strange things. His left hand started to shake, as if it was going to move independently of its own volition.

"So, what?" he asked Shelly. "Am I just meant to believe everything that you all are saying to me? That I'm not really me, just an echo of someone you all know?"

"Not all," Shelly said, smiling. "Linda doesn't have a clue who Filthy Henry is either."

"That meant to be funny?"

Shelly nodded her head.

"Yeah," she said. "Worst of all, if you were him right now, he would have made that same joke."

"Well then why don't you let him into your....sorry that was about to go down a very dirty and sordid path."

217

"Not unlike how Filthy would have gone," Shelly said.

She slid the little figure across the counter towards his left hand.

"Listen," Shelly said. "There are some things in the world that just suck. Holy folk will tell you it is all part of a Big Plan, that some Higher Being is masterminding every single move we make. But that's a crock. I've met gods, one of them just loved reading books and the other was a fat guy with a magical cauldron that made food. Neither of them was a puppet master. I will say this though, not everyone gets a chance to help the world and make the holy nutters think they are right."

Quinn picked up the toy detective and started twirling it over and over in his hands.

"You've met gods?" he asked.

"Yep, both good and bad," Shelly said. "But right now, there is something stalking the streets of Dublin. They are going around taking people's memories, possibly causing them to end up at the hospital with you. Everyone in this room would like to make it stop, but the problem is one person in this room isn't in the right frame of mind."

"Or body," Quinn said, feeling a faint smile touch the corners of his mouth.

"Or body," Shelly agreed, grinning. "Now, I'm fairly new to this whole magic thing. But I know that you didn't just happen to appear out of thin air the moment Filthy Henry's spirit left his body. You are, on some level, a part of him. It's the only thing that makes sense. So, while you might not be behind the mental wheel any more, you are at least going to be in the car."

Quinn frowned and stared at the blank face on the toy detective. Whether or not the spirit of a fairy detective resided in the figure was, at least in Quinn's opinion, just hearsay. There was nothing fantastic about the toy, no glowing sparks or wonderful

218

aura that...

Then it happened. He blinked, just like before when Bosco had been talking about fairies outside the common room window. One second the world was completely normal, the next there was a subtle shift in the visual spectrum. Without touching a hidden button or flicking a tiny switch the toy detective began to glow. A faint, blue, outline that pulsed gently like it was matching the rhythm of something. Beating in time to...

"...holy crap," Quinn said.

"What is it?"

He held up the figure in front of his face and stared at it, slightly mesmerized by the blue glow.

"The glow, or aura, or whatever, around this," Quinn said. "It's pulsing in rhythm to my heartbeat."

"Well it does contain part of you, so I guess that makes sense."

Quinn closed his eyes and dropped his head. He could feel his shoulder's slump. Being a Blank Slate meant he had no memories of his mother. This in turn meant he had no idea if his mother would be proud or not of her son sacrificing himself for the Greater Good. But Quinn knew, deep down, that doing something to help others, regardless of the cost to yourself, was the right thing to do.

He clutched the toy detective firmly in both hands and slowly nodded his head.

"You're sure Filthy Henry will be able to catch whatever is going around stealing the memories from people? To help the other Blank Slates?"

"If he can't," Shelly said. "He will do his very best to annoy the hell out of whatever is stealing memories. So much so that going into hiding will be its next move. If nothing else, Filthy

Henry is good at winding people up to the point that they don't want to be around him any longer."

"Good enough," Quinn said, opening his eyes and looking over at her. "I'm in, I guess. How do we do this?"

Shelly's expression went blank, like she had been asked to solve an incredibly complicated mathematics equation using only her fingers.

"Em…," she said.

# Chapter Ten

Sometimes the urge, the desire, to collect was easy to ignore. Not like when he went to ground for a few years, hiding from the world in order to take a break. Those sabbaticals from everyone were sated with one big collection, like a bear going into hibernation. Now there was no such easy way out, hibernating was not an option. It was like being on a diet while a little voice in the back of your mind whispered to you about cake. How good the cake was, how tasty it looked. How that this cake, above all other cakes, was actually calorie free and you should really have two slices of cake. Sure it was even a gluten free cake, a third slice would hardly make a difference.

Would it?

It felt like a little buzz in the brain when at its strongest, making all other thoughts secondary until a collection took place. Sometimes, if he concentrated, it was possible to hear them, all the previous Collections. Hundreds of voices telling their stories over and over. When he had trouble falling asleep he just let them chatter together. It worked better than counting sheep. It helped, definitely, that the voices were not screaming for freedom or vengeance. They were simply personalities without bodies, unbound verbal historians.

But the desire to collect another story needed to be suppressed, at least for now. A meeting had been requested. A meeting which had not taken place for a number of years.

Thankfully the old espionage tropes were ignored. There was no shady alleyway or trench-coat and matching fedora to be found. The meeting venue was in a public place, that way nobody would even question what was going on.

He had found a seat by the window of the coffee shop, staring out and watching all the stories, also known as people, passing by. Tales that could be collected and most likely should be. It did not matter if all the stories in his collection were not epics. A story was a story and, at the end of the day, it was the receiver of the tale that put the true value on it. What one person may class as a classic piece of narrative work, another would as soon wrap their fish supper in. Besides, he had his List to work through. Names of people whose stories must be collected. Stories that had a greater value above all others. As long as those stories were definitely collected, everything would be fine.

Even if time was getting a little short.

As the waitress brought down his order he took out two blue, latex, gloves and pulled them on. These had been the most ingenious thing ever invented. With a satisfying snap of the material closing around his wrist, he picked up the coffee cup and took a sip of the hot beverage. Content in the knowledge that no fingerprints would be left behind.

"I have no idea how you drink that muck."

He looked left and saw his contact walk by, taking up the only other seat at the table. She smiled at him, a mouth filled with blackened teeth. A smile dentists would have nightmares about. Small children would have ran home at the sight of such a decayed grin and brushed their pearly whites vigorously in order to avoid a similar smile.

The waitress returned, visibly recoiling at the sight of his contact, and put on a brave face.

"Anything to eat or drink?" she asked the new arrival, her gaze fixed firmly on the notepad in her hands.

"Just tea," Blacksmile said. "Black."

Without saying anything else, the waitress left their table and walked briskly back towards the kitchen.

"You know if you're going to drink black tea you should really just give coffee a try," he said.

His contact narrowed her one good eye and glared at him.

"Let's not forget how this arrangement works," she said. "You know why I am here?"

He shrugged. When the message had magically formed in front of his eyes two hours earlier he had not given it much thought. If a meeting was requested it was either to clarify things or complain about stuff. Nobody sent secret notes to arrange for ideal chit-chat.

"You let him get away," she said. "After taking him out of the equation in the most perfect way possible, you stupidly allowed him to be rescued. Right from under your nose."

"That is hardly my fault," he said, slowly placing his cup of coffee back on the table. "Your magic didn't effect him the same way it has done everyone else for centuries. He is in here, amongst all the other voices. Saying the same thing over and over again. But something was left behind in his body, enough that it made him curious. What else was I meant to do? You said killing him would cause more complications for us than it was worth."

"You could have continued siphoning from him."

"I did!" he said, getting annoyed. "Don't think I didn't come to that conclusion on my own. He just reset slightly but always the personality remained. I don't see what you're worried about, he didn't learn anything and if he had stumbled across something I made sure to remove it on a weekly basis. The fairy detective that you worried about is in my head, I'm sure of it."

He tapped his left temple twice, grinning.

Blacksmile raised her hands, showing her gnarled and horrific fingers, and ran them through her straw-like hair.

"It doesn't matter if he did or did not find anything out. I've

223

been following his little mortal friend and she has stumbled onto this arrangement. Found one of your unimportant victims with her memories all removed. You've gotten sloppy in your old age."

"I've gotten more careful, if anything," he said. "You just need to figure out how much energy will be enough for phase two."

The waitress returned, dropping off a mug of black tea.

"We're nearly there," Blacksmile said, taking the mug in her left hand. "But you need to be careful. The amount that needs to be collected is still important. Any less and we risk ruining the ritual. Make sure to complete your List before the deadline, but consider doing it from the shadows. Stealth might not be the worst idea at this stage. Abandon your disguise, it was only so people didn't question where your host had gone."

He nodded.

"I understand my part, crone" he said. "You just keep an eye on the fairy detectives."

As the crone started to sip from her drink, he found the urge to collect intensify. A collection, from The List, would be required very soon.

#

Shelly and Filthy Henry, or Quinn if she was being pedantic, walked back over to the table where everyone else still sat.

"I can talk to people, okay?" Shelly said in response to the questioning look from Elivin.

"Hey, never doubted it," the leprechaun said. "Just amazed you talked this guy into basically committing Filthy Henry-kiri is all."

"Is that a horrible pun on harakiri?" Shelly asked Elivin. "The Japanese ritual suicide by disembowelment? That is really reaching."

Elivin shrugged, her smile telling the world that at least she found the pun funny.

"She made a valid point about catching the bad guys," Quinn said, pointing at Shelly. He flung the toy detective onto the table and pointed at it. "How do we do this?"

Bunty Doolay steepled her fingers and stared at the little statue.

"I'm not entirely sure," she said. "Usually a *coimeádán spiorad* just unlocks itself once returned to its rightful owner. But then this one is different."

The *Sídhe* reached over and lifted the figure up.

"You've mentioned its uniqueness before," Shelly said. "That doesn't mean a whole lot to the people sitting at this table with no experience of spirit containers."

"Oh is that what that translates into," Linda said. "God, my Irish is really dreadful. But I suppose that's what happens when you don't use a language everyday of the week."

"Yea," Shelly said. "You start to pick it up again when dealing with the fairy folk."

Bunty tossed the toy lightly into the air, where it decided to immediately disobey the laws of physics and float. No upwards movement, no downward tumble because of gravity. The toy literally just hung in the air a few inches above the table while Bunty Doolay slowly waved her hands around it. Her long, elegant, fingers gracefully moved above and below the toy.

A thin, wispy, line of green light slowly extended from the toy and floated through the air, connecting with Quinn's chest. He looked down at the line and batted it away with his left hand, to no avail. In an attempt to be clever he placed his right hand flat against his chest, covering the spot the line touched. The line simply moved up his chest, passing through his hand.

Quinn, apparently not wanting to be bested by a line of magical light, put his left hand above his right and blocked the line once more. This had the interesting effect of causing the line to retreated away from him for a second, before the end of it split into a hundred little lines. Like the end of some frayed rope. Each piece shot forward and touched every part of Quinn's chest at the same time.

He looked over at Shelly.

"Worth a shot."

"I dunno," she said. "I'm guessing somehow Filthy Henry, even though he is currently in a toy, was controlling that line."

"He is," Bunty Doolay said, rotating her hands around the toy. "The connection is always under the control of the spirit inside. But...ah, here we go. First difference found."

"What is it?" Elivin asked, her tone sounding like she was genuinely interested.

"Filthy Henry isn't a full fairy," Bunty Doolay began to say.

"A full fairy?" Linda asked.

Shelly reached out and gently patted her hand.

"Don't worry about it. He's a half-breed, only one of his kind. Nothing majorly complicated but I really need to hear the rest of what she is about to say so zip it. Please."

It was rude, but Shelly had learned from dealing with the fairy detective that sometimes you needed to be rude in order to get your answers quickly. Otherwise questions became tangential conversations which just delayed everything. Linda seemed to take the subtle hint in her stride and settled back in her chair.

"A full blood fairy would have been able to create their *coimeádán spiorad* so that it was a self contained thing. No external power source, keeping the spirit inside safe until the end of time. Filthy, however, had to create a siphon for his magic.

226

That little line there is an ongoing spell, giving just enough power to the toy figure to keep the protective and container spells working. He must have put some extra magic around it so that it remained undetectable unless close to his body."

Shelly looked over at Filthy Henry.

"But he couldn't have done that for weeks," she said. "He needs to eat more than a normal daily amount for a person so it gets converted into magical energy."

"The jelly pots," Linda said. "He must have had four or five of them a day."

"That would do it," Bunty Doolay said, twirling her hands around the toy detective again. "Enough magic drained to power this, with the jelly being converted to keep his physical body topped up with magical energy. Well now...that explains why it hasn't just restored his spirit. He put a lock on it."

She plucked the figure out of the air and tossed it over to Quinn, the green lines fading away in the process. He caught it in his right hand and tapped the toy thoughtfully on his bottom lip.

"I take it that isn't normal?" Shelly asked.

"No need, really," Elivin said. "You get your spirit into a container it is meant to be a short term thing, just while your body heals from the brink of death or you get a new body. They're not generally used as a hidey-hole."

"So, how do I open it then?" Quinn asked Bunty Doolay.

"You say the passphrase that was placed on the spirit container when the spell was originally cast."

Everyone around the table went quiet, glancing at each other before all eyes turned to the *Sídhe* once more.

"Em," Quinn said after nobody spoke for the better part of a minute. "If I can't remember that I am not me, how am I meant to know what the passphrase is?"

Bunty Doolay frowned and pushed her chair back from the table.

"What do you want from me? I don't know everything," she said, standing up. "Better get your thinking cap on."

#

Collins Barracks, located in the Arbour Hill area of Dublin city, was the architectural equivalent of a 'hand-me down'. Built in 1702, it originally was used as a military barracks by British forces who occupied Ireland at that time. When the Irish Free State came into being, in 1922, the barracks changed ownership and housed Irish garrisons for a time. But as Ireland decided to be a neutral country, whose army should be housed in more modern complexes elsewhere in the land, Collins Barracks was handed over in 1997 to the good people at the National Museum of Ireland. Since then it had been home to wondrous displays of art, crafts, even currency. An ever rotating exhibit for the crowds to come and see.

Even though it was the middle of autumn and heavy, charcoal grey, clouds hung overhead, threatening rain, the museum grounds were busy. Given the location of the barracks there were a number of public transportation options people could use to get to it, both by bus and using Dublin's light weight tram system. Clever entrepreneurs had set up historical tour companies with all the places of interest being on the Luas Red Line or Green Line. Once or twice a week representatives of these companies 'forgot' to purchase the tickets for their tour group. This would result in them throwing a little improv into the tour at the sight of a ticket inspector getting on the carriage. Everyone in the group would jump off a stop or two earlier than they needed to. After all, dodging your fare was part of the genuine city-touring experience.

Who would want to miss out on that?

Some more wily tour guides would even pretend that they

were being slightly absent minded and the early stop was a mistake.

"Oh, I always do this," such guides would say. "I mix this stop and the one we are going to up all the time. Ah well, next Luas is in ten minutes. Not that long to wait. While we do, let me tell you the fascinating history of this lamppost..."

Not that Jeffrey O'Brien cared how people came, or indeed were coerced into coming, to Collins Barracks. Just as long as they came, that was the main thing. Walked through the old gates, towards the imposing granite buildings, intent on soaking up history and culture. If they bought some of the overpriced souvenirs from the gift shop on their way out, all the better.

As curator for the museum, Jeffrey liked to focus on how to get people in through the doors. A lot of the exhibits had been in place for far too long by the time he stepped into the role of curator. Even he, a self proclaimed lover of all things historical, took umbrage at the fact that the rotation of artefacts had been so slow. Museums, his his view, would be better if they follow the same business model that stores did, frequently changing displays to get repeat foot traffic from the same people.

If you displayed it, they would come.

It helped, Jeffrey felt, that his own family history was so rich. Stretching back to the time of the High Kings of Celtic Ireland. This meant a love of sharing history with others was ingrained in his very soul. What better qualifications could you ask for in a curator?

Aside from the obvious educational ones that showed the curator deserved to curate, of course.

Jeffrey fixed his bow-tie in the full length mirror which hung on the back of his office door, opened the very same door, and stepped out. Every afternoon, at around three o'clock, he took to the floor. It filled him with such a sense of pride to walk through the museum's various wings and halls, mingling with the patrons.

Sometimes he would engage them in conversation, so that they could ask questions about a particular object they were looking at. Other times he made sure that his bronze name badge was polished to perfection, so that when he stood underneath the overhead lights it shone and drew the attention of people around. Then they would approach, like moths to his educational flame, and seek out his knowledge.

The three o'clock stroll gave Jeffrey a great sense of achievement and pride in his work. If at least one person was engaged in conversation it was a successful walk. He would have imparted some information and made the world a more educated place.

As he made his way through the south wing of the museum, Jeffrey smiled. A bus of school children had been dropped off, the sort of kids all museum curators wanted to visit their place of work. Young enough to find everything in the glass cases amazing but old enough to understand you looked but did not touch. A group of seven children ran past him, going in the opposite direction, quickly followed by their teacher. Jeffrey gave the young man a polite nod as they passed each other and carried on his way.

Jeffrey stopped for a moment at a display of ancient coins that had recently been taken out of storage. They had been unearthed during some routine roadworks in the mid-lands and were breathtaking to look at. He clasped his hands behind his back and slowly examined each one.

"They are truly exquisite."

"That they are," Jeffrey said, looking at the reflection of the man standing beside him.

The three o'clock stroll; it never failed.

"These are from Celtic times, if I'm not mistaken."

Jeffrey silently thanked whatever Higher Power organised

events in the universe. While the three o'clock stroll was always a sure-fire conversation starter, it was rare to get a fellow lover of history at them. Most of the time it was a tourist or a student writing a report, chatting to get a small bit of information. Never someone who knew what they were really talking about.

"You have a good eye," Jeffrey said, straightening up and turning to face the museum patron. "Are you in the trade? A collector maybe?"

The patron scratched behind his ear, his hands in blue latex gloves, and leaned in a little closer to the display. Gloves liked that were always worn by true historians Jeffrey found, even the hobbyists. It meant the man was familiar with handling precious items. This three o'clock stroll could turn into the most interesting conversation in a long time.

"No," the patron said. "But I've seen them before. Used to handle them, back in the day."

That was not such a bad answer to get. While it meant he may have had no actual interest in coin collecting, the patron could still have worked as a trader or broker who dealt in similar items. Such people still needed some sort of information on what they were trading, otherwise how else would they get the true worth of a thing?

"Well, I'm glad that the display brought you here today," Jeffrey said.

The patron looked over at Jeffrey, smiling.

"Oh, it didn't bring me here today," he said. "In fact, I've no interest in them at all. No, you see, the thing that brought me to this place today was you."

Jeffrey looked at the patron, confused. Nobody from head office had mentioned an inspection.

"Um, I'm not sure I follow," he said.

231

"Well you wouldn't," the patron said. "I doubt you have any idea how far back your family tree extends. But let me tell you I have spent a long time pruning that tree. It is something of a personal hobby for me."

Something about the man's tone made Jeffrey feel uneasy. There had been a coldness to the man's words. He decided right then that, sometimes, the three o'clock stroll could be cut short. Especially if a guest of the museum was being a little creepy.

"Well, if you go one floor down, we have a fantastic genealogy exhibit for you to enjoy," Jeffrey said.

"I'm sure you do," the patron said, his eyes twinkling a dazzling red in the light from the display cabinet. "But, as I said, your family tree is very interesting to me. So, Jeffrey. Tell me your story."

#

People could have holes in their memories for a number of reasons, but when you had more holes than memories it made it very hard to recall anything. Quinn knew comparing his memory to Swiss cheese would have been an insult to Emmental cheeses the world over. But the problem still remained; a passphrase had to be recovered with no clue as to what it might be.

Bunty Doolay had basically just told Quinn to start a treasure hunt while neglecting to give him a map with a conveniently placed X. The *Sidhe* had also declined to tell him what the treasure was.

Which was why Quinn had spent the last hour sitting in a booth at the back of Bunty Doolay's Bar, staring at the little toy detective.

The toy just stared right back, or at least it would have if the face had eyes. Yet still they both engaged in the never ending staring contest, one seeking secrets and the other unwilling to give them up.

Everyone else had left him alone for the hour. Nurse Faul had mentioned she was feeling a little bit tired and suddenly fell asleep. Elivin had winked at Shelly just as the nurse's head rested on the table. Bunty Doolay had disappeared, literally vanishing into thin air. In terms of support for ideas, no matter how crazy such ideas might be, the ladies were not exactly stepping up to the plate.

Quinn scratched at the back of his neck with one hand and picked up the toy detective with his other. The glow had failed to return around the figure, although Quinn was not entirely sure if he had full control over that ability or not. Then again he had no clue if the glow would have made it any easier to remember a secret passphrase that he had no memory of. Even if, through some insanely lucky sequence of events, he remembered a passphrase right now from his previous life who was to say it would be the right one?

He turned the toy slowly around in his hands, closely examining it. Not one single part of it moved in any direction. There was no give to the plastic at all, preventing bits from being bent. Nothing could be pushed in, ruling out any hidden buttons. It looked like the only way to unlock the magical container of madness was with the secret passphrase.

"Shelly," he said, loudly. "Could you come down, please?"

The sound of her chair legs being pushed along the wooden floor was the only response he got. Shelly walked down towards his booth and slid into the empty seat opposite. She nodded at the toy detective in his hands.

"I'm going to guess that you still haven't figured out how to open that yet," she said.

Quinn nodded.

"I'm sorry," he said. "I've tried, honestly I have. But this is like trying to figure out how long is a piece of string."

233

"Twice the length from the middle to one end," Shelly said, far too quickly for it not to be a rehearsed answer.

He thought about her response for a moment and found himself smiling. It was a good. Totally correct, without getting into the specifics of pesky things like actual measurements.

"Good one," Quinn said. "But seriously, how am I meant to do this? I don't even remember being Filthy Henry and everyone is expecting me to know, on some genetic level or magical membrane or some such crap, what passphrase he would have used to seal this thing shut. Is that honestly the best plan we have?"

"It is the only plan in town at the minute," Shelly said, settling back into the seat and crossing her arms. "I'm not saying that makes it a good one, but beggars can't be choosers."

Not for the first time in the past hour, Quinn thought about how they badly needed another plan. The current one was up there with skydiving into the middle of the Amazon rainforest, stumbling across a tribe that had no exposure to the modern world for generations, and asking to charge your smartphone so you could use the online maps. Even stringing together that most horrible of similes had taxed Quinn's brain greatly, using information he had only learned in the last few weeks from magazines in the hospital. If he had to rely on newly acquired information to come up with thoughts like that then surely he would have to…

"Tell me about him," Quinn said to Shelly after an idea popped into his head.

He placed the toy detective back down on the table.

"What?"

"Tell me about Filthy Henry. Maybe if I learn something about the person I am meant to be I will be able to take a stab at this passphrase. You know, an educated guess based off all the

234

information I have at my disposal. At the minute my Filthy Henry info is limited to the fact we look the same, on account of being the same person apparently, and that he can do magic. Not a lot to go on."

Shelly shrugged her shoulders, nodding her head at the same time.

"That's actually not a horrible idea. Sort of like a mental jump-start for your memories. I mean muscle memory might apply to the brain as well, right? Even if you don't have the memories, the brain might have something in there still."

So, Shelly began to tell Quinn all about Filthy Henry. She started at the very beginning, a very good place to start. About how her first encounter with the fairy detective had been after she hired him to find her talking cat. Quinn decided to not interject and ask what the hell Shelly was on about with regards to a talking cat, considering how the day had gone so far.

It was a story of pure insanity. Shelly and Filthy Henry had searched all over the city for the cat while at the same time working on a case involving a couple of dead crooks in a warehouse. They had chased after vampires and even confronted some big wig author called Bram Stoker. The climatic battle between Filthy Henry and the vampiric author took place on Grafton Street, late at night. During the fight Stoker had done something that the fairy detective was unable to prevent; he killed Shelly. Picked her up like a rag doll and flung her into the nearest wall. Ending Shelly's life in a brutal and horrible fashion. Filthy Henry had not taken too kindly to it. After destroying the vampire author with some dangerous and powerful magic, the fairy detective used a wish, granted by the King of the Leprechauns himself, to bring Shelly back to life.

A minor detail which the fairy detective decided to never tell Shelly.

They worked another case a few months after the secret

resurrection, involving a murdered god. That had turned out to be a ploy by some evil gods, who lived under Ireland in a magical prison realm, to try and rewrite History itself. With Shelly's help, Filthy Henry solved the case and saved the day.

As Shelly told Quinn about their last big case together, involving a murderous time travelling queen and the legendary hero of Ulster Cú Chulainn, he realised he had stopped blinking. It was just hard to not be so surprised by the tales Shelly was relaying. During their last case Shelly had stumbled upon the truth about her actual-death experience, the information causing a rift to form between herself and the fairy detective.

Quinn could tell she was putting on a brave face, but as Shelly told the final bits of her story he could hear the quiver in her voice. Her eyes began to water, ever so slightly. Pulling a tissue out from her back pocket, Shelly dabbed at the bottom of her eyes and sniffed very loudly.

"I thought he was my friend, you know?" she said. "Like, I find it very hard to make friends. I always have. Seeing fairy creatures, even before Filthy Henry gave me full control of the ability, made me a sort of oddball to be around. I never trusted anyone, not really. Until he came along. Then he went and did that and sure, it was nice not being dead and all. But he could have told me. You know?"

He did not, due to a lack of experiences in that particular area of life. But it was clear that this act of friendly betrayal had hurt Shelly more than even she realised. As she sat there, gently sobbing away to herself, Quinn reached across the table and clasped her left hand in both of his. Shelly looked over at him and smiled a sad little smile.

"I'm not him," Quinn said. "But I am wearing his face. So, for what it is worth, from the face of your friend who betrayed your trust like that. Shelly, I'm so sorry."

The toy figure started to wobble back and forth on the table, a bright blue glow coming from within its plastic body. Shelly and Quinn, still holding hands, stared down at the little detective as it began to bounce on the spot. Like a drop of water splashed onto a warm frying pan, the toy figure started to hop around the table randomly. Each move it made caused the blue glow to intensify, until all details of the figure were obscured by the mysterious light from within.

With a final hop towards Quinn the glowing blue light rose up from the toy and floated above the table. It began to expand outwards and upwards, forming a blue cloud of light over the table. The cloud drifted up on unfelt winds so that it was directly in front of Quinn's face. He stared into it and was amazed at the beauty of it all.

Tiny dots of bright blue light nestled inside the cloud, like dazzlingly brilliant stars in space. Each of them pulsed slightly, sending waves of light through the cloud. Around the edges of this little display, the blue light had grown darker. Defining an outline of sorts around the cloud. It was, quite simply, the most beautiful thing Quinn had ever seen. Without consciously thinking about it, he let go of Shelly's hands and reached out to touch the cloud. As his fingers came closer the cloud began to shrink, folding in on itself. Each of the little blue stars rapidly moved towards the centre of the cloud, while the waves of light began to bounce around faster and faster with each pulse. Within a minute the entire cloud had collapsed completely, leaving behind a dark blue sphere, roughly the size of a marble, floating in the air.

"What do you reckon this is all about?" Quinn asked Shelly, lowering his hand and leaning towards the blue sphere. "Did I get the passphrase right by accident or something?"

"You must have," Shelly said. "But what that blue ball is I don't..."

Before she could finish her sentence the blue sphere shot forward, moving at great speed directly for Quinn's forehead.

Leaving him no time to react at all, he could but watch as the sphere slammed into his head, knocking him back into the seat.

Then the world went dark.

#

It had been very satisfying visiting the museum. More so because the Collection had not taken long. When the universe aligned in such a wonderful way you never questioned how things worked. You just enjoyed everything going perfectly.

Today had gone particularly well, considering the location. In general Collections in very public, populated, places were tricky. There was the risk of drawing the attention of people nearby. Not that this was a huge problem to deal with, it just meant some insignificant stories had to be Collected as well, to silence the witnesses. Those sort of encounters soured things. But in a museum, with people all around, to get the Collection and have nobody interfere. Well that only made the entire experience much more fun.

One more name taken off The List. At the end of the day that was his main agenda, to finish The List. True other people had a vested interest in his work, but they were just after the power that each Collection gave him. The satisfaction of taking a story from a person who had wronged him, whose entire family had wrong him, that was just for his enjoyment.

At the entrance to the gift shop he paused. He felt momentarily light headed. Something had just happened, inside his mind. An event which never usually occurred after a successful Collection. It almost felt like something had been removed, but what exactly he could not tell. Looking around the immediate vicinity revealed nothing to worry about. Nobody was even paying him any attention. He shrugged and put it down to the excitement of the day.

Strolling through the gift shop on the way out, he gave the girl behind the counter a smile.

"It's going to be a fantastic day," he said to her.

# Chapter Eleven

Filthy Henry opened his eyes, stared ahead, and felt his body jolt. It was good to feel that again, to have the sensation of a body which was not just made from a solid piece of plastic. This realisation hit him the instant he opened his eyes. The last few weeks had not been spent in some sort of perfectly created magical prison, they had been spent in his own spirit container. For some reason this information had been missing while inside the *coimeádán spiorad*, yet now he knew that was exactly where he had been. Not captured or held in a strange, impressive, prison. But safe in a spirit container of his own making.

Why those memories had not come along with him was something to look into later. Nothing in Filthy Henry's research mentioned memory lose or confusion while inside the container. Yet it had clearly happened.

A curl of grey mist drifted before his eyes. This was unexpected, since Bunty Doolay did not allow smoking, magical or hazardous to ones health, in her bar. Filthy Henry slowly sat up, rested on his elbows, and looked around.

Everywhere was in darkness, the only thing visible being a swirling cloud of mist along the ground. It drifted in every direction at the same time, never gathering in the same location for more than a second. That was fascinating, but not nearly as much as the lack of anything else.

A great, vast, open space with nothing in it at all.

There was no sign of Shelly or Bunty. No pub furniture. No pub even. Just endless darkness and the mist.

"Well now," Filthy Henry said, climbing to his feet and

looking around. "At least I'm dressed and wearing my trench coat, I guess."

The mist parted as he rose, before rushing back in to obscure his feet from view.

A scary thought popped into Filthy Henry's mind, concerning the creation of his customised *coimeádán spiorad*.

Generally only full-blood fairies created spirit containers, due to the vast amounts of magical energy they required to ensure *coimeádán spiorad* was made correctly. The fairy detective, on the other hand, had a limited amount of magical power in his body on account of his half-breed nature. After pouring over some ancient tomes and having chats with the various fairy folk who tolerated him, Filthy Henry had come to the conclusion that creating a spirit container was not a time sensitive task. It did not have to be crafted in one sitting. He had broken down the various steps and, with a notepad, worked out some thaumatology equations to come up with the required amount of energy each part required.

This not-so-small feat of mental magical arithmetic had equated to four boxes, each containing a dozen doughnuts, and a couple of weeks of late night spell casting. All to craft a *coimeádán spiorad* that had never been crafted before, one fit for a half-breed.

Doubt, however, was now creeping into his thoughts. Filthy Henry had, a long time ago, come to the realisation that, despite being the only human with actual magic in his veins, the spells he could cast were limited. By and large he had made his peace with this Fact of Life decades ago. After all, being able to conjure fireballs with your hands was still an impressive party trick to have in your repertoire. Just because your invisibility spells only lasted a couple of minutes did not in any way mean your explosive magical abilities were something to sneer at.

But, what if a limited capacity for magic meant spells could not be cast or enchantments performed in stages? Working out how much magic would be required was one thing, but Filthy Henry wondered did thaumatology sums, magical maths, account for entropic decay? Just because a spell was cast in the morning and the caster had to recharge during the afternoon, did the initial spell retain the same amount of energy? If the equations did not factor this in, then when the *coimeádán spiorad* had been under construction magic would have leaked out of it for days at a time. Which meant the unique, first of its kind, spirit container was probably as safe as a nuclear power plant built over an active volcano.

As his thoughts went down these scary lines of thinking, Filthy Henry began to have serious doubts about whether or not the *coimeádán spiorad* had even worked to begin with. He definitely had been inside it, of that there was no doubt. But inside it and missing all the memories about the spirit container. That was not how they were meant to work. What if it had just broken down now, completely failed to keep his spirit inside?

That might explain why there was nothing to see but darkness and a strange grey mist. The fairy detective's spirit container had released him back into the world, sans a body for his return.

"Oh crap!" Filthy Henry said into the darkness.

"Hang on," a familiar voice replied. "You're meant to be the big damn hero everyone wants and you haven't figured this out yet?"

The fairy detective twirled around on the spot, his trench coat spinning in the movement, and caused the mists to bellow up from the ground slightly. He could not see anyone else.

"Figured what out?" Filthy Henry asked into the darkness. "Am I dead? Pretty sure my dad would have shown up if that was the case. Be sort of rude not to, really."

"I would have liked to see that," the unseen speaker said. "No, you're not dead. But right now, we need to talk."

243

"Okay," Filthy Henry said, squinting at the all-encompassing nothingness to see if he could pick out any details. "Let's talk."

In his line of work, the fairy detective was used to things attacking him from a blind spot. Generally, the bad elements of the world, be they fairy or human, preferred to not give their victims a chance to survive. Why attack somebody head on when you could stab them in the back? What these nefarious elements of the world failed to realise was that Filthy Henry liked to blow such attackers up.

Sometimes the only way to stop a bully was to turn around and punch them square in the nose. With a fireball!

Keeping his right hand close to his side, Filthy Henry slowly began to conjure up a fireball. He was pleasantly surprised, and a little bit relieved, to discover the spell actually started working. The longer he had to create it, the more powerful it would be, without the need for a massive, and draining, burst of magic. It was one of the few spells the fairy detective had managed to master.

There was a rush of wind, the mists spread apart, and the speaker was suddenly standing in front of Filthy Henry. Wanting to use the element of surprise to its full advantage, the fairy detective flung his right arm forward and launched the fireball at the new arrival. It flew, the grey mist curling in the fiery sphere's wake, and raced towards its target. A target who, without even flinching, casually reached forward and plucked the fireball out of the air as if he had just caught a tennis ball.

Filthy Henry did the only thing he could think of in his current predicament and stared, mouth wide open, at the figure before him. The figure who was idly looking at the fairy detective's fireball like it was a freshly picked apple.

"Well that is neat," the figure said, turning the fireball around with a flick of the wrist. "Was I able to create these? You get told you have magic in your body, but it sounds like a crazy idea.

Then again, when you get told this in a mental hospital I guess you'd doubt if it was insane or not."

Very few fairy creatures possessed the ability to catch another fairy's spell, particularly one that was meant to injure a person. Some of the truly powerful races, like the *Sidhé*, could give the impression they possessed such abilities. However, all they were doing was very impressive sleight of hand. They would conjure a shield around their hand in such a way that it acted like a baseball mitt.

The fairy detective assumed that the old Celtic Gods could catch fireballs with ease, but that was a god. It would have been more surprising to discover that a god could not catch a simple fireball. So, for this mysterious figure, in this strange place, to display such a skill made Filthy Henry a little bit worried.

"Who are you?" he asked.

The figure brought the fireball closer to their face, revealing features generally seen only in Filthy Henry's reflection on shiny surfaces.

"I'm you," the copy said. "I go by Quinn."

Since dropping his mouth open in shock had already been the response to seeing his fireball caught, Filthy Henry did the only other action open to him. He blinked rapidly and shook his head.

"Run that one past me again," he said.

"I'm you, sort of. I don't fully understand it myself to be honest," Quinn said, playfully tossing the fireball up and down in the air. "When you left my...your...our...body, I arrived. Maybe 'appeared' is a better word, 'arrived' suggests that I was outside and got dropped off when you left. I've been in it ever since. Your body, that is. Figured we should have a chat before you get back behind the wheel."

Filthy Henry looked around at the grey mist and the darkness, then back to Quinn, when it all suddenly clicked into place. He was back in his body, or rather a loading area of sorts. This place was inside his mind, a representation of something to allow two consciousnesses to exist at the same time. Presumably a place created by Quinn.

"OK, sure," Filthy Henry said, walking over to stand near Quinn. "What do you want to talk about? I hope you're not expecting some sort of time-share situation. It was my body before you got your mental mitts on it."

Quinn tossed the fireball up into the air and caught it with his other hand.

"Yea, I'm strangely not all that upset about giving you back your body," he said. "Once your spirit returned I realized that I was just a part of you, not a separate entity. As you started to regain control I was able to use your knowledge, that's how I performed this little trick. Right now we are having a conversation in between a second. Conversing at the speed of thought."

"Speed of thought," Filthy Henry said, smiling. "We're just a couple of neurotic neurons firing around in my head, is that it?"

Quinn nodded, stretching out his hand and offering the fiery orb to Filthy Henry.

"Alright, I'll ask again," the fairy detective said, reaching over and picking up the fireball. "What do you want to talk about?"

\#

Everyone had gathered around Filthy Henry after his spirit container released the little ball of energy. Elivin stood on the seat beside Shelly, peering down at the forlorn figure. Bunty Doolay and Linda stood at the end of the table, looking at Filthy Henry with concerned expressions. On the table, the little toy detective lay motionless. It no longer gave off any trace of magic. Whatever it had once been it before, it was now back to being just another tacky piece of plastic.

The fairy detective lay slumped back in his seat, motionless. He had been that way for nearly two minutes. Shelly was unsure if this was normal or not, but like everything in the Fairy World the safer course of action was to never assume normality in anything. If a fairy walked in off the street and told you the sky was green you both accepted that this could be possible and, without making it obvious so as to avoid offending, went outside and checked for yourself. She looked over at Bunty Doolay but, as usual, it was impossible to get a read from the *Sidhé*.

"Okay," Shelly said. "What do we do here? Did we just trick Filthy Henry into killing himself with some sort of magic bullet?"

"No," Bunty Doolay said, shaking her head slowly. "That must have been how he wanted his spirit to return to his body. Quickly. I guess he never factored in being so close to the container when it was opened."

"Yea, because next time I do that I will be making it from fluffy pink clouds and unicorn farts," Filthy Henry said, groaning with discomfort as he hauled himself back upright in the booth. Rubbing at his forehead, the fairy detective looked at the faces around him. "I'm baaaaaacccckkkkkk!"

Bunty snorted, turning away from the table. Shelly caught the hint of a smile on Bunty's face before the *Sidhé* was looking at something behind their little group. Elivin dropped back down onto the chair and put her feet up on the table, the big green combat boots banging loudly on the wood. Linda stared blankly at everyone, before looking directly at Filthy Henry.

"Quinn?" she asked.

"No," the fairy detective replied, taking his hand down from his head and smiling at the nurse. "But he is in here, somewhere. Before we swapped seats he asked me to convey his gratitude to you, Nurse Faul. Says you did a great job and he really appreciated everything over the last few weeks."

"How do we know it's really you?" Shelly said. "We don't

know who was in that spirit container. It could have been an evil spirit that was just waiting for an empty head to show up in order to occupy it."

The fairy detective held out his right fist, turned it so the knuckles pointed downwards, then opened his fingers. Instantly a ball of fire appeared, hovering just above the palm of his hand. He smiled as the flames flickered brightly without setting anything afire.

"If you can show me another ruggedly handsome fairy detective, with a penchant for setting things on fire using these balls of delight, I'd be impressed," Filthy Henry said.

Shelly rolled her eyes.

"It's him," she said. "Nobody else would describe themselves with that stupidly sentence. Excuse me, Elivin."

The leprechaun stood up on the seat once more, allowing Shelly to slide out from the booth. Shelly walked over to the bar and sat down on a stool near the end of the counter.

Now things had gotten complicated, which was never going to make solving a case easy. Filthy Henry was back in his body. That was good, because they definitely needed his particular brand of magical detective work. But it meant that Shelly needed to work with the one person in the world who had kept the biggest of secrets from her.

A knock on the bar counter to her left drew Shelly's attention. She turned to see Filthy Henry standing there, an expression on his face that suggested he was not comfortable saying what he was about to say.

"Welcome back," Shelly said. "I'll put the invoice in your mail, since technically I took the case to find you."

"Well, I never did charge you for finding your cat," Filthy Henry said, raising an eyebrow at her. "So, how about we call it even?"

"Even!" Shelly said, spinning the stool around so that she was facing him directly. "Are you being serious right now? You kept the fact I died from me for over..."

"I'm sorry, Shelly," Filthy Henry said cutting her off mid-sentence, holding up his hands with the palms facing out. "I really, truly, am. I shouldn't have decided you didn't need to know you died. I'm not a god. I don't even like the ones I actually know. I had no right to keep that from you. At the time I thought I was doing the best by you, but you're right. I should have told you the minute things settled down and we'd buried Kitty Purry. I should have helped you through it. Like a friend would."

He bowed his head, dropped his hands, and let out a deep sigh.

It hit Shelly like a flock of Leerlings smashing into her head. She actually felt the stool wobble beneath her.

For as long as she had known the fairy detective, Filthy Henry had always been consistent with one very bad character trait. He rarely, if ever, apologised for his actions. The self appointed defender of human and Fairy Worlds, Filthy Henry walked through life with very little regard for his actions. Over the decades he had accumulated no real friends and the few people, fairy or human, who regularly dealt with him merely tolerated his presence. All the while he cast spells, disrupted evil plans and generally walked around like he owned the place.

Shelly had considered herself to be his first, true, friend. Even though the fairy detective did everything in his power to dissuade her of this notion. They worked on some small cases together, solved a few bigger ones, and even saved the world twice from nefarious powers. In all that time, through all those challenges, Shelly had never questioned that, on some deep level, Filthy Henry thought of her as a friend. When he had revealed, through a painful spell cast on him by Bunty Doolay, that Shelly had died and been resurrected it changed things between them. Somebody she once considered a friend had basically lied to her, for nearly

249

two years. Then, to compound the hurt, he had not even bothered to say sorry properly.

Until now.

If all it had taken to get a truly heartfelt apology from Filthy Henry was the, relatively simple, act of getting his spirit removed from his body, Shelly would have done it months ago.

"Oh…," she said, with no idea of how to proceed from here. "Em..."

"Look, I don't want you to just instantly forgive me or anything," Filthy Henry said, sitting down on a stool across from her. "That would be expecting way too much. What I want is a chance to get things back to how they were."

"Hold on now," Shelly said. "If anything, I want things to go back to how they were with some improvements. Partners in Celtic Investigations, not just a lackey."

"Whoa," Filthy Henry said, leaning back on the stool in an exaggerated dramatic pose. "I didn't kill you! I brought you back and..."

Shelly decided not to let him finish speaking. She slapped him in the face, relishing the sting in her hand afterwards.

"Just shut up," she said, holding her fist under his nose. "Agree that we become partners, full partners, and start showing me a bit of respect. Do that and I will start to consider forgiving you."

"Start to consider?" Filthy Henry said, rubbing his freshly slapped cheek.

"Best offer, take it or leave it," Shelly said, crossing her arms.

Filthy Henry seemed to, genuinely, start thinking about what she had just said.

"Are you bloody kidding me?" Shelly practically shouted.

"Okay, okay!" the fairy detective said, making calming motions with his hands. "I'll do it. Quinn said that I had been a full-on idiot and I needed to properly apologise. So I will do it, if that's what it takes."

"Good," Shelly said. "You spoke with Quinn?"

"Long story," Filthy Henry said, tugging at his hospital garb. "Literally. Somehow he managed to talk to me for what felt like three hours in only a few seconds, it was mental. Also literally. I don't suppose you brought one of my suits along, did you?"

#

"So you're saying to me that I'm to now call you 'Henry'?"

"Filthy Henry."

"I'm not calling you 'Filthy' anything."

"Well that's good, because my name isn't 'Filthy Anything'. It's Filthy Henry and has been since I took it up."

"Filthy!"

"What, Shelly? Honestly, I'm only back in my body a wet second and already you're shouting at me like I've done something wrong. How would you like it if somebody went around not calling you by your proper name?"

"I don't like it," Shelly said. "You've yet to tell anybody my correct surname as it is. You either just introduce me as 'Shelly' or make up some horrible name that isn't even close to my actual one."

"Really?" Quinn, now going by the name 'Filthy Henry', asked. "That doesn't sound like me."

"My name is Shelly..."

Filthy Henry waved his hands in the air wildly, then scratched furiously behind his left ear.

251

"We don't have time for that now, Mary," he said.

"Shelly Mary? Seriously?!"

"We have a human amongst us that needs to be brought up to speed quickly as to why I won't be responding to the name 'Quinn' any more," Filthy Henry finished, turning to look at Linda. "Look, I chose the name 'Filthy Henry', so you're alright to use it."

Linda felt very uncomfortable. True, she had not exactly been in her comfort zone for the last few hours, but that was largely down to the fact that an honest to God leprechaun had paid her taxi fare. Then, to top it off, a stunningly beautiful elf-like creature appeared in the street and invited them all into her pub. Her pub, which could be accessed without the pesky requirement of having to actually walk into it. Instead the world just shifted around you. One second you were standing outside, the next you were in a pub. By magic. Which is what it had been. Magic. Plain and simple. Magic, which had also been cast on her so that she would easily accept that magic was a thing in the world.

Magic which, right now, Linda was beginning to think had worn off and left her mind back in control of things once more.

Either that or she was having her first nervous breakdown. Medically the second scenario made sense, because in reality how could magic be a thing? But that made Linda question things she would rather avoid, since not everything that had happened today could easily be explained by a mental issue.

Like Quinn, for example. Only moments before he had been sitting in the pub, talking to them as normal. They had given him the toy detective, sent him down to play with it. Linda had taken a short nap and, upon waking up, everything suddenly changed. It was not even an act, like Quinn pretending to be somebody else. Everything about him was different. His posture, the expressions on his face, the way he spoke. Even the light in his eyes had changed. If Linda did not know better she would have guessed that the man sitting in front of her was just Quinn's identical twin.

That assumption made sense. At least it was a thing you could agree was possible.

What did not make sense was that his actual personality had been contained inside a little toy detective and, after uttering the correct magical phrase, been released. Quinn had been there, a person in his own right. Yet now he was gone, leaving behind...

"Filthy Henry, the fairy detective," Nurse Faul said, wondering if maybe this was all some elaborate practical joke with hidden television cameras everywhere. "The same fairy detective that you...Quinn...the other you...em..."

The fairy detective reached over and patted Linda reassuringly on the hand.

"If it's any consolation you're doing very well, considering the circumstances. Most people would have tried to run out of here screaming by now. Shelly took a long time to come around to things herself," he said.

"Hey, that's not true! You didn't warn me about the fairy vision when you gave it to me," Shelly said, crossing her arms and glaring at him.

"I'm pretty sure I did warn you," Filthy Henry said.

"Can we speed this along please?" Bunty Doolay asked. "There are a few too many humans in the bar for my liking and two of them are thumbing their nose directly at my barring list."

Filthy Henry looked over at Elivin.

"You?"

"My dad," the leprechaun said, shrugging her padded shoulders. "Apparently getting barred is family wide now. Did you know that?"

"Well, knowing your father, I can't blame Bunty," Filthy

Henry said. "I'd ban the whole family too."

"You know Elivin and her dad?" Shelly asked.

The fairy detective nodded his head.

"Can we all please focus," Bunty Doolay said. "Too many humans, remember?"

"Are you talking about me?" Linda asked.

Everyone else just stared at her in silence.

"I'll take that as a yes."

"Look, don't take it personally," Filthy Henry said. "Bunty Doolay's Bar is sort of a fairy only pub. Shelly is the only human who has ever been allowed in through the doors."

"You're human," Linda said, pointing at him.

"Half-human, half-fairy," the fairy detective said. "Half-breed is the medical jargon. A filthy abomination in the eyes of the fairy folk."

That made about as much sense as everything else which had happened today. Including the fact that Quinn, now Filthy Henry, had made a fireball appear in his hand. Linda decided to just stop bothering with logic.

"So, Quinn is gone, you're Filthy Henry and I'm in a magical pub with a fairy and a leprechaun."

"Plus me," Shelly said. "But yes, that's about the height of it."

"Okay, gotcha," Nurse Faul said, pulling out a chair and sitting down. "I've got to stop working so many night shifts."

"Em, can we get back to the other case?" Elivin said, leaning against the back of the booth.

"What case?" Filthy Henry asked. "The case of the missing ruggedly handsome fairy detective? That one was solved already.

254

Good job Team Fairy, drinks all round."

"No drinks," Bunty Doolay said, a stern tone to her voice.

"Worth a shot," Filthy Henry said.

"Oh for the love of God will you shut up for one minute!" Shelly snarled. "I am already regretting putting you back in your body."

"You didn't put me back," Filthy Henry said. "Technically I did. Your role in the entire affair was to give me the tools. But, seriously, what's this other case?"

Bunty Doolay walked over to the bar, flipping up the counter door and stepping behind. Shelly pulled out her notepad and dropped it down onto the counter in front of her, pulling out the pen from the spiral ring along the top. Linda looked around at everyone, with no idea what was going on at all.

"Linda," Shelly said, pen at the ready. "Care to bring the ginger one up to speed on your case?"

#

Filthy Henry glanced over at Shelly's notepad and noticed that the page she had opened was covered in notes. Not just some random scribblings or a shopping list that was likely to never be completed, but actual notes. Case notes, like she used to take when they worked on magic related crimes together. If anything, her notes had improved since the last time they worked together. More ordered it seemed.

There were even little diagrams.

It had been a tough few months without Shelly in his life. Not that Filthy Henry would admit that to anybody, even under torture. But when you had very few friends in the world one of the good ones just cutting you out entirely stung.

Badly.

Being stuck in the toy detective, now that he remembered that was where he had been, for weeks had left Filthy Henry with a lot of time to think about things.

Before going into the container he had heard rumours that there was another fairy detective in town and you did not need brilliant investigative skills to work out who that was. From all accounts Shelly had been doing a good job on her own. The cases that people came to her with had been small fry affairs, nothing that required magic and spells at the ready. She had even worked around her magical handicap by going to Dru the Druid and purchasing various charms from him. All in, Shelly had become a friendly fairy detective.

But Filthy Henry was unaware Shelly had been working on a big case.

He spied the first word scribbled onto Shelly's notepad and read it, upside-down. Somewhere in his head the remnants of Quinn sparked a neuron or two, giving Filthy Henry access to a memory that was not one of his own.

"Blank Slates," Filthy Henry said out loud. "That's what your case is about?"

Shelly nodded, her eyes fixed on Linda.

"Linda here works in the hospital where several patients have shown up without their memories. The staff called them 'Blank Slates'. You were one for a while."

"A particularly unique one," Linda said. "Since you showed up and at least could remember your name was Quinn, even though it apparently it isn't. Others, we only found out their names after family members showed up and identified them so the Guards could close out a missing person case. Although Bosco Burns showed up missing half of his memories and rambling on about seeing fairy creatures all around the place. Which I guess isn't so far fetched now. We just never officially classed him as a Blank Slate, since he didn't exhibit any of the same symptoms. Bosco arrived before Milton did, so he wound up seeing Dr. Flynn."

Filthy Henry eyed Elivin. Himself and the leprechaun bounty hunter had interacted on a professional basis a limited number of times and only a handful of ones from a personal perspective. But the fact that she was here meant that her current target overlapped with Shelly's case.

"You know what they are on about?" he asked her.

"Yep," Elivin said. "I explained it all to Shelly. Something has been going around Ireland for centuries, stealing the memories of mortals for some reason. I never could corner…whatever it is. Shelly stumbled upon the trail and we teamed up."

The fairy detective scratched thoughtfully under his chin.

"That's the same case I was working," he said. "I'd found some entries in an old journal, written by the last proper group of druids on the island, and started digging into it. Kind of like a hobby-case on account of my workload being fairly light due to some new competition in the field. I even caught it trying to steal the memories from somebody, Bosco as it happens. It ran off and I chased after it but it got the better of me, that's how I ended up in my spirit container."

"Are you saying that something is going around taking people's memories? For real?" Linda asked, her voice a little on the high-pitched side.

"After everything you've seen today, I can't believe that you find such a possibility to be insane," Filthy Henry said.

"Hey, quiet you," Shelly snapped at him. "This is my case, you're riding shotgun on it. Understood? Now, Linda. Can you tell me everything you know about the 'Blank Slates'?"

"Wait one second," Filthy Henry said, bringing both of his hands up to his cheeks and gently touching his face. "Do I have the makings of a poor man's beard going on?"

257

"Ignore him," Elivin said. "Man, that really is a phrase that gets used a lot around the half-breed. Starting to wonder if bringing him back was a good idea. Linda, over to you."

Linda started to tell them all about her case.

#

After Nurse Faul had finished telling them all about the Blank Slates, how they kept appearing at the hospital, nobody spoke for a couple of minutes. During the recounting Shelly updated and reorder her notes. Elivin had listened to everything Linda said, whispering to Shelly from time to time when something was mentioned that the leprechaun deemed important. These little snippets were scribbled down onto a new page, underlined a few times for good measure, then thrown into the mix of other bits of information. Filthy Henry remained silent throughout.

Apparently Quinn's long, but short, talk had left an impression on the fairy detective.

"So, what you're saying...if you'll permit me, Shelly?" the fairy detective said. "What you're saying, Linda, is that people have just been showing up to your hospital with absolutely no memories at all? But they still can do some impressive things, given they have been reset."

"Sort of," Linda said. "They come in with no personality at all, as if all the memories about their families and who they are have been removed completely. They can still speak, they understand maths and the likes. I dunno, it's really hard to explain. It's like the parts that made them...them...have been removed from their minds. Their episodic memories. But everything else is still there. If you follow."

"I don't," Filthy Henry said, shaking his head quickly and settling back into his seat. "And that's coming from somebody who spent the last few weeks inside a toy."

"I've seen these sort of people before," Elivin said. "When I

258

was tracking this thing, the few times I got close it had left a dozen or so people like this in its wake. Once or twice they accidentally found their way back home and people would help them. The skills that they had, mainly ones that were muscle memory, remained intact. They just had no personalities at all."

"I was called out to look into a person just like this the other day," Shelly said. "It's how myself and Elivin met. The woman was in a coffee shop but had no idea who she was or where she was. Like...amnesia."

The fairy detective frowned.

"But amnesia isn't something that goes around the air, waiting to strike at people," he said. "It's a condition, usually brought on by some traumatic event."

"True," Elivin said, nodding. "But you said you caught the thing in the act before being kicked out of your body. Spill."

Shelly knew what was going to happen next. Filthy Henry, unable to help himself, would smile that cheeky smile he used when other people in the room were meant to be impressed by his skills. At least that was what he thought the smile represented. Usually the smile he used, right before showing off, annoyed anyone who seen it. Those unlucky few who had witnessed the smile multiple times found the desire to punch the fairy detective in the teeth quickly rise up in their list of things to do. Shelly herself had imagined smashing the smile in, numerous times, over the last couple of months.

But, on reflection, that desire may have been less to do Filthy Henry's attitude and everything to do with him being a lying toe-rag.

Right on cue, the fairy detective flashed his irritating smile at everyone before clearing his throat.

"The reason I made my own spirit container was because I had a theory about what this thing does when it steals a person's personality. It is not so much taking the memories as taking the spirit, the essence, of what makes a person who they are. I say essence, medical types say episodic. Anyway that's why educational memories mostly remain behind, along with muscle memory. You can be a bloody good carpenter but an outright jerk at the same time. The two are mutually exclusive."

"You can be a mediocre detective and an outright jackass," Shelly said, smirking.

"You can," Filthy Henry said, obviously holding back a cutting remark. "The point is, it isn't damaging the person when the spirit is removed. But if you have a handy container lying around, with a little forethought, you can prevent your spirit being pulled out of your body."

Linda looked up at the ceiling, thoughtfully.

"Em," she said. "You did have your spirit pulled out of your body."

"Well, yes," Filthy Henry said. "But the second it left my body the container pulled it in. Keeping it safe. It didn't go wherever everyone else's spirit is going. Although maybe some of me did, because I definitely did not know where I was until I returned to my body. Although those memories have come back, so that's positive. Means we can probably restore everyone's memories."

"What was the big difference with you and everyone else Bunty Doolay said from behind the bar counter. "How come you seemed to have a personality left behind? Is Quinn your dirty little split personality you've never told anyone about? Dr. Quinn and Mr. Half-Breed?"

Shelly was not entirely sure, but something about the fairy detective's expression suggested that Bunty Doolay had hit on a topic he would rather avoid speaking about.

"So," Shelly said, clicking the end of her pen so the nib retracted. "Where do we go from here?"

"What do you mean?" Filthy Henry said. "I can't conjure up three spirit containers to keep us safe. My one has been used up, you don't get to reuse them. We go nowhere from here. Whatever is out there doing this, this...memory stealing...it gets a free pass."

"What?" Elivin said, standing upright on the seat. "This whatever is out there?You mean to say you didn't even get a look at what it was sucking the soul from your body."

The fairy detective shook his head.

"I was blind-sided. Something fell over behind me, just as I was closing in on whatever-this-is. Next thing I know I'm in my spirit container not knowing I am in it."

"Was it human or fairy?" Shelly asked.

"That bit I can tell you," Filthy Henry said. He sounded worried. "It was human, or human shaped at least. As I got closer to it I had flicked on my fairy vision, but no aura appeared around it. Whatever it was, it was definitely not a fairy creature."

"That can't be right," Bunty Doolay said. "You're trying to say that there is a human going around out there stealing the memories right out of people's heads? Unless it's a druid with a fairy sponsor, that isn't likely to happen. Even then, Druid's couldn't channel that much power from a sponsor to do something like this. I'm not even sure if they had a god as a sponsor it would be possible."

Filthy Henry turned in his seat and shrugged a shoulder in Bunty's direction.

"I don't know what to tell you," he said. "The thing that I was chasing after it attacked Bosco was human. All the way through. No spells coming off him that I could trace. I thought it was something else, a race that I had never encountered before, but then the bin beside me fell over and I looked to see what had knocked it..."

He paused, staring at something in the distance. Shelly had

261

seen the same expression on his face before, the one that meant he was thinking about something. Trying to recall a detail that may have been dismissed earlier as nonsense and was now suddenly, probably, important.

"What is it?" she asked him.

"There was something else in the lane-way with me," Filthy Henry said, looking over at her. "That's what distracted me. I had this feeling that something was...watching me. Right when the bin fell over, that's what I was thinking. The hairs on the back of my neck stood up because while I was tailing the memory thief something was tailing me."

Linda shivered on her seat.

"If it's all the same to you I'm going to have another little lie down," she said. "I've had enough ghost and fairy stories for one afternoon."

# Chapter Twelve

It was raining. This was a common enough event for most parts of the world, but in Ireland it sometimes caught people by surprise. Despite there being a weather report at the end of most news bulletins, it was widely considered by the Irish to be an 'at best' attempt at reporting the weather. If the report said it was going to be clear skies and warm temperatures for the entire day an Irish person would pack a brolly and jumper, just in case. Most of the time those 'just in case' items would be brought into service. When that happened it allowed the person to walk among their peers with an air of smugness, particularly if said peers had not packed similarly useful items.

Still, being caught out in the rain was a mild irritation that had to be lived with. It did dampen one's mood, however. Although there were other things that could ruin a person's mood. Such as your afternoon stroll, a reward for yet another successful Collection, interrupted by people who should know better.

"What did I say about doing another Collection in public?" Blacksmile asked.

"Not to do them anymore since the fairy detective escaped the hospital and our deadline was fast approaching," he replied.

"Yet what did you do, exactly an hour after we spoke?"

He had been around long enough to know questions of that nature did not need to be answered. Blacksmile was fully aware that a Collection had taken place. She merely wanted to chastise the doctor for disobeying her.

Sitting on Blacksmile's shoulder was a small rag doll, the mere sight of which was unnerving to say the least. At this stage the thing was hundreds of years old, evident by the wear and tear it showed, yet there it sat like a hideous parrot. Two buttons stared at him, fixated on a spot right between his eyes. At least that was the impression the buttons gave, that they were staring. The mottled, brown, cloth material had seen better days, as had the brown wool that was meant to be the doll's hair. A long, wide, cut split the face open and acted like a mouth. It was the bastard love-child of a muppet and a sock puppet.

A puppet that needed no human interaction to sit on a shoulder and stare with button-eyed judgement.

"If we miss this window because you get captured then we're stuck doing this for another two thousand years. I can tell you right now, you won't enjoy a single minute of those years."

That part made the doll even more unsettling. It could speak. The voice was hard to describe, like a mouth made by two wet fish slapping into each other. Of course, a speaking doll was hardly an oddity in this day and age. Most children could walk into any toy shop and scream the place down until their parents bought them one. Cute little creatures with tiny computers inside that repeated lovely phrases over and over. Imitations of life.

This doll, however, was completely different. It contained no computer parts, never repeated the same phrase and was not something one would consider 'cute'. Both physically and when you factored in the personality it had.

"I'm not exactly horsing around out here," he said to the doll. "But neither of you have to deal with the urge to collect stories. Lately it has been getting too strong to ignore, even after I tick somebody off The List. But don't worry, I made sure there were no witnesses around. I know you both have grand plan that you want to see completed."

"Just make sure you don't forget that," the doll said, jabbing her handless arm in his direction. "Be extra careful finishing off your precious List."

264

"She's right," Blacksmile said.

"She? Whose she? The cat's mother?" the doll asked.

"What?" Blacksmile said to the doll

"I never got that either," he said, pointedly. "'She' is just a pronoun, like 'he'. How come when a man is described as 'he' they don't reply with 'Whose he? The dog's father?'"

"What?" both Blacksmile and the doll asked in perfect unison.

"I'm just saying. You don't see men going around the place complaining when somebody uses the word 'he'. As a story-teller, my original trade, I find that most fascinating. Like, when did that lark start? Was there a meeting in the town hall centuries ago and all the women-folk voted that they no longer liked their pronoun?"

The doll turned its battered sock-like head, its button eyes focusing on the head of his accomplice.

"Are you hearing this too? I can never tell if the wool and straw in my head muffles the sounds."

"No," Blacksmile replied, never taking her gaze off him. "I can hear exactly what you are hearing. Maybe after all this time his little mortal mind has finally snapped."

He groaned, loud enough for them both to make no mistake about what the sound was.

This was only the fifth time all three of them had met since their pact was formed. Usually only one of them approached him, either with new instructions or a message about being sloppy and needing to hibernate again. Sometimes it was to warn him about an impending Pedigree Collapse, a phrase he had coined, with a particular family tree he had been working on for years. Those were always tricky, you wanted to avoid them, but at the same time it was exciting to see how close to the edge you could get.

Although there had been that Pedigree Collapse back in the

1800s when he had wiped out an entirely family line. But three of the people had been on his List, only a mad-man would pass up an opportunity to take them all in the same decade.

When the three of them did meet at the same time, however, it always seemed to involve a little bit of two-on-one attacking. Generally the two of them attacking the one of him. He had never figured out exactly what prompted these tag-team attacks, but they did entertain. For all their bluster, covert instructions and threatening reprimands, the pair never could truly punish him because of one simple truth: they needed him to complete their plan.

They needed him a lot more than he needed them.

That last point may not have been entirely true, he realised. Magic was a fascinating thing, truly a wonder to behold. After discovering the Fairy World existed he had been in awe. Tasks which took mankind minutes to achieve, a fairy could do in seconds. Even now, in the modern day, the Fairy World was still something wondrous to behold. It was the magic of his accomplice, his sponsor, that kept him alive and gave him his unique abilities.

Abilities he had used to get revenge on the descendants of his enemies for years. A most satisfying endeavour. None of the victims, at least the ones from his List and not just the random commoners he used to curb the hunger in between bigger Collections, ever truly knew or understood why they were chosen.

He was not a monster. Right before their stories were pulled from their bodies he would explain it to them. Nobody every believed him, why would they? In this modern world things like fairies and magic were the stuff of myths and legends. The very stories he himself once told were now used to put young children to sleep.

"I miss being a seanchaí, you know that?" he said, wistfully.

Neither of them responded for a minute.

"You were never a story teller," Blacksmile said. "You were a trainee and nothing more. Stop having deep and meaningful thoughts about pronouns and go finish what you started. With the fairy detective presumably back in play we have to be careful about how we proceed. You most of all. From now on keep a low profile and no more Collections in public places, it's too risky. Even the little ones you do as snacks. In fact I think you should avoid being out in public at all until the final Collection. You don't know Filthy Henry like we do, but he has a nasty habit of ruining the best laid plans at the last possible second."

"It's really irritating," the rag doll said.

#

Dublin City, being the modern metropolitan city that it was, had a public transport network. This network was made up of buses, trains and the Luas. None of which catered for travelling across the city, at least not in a logical manner. If you wanted to go north to south or east to west, you were covered. If you needed to do something insane, like go from a northern point to an eastern one, you had to come into the city, walk a bit, find the next mode of transport, and off you went again.

Nothing made this lack of planning more obvious than the Luas. During construction of its two lines, since no modern transport network would ever need more than two lines, the public had been left wondering one thing: Why were the lines not connected? There had been a Green Line constructed and a Red Line, but it appeared that the planners had taken a sentence from the movie 'Ghostbusters' a little too literally.

They made damn sure to 'not cross the streams'.

The attitude in Dublin City Council when planning the Luas had apparently been if you needed to get from the Red Line to the Green Line you could bloody well walk it. Exercise was good for you, after all.

Thankfully smarter heads prevailed and work had finally begun, years after both lines were finished and fully functional, on the Interconnect Project. A feat of wonderful engineering designed to connect the two lines and remove the need for people to walk between stops. This had, of course, been met with two kinds of mood typical to many residents of Dublin City. Those that cheered the project on as they looked forward to making full use of the Luas and the rest who drove on the mean streets of Dublin, viewing the project as nothing more than a continuation to the perpetual roadworks.

Roadworks, some people in Ireland would have you believe, was an ancient Irish word meaning 'Huge delays that cost the tax payer money and go on forever without ever benefiting the public". It was entirely possible something was lost when directly translated into English.

Filthy Henry, being an astute detective in general matters as well as fairy related ones, knew that the Interconnect Project was in full swing. More than that, he knew the route from Bunty Doolay's Bar back to his office, if they were to take a taxi or bus, went right by the current phase of Luas works on O'Connell Bridge. This meant the journey would take much longer than normal and be twice as irritating to boot.

A factor of irritation he pulled out of thin air, true, but felt was apt for the given situation.

Walking was an option, of course, but Filthy Henry did not want to be seen strolling the streets of Dublin dressed only in his hospital attire. He had a reputation, of sorts, to maintain. Plus, he wanted to get back to his office quicker than walking would allow. Meaning some form of other transportation was required.

Filthy Henry figured he had just the plan to get around this transportation conundrum. A plan that involved a teleportation spell. One which would move them, all in the literal blink of an eye, back to his apartment on Middle Abbey Street.

Normally casting such a spell on a human was a taxing effort for the fairy detective, given his half-breed nature. Moving a pair of humans, along with himself, with a leprechaun in tow would have pretty much destroyed his body. Filthy Henry had never really pushed his magical limits before, but he had been told that the results would have been of the fatal variety.

Luckily, the fairy detective was able to employ other skills in situations like this. Skills that could get a free teleportation spell cast on everyone with no magical effort on his part at all.

He would annoy Bunty Doolay.

Shelly and Elivin had gone off to sit at another table with Linda, asking her more questions about the Blank Slates. Clearly Shelly had spent the last few months watching how detectives on television shows found their suspects. By asking the same thing over and over, only varying the phrasing and words slightly, until eventually the perp snapped and just straight up confessed in order to stop the endless questioning.

In the real world that form of interrogation did only one thing. Got the person being asked the question worked up so much that they stopped talking entirely.

Filthy Henry looked over at the *Sidhe* and made sure not to smile or grin. Nothing that would give the game away. Bunty was many things, an idiot was not one of them. Plus, she had known Filthy Henry longer than most people. She would be able to spot his tell a mile away, even without magical powers. In order to get a free teleportation spell out of her, trickery would be required. Something that the fairy detective felt was a little unfair, truth be told. Bunty Doolay's magical abilities were near limitless. Fairies, or at least the races that could cast proper levels of magic, had an almost endless supply of energy to draw from. They would tire from continuous use of their magical powers, but it was not as deadly to them as it was for a half-breed.

The fairy detective slid out of the booth and walked over to the bar counter, taking up residence in his favourite stool at the end.

Since first darkening the doors of Bunty Doolay's Bar, Filthy Henry had always sat in the same spot. While the pub itself was considered by all races as neutral ground, a consideration backed up by the harsh and swift justice dealt out by Bunty Doolay, that did not prevent brave fools trying to do bad things. A stool positioned far from the front entrance, with walls to cover rear approaches, was preferable for a half-breed. Particularly a half-breed that was not meant to be alive. A half-breed who made a habit of annoying uppity fairy creatures at every opportunity.

After all, someone had to do it. For the sake of humanity.

Bunty was stacking some bottles, containing various fairy alcoholic beverages, onto the glass shelves behind her. In a typical pub this would have involved a person lifting bottles out of a box and physically placing them onto the shelves, aligning the bottles perfectly so the labels were clearly on display. There would have been a lot of bending at the knees, maybe even a step ladder to allow the higher shelves be reached for people of short height. In Bunty's the bottles just floated up out of the box themselves. It was like watching a Disney movie in real-life. Filthy Henry half expected a nearby mop to suddenly stand upright and start cleaning the floor.

"No," the *Sidhe* said, gesturing with her left hand at an empty box while writing something down onto a pad that floated near her right hand.

The box slid across the floor, unaided, and another one took its place. The flaps opened and once more bottles began to float up into the air, drifting towards empty spots on the shelves.

"They respond to verbal commands?" Filthy Henry asked, knowing straight away that she had been talking to him.

Bunty Doolay shot him a dirty look, then turned her attention back to the inventory work.

"Come on," the fairy detective said. "You have to admit you missed me a little bit. No?"

"I missed you like I miss a cold," the *Sídhe* said, a hint of a smile touching the edge of her mouth.

Filthy Henry took that smile as a positive and started to trace around a knot on the wooden counter with his finger.

"Still not hearing a complete negative in there," he said. "Come on, just admit it. Things are a little bit boring when I'm not around doing my investigating and stirring up some trouble. Trouble that ultimately results in saving the world from impending doom."

Bunty Doolay watched the last bottle float into its home on the shelf, jotted down some final numbers on her levitating ledger, and with a wave of her hands dismissed the tools of stock taking from her personal space. The empty boxes folded in on themselves, before lifting off the ground and dropping into a bin under the bar counter. With a twirl in the air, as if being held by an invisible assistant, the ledger drifted upwards and found a home on an empty shelf above all the bottles. The *Sídhe* turned and strolled down the bar, her hips swaying hypnotically.

For a moment Filthy Henry tried to figure out just how long he had been away from his body. He had never once denied that Bunty Doolay was by and far the most beautiful thing that ever walked the face of the Earth, but they were from two different worlds. Literally.

Well half of one world, if you wanted to get pedantic about details.

Yet now it was as if Filthy Henry were seeing her for the first time all over again. Either that or Bunty was purposely walking in a very alluring and slightly exaggerated manner to set him up. She came over and rested her arms on the bar counter, leaning slightly forward as she tended to when they would chat privately.

271

"Okay, smart-hole," Bunty said, smiling ever so slightly. "I missed telling your ugly mug that you were barred from here and to stop trying to find loopholes. Better?"

Filthy Henry grinned.

"You know I only play along with that barring lark because I don't want you to lose face in front of the other patrons, right? I mean, I don't do terrible stuff on a regular enough basis to warrant the amount of times I've been barred."

"My bar, my barring," Bunty Doolay said.

They looked at each other for a moment, neither speaking.

In a world with fairies and humans you had to take a few things at face value. Fireballs could be conjured out of thin air. The swan staring at a young couple kissing may very well be a Leerling with some voyeuristic tendencies. Mortals could walk down a busy street and navigate around races of creatures they simply did not see. All of this, and more besides, were just part of the normal aspects of a planet home to two distinct worlds.

Other things, Filthy Henry had learned, you did not take for granted. Like being accepted.

From an early age, even before his powers manifested, the fairy detective had always found it hard to fit in. His mother, a mortal woman with no trace of magic in her at all, had done her best as a single mother growing up in Old Ireland. 'Old' being a nice way to describe the country nearly one hundred years ago. Filthy Henry usually used the phrase 'Judgemental Ireland'.

A century ago people with no proper education or understanding of the human condition fell into positions of power and authority, lording it over everyone as if they had a God given right to do so. Being a single mother after your husband died was one thing, that could be accepted in Judgemental Ireland. A woman with a child and no husband or father in the equation at all? Well that was frowned upon and in some cases dealt with in harsh and very questionable ways.

But when it was your government and political leaders, figures put into authority for the good of the people, doing the rotten deeds such ways could not be questioned by the public with any great effect. It was renamed 'for your own good' and that was that.

Filthy Henry's mother had avoided going to the laundries ran by nuns, where other young mothers ended up while their kids were sent to other families or orphanages, thanks to a little help from his fairy father. An amulet worn by the fairy detective's dear old mammy made people never question her household arrangements. It did not make her invisible, like one of the fairy folk, to other people. They just did not stick their noses into something that was none of their business to begin with. This meant she could work and keep a roof over her and her son's head, without some busybody coming around looking to split them up 'for their own good'.

The amulet, however, did nothing to stop the fairy folk getting involved in their lives. Either turning the milk sour or making the fruit go bad a lot quicker than it normally would. Things like that were noticed by others in the village and, as tends to happen when the uneducated masses turn to uneducated leaders, talk of curses began. Obviously Filthy Henry and his mother were cursed or lived in a cursed house.

Try going to school and making friends with that hanging over your head.

Which gave the fairy detective his first taste of what it would be like living in both worlds but being part of neither. A life of growing up with no confidante, of being excluded as the other children all formed bonds that would last years.

That was why Filthy Henry valued Bunty Doolay's friendship so much. When all other races dealt with him out of necessity, she did it out of mutual respect. True, ninety percent of his time was spent winding her up or abusing the friendship in return for her magical abilities. But that still left ten percent of the time for genuine friendship. She was a very attractive anchor in the sea of chaos that made up his life.

"You okay?" Bunty asked, her brow creased with a slight frown. "You sort of went away into your head a little there."

Filthy Henry blinked twice and stared into the completely blue eyes of the *Sídhe*.

"Yep, fine," he said, quickly. "Look, I was going to try and pull one of my usual stunts. But I'm not now. Is there any chance you could teleport us over to my apartment?"

Bunty Doolay looked incredulously at him.

"Are you serious? No con? No trick? You sure you're feeling OK?"

He nodded.

"Alright then," she said. "I should open up soon anyway. Won't look good if I have two humans and a half-breed in here."

"True," Filthy Henry replied. "Usually just having the half-breed is bad enough. Wouldn't mind if you could help me shave during the teleport. You know I hate this rodent graveyard on my face. It's why I never try growing a beard."

Bunty stood up straight and raised her hands above her waist. With one hand aimed towards Shelly, Elivin and Linda, the other pointed at Filthy Henry, she started to make intricate patterns in the air with her fingers. Trails of lights appeared, forming in the wake of her hands and floating in the air. Blue and purple threads, looping in amongst themselves and interlocking with each other.

It was like watching Da Vinci paint while high on drugs.

As the threads of light tightened, forming a thick band that started to pulse with magical energy, Filthy Henry stood up from the stool.

"Not going to say it before we go?" he asked.

The *Sidhe* smiled at him above the spell.

"You're barred for bringing all this crap into my bar."

Before the fairy detective could even reply, the world changed rapidly. Like paint being flushed down a toilet, all the colours swirled around him. There was no sense of movement or motion, but he knew that when everything settled back down Bunty's Bar would be nowhere in sight.

The joys of having real magic.

#

The first thing Shelly found odd was the table.

As tables went it was a fairly normal piece of furniture. There was a large, flat, part that things could be placed on so they did not just fall to the floor when let go. Four legs were attached to this broad section, helping to keep it upright and thus aid in the task of not having things drop to the ground from a slight height. Given it was a wooden table there were the obvious signs of wear and tear on the surface. Chips from the edge, some coffee stains that had been allowed to seep into the wood. All in, it was a perfectly fine, serviceable, flat, rectangular, four legged wooden table to be seated at.

Except a second before it had been a round table with only three legs.

Both Linda and Elivin noticed the sudden transformation at roughly the same time as Shelly, each pushing back from the table and examining it like monkeys before a black obelisk which had appeared out of nowhere. They looked at each other, then at their surroundings.

Surroundings which now looked nothing like a pub and everything like the interior of a bachelor's flat. A bachelor's flat complete with that questionable smell of socks in dire need of petrol, a lit match and some washing. In that exact order.

"Oh," Elivin said, looking around with an expression of awe. "She actually is really good, isn't she? Like, there was no hint of it happening at all. She's a damn artist."

Linda frowned.

"I'm sorry," she said. "Have the drugs worn off now and I'm back in the land of the mentally sound and coherent? Were we in this flat the entire time and it was only the mushrooms you slipped into my drink that had me seeing magic and fairy creatures?"

Shelly shook her head and stood up from the table.

"No, we were teleported here by Bunty Doolay. Guess we overstayed our welcome. Also, you think you had mushrooms?"

"Slipped into my coffee, shortly after you arrived," Nurse Faul said. "I was sort of banking on it to explain why I was suddenly insane."

Shelly turned and walked out of the kitchen, down the hallway, towards the sitting room area. She passed the open bedroom door, which revealed Filthy Henry buttoning up a white shirt. He smiled at her, tucked the shirt into his brown suit trousers, and stepped out of the room.

"Can't beat wearing your own underwear, know what I mean?" he said, marching down the hall towards the sitting room.

The fairy detective picked up a pair of shoes from beside the sofa, taking out two rolled up black socks and pulling them onto his feet before putting the shoes on. He spotted a tie on the coffee table, tugged it free from the pizza box it rested beneath, and started to tie it around his neck.

"So," Filthy Henry said. "How was it? Enjoy the experience of a proper teleportation spell?"

"I've been teleported before," Shelly said. "By you. Plus we had that coin last year from Dagda."

"Yea," the fairy detective said, tightening the knot slightly and sliding it up so that the top button of his shirt could be left open. "But I can't teleport another person without making them puke their ring up on the other end. Dagda's coin wasn't so much teleportation as it was folding two points in Ireland together so that you could just 'step' from one to the other. What Bunty did just now is an art form."

"Really?" Shelly asked, genuinely interested in how Filthy Henry had come to that conclusion.

"Of course," he said, settling back into the sofa and closing his eyes. He seemed content. "Not only did Bunty Doolay send us halfway across the city, but she also positioned us in different spots so that we were nearly in the exact places we left. You three at the table, sitting down, having a conversation. Bet you didn't even realise anything had happened until you spotted the table was a different shape."

"She placed us inside your flat," Shelly said. "What about your wards that stop that from happening? I mean I know Dagda came in past them without any problems, but he is a god after all."

"Oh, yeah, them," Filthy Henry said, blushing slightly. "Bunty is sort of ... on the guest list. She can get around the wards."

"Really?" Shelly said, enjoying the fact that the fairy detective was clearly uncomfortable with the conversation. "Why ever would that be?"

Filthy Henry opened his eyes and stared at her.

"Let's not play teenage school-yard gossip, shall we? Bunty shaved me during the teleport, right?" he asked, rubbing his face.

Shelly grinned at him and nodded her head, shrugging her shoulders at the same time.

"It's like you never had facial hair at all," she said.

Linda and Elivin came walking down the hallway, moving past Shelly, and stood beside her. The nurse looked around the room, clearly appalled at what she saw.

"Qui...Filthy," she said. "If this is the state of your home it is no wonder you lost your mind. I would want to forget a place like this as well. Have you not heard of that new fangled thing called 'cleaning'?"

Filthy Henry ran his hands through his hair and sat upright on the sofa.

"Look, I live how I live and I haven't had any complaints yet," he said. "I fight fairies and take names, while living in squalor."

"You can say that again," Elivin said, edging away from a mound of dirty clothes. "You know you could just clean using your magic, right?"

"This isn't a bloody Disney movie," Filthy Henry said. "How much magic do you think it would cost me to do something like that?"

The leprechaun bounty hunter held up her hand and conjured a bright ball of white light. At its appearance Shelly got an overpowering whiff of cleaning products, like they were standing back at the hospital. Even Linda, judging from the deep sniffs she was taking through her nostrils, noticed.

"Get rid of that," the fairy detective said, pointing at the ball of energy.

"Or?"

Over by the front door of the apartment stood a bookcase. It was home to a number of books, a collection of dirty dishes and three hideous statues that looked like they had been made by a blind dog. One of the statues started to wobble back and forth on the spot. Shelly watched it, surprised at the suddenly animated inanimate object.

"I'm warning you," Filthy Henry said, nodding at the spell Elivin was still casting.

"Listen here, half-breed," the leprechaun said. "I don't tell you how to cast your muck-savage magic so don't tell me how to use mine."

The statue picked up a little speed, the wobbles turning into full on noise producing movements. Each move was now accompanied by an audible tap on the shelf. Linda and Elivin both looked over at the statue, right at the moment it fell and toppled towards the floor. As fragile clay objects tend to do when they fall from a height, the horrible statue shattered into pieces. Except instead of little parts spreading across the floor they rose into the air, changing into coloured bits of floating goo. This goo spread out in the air slightly, then raced towards Elivin, growing larger in size as they neared the bounty hunter.

Before she was able to react, Elivin was covered completely in the goo. It slid across her body armour, joining together to form a grey plaster shell around her. As the last part of her disappeared beneath a bumpy casing, the white orb vanished from sight. There was a slight hiss from the plaster, the cracks along the shell slowly closed, and Elivin was replaced with a horrible bounty hunter-sized statue.

"What the hell was that?" Shelly asked, staring in disbelief at the encased Elivin.

Linda backed away from the leprechaun, looking terrified.

"Security system," Filthy Henry said. "Fairies can't cross over the threshold of my flat because of the wards I've put in place. But just in case they do get around the wards I've a few little tricks in place. Once the security systems detect magic that is not mine they kick in. That's actually the nicest of them."

"Didn't work with Dagda," Shelly said, stepping closer to the encased leprechaun and gently tapping on the grey shell.

From within the cocoon Elivin mumbled something that nobody could hear clearly through the shell.

"The fat man never did anything in here," Filthy Henry said. "Besides, he is a god. Not entirely sure if it would work the same with him."

"I'm sorry, are we just going to leave her in there?" Linda asked. "Can she breath?"

The statue-Elivin started to rock a little from side to side. Filthy Henry got up from the sofa and walked back towards the kitchen. They heard cupboard doors being opened and slammed closed, while large objects were moved around. He returned with a hammer in his left hand and a long, flathead, screwdriver in the right. The fairy detective walked around and stood in front of the shell, placing the tip of the screwdriver roughly where the leprechaun's forehead would be. Two gentle taps with the hammer and the tip broke through the shell, creating cracks all over the outside. With a light rap from the head of the hammer, the shell shattered in a cloud of dust and pieces, freeing Elivin.

She shook her head, dust falling out of her short hair, then glared at the fairy detective.

"It's no surprise why nobody likes you," Elivin said, curtly.

"I don't lose much sleep over it. Don't mind the mess, I'll clean up later."

He fell back onto the sofa and let out a contented sigh.

"Right, Ms. Fairy Detective," Filthy Henry said, tilting his to look at Shelly. "It's your case. Let's get cracking."

"Was that a dig at me?" Elivin asked, wiping some remaining plaster pieces from her padded shoulders.

The fairy detective propped himself up on his elbows.

"How could that have been a dig at you?"

"Because you had to 'crack' me open just now," the leprechaun said, taking a somewhat overly aggressive stance Shelly felt.

"No," Filthy Henry replied. "It's a turn of phrase. Dagda above go straight to eleven why don't you."

Shelly was not sure exactly what happened next. Later, when she had time to think about things in a less tense situation, all she could recall for certain was diving back into the hallway. She slid across the floor, away from the living room, while Linda dropped to the ground and rolled under the dining table.

#

Filthy Henry was not a huge fan of music, at least not the sort that had lyrics. Words, he always felt, belonged in books and stories. Music should just be the instruments and the listeners own imagination. This was not to say that the fairy detective shunned lyrical music, far from it. He just enjoyed the instrumental stuff more. Mainly because when a song got stuck in his head the lyrics tended to pop up at the oddest of moment.

Case in point, one second after Elivin had taken insult over absolutely nothing, 'Ballroom Blitz' popped into his head. More accurately the lines 'It was like lightning; everybody was fighting.'

An arc of red lightning flashed towards him from Elivin's outstretched hands. Filthy Henry reacted by conjuring a small shield at his feet, curving it so that the electrical spell would be deflected around his body. As the red fingers of energy struck the shield they were redirected harmlessly away from him. The fairy detective rolled off the sofa and dropped to the floor. He saw Shelly and Linda take cover and was grateful for small miracles. Protecting himself was going to be hard enough against a leprechaun, never mind trying to keep two mortals safe as well.

Elivin made a gesture with her right hand, flicking the fingers out, and five tiny, blue, fireballs appeared over each fingertip.

281

"Fancy," Filthy Henry said, before quickly getting to his feet and diving behind the sofa so that his back was to the wall and the midget murder machine was on the opposite side of the room.

"Everyone thinks my name is so bloody funny," Elivin said. "Mispronounce it and all have a chuckle at my expense."

"Well if the angry shoe fits," Filthy Henry shouted from his hiding spot.

He looked around the room for anything that could be used to make this bad situation bearable. On the book shelf by the front door there were two remaining protection statues, which had both started to wobble back and forth. Neither of them was going to be able to fool the leprechaun again, Filthy Henry felt sure about that. Plus they took far too long to activate. That was something to look into at a later date. A date that did not involve an angry leprechaun lobbing death spells around his apartment.

But while they lacked a speedy sort of execution, both statues represented something else to the fairy detective. A plan that required less magic on his part to execute, while at the same time ensuring his pasty white backside was not hit by Elivin's fireballs. He reached towards them with his left hand, fingers outstretched, and pressed his back firmly into the side of the sofa.

"*Atreorú uaim,*" Filthy Henry said, sending a minute amount of magic into the spell.

Both statues started to wobble faster, preparing to unleash their magic. The fairy detective counted to three under his breath and then, bracing his left leg against the apartment wall, quickly pushed himself up from the floor and vaulted over the arm of the sofa. He ran along the seat cushions with all the balance of a one legged acrobat. Elivin stared at him, anger clear in her eyes, and flicked her fingers towards him. The action launched each of the tiny fireballs directly at Filthy Henry.

Things seemed to happen in slow motion then.

Filthy Henry brought his right forearm up so that it passed across his chest, clicking the fingers on his right hand in the process. The statues simultaneously exploded, just as the first one had done before. Each of the chunks flew through the air towards Filthy Henry's arm, gathering together and expanding outwards. In a second they had formed a large stone circle attached to the fairy detective's forearm, resembling a crude shield. As the last chunk slotted into place, Filthy Henry dove over the second arm of the sofa, crude stone shield held before him, and crashed into the five little fireballs.

Each one exploded against the stone surface, leaving little dints and clouds of grey dust behind as they did. With enough shield to still act as protection, Filthy Henry fell on-top of the bounty hunter before she could move out of his path. He slapped his left hand on the edge of the shield.

"*Ar ais le chéile tapaidh!*" Filthy Henry shouted.

The shield dissolved, pouring down onto Elivin like dark grey paint, before it hardened once again. As the new shell encased the leprechaun completely from the neck down, Filthy Henry rested his head against her forehead and sighed.

"Just once it would be nice if you lot didn't automatically go into 'murder mode'," he said. "I mean, what would your father think?"

Elivin, her face a bright shade of red as she huffed and puffed in her new confinement, glared at him.

"Well you'd know," she snarled. "Aren't you and him besties all because he brought your girlfriend back from the dead."

"Say that again?" Shelly said, cautiously coming down the hallway and checking around for any stray fireballs that might have been flying around.

Filthy Henry looked up at her and smiled.

"Oh, didn't she tell you?" the fairy detective asked Shelly. "Elivin's dear old dad is Lé Precon."

# Chapter Thirteen

He sat in his office and stared out the window.

On the desk was a journal; his journal. One which he had kept for many years, never allowing another soul to read it. It was a very important journal, containing the details of what most people would have called their Life's Work. Then again, most people only had one life within which to complete such things. He had had a life and more besides, working within the constraints of Blacksmile's rules.

Turning a page he saw the final name on his List. A List that had taken a lot of time to create and keep up to date. A very important List, one that changed and evolved as the decades rolled by. Not many people would have put the effort into maintaining such a List, rather marking the names off as they succumbed to the passage of time. But he had always envisioned doing it this way. True satisfaction could only be achieved by crossing out a name on The List personally, while the person who owned that name had no idea why they were picked.

The last name, however, had to be handled with care. Once their stories were Collected there was nothing left to do. All the Collected stories, all the potential energy stored within his body, would need to be released and his sponsor would have no use for him anymore. Unless there was some way to convince Blacksmile to keep him around afterwards.

A knock at the office door brought him out of his thoughts.

"Yes, yes?" he said.

The door opened and a young nurse entered the room.

"Sorry, doctor," she said. "Actually it's a cover-appointment.

Dr. Flynn is out sick today so he asked would you mind seeing two of his patients this week. One had a session booked in for today."

He closed the journal and pulled out a desk drawer, dropping the journal into it.

"Who is the patient?"

"Bosco," the nurse said. "Bosco Burns."

Bosco, who had been friends with Quinn. Quinn who had been some strange substitute in the fairy detective's body. Well it seemed that poetic justice had its own sense of humour after all.

"Oh we've had a conversation in the past. I'd be happy to help," Dr. Milton said. "Bring him in. I can't wait to have a chat with him."

#

Filthy Henry propped Elivin upright, leaning her encased body against the wall. She looked like a strange sort of living sarcophagus. It had taken her nearly fifteen minutes to calm down enough so that her cheeks returned to their normal colour. Not that this, in any way, made the fairy detective consider releasing her from the stony shell.

Shelly knew that was his way of showing the leprechaun who was still in control of things. A fairy lording their full-blood magic over Filthy Henry always received the same reaction from the fairy detective. Smart-ass remarks and a childish display of his own magical abilities that would just annoy a fairy rather than do anything truly impressive.

Linda and Shelly cleared away some of the food containers and various bits of bachelor detritus from the dining table, righted the chairs, and sat down. Linda kept staring at Elivin, only looking away when the leprechaun glared at her. Shelly sat down in the chair nearest the bounty hunter, to put a neutral face between her and Filthy Henry. The fairy detective perched against the back of the sofa, dusting away tiny bits of the stone shield from his shirt sleeve.

"Right," Shelly said after nobody said anything for a couple of minutes. "Now that the big magical muscle-flexing has concluded. Shall we get back to the case?"

Filthy Henry gave a curt nod. Linda pulled her stare away from Elivin long enough to give an affirmative shake of her head. The encased leprechaun bounty hunter wobbled slightly, which Shelly assumed was a shrug of the shoulders. All the players were back in the game, at least for the minute. Anything that kept fireballs from whizzing around the apartment was viewed as a win in Shelly's eyes.

It would have been easier to herd blind cats.

"So, first things first," Shelly said, her trusty notepad placed on the table with the pages opened to the current case. "We need to figure out who this memory thief is..."

"It's the doctor," the fairy detective said, examining something under his left thumbnail with great interest.

Shelly sighed.

"What?" she asked.

"The doctor. Your man who runs the loony farm I was in. That's who Elivin has been looking for all these centuries. All she needed to do was hire me and everything would have been solved years ago."

"I will pop your ginger head like a pimple!" the bounty hunter snarled, rocking in her shell. "Once I get out of this...mark my words. Is it dampening all my magic somehow?"

"Yeah, yeah, yeah," Filthy Henry said. "Course it is dampening your magic, otherwise you could escape."

"Would you two calm down and stop with all the magical bravado. You're impressing nobody," Shelly said, turning her glare from one to the other.

"I'm sorta impressed," Linda said. "I mean those tiny fireballs were pretty cool and that's not even the first bit of magic I've seen today. Kinda scary, watching them fly around. But still cool."

"Linda...work with me here," Shelly said, giving her a pleading look. "Fairies are basically kids hopped up on sugar. Pixie sticks if you will. They need very little encouragement to make things difficult for us."

"Hey! I resent that remark," Elivin said. "If anything I'd rather you monkey folk weren't around so we could just enjoy our country. It's your man over there who is an overgrown child."

They all looked at Filthy Henry, who was now chewing on the thumbnail he had previously been examining.

"What?" he mumbled, thumbnail firmly between teeth.

In some ways Shelly was happy to have him back. Once people realised how unbearable he was her fairy detective business would start booming with new clients. Being in a niche market only worked if people liked you in said niche.

"How do you know that the Dr. Milton is the thing we are after?" Shelly asked, looking away as Filthy Henry continued to chew on the nail end.

"Oh, I don't," the fairy detective said, before spitting out a bit of nail on the floor and appraising the thumb once again.

Shelly frowned. Out of the corner of her eye she saw Linda do the same thing and would have guessed Elivin was also exercising her eyebrows and forehead muscles.

"Go again?"

"I don't," the fairy detective said. "It's an educated guess."

"Based on what?" Linda asked. "Not that I think you're wrong...there is something about him that I've always found creepy. Just could never put my finger on it."

"Well think about it. New doctor shows up at a hospital just as an influx of patients with vanished memories start appearing. He is the only person dealing with them at all and they consistently fail to get any better while also, sometimes, seemingly reset to the condition they arrived in. It has to be the doctor."

The stone encased around Elivin made a grinding sound as the leprechaun slowly nodded her head.

"Makes sense, actually," she said. "If he is going around the country stealing memories straight out of people's brains, then maybe there is some sort of connection to him? If they get reset regularly it could be him tapping off them, stealing the newly formed memories."

Shelly mulled it over for a minute, ideally clicking her pen.

A new doctor showing up right when there had been a spike in people losing their minds did seem a little too coincidental. Like a badly thought up plot from a mystery writer, one who did not like to come up with too many clues when it came to explaining who the bad guy was. If Filthy Henry was referring to Dr. Milton then something still did not add up.

But then again...

"Why did you come looking for me?" Shelly asked Linda.

Nurse Faul looked away from the fairy detective and frowned at Shelly. She shook her head.

"I don't get what you mean," the nurse said. "Don't you remember? I didn't came looking for you, I came looking for a fairy detective. Qui...well Filthy Henry, I guess, wanted to talk to the fairy detective about something he had noticed going on in the hospital."

"But what was going on?" Shelly said. "We never did get around to talking about that. Why come looking for a fairy detective instead, or any detective, instead of going up to your supervisors or somebody else in a high ranking position?"

Filthy Henry sat on the back of the sofa, balancing on the cushioned edge by placing his feet against the material.

"The patients were being reset," he said. "The other Blank Slates."

"Blank Slates?" Elivin asked.

"That's what we called ourselves," Filthy Henry replied. "The other guests, patients, in the ward."

"On account of having no memories," Linda chimed in.

The fairy detective nodded.

"You thought something was going on, but needed to get proof about what before approaching your seniors. That meant a detective, but not any old detective. When one of the Blank Slates started talking about a fairy detective you figured what the hell," Filthy Henry said, look across the room at Linda.

"Well we couldn't prove that the patients were being harmed in any way, nothing physical was showing up. Nobody else on the staff wanted to listen to me. So yeah, I guess you're right. When somebody under your care starts saying they want to speak with a professional, even if it was with a made up title, you take a chance."

"It still doesn't mean that Milton is the guy who has been running around for centuries stealing people's memories," Shelly said. "All that means is he is a creepy guy who had raised a red flag with your alternate personality for whatever reason."

"You know what I say about magic and coincidences," Filthy Henry said.

"Dagda above, are you still prattling on with that tired old expression?" Elivin said, shifting about inside her stone confinement as she looked down at the outer layer.

"So it's the doctor?" Shelly said, writing his name down on her pad. "Somehow, at any rate. Suspect number one."

"Seems the most likely person to go at the top of your list," Elivin agreed.

"Oh no, it definitely is him," the fairy detective said. "Quinn found a secret notebook in Milton's office. It basically documented the whole stealing my memories thing and how he kept resetting Quinn's memories as well. Yeah, totally Milton."

"What?!" Shelly said. "You're only mentioning this now?"

"Well in my defence I wasn't exactly in my full faculties, on account of being trapped in a toy detective," Filthy Henry said. "Quinn didn't know what the hell he was reading. Plus I think I left the notebook back at Bunty Doolay's when she teleported us here. So there's that..."

"That is the dumbest thing I've heard you say...today," Elivin said.

"Sure, I can see that," the fairy detective said back, smiling at the leprechaun. "But I think we are all forgetting one very important thing that still needs to be figured out."

Nobody at the table spoke. The fairy detective seemingly took this to mean they all wanted to hear more.

"Why has this guy been running around Ireland for hundreds of years stealing the memories out of people's heads? More importantly, is there a connection between the victims?"

That caught everyone a little off guard. Up until now, Shelly and Elivin had just spent the time trying to figure out who it was doing the memory stealing. Now Filthy Henry was making them attempt to figure out a motive for it as well. As if stealing memories for the sheer joy of it was not a reason in itself.

To make matters worse the fairy detective was sitting there with that grin on his face. The one reserved for those times when

Filthy Henry felt like the smartest guy in the room.

"Somebody crack this bloody shell open so I can punch the smug git in the face," Elivin said.

#

Linda had heard crazier sounding plans, but that was due to the calibre of patients she generally worked with. Once, her second year out of nursing college, two patients had tried to convince her that they had a foolproof plan to escape from the hospital. All it required was a torch that one of them had hidden in his room. The only reason they had even bothered mentioning this to her was because they needed a third party to settle an argument for them.

Their plan was simple. One patient would hold the torch and shine the beam of light across from the roof of the hospital to the outer wall. The other patient would then walk across the beam, catching the torch from a throw made by the first patient, and hold it so his partner could follow in the same manner. Their disagreement stemmed from the fact that neither fully trusted the other and both assumed that whoever was holding the torch first would turn it off when their associate was at the half-way point.

Despite trying her best, Linda was unable to get either man to grasp the concept that nobody could walk across a beam of light. Then again, the things she had seen in the last few hours, who knew? Maybe those two patients had been a lot more clued in to how the world really worked than Linda ever would be.

The pair of patients decided then to put the plan on hold until they each had a torch. That way whoever was walking across the beam would have a backup. Just in case.

That plan made a whole lot more sense than the one currently underway.

Shelly and Filthy Henry were big on proof, particularly because it made closing their cases so much easier to do. Elivin also seemed inclined to believe a person, be they fairy or human, was innocent until proven guilty. As such, all three agreed that just because Fluid's arrival at the hospital was very coincidental, they were still going to need some evidence of his involvement in the memory stealing. Apparently the notebook was not iron-clad enough for them, they wanted to catch him in the act or find something else incriminating. There had even been mention of questioning Milton directly, see if he tripped up and revealed something he probably did not want to. To do that the three of them decided that Filthy Henry was going to return to the hospital, pretend he was still Quinn, then go into Fluid's office and dig around.

The return to the hospital had been the part of the plan that made the least bit of sense. Shelly and Filthy Henry figured that they could just go back to the hospital, along with Linda, and sign Quinn back in without anybody wondering why he had been outside in the first place.

Right then, Nurse Faul felt like she was standing on a beam of light and the fairy detectives were about to turn off the torch.

With a crunch of gravel under the front wheels, their taxi came to a stop at the automatic doors of Saint Patrick's. Everyone climbed out of the car, Filthy Henry paying with money that Linda had no idea where he kept in his pocket-less hospital patient garbs, and stood to the left of the entrance. The taxi pulled away.

"I literally had only gotten back into my suit," Filthy Henry said, adjusting his hospital clothes. "Everyone know the plan?"

"You look lovely in those," Elivin said, using magic to present herself as a small girl to the world. "Just don't get them wet, my spell doesn't work when it comes into contact with water for some reason."

"Thanks, pint-size," he said. "Isn't there some saying about the clothes making the man?"

"Nobody cares," Shelly said, looking around. "You and Linda get in there, look around the office and..."

As she trailed off everyone else turned to look at Shelly. She was staring across the grassy area in front of the main doors, towards one of the other buildings in the complex. Linda tried to see what was so interesting, but could not spot anything that would have caught a person's attention so fully.

"Whatcha looking at?" Elivin asked.

"Nothing, just thought I saw...something," Shelly said. "Something looking at us. I must need coffee."

Shelly rubbed her eyes.

"Let's leave Shelly outside," Filthy Henry said. "Elivin, why don't you stay out here with her?"

"Why's that then?" the leprechaun bounty hunter asked, looking slightly annoyed.

Linda decided to jump in before a re-enactment of the apartment fight took place.

"Just a wild guess," she said to Elivin. "But you tend to get annoyed a little quicker than most people. That might not go in our favour if we are trying to be discreet."

Elivin started breathing heavily through her nose.

"Get over yourself," Shelly said. "Count to five and walk it off."

The bounty hunter said nothing. She walked over to a nearby bench and sat down.

"You going to be okay out here for a bit?" Filthy Henry asked Shelly.

She nodded.

"Yeah," Shelly said. "I'm just seeing things is all. Been using the fairy vision a lot lately, might be forgetting to turn it off. Go on, I'll be grand."

He smiled at her, then reached out and patted her on the shoulder.

"Okay, Linda," the fairy detective said. "Let's return me to this place of fun and madness."

#

It was funny walking through the doors of the hospital and into the foyer. Filthy Henry both had and did not have memories about his first time entering the building. Quinn had created the memories originally, whatever that persona actually was. Now they occupied little bits of the fairy detective's mind. Almost like a mental sea had washed up some memory detritus onto his cerebral shores.

Without having ever set foot, mentally at least, into the hospital, Filthy Henry knew exactly where they were going. It was a surreal sort of déjà vu. The sensation of having done something before while definitely being sure it had been done before, just with somebody else driving the cranial car.

Nurse Faul guided him towards the admissions desk, waving at the young lady behind it. The young woman looked up and smiled as Linda cupped Filthy Henry's right elbow and gently pulled him towards her.

"Evening, Sarah," Linda said to the young woman.

"Is it? I've been working a double, you lose track of time in here," Sarah said. "Even with all the windows to see the world outside."

Nurse Faul laughed, a chuckle clearly reserved for co-workers and their in-jokes. Nothing funny had been said, but you understood the suffering that was being referred to.

Filthy Henry groaned. One of the great things about working

as a fairy detective meant you did not have to worry about all this social interaction of co-workers. Mainly because detective's worked better alone, with a folder full of useful contacts upon which to call. He smiled at Sarah, trying to catch her attention in order to get things moving.

It did not work.

"Did you see we got a few more Blank Slates in?" Sarah asked Linda, shuffling around some papers on the desk.

"Since I left yesterday?"

"Yep," Sarah said. "Three. One of them looked really familiar though. Like I'd seen him before or met him somewhere or something."

This caught Filthy Henry's attention.

"How do you mean?" he asked. "Like, you've seen them around Dublin or something?"

Sarah swivelled her chair to look at him, then frowned.

"Quinn? What are you doing out from the ward? Were you outside?"

Filthy Henry opened his mouth to respond, then had second thoughts. Quinn would not have given a snide comment back.

"I had to take him out for a family thing," Linda said to Sarah. "There should be a temporary discharge form somewhere back there. Dr. Milton filled it in for me."

Sarah rolled her eyes at the mention of the doctor.

"Fluid? That guy gives me the creeps," she said, searching around the desk. "He always seems to be trying to figure out what is going on in your head. But like...with mind-reading or something."

"It might be over there on the right, under the binders," Linda said.

"No, I looked under them just now. If it's anywhere it is mixed in with the..." Sarah said, searching amongst the pages in a small tray.

"FOR THE LOVE OF GOD WOMAN WILL YOU CHECK UNDER THE BINDER!" Filthy Henry shouted, cutting her off.

Both Sarah and Linda slowly turned their heads towards him, staring with eyes wide open and shocked expressions on their face.

"Fi...Quinn," Linda said. "I think you're a little overexcited. Maybe use your indoor voice until we get you back to your room. You can take a nap then."

Filthy Henry sighed, put on what he hoped passed for a contrite look, and nodded his head in agreement.

"Sorry," he said. "Bit frazzled. Outside was...a lot to take in."

Sarah frowned at him, reaching over and lifting the binder up.

"You know what, I bet Fluid didn't even drop it down," the desk nurse said. "Let's us nurses stick together against the medical man. Just drop it in before you go home and I will say it got stuck under a book or something."

"You're a star," Linda said, winking at Sarah.

"Don't mention it," Sarah said, reaching under the desk. "I'll open the door."

An electric buzz sounded, signalling that the double doors beside the desk were now unlocked. Linda and Filthy Henry walked over, Nurse Faul opening one of the doors and guiding the fairy detective through. Once on the other side of the door it slammed shut behind them, the lock slidding back into place with a loud click. The smell of medically strong cleaning products assaulted the fairy detective's nose so much he was sure nostril hairs were being burnt off.

The walls of the hospital were coloured a typical sterile white, the floor made up of tiles with little flecks of black in them. All of this was both new and old information, interpreted by his brain simultaneously. A strange sensation. At times, looking around the hallway, Filthy Henry could clearly see places that Quinn had stood.

Filthy Henry wondered if the strange, alternate, persona was still knocking around inside his mind. After all, if the definition of being alive was 'I think, therefore I am' then Quinn had been very much alive. Just occupying a body he had absolutely no right to. Once the case was over Filthy Henry fully intended to figure out just how he had a backup personality waiting in his skull, ready to go when something happened. Had it always been there? With his return was there enough room for everyone one, mentality, to continue existing?

Filthy Henry was not completely sure, but he could have sworn that somewhere inside his skull there came a slight chuckle.

"Huh," the fairy detective said, stopping in the middle of the hallway and looking around.

Linda turned around and looked at him, obviously slipping into medical mode and examining him visually like a nurse would.

"Everything alright?"

"Yeah," he said, shaking his head. "Just got lost in my thoughts for a second."

"You sure you're up for this?" Nurse Faul asked. "I mean I am not going to pretend to understand completely what is going on, but you're only just back in your body. Maybe you should have rested for a bit first?"

Filthy Henry continued walking, falling into step beside her.

"No, let's stick with the plan. The main thing to remember is I

298

don't want to spook the guy. If he has been around for centuries we need to be careful he doesn't rabbit on us."

"Rabbit?"

"Yeah, run away and hide down some hole. Like a rabbit. Let's be clever about this. I will go back into the common room and hang out around the other Blank Slates. Maybe even see if I can figure out what is effecting them on a magical level. You go into Milton and tell him I need a session or something. Just get me into the office. Once I'm in there I will act like Quinn, see what is what and then, all things being equal, throw a few fireballs around the place."

Linda stopped walking and reached out, grabbing Filthy Henry by the arm and yanking him back towards her so that he nearly lost his balance and toppled over.

Her expression was stern and disapproving in equal measures.

"There will be no fireballs in this hospital! Understood?"

Something about her vice like grip, coupled with the anger in her eyes, let Filthy Henry know that she was not messing around. You did not get to be a nurse in a hospital that cared primarily for people with mental health issues without a will of iron, he supposed.

"Okay, okay," the fairy detective said. "No fireballs. But I can't make any promises for Milton. Assuming it is him, of course."

This appeased Nurse Faul somewhat. She let go of his arm and pointed at a door on the left.

"Head in through that door and sit your backside down. Don't rile any of the actual patients up, they need to rest when in here. I'll go and see if the doctor is in."

Filthy Henry did as he was told, pausing at the door.

"You know you're a tad scary now we are on your home turf,"

he said back to Linda.

Nurse Faul just stared back at him.

"I've got access to a lot of powerful sedatives," she said, coolly. "Don't get any of those people worked up while you wait."

"Yep," Filthy Henry said, pulling the door open. "Scary."

#

Shelly sat with Elivin on the wooden bench just beside the hospital doors. Around them the hospital grounds were a hive of activity. Ambulances came and went. Cars dropped off or collected patients. Groups of nurses, young and old, walked by in their scrubs. Some chatted, clearly having a good day as they laughed together, others were more sombre, suggesting that not everything had been rosy during their shift. Doctors clearly just out of university ran by, their short, white, lab coats proving to be little protection against the wind. More senior members of the medical profession appeared from time to time, leisurely walking to wherever they were going.

It made for some fascinating people watching.

As an artist, something Shelly still claimed to be, at least to herself, she would often just spend time people watching. When working on her art project trips out to the airport, down to the docks or even just into Heuston Train Station in Dublin had been regular outings. You went, you sat, you grabbed a coffee and just watched the complicated and chaotic world go by. Everything connected in some minute way that nobody could ever truly grasp. All the while her artist's eye would take in details, both consciously and subconsciously, so that later it could be painted.

In all her years working as an artist, Shelly had never once come out to a hospital to do her people watching. A fact which only now was striking her as odd. Travel hubs all had the same generic story behind them. People departing or arriving, families and friends reuniting or splitting up. But hospitals had a very different story to tell and Shelly was trying to soak it all up for later.

Which was how she had spotted *it*.

Most people going about their business rarely paid attention to those around them. The world turned and folk just lived out their lives, only interacting with others when the need arose. It was what made people watching such an interesting hobby. Human nature meant that nobody paid any attention to somebody not directly involved in their life. It was similar to how the human mind adjusted to magic being in the world. Magic was there, the brain just sort of filtered it out. Likewise when somebody was people watching the ones being watched did not really notice. Sometimes they might get a 'feeling' that they were being observed, but it never went much further than that.

But if you were people watching then that meant you had the edge on other people who were also people watching. You could notice when the observer became the observed.

It had started as a feeling somebody was watching her, one Shelly could not ignore. After three slow, casual, gazes around the grass area Shelly zoned in on who was looking at her. Without making it too obvious, Shelly looked about again, lingering a little longer on her own observer, before continuing to watch a young couple walk by.

On the far side of the quad, standing beside a building that looked like it was a small bike shed, was an old woman. She had been watching Shelly and Elivin for the better part of twenty minutes, ever since the others had gone into the hospital. The old woman was doing very little to hide the fact she was watching Shelly and the bounty hunter. But, for whatever reason, Shelly thought there might be more to the woman than merely some old lady out for a stroll and a casual session of people watching.

Closing her eyes, Shelly mentally flicked on her fairy vision to see the magical side of the world.

301

Around Shelly nothing really changed, which was somewhat unusual. Most places, particularly the cities, in Ireland all had a high concentration of fairy folk. But the hospital grounds lacked anything magical at all. Maybe it was something to do with the hospital itself and what it represented. Fairies generally used healing spells to get better, anything from a broken bone to a cold could be solved with magic. Even death was only a temporary thing for certain races. Shelly was living proof of that. So, she concluded, buildings filled with sick and dying humans may have been a little too much mortal reality for fairy folk to deal with.

Aside from the fairy standing by the bike shed watching them.

Shelly adjusted the level of her fairy vision, increasing what she could see. It was a self taught trick, one that came in very handy from time to time. By upping the amount of the magical spectrum she was looking at, Shelly could see the aura of a fairy creature. Sometimes these were nothing more than dazzling display of colourful energy. In the case of a Leerling their aura seemed to be composed of feathers that appeared and disappeared around them on rays of white light.

Then you got the horrible auras, like the one surrounding the old woman. It was made up of black smoke that swirled around her, coming up from the ground in puffs. Strangely, the woman did not change her appearance when viewed through the fairy vision.

"Must look human enough to not require an illusion spell," Shelly said to herself.

"Who doesn't need an illusion?" Elivin asked.

Shelly looked at the leprechaun in her disguise as a girl, then nodded in the direction of the bike shed.

"Have you been napping while we sat her? There is a fairy over there...."

The old woman was nowhere to be seen. A fact that Elivin

pointed out with a cheeky grin on her face.

"I don't see anybody," she said to Shelly. "Maybe you need a nap? Do adult humans take naps or is that just the little humans."

Shelly glared at her.

"So, magic just makes you all jerks is it? Here was me thinking it was just Filthy Henry."

# Chapter Fourteen

Nurse Faul passed some other night-shift nurses, clearly exhausted from working the late shift, sticking around in order to help out some of the nurses on day shift. Comrades in suffering arms. All of the patients were either in their rooms or back in the common area. Nobody ventured out into the garden from the ward, mainly because the Blank Slates usually forgot that there even was a garden.

Turning onto the corridor where the doctor offices could be found, Linda began to form her plan.

Thankfully this part could be kept as simple as the day was long. All she had to do was go into Dr. Milton and tell him that a patient had requested an emergency consultation. It was the most natural thing a nurse could do. No red flags could possibly be raised. Patients asked for spontaneous chats with their doctor all the time. This did not, in any way, guarantee the patient would get their consultation. It was just the nature of the beast. But a good nurse, one who truly cared for the patients under their care, could talk any half-wit doctor into taking the request seriously.

After that it would be all down to Filthy Henry.

Which was a thought that did not instil great confidence in Linda.

If it was Shelly going in, trying to find some evidence that Dr. Milton was up to no good, Linda would have had no problems. Filthy Henry, on the other hand, gave Nurse Faul no warm and fuzzy feelings at all. After being back in his body no longer than three hours he had annoyed a leprechaun so much that a literal fire-fight broke out. That did not exactly scream 'this person is subtle' to Linda. Still, Quinn had thought there was something odd about Fluid. Filthy Henry thought there was something iffy about the doctor. Even the nursing staff thought things did not completely add up when it came to Dr. Milton. So, if she had to get Filthy Henry into the office, then into the office she would get him.

She arrived at a closed office door, with Milton's little sign moved into place to indicate he was in session. Linda checked the watch which hung from her uniform pocket and saw that it was coming up on the top of the hour. Fluid never let a session run longer than an hour. He was very particular about that. Which meant that whoever was in the office with him right then was nearing the end of their consultation.

Linda decided to wait, rather than barge in. Again, to ensure nothing rattled Fluid at all.

Three minutes later, time was up. She waited patiently at the door, but it did not open.

This was slightly strange. In her experience doctors generally had so much on their plates they rarely let appointments run over. If anything, they tried their very best to wrap things up as quickly as possible. Sometimes even cutting sessions short if they could. Not that this was a common practice amongst those in the medical profession. After all, there were always going to be one or two doctors who cared more about the patients than the turnover.

Fifteen minutes later, however, and Nurse Faul was starting to wonder if anybody was actually in Dr. Milton's office at all. She checked nobody was coming down the corridor in either direction, then slowly approached the door and knelt down close to the keyhole. Closing her left eye tightly, Linda peered through the keyhole into the room. The narrow field of view allowed her to see the edge of Fluid's desk and the shrink sofa that was in the office. Bosco was lying face-up on the sofa, staring with eyes wide open at the ceiling. It was hard to be sure, but Linda could have sworn there was a little drool coming out of his mouth. Like he had been heavily drugged.

That, however, was not the most interesting thing Nurse Faul could see through the keyhole. No, that honour went to the stream of red lights that were flowing like water from Bosco's head towards Fluid's desk. Lights that had no discernible source and looked strangely like magic.

If Linda had not seen fireballs conjured out of thin air earlier that day, she would have assumed the lights were just some new tech. Now she knew better and, if nothing else, this was concrete proof that Fluid was in fact the thing they were looking for. But the nurse in Linda made her want to stop whatever was being done to Bosco immediately. Rescue her patient first, work on getting Filthy Henry in to deal with the bad guy second.

Linda stood up straight and knocked rapidly on the door. She did not wait for a response from the other side, grabbing the handle and turning it. As the door swung inwards Linda saw a final thread of red light float through the air, into Dr. Milton. Rather than acknowledge what she had seen, Linda focused her gaze on Bosco Burns and did not mention the lights.

"Is he alright?" she asked, motioning towards the forlorn figure on the sofa with a nod of her head.

"Em, what? Yes, yes, of course he is," Dr. Milton said, shaking his head as if he had only woken up. "Didn't you see the sign on the door saying I was in session?"

"I did," Linda said, walking over to Bosco and checking his pulse. "But I didn't hear you talking so I figured it was alright to come in. Are you sure he is okay?"

Fluid started to shuffle papers around his desk, avoiding eye contact with her.

"Oh he got into...a...fugue state, after telling me some....stories," Dr. Milton said. "Medical term, you can look it up later. I must let Dr. Flynn know it happened when he comes back from his sick leave."

Linda helped Bosco to his feet. He moved with a groggy pace, as if drunk. She slid an arm around his back, gripping tightly to his hospital top, and started walking towards the door.

"I'll bring him back to his room," Nurse Faul said to Fluid. "But I was looking for you."

"Oh yes?"

"Yea. Quinn was wondering if he could have a session today. Said he was feeling a bit fuzzy and to be honest I don't think he is acting like himself."

Lies were always easier to tell when there was a bit of truth to them.

Dr. Milton stopped moving the pages around his desk, an obvious attempt to appear busy, and looked directly at Linda.

"Quinn wants a session? He did miss his last scheduled session, must have been those visitors he had. How exactly is he not like himself?"

Linda paused at the door, resting Bosco against the frame. For such a skinny individual he weighed a tonne. The next time she needed to do something like this, the person looking to get into an office they had no business being in could help carry the doped patient.

"Oh, you know," she said. "Saying stuff that doesn't make sense. Keeps talking about a fairy detective. To be honest I think he needs to see you."

She was not sure, but Linda could have sworn that a smirk crept across Dr. Milton's face.

"Well then, bring him in," he said. "After all, the patients must come first."

It sounded like a genuine statement.

"I'll bring him right down."

There had either been a change in the light or Linda was seeing things, but she would have sworn on a Bible that Fluid's left eye started to twinkle with a red light.

"Excellent," Dr. Milton said. "Just wait a moment though. I need to have a word with you about something."

#

Filthy Henry was not entirely sure what to make of the Blank Slates.

An entire room of people, none of which were interacting with each other. They were not even interacting with things in the room. His memories from Quinn revealed this was just an average day at the hospital. Blank Slates blankly staring at the walls and doing nothing. So emptied out at a mental level that they did not know they were getting bored.

In a way, the fairy detective guessed this was a nice state of being. No worries, no concerns. Any problems you had in your life forgotten, completely and utterly. All you had to do was breath and look around at others who also just needed to continue breathing. The pressures of everyday life a distant memory. A memory that was not even in your head to begin with.

On some level, Filthy Henry could not help thinking that maybe the memory thief was doing these people a favour.

"Of course he isn't," he said to himself, since nobody else in the room was paying him any attention. "He is the bad guy. He has to be stopped."

But still...

Linda entered the room, half-dragging, half-carrying Bosco with her. Another bit of information that Filthy Henry owed to Quinn's memories.

Bosco Burns, according to Quinn's memories, had been one of

309

the few patients he had managed to strike up a friendship with. Seeing him come into the room, the fairy detective recognised him from outside the hospital as well. He was definitely the victim who Filthy Henry had saved from the memory thief.

Nurse Faul brought the patient over to a sofa and dropped him onto an empty cushion. The patients on either side moved to give him some space, looked from Bosco to Linda and back again, before returning their gaze to the floor.

"Em..." Filthy Henry began.

Linda looked at him.

"I've seen something today," she said, quickly. "Something that doesn't make sense."

"What's that?" he asked.

The nurse made sure Bosco was settled on the sofa, then looked at Filthy Henry.

"There were some lights, back in Dr. Milton's office. Floating through the air."

This sort of thing tended to happen when normal people got involved in the fairy detective's line of work. Typically, humans went around unaware of the magical world. Fairies were the stuff of stories and nothing more. But if you began to regularly interact with the Fairy World, even unintentionally, the human mind stopped filtering out the magic it saw. Repeated memory adjustments just required more work than a brain was willing, or capable, to do. Generally, being removed from a magical situation allowed the mind to settle back into what it considered 'normality' after a few days. Everything that had been seen and heard fading into distant, uncertain, memories. Eventually even the memories became nothing more than ideas for stories, tales to be told on a dark night to amuse young children.

Seeing the Fairy World this way was not exactly the same as having fairy vision, like he and Shelly possessed. That was an ability to see the magical side of things whenever you wanted, the mind not adjusting afterwards. This was more like having a case of temporary insanity, while still being completely sane.

Linda had witnessed enough magic lately that her mind was allowing her to continue seeing it directly. Whatever lights she had seen, if no obvious source could explain them, were more than likely a spell that Fluid had been casting. Judging by the slightly stupefied state Bosco was in, this was a safe conclusion to make.

"Magic, most likely," Filthy Henry told her. "Don't worry about it. Once we're all clear and close the case, you will be back to normal."

"I see," Linda said, looking around the room.

Something about her expression reminded Filthy Henry of an artist as they looked at a room filled with their own art. Nurse Faul clearly took great pride in the care she provided her patients. Each of the Blank Slates were more healthy under her watchful eyes than if they had been anywhere else.

"Are we on?" Filthy Henry asked.

Nurse Faul stopped her slow look around the room and stared at him for a moment.

"Oh, yes, yes of course," she said. "All systems go. You just go on down to his office there and Dr. Milton will see you."

Filthy Henry frowned.

"Shouldn't you bring me down? Just to make sure we don't spook him."

"No, I've to go do...nurse stuff," she said. "Patients often just walk into the office without a nurse escorting them. You know where it is, right?"

One of Quinn's memories popped up unbidden, the path to Fluid's office from the common room.

He nodded.

"Yea, I got it."

"Good," Linda said, eyeing the far door out of the room. "I've to go and do nurse stuff. Like I said. Then I will catch up with you later."

She did not wait for a response from him. Turning around, Linda walked over to the door and left through it. Filthy Henry watched her go, then looked at Bosco.

Filthy Henry knelt down in front of Bosco, trying to catch his attention. Bosco simply stared through him, vacantly looking at nothing at all.

"I'll get this guy," the fairy detective said to his alternate personality's friend. "Something tells me I'd have a splitting headache if I didn't make sure you were looked after."

Somewhere in Filthy Henry's mind there came an awareness of agreement. Which was, he knew, a concept that made very little sense. After the case was solved, he was definitely going to have to investigate if there was a back-seat driver currently in his mind.

#

"I'm telling you, something was watching me," Shelly said.

"I am not saying there wasn't. What I am saying is how do you know it was definitely a fairy? Other things can have magic swirling around them. Humans under a spell, for example."

Shelly looked at Elivin and could feel her level of annoyance rising. Not being believed when you told people you could see things nobody else could was one thing. Not being believed when you told a thing nobody else could see you were seeing something was a different kettle of fish entirely. If anything, Shelly felt that a leprechaun bounty hunter, currently presenting herself to the world as a little girl via a magical spell, would have given her the benefit of the doubt.

"Are you serious right now?" Shelly asked her. "I have fairy vision. I can see fairies. Magic. Auras around creatures. I've been using it for years. I'm telling you something was watching me over there."

Elivin shook her head.

"Look, there is a reason that mortals don't get to see the Fairy World after they reach a certain age. It makes them go a little bit loopy. The ones that can continue to see it, they lose their grasp on reality. As in always. I know Filthy Henry gave you the fairy vision because you could sorta still see fairies on account of being an artistic sort, but I don't think that was the best idea he's ever had."

This was a topic of conversation Shelly had been wondering about for the better part of a year now. Before, her fairy vision had been a gift from Filthy Henry. A spell he had cast and one, Shelly presumed, was forever going to be tied to him. After her actual-death experience and resurrection, the ability to see the Fairy World had become part of her. This either was an accident on the part of the leprechaun whose wish had brought her back to life, or a deliberate act. Either way, Filthy Henry was no longer required to allow Shelly to see the magical way of life that existed right beside the plain old human world. But, ever since learning about the supernatural adjustments made to her body, Shelly had started to wonder if there would be negative effects.

After all, presumably there was some sort of psychological reason for adult humans to not see the Fairy World. Maybe that was why people with a slightly tenuous grasp on sanity wound up letting go. Seeing fairy creatures drove a person crazy. Hell, spending thirty minutes with Filthy Henry was enough to make anybody go mad in the head.

Maybe being able to see the Fairy World whenever she wanted had started to damage Shelly's mind. Meaning it was entirely possible there really had been no fairy across the green watching her.

"You're saying that my fairy vision is now dangerous...to my health?"

Elivin chuckled.

"No, you idiot," the bounty hunter said. "Mortals shouldn't see our side of the world. Your primitive brains can't handle it. I bet you just got paranoid at a Leerling that was changing back into their human form."

"I know what a Leerling looks like," Shelly said, annoyed at how flippant Elivin was being.

Beside them the automatic doors whirred open and Linda stepped out. She headed down the path towards the main road out of the hospital. Shelly and Elivin both watched her for a few seconds. Nurse Faul did not even look back in their direction.

"Linda," Shelly called out. "Is there a problem? Filthy Henry get in alright?"

Linda stopped walking and looked over at them.

"What? No, no problem," Nurse Faul said.

No further conversation seemed to be forthcoming from her.

"Everything okay?"

Linda nodded her head quickly, then pointed over her shoulder.

"Yes, yes, everything is fine," she said. "I'm going to go and do some nursing and then head home for a bit."

"Home?" Elivin asked.

"Yes," Linda said. "I think the excitement of the last few days has just gotten to me. I need to get some rest. Too many double shifts, lots of working with fairy detectives. You know...under

314

funded health service and all that."

Shelly shrugged her shoulders and gave a nod of agreement.

"Probably not a bad idea, all this fairy stuff can be a lot to take in after a decent sleep. Go and get your head down for a bit, I'll give you a call later," she said. "Let you know what we find out."

Nurse Faul smiled, a little on the fake side of the emotional spectrum Shelly thought, then turned and continued on her way out of the hospital grounds.

"Did she seem a little peculiar to you?" Elivin asked.

"She has seen some crazy stuff in the last few hours," Shelly said. "Can't have been easy taking all that in while also working in the health service."

"Maybe," the leprechaun said. "But you're seeing things that aren't really there and you seem to be doing alright."

Shelly groaned and rolled her eyes. Being rude definitely had to be a requirement for membership in the world of fairies and magic. It was the only explanation for how they all spoke to her. At this stage the only fairy that seemed to talk to her in a half-way normal manner was Bunty Doolay and Shelly was positive the *Sidhé* hated her.

"Bloody fairies," Shelly mumbled under her breath.

#

Filthy Henry stood outside Dr. Milton's closed office door. He did not want to just barge in, fireballs blazing, to take down the bad guy. Mainly because of a dumb promise made to a nice nurse. Catching Fluid unaware was going to be the best approach to this entire endeavour. A simple containment spell, maybe even an overpowered sleep enchantment, would do the trick. Something cast when the bad doctor least expected it.

Which meant going in, pretending to be Quinn, and striking when Fluid's guard was down.

All requiring a level of acting that the fairy detective was not entirely sure he could pull off. Even growing up, Filthy Henry always tried his best to avoid being in school plays. When avoiding them was a non-runner he would take on as small a part as possible. Like a tree. No lines. Limited movement. Participation award at the end of it all.

Such awards being the only way his acting would win any accolades.

Filthy Henry stepped up to the door and knocked on it. A mumbled reply came from the other side. The fairy detective opened the door and stepped into the office.

Dr. Milton was sitting behind an oversized wooden desk, looking flustered as he sorted through some sheets. He glanced up at the fairy detective and frowned.

"Yes?"

"Em, Nurse Faul said I could come in for an emergency session," Filthy Henry said. He pointed at his own chest. "Quinn."

"Quinn..." Dr. Milton repeated back, lifting up a folder from the stack to his left and flipping it open. "Yes, yes. Right. Sit...lie...do the thing. On the sofa. Then we can begin."

The fairy detective walked over to the sofa and lay down on it. He slowly started to conjure up a potent sleeping spell in his right hand, keeping it obscured from the doctor's desk. By taking his time to cast the spell it would be less of a drain on his internal magical energy, while also intensifying the strength of the spell. Conjuring this thing for five minutes would make it powerful enough to knock Milton out for a couple of hours.

Filthy Henry shifted around on the sofa, dropping his spell arm over the side for some extra obscuring, and looked at the doctor.

"What's up doc?" he asked, smiling.

Fluid closed the folder in his hand and leaned back in his leather chair. Nothing screamed over-compensating doctor more than a huge fancy-pants leather chair. As if sitting on a throne made from treated cow skin improved a person's ability to do their job.

Something about Fluid's manner did not sit well with the fairy detective. Using Quinn's memories, he was fairly sure that the bad doctor did not slouch as much as he currently was. For that matter Filthy Henry noticed that Fluid seemed slightly flustered, as if he had just woke from a nap.

The doctor shifted more pages about the desk as the search for whatever it was Dr. Milton wanted continued. Folders, neatly stacked, were knocked over, the resulting mess stared at.

Not that any of this was really important. While Filthy Henry had never met the man in person, so to speak, Quinn had. The alternate persona had attended a number of sessions with Milton and each one always involved the same thing. Magic seeping into his mind and removing any of the newly formed memories Quinn had made, effectively resetting him each and ever time. Not a complete memory steal, more like a delta sync. Removing just the newest memories formed. Quinn, on account of the memories being removed, never remembered this happening. In fact it was because Filthy Henry had returned to his body that he knew Quinn's memories were missing bits. A third party able to look at the memories from the outside, so to speak. Even now, lying down on the sofa, the fairy detective was learning something new about Quinn's time in his body.

Each time Fluid extracted memories from Quinn an intense migraine-type headache kicked in, effectively breaking the connection between patient and doctor. That was how most of their sessions ended, with the fairy detective's body using these headaches to keep the Quinn personality intact.

More stuff to look into when the case was solved. Which, after the fairy detective cast his sleeping spell, would be very soon.

Just being able to say that he, Filthy Henry the half-breed of Ireland, had solved Elivin's case after only working on it for a few months would be amazing. Nothing was more enjoyable than telling a fairy creature that what they had not been able to achieve in centuries, a half-human half-fairy had managed in less than a year. Since he had taken on the case himself, effectively being his own client, Filthy Henry felt winding up Elivin would be suitable compensation for his services.

"Quinn?" Fluid asked, looking over the top of his glasses at Filthy Henry.

"Yep," the fairy detective said, still slowly creating his sleeping spell.

At this stage the magic in it would have been able to take down a dragon for a few hours. He held the energy in place and stopped feeding into it. The aim was capture, not comatose.

"Right," Fluid said. "But what's your last name. I don't have a file sitting here with just Quinn written on it."

"Em," Filthy Henry said. "I don't have a last name. I'm one of the Blank Slates, remember? We recall nothing at all. I think we all just go by first names, unless we had identification when we checked in. Think one of the nurses said that family members sometimes come by and help identify us. Nobody did with me. Unclaimed baggage, that's me. I suppose Quinn Unclaimed could be my name."

Dr. Milton took up a pen and started jotting some notes down on a nearby pad. He looked at Filthy Henry every couple of scribbles, then back at the notes. After roughly a minute the doctor stopped his writing and stared down at the page before him. He arched an eyebrow, then looked across once more at the fairy detective.

"Have we met before?"

318

Filthy Henry smiled. This guy was good, not brilliant but definitely up there in the smarts department. Rather than act like this was more than a simple therapy session, the bad doctor was going to start acting like he had never met Quinn. Not the most imaginative of plans, but possibly something that would make lesser detectives look elsewhere for their culprit. It was just a shame that Dr. Milton was going up against Filthy Henry.

Shelly would have fallen for it, no question.

In a way, the fairy detective felt bad for the doctor. There he was, sitting behind his desk on his dead cow skin throne. Probably content with the little bit of power he had, relishing the ability to steal memories straight from a person's mind. In walks one of his victims, fully restored but performing at amateur levels of acting to pretend he was not back in control of his body.

They both were playing an intricate, delicate, game of cat and mouse. Except now the mouse had hit the gym and learned to work a shotgun.

"We have, doc," Filthy Henry said, eyeing up the doctor.

At any minute now magic was going to start flying around the room. Timing would be everything.

"What's today's date? I seem to be all mixed up with my mental calendar," Fluid said. "Why are you looking at me like that?"

"The better to catch you with your trousers down, my dear," Filthy Henry replied.

Fluid leaned back in his chair, the leather creaking loudly again, and reached up to take his glasses off. If ever there was a precursor for somebody to fire something out of their eyeballs, that motion was it. Filthy Henry had seen enough movies about adopted alien superheroes to know that glasses got in the way of heat rays shot from the eyes.

The fairy detective rolled off the sofa, in the direction of the desk, and brought his right arm up in the movement. He straightened it and, at the height of the roll, launched his spell towards the doctor's head. The purple orb of bright light, roughly the size of a tennis ball, flew through the air quickly and smashed into Fluid's face. It caused Milton to snap his head back, the light passing through his skin and into his skull. When the last of the orb entered the man's head, his eyes rolled backwards and he slumped forward in the chair.

Filthy Henry fell to the carpet, sprang up to his feet quick like a bunny, and turned to face the desk. He had timed it perfectly. Fluid dropped his head to the desk and began snoring.

"Well now, I should just put people asleep more often," Filthy Henry said to himself, immensely proud with how the spell had turned out.

Fluid snored in his seat, out for the count.

#

"All I'm saying is, the human mind filters out fairy stuff for a reason."

"Seriously? Are we seriously having this circular conversation? I've been doing this for nearly two years, with no psychosis manifesting. I'm good, alright?"

Elivin shrugged and sipped from her milkshake.

She had conjured two of them out of thin air, giving one to Shelly. It was the most delicious strawberry milkshake Shelly had ever tasted. Not that she was willing to admit this to the leprechaun. Fairies had a tendency to take compliments as their God given right.

They sat in silence and drank their milkshakes. Medical staff and civilians alike walked past, some smiling at them as they went by. The automatic doors groaned on their motors as they opened, allowing Filthy Henry to come out of the hospital pushing a wheelchair before him. He stopped just outside, looked around until saw Shelly, then turned the wheelchair and pushed it towards the bench.

Beside Shelly, Elivin leaned forward. The straw of her milkshake was stuffed into the left side of her mouth, her right cheek inflating and deflating as drink was sucked out of the cup.

"Hey," Filthy Henry said, leaning back and examining the bottom of the wheelchair. He clicked the break into place with his left foot, then smiled at them both.

"Filthy?" Shelly said.

"Yes?" the fairy detective replied.

Nobody said anything for a minute. The only sound coming from Elivin's straw as she sucked up the last molecules of milkshake.

"Half-breed, have you just stolen a human and put them in a wheelchair?" the bounty hunter asked.

Filthy Henry looked at the occupant of the wheelchair, then back to Shelly and Elivin.

"It's him," he said, pointing at the sleeping person. "Milton. I caught him. I managed to solve the case you've been working on for a few centuries, Elivin."

The leprechaun ideally tossed her cup into the air. It vanished in a puff of green smoke that drifted away on the breeze. She scooched forward, dropped down from the bench, and walked over to the wheelchair.

"Beginner's luck," Elivin said, peering at the man in the wheelchair.

"More like 'send in a professional when an amateur can't get the job done'," the fairy detective said.

"Filthy! You can't just go into a hospital and kidnap people. How did you get him out without anybody seeing or asking questions?" Shelly said.

Holding up his left hand, fingers outstretched, Filthy Henry brought it over Milton's head. He wiggled his fingers briefly. In the wheelchair Doctor Milton sat upright, shook his head, then slouched to the right and let out a sigh.

"That's how," the fairy detective said. "I cast a sleeping spell on him to knock him out for a couple of hours, then any time somebody was looking at us we did our best 'Weekend At Bernie's' impression."

"Weekend at what?" Elivin asked.

"It's a movie," Shelly said. "Basically this guy Bernie is dead and two idiots pretend he is alive for an entire weekend through trickery. You don't watch human movies?"

"Some of us do," the leprechaun said. "But then the special effects always look worse than something a baby fairy could conjure up. Sort of ruins things a little."

"I'm sure it does," Filthy Henry, his voice heavy with sarcasm. "Anyway, I walked around for about twenty minutes trying to find Nurse Faul. She isn't anywhere inside, said she was going to do nurse stuff while I carried out the plan."

"She left about forty minutes ago. Came out, said she was going home. Tough day and all that."

Filthy Henry frowned.

"Okay," he said. "Bit strange. Sort of figured she would have seen this through to the end. Anyway, let's get going."

"Where? You turning him in?"

The fairy detective shook his head.

"No," he said. "I need to figure out what makes him tick and see if there is some way to reverse what he has done to the people in there. Meaning we need to get him to a holding area."

322

"Bunty's?" Shelly said. "I think we may have over stayed our welcome with her earlier. She probably won't be too pleased to see us bringing in the bad guy."

"Nah, not Bunty's," Filthy Henry said, smiling. "I've another place in mind. Just need to figure out a way to teleport inside."

# Chapter Fifteen

Closing time was something of a ritual, just not one everybody enjoyed.

For patrons of a public house, closing time meant the beer taps no longer flowed and the bar-staff would only serve you water. In Ireland there was the concept of a lock-in, which was basically just a bar-wide agreement for everyone, both patrons and staff, to continue drinking with the doors locked and the lights turned down low. To those outside, the bar was closed for the night. The people inside continued to be merry, just quietly so that no Garda could hear. Not every pub partook in this unofficial tradition however, meaning closing time was the death kneel of a good night out. People had to finish up and leave, in search of taxis or fast food or possibly an alleyway because they had forgotten to use the bathroom before leaving the pub.

In terms of shops, closing time was slightly less traumatic. Unless you were a shopaholic and the tills had all been switched off. Shoppers would be informed the store was closing, instructed to head towards the nearest checkout in order to make their purchases, and repeatedly told in a polite manner to get the hell out. There was no such thing as a lock-in when it came to shops, primarily because after you made your purchases there was not a lot left to do in a closed shop.

Unlike being locked in a pub for the night.

Dru the Druid, purveyor of magical things and useless crap with mumbo jumbo names, loved closing time. The normals, those humans with no idea about the Fairy World, who searched his shop for items mystic would make impulse buys and leave in an orderly fashion. Right after he slid the bolts into place, locking the door, a pleasant silence came over the store. The druid always smiled at this time of day.

Mainly because the 'closing time sales', as he called them, always had the same problem with their receipts. None of them allowed for an item to be returned, all because the date of purchase was somehow from Victorian times. A point nobody noticed while walking out the door.

He walked over to the cashier counter, reached beneath it, and flipped some switches just underneath the top. Around him display lights over units turned off, while two dragon statues in the front window remained brightly illuminated. Peace and quiet reigned

Dru reached into the left pocket of his robe and pulled out a small piece of white marble. He placed it on top of the cash register and tapped it once. A soft light came from within the stone, casting a gentle glow over the counter. As security systems went, this was both elegant to look at and easy to use. A simple glamour spell that made any would-be thieves see nothing when they looked directly at the counter. It was kind of hard to steal the cash in a register if you could not see said register.

The druid walked down the shop floor, through the rows of trinkets and knick-knacks that did very little in the way of proper magic, towards a door set in the back wall. It was the second Thursday of the month and that meant some Druiding was on the cards. He picked up some beeswax candles from a shelf by the door, pulled a key out from his pocket, and unlocked the door. Opening it, Dru went to step inside and stopped when he found the way blocked.

"Well that saves me having to eat a doughnut to unlock the thing," Filthy Henry said, grinning.

"Oh for Dagda's sake!" Dru the Druid swore.

"Hey, Dru," Shelly piped up from inside the room.

326

"How do you people keep teleporting in here? I mean seriously! I've so many wards around the shop it basically is more magic than mortar at this stage."

A little girl stepped out from behind Shelly and smiled at the druid, right before she shimmered. Actually shimmered, like a heat mirage. When the shimmering stopped the little girl was nowhere to be seen any more. In her place stood the leprechaun in green body armour, like a terrifying tiny S.W.A.T. team member, who had been with Shelly the other day.

Sweat lined her forehead and she seemed to be panting.

"No," Dru said. "Not happening. Don't care that you two suddenly have a leprechaun on the staff. You can't get through these wards unless your Dagda himself."

"He's right," the leprechaun said. "There are some seriously good wards around this place. Powerful ones."

Filthy Henry turned and looked at her.

"Meaning what, Elivin? I seem to remember you teleporting the four of us here. How did you get through the wards if they are so good?"

Elivin looked up at him and tapped her nose conspiratorially.

"Trade secret."

Filthy Henry looked back at the druid and shrugged.

"Does that clear everything up for you?"

Dru could feel a headache starting to build, right in the centre of his forehead. At this stage he was fairly sure they were migraines, triggered by close proximity to Ireland's foremost annoying fairy detective. Most people just had to avoid things like chocolate, cheese or stress. Dru had to keep a sentient being away from his person in order to not get mind numbing pain in the brain.

"Did you say four people were teleported? You know what? I don't care. Get out," he said, exasperated because he knew exactly how the conversation was going to proceed.

Shelly chuckled. Actually chuckled, then reached past the fairy detective and patted Dru on his shoulder.

"You know that isn't how this goes," she said. "Now come on, we need some supplies."

The druid hung his head, felt his shoulders sag, and walked through the door. Filthy Henry and his cohorts walked down the stairs ahead of him, showing far more familiarity with the basement of Dru's store than he was happy with them having.

One of the useful features of The Druid Stone was the basement in the building. Back in the good old days, when Dublin was being built from the ground up, basements had been very much in vogue. Cellars for storage, mainly favoured by pubs and bars, had been dug out of the earth and built. A lower level, kept away from sunlight and generally safe from any ne'er-do-wells. As rows of buildings were built together, basements and cellars were added purely out of laziness on the part of the builders. As such, a lot of the older buildings around Dublin had basements.

Dru had set up shop on Parliament Street mainly because of the basement. It was a perfect extra level to have where magical things could be done securely and secretly. After all, who ever heard of a druid doing their naked moon dances in public? Sure, it may have been all the rage back in Celtic Times. A bunch of men de-robed and frolicking around hilltops in order to commune with the Fairy World. But that sort of thing was greatly frowned upon now in modern society. Hence why a basement was much more appealing.

As basements went, the one beneath The Druid Stone was actually quite charming. The floor was covered in thick, heavy, rugs with intricate Celtic designs all over them. They were not cheap rugs either. Dru had decided to spare no expense when it

328

came to the place he would be spending large amounts of time dancing around in his birthday suit. Tapestries adorned all the walls, depicting some scenes from Celtic legends. On the far wall, directly opposite the stairs, stood a large oak bookshelf packed with books and tomes. The shelves had warped so much that sometimes Dru thought it looked like a kid who had eaten too much cake. All the light fixtures were those modern style ones with the candle shaped bulbs in them. More for atmosphere than any practical feature, but with the fancy rugs the druid had decided against using candles.

Wax was so hard to get out of anything you cared about.

Some solid wood chairs were spread around the room, intended to be used by a druid circle. Sadly, the days of druid circles were long since past. In the centre of the room some of the rugs had been carefully arranged to leave the stone floor exposed. Over the course of a month, Dru had chiselled into the stone some ancient and mystic Celtic symbols and designs, creating a personal circle of power that he could use for his rituals and magic. For a non-artistic minded individual, Dru was very proud of his work.

"Who the hell is that?" he asked, pointing at the man seated in a wheelchair in the centre of the ritual circle. "Plus, why is my circle glowing?"

"That's the bad guy," Filthy Henry said, extending his left hand towards the man and wiggling his fingers.

The man in the wheelchair, who was leaning forward and snoring, wiggled the fingers of his left hand.

"He's asleep," Shelly said. "Filthy is enjoying a 'Weekend at Bernie's' spell a little bit too much."

Dru the Druid stared at the man, unsure of what to do with this new information. Instead he pointed at the lines chiselled into the stone floor that were glowing with a soft, yellow, light.

"That's me," Elivin said.

She had taken up a seat at the bottom of the stairs on the last two steps and was just watching everyone.

"Holding spell?" Dru asked.

The leprechaun nodded.

"You're pretty smart for a druid," she said.

"Yeah, well. I've been involved in this game for a while."

He walked over to the nearest chair and sat down in it. This was definitely not what had been on the cards for the night's entertainment. If he was being brutally honest, Dru would not have teed this up for the month's entertainment either.

"So," the druid said, rubbing the ball of both palms into his eyes. "What's going on and why am I getting dragged into it? Also where in Dagda's name have you been, Filthy?"

Filthy Henry cleared his throat with a theatrical cough and launched into a story as mad as anything else Dru had heard from the fairy detective. It involved a creature going around Ireland for centuries stealing people's memories. Patients turning up at a hospital and being 'fed' on periodically, like a memory vampire. Some sort of connection between the victims that nobody was able to fully figure out and Filthy Henry developing an alternate personality that everybody seemed to prefer over his actual one.

This last bit Dru did not find hard to believe, actually. If personality transplants had been a thing, the online funding page would have reached its target in minutes to get Filthy Henry a nicer personality.

"Still not getting how this involves me," the druid said, pushing out his bottom lip and looking at each of them in turn. "You can't just teleport into my basement with somebody you have, basically, kidnapped and expect me to just run with it. There are still laws we have to follow. Mortal ones. Laws of the land!"

"Just like there are Rules," Filthy Henry said, managing to make the capital 'R' audibly noticeable.

"Nice emphasis on the lettering there," Elivin said.

"It's what I do," the fairy detective replied.

Dru felt his headache getting worse. Right now he could see his entire night being dragged into another of Filthy Henry's madcap schemes to save the world. While it was true that such an activity was a worthy enterprise to be involved in, Dru would have preferred if he was not personally involved in it. The last time he had assisted the fairy detective they ended up travelling to Carlingford and training the wrong person, all so the same incorrect-hero could do battle with a power mad queen. A queen who had time travelled and was hell bent on ruling the land with a magical iron fist.

It ranked very highly as the worst trip outside of Dublin Dru had ever taken. For starters it involved far too much personal violence towards the druid and lots of walking.

Druids were not made for walking, it inhibited the cultivation of a pot belly. Pot bellies were very important for the Druiding types, as it was a sign of how little exercise they partook in while researching things. More importantly, it was a matter of pride to have a bit of a gut when involved in druid work. The bigger the gut, the more important the work being done.

Right then, Dru was not feeling in a very energetic mood. At least not enough to help the fairy detective.

"Get out," he said, again.

All three of them laughed at him. Just laughed, like they had heard the funniest joke of all time. Filthy Henry even wiggled his fingers and made the man in the wheelchair appear to laugh. They all chuckled for a solid twenty seconds, then stopped.

In the wheelchair the man's head slumped forward once more.

Dru figured it might be easier to get rid of them all, since they clearly were showing him no respect, if he pretended to care what they were up to. Ask what help was required, then come up with a plausible lie to get out of helping. The age old trick used by husbands the world over. 'Do you need any help with the dinner? Woops I forgot I have to go and see a dog about a man...'

"Why did you bring him here?" the druid asked Filthy Henry.

"Simple, I don't have a circle of power inscribed into the stone floor of my apartment. Mainly because I don't have a stone floor in my apartment," the fairy detective said. "I need to contain this guy in something more than just a jail cell or salt ring."

"So you brought him here to use my magical containment circle?" Dru said, with some disbelief.

"Yep," Shelly said. "Elivin said it would have taken too long to carve out our own ritual circle, but powering your ready made one was no problem. Apparently she sensed it was here on our last visit, so that worked out well for everyone involved really."

"Glad to be of service," the druid said, hoping the sarcasm came across nice and thick.

"Knew you would be," Filthy Henry said, clearly oblivious to the sarcasm.

"What was the bit about the doughnut then?" he asked the fairy detective. "Since you had the short one over there to use her magic on the circle."

"Oh bloody hell," Shelly said, closing her eyes tightly and rubbing her temples with the thumb and finger of her left hand. "It's like he completely forgot what happened last time they met."

"What did you just call me?" Elivin asked, slowly standing up on the bottom step.

Dru the Druid had been involved with enough of Filthy

332

Henry's case to know when the mood of a room changed. Generally said mood belonged to the proprietor of a mystical emporium located in Dublin city. Particularly when the fairy detective was known for coming into Dru's shop to get supplies without actually paying for them.

Now though, Dru knew the mood of the room had changed for radically different and slightly dangerous reasons. Elivin had clearly taken insult at something just said. The druid mentally played back the last few words uttered from his soon-to-be-in-hot-water mouth and spotted the phrase instantly.

Hanging around a smart arse like Filthy Henry clearly had negative effects on people, it seemed. Prolonged exposure to his surly and sarcastic ways could result in a person taking up the same disliked traits.

Elivin stepped down from the stairs and stared at the druid.

"Say it again," she said, quietly.

Dru swallowed.

"I'd rather not," he said. "In fact I'd like to retract my previous statement about anybody, fairy or human, in this room that may have caused insult."

"Apology accepted," Filthy Henry said.

"Filthy!" Shelly snapped at him.

"Fine, fine," he said. "Elivin, calm down. He didn't mean anything by it. Dru, to answer your question from before. I was going to teleport your door out of the shop so I could go in and get some supplies."

The druid, glad that he had maintained control of both the situation and his bladder, frowned.

"Why wouldn't you just teleport the lock and leave the door? Maybe even just use a tiny bit of magic to unlock it? You know the only magically protected locks are on all the external doors."

Filthy Henry shrugged.

"Where's the fun in that?"

"Oh for Pete's sake! Can we get on with this?" Shelly said, looking from Dru to Filthy Henry.

"I'm going to have to help, aren't I?" the druid asked.

Elivin leaned against the basement wall, beside a tapestry depicting the Cattle Raid of Cooley, and nodded. She crossed her arms, the padding of the armour making her look like she was a miniature version of The Hulk. Without saying a word, the leprechaun's body language answered Dru's question.

He sighed.

"Fine," Dru the Druid said. "What do you need?"

#

Filthy Henry did enjoy when his cases caused Dru the Druid to get involved. Not because the druid was in some way integral to crime solving, far from it. It was due to all the fun that could be had winding the bald mystic man up. Each time was just as enjoyable as the last. The fairy detective would show up, invariably ruining Dru's day my merely existing, then explain the situation. There would be some back-and-forth banter, Dru would put up a weak counter-argument as to why he would not help and then change his mind.

Usually, the last few times, Shelly would have been the person who convinced Dru it was easier to just help. Sometimes this was achieved through violence, others she talked him around. Having Elivin change the Druid's mind without even saying a word was a nice twist on things.

Kept it all very fresh.

What they were attempting to do here was not overly complicated, thankfully. Having Dru's ritual circle already in place and powered by Elivin made things much easier.

334

Containing Milton, whatever he was, would have taken a lot more from the fairy detective than he was willing to admit. Which would have seriously limited the other spells he could have used for the remainder of the day. Making an interrogation of a magical creature somewhat difficult.

Powerful beings connected to the Fairy World rarely feared the same things mortals did.

They did, however, react much better to spells that forced them to tell the truth about things. The only problem was the amount of magical energy Filthy Henry needed to cast such spells. Thankfully there were ways for the fairy detective to bolster his power temporarily, methods which could be used to focus the smallest bit of energy and put it to the fullest of uses. He only required some simple, everyday, mystical objects. Ones easily procured from any magic shop in the city.

Luckily, his good buddy Dru the Druid happened to run such a shop.

"You know some day you're going to have to start being nice to him, right?" Shelly asked, as if she had been reading the fairy detective's thoughts.

Filthy Henry smiled.

"Nah, why would I need to do that? He loves our little sparring acts. Didn't you see the happy spring in his step when he went back upstairs to get the bits we need? Loves the banter I tell ya."

Still sleeping away in the wheelchair was Dr. Milton. Filthy Henry had asked Linda why they called him Fluid once, back when he was Quinn. The story had been humorous but not exactly gut wrenchingly good to hear. A poor play on the doctor's surname and a cleaning product called Milton Fluid. Now though, knowing that the man in the chair was actual a centuries old memory thief, the nickname was taking on a completely different meaning. Fluid seemed very apt for a man that had been hard to capture; like trying to pick up flowing water with just your hands.

Footsteps on the stairs drew all their attention. Dru had returned from the shop floor, carrying a battered cardboard box in his hands. It was like watching a drunk penguin descend the stairs. He inched one foot towards the edge of a step, then stepped down and brought the other foot along. Rinse and repeat for what seemed an age but was only a minute. At the end of the stairs the druid skittered around Elivin, who had taken up her seat on the bottom step once more, and walked over to Filthy Henry.

"Just put it on your tab?" Dru asked.

The fairy detective frowned as he took the box from the druid.

"I thought I cleared that already."

"That doesn't mean you get stuff for free eve....you know what? Forget it."

The druid marched over to his chair and dropped down into it, sulking like a big baby. If a baby was as bald as a coot and pushing fifty, of course.

"One of these days you two will just kiss and make up and work cases together without all this drama," Shelly said. "It will be like a bunch of super heroes coming together, reluctantly, to form a team and save the day. I think I might die from shock when it happens."

"Don't worry too much," Elivin said. "If that happens I'm sure Filthy Henry will just go and do another job to get himself a leprechaun wish. Bring you right back."

It was safe to assume a pin could have been heard drop in the room at that moment. In fact the pin itself would have been capable of hearing atomic pins dropping, that was how quiet the basement had gone. Everyone turned, except for Fluid who was still knocked out, to look at the leprechaun. She met each stare in turn.

"Too soon?"

"Little bit," Filthy Henry and Shelly said, nearly in unison.

They glanced at each other, the fairy detective breaking the look before things entered awkward territory. He walked over to a table and dropped the box down onto it, taking the contents out slowly. Some sea salt, in what looked like a novelty container meant to be in the shape of a dragon. When you shook it the salt came out its nostrils. A box of chalk, the label of which read 'Causality Chalk'. Filthy Henry picked it up, rattled the contents a little, then held the box out towards Dru.

"This is just chalk, right? You've made up a label and a brand?"

The druid shrugged his shoulders.

"Does it matter?"

"It doesn't, really. I'm just trying to figure out who is dumb enough to buy it," Filthy Henry said.

Five large candles, made from beeswax, were next to be taken out of the box. There was nothing particularly interesting about them, other than the price tag. Since Dru the Druid merely sold the candles, not at all being involved in the manufacturing of them, Filthy Henry knew there was no way they could cost what he had priced them at. If the fairy detective ever actually paid for things when he needed them, seeing the cost of these candles would have made him pay in instalments. Last of all he took out a ball of purple twine out.

All the components for a bit of magic.

The ritual itself was a fairly simple. Holding spells could easily be cast using a bit of salt, spread around in a circle, and infused with a touch of magic. Such containment magic was ideal for keeping a small creature or object in place, like they were trapped in an invisible glass jar. Until the circle was broken, whatever was contained within stayed there. However, for bigger

337

creatures you needed to embellish the spell a little. Dru's fancy circle was great, but only as a source of power. Not that the druid even knew how to correctly use the circle. For him the circle was just pretty designs carved into the ground, somewhere to park his bare butt when some druid chanting was required.

To somebody with magic, the ritual circle was something that could be charged up and used to break the laws of thermodynamics. A magical battery to power a long term spell, magic that could do some serious work on a fairy creature.

Filthy Henry started to place the candles down around the circle at five points, watched by everyone in the room as nobody volunteered to help him. Once the last candle had been placed he picked up the box of chalk, opened it, and pulled out a stick. He slowly began to draw lines between the candles, criss-crossing some of them by going through the ritual circle on the floor. After a minute he had drawn a five-pointed star, the tip of each point topped with one of the candles.

"Bit Satanic," Dru said.

Shelly tutted.

"You really are the worst druid I've ever met," she said.

Filthy Henry let out a titter of laughter.

"Have you met many?" Dru asked.

"One," Shelly replied. "But even I know that the pentagram is a symbol used by pagans and druids to represent the five elements. You're thinking of the inverted one that was bastardized for Satan worship."

Dru looked over at Elivin.

"She's right," the leprechaun said. "I'm embarrassed for you."

"Hang on just one second," the druid said, pointing down at Filthy Henry's floor art. "That is an inverted five-pointed star, ergo pentagram."

The fairy detective pocketed the stick of chalk and dusted off his hands.

"How in Dagda's pot belly is that inverted?"

"There," Dru said, pointing to the near candle to his chair.

Shelly tutted again, louder this time. Filthy Henry figured this could be entertaining. An argument between Dru and Shelly never ceased to end badly for the druid.

"I'm not a practitioner by any stretch, but I'm an artist. Using that talent I can tell you that star has been drawn with the top point aligned north, which is that wall over there with the hanging tapestry of the Children of Lir. You utter moron."

Filthy Henry looked over at Dru and grinned. The druid looked from the star to the tapestry on the opposite wall and back again, confusion clear on his face.

"Uh...." Dru said.

"I'd quit while I was behind if I were you," Filthy Henry said, going over to the table and taking up the ball of yarn.

He tugged at the ball and began to unwind it. Carefully, Filthy Henry wrapped some yarn around one of the candles. Once it had six loops tightly around it, the fairy detective started to walk to the next candle, keeping the yarn tight as he went. Another six loops kept the yarn secure so that the line between candles was tense. He repeated this for all the candles until there was a line of yarn between each of them, forming a pentagon on the edge of the ritual circle. From the last candle Filthy Henry brought some excess yarn down until it touched the glowing edge of Dru's design carved into the ground. There was a spark from the floor as energy jumped into the yarn, travelling up the excess and racing around the candles quickly. Each of the candles flickered into life, their wicks now home to bright green flames. Filthy Henry tossed the remainder of the ball back over to the table, then placed his right hand on the edge of the ritual circle.

339

"*Rud é go bhfuil an rud*," he said, drawing from the magic Elivin had supplied into the ritual circle rather than taking from his own internal supply.

The chalk lines began to glow faintly, white light that brightened Dru's somewhat gloomy basement workshop.

"We good to go?" Shelly asked.

Filthy Henry nodded.

"Good to go."

Dru the Druid rose from his seat and walked over, stopping a foot from the nearest candle. Elivin came and stood beside the fairy detective. Shelly remained in her chair, put took out her trusty notepad and pen from her jacket pocket. Everyone looked at Fluid in the wheelchair, as around him the containment spell pulsed.

"I get the candles and the pentagram," Elivin said. "What's the yarn for?"

"Personal customisation," Filthy Henry said. "Not sure if it will work, but you never know unless you try."

Now came the fun part: the questioning.

Over the years Filthy Henry had very little opportunity to cast a proper holding spell, powered by a ritual circle, with his intended target actually in the circle at the beginning. On those few occasions when he had performed one it had been not nearly as extravagant as this. Previously it had been a circle of salt containing only a wisp, hardly something to brag about.

In many ways the fairy detective was not even sure if this would work at all. Milton was an unknown. He was definitely mortal, there was no denying it. Looking at the bad doctor with his fairy vision, Filthy Henry saw none of the usual telltale magical signs usually associated with fairy creatures. Which meant one of the questions to ask was most certainly going to revolve around how Milton had been stealing memories.

The source of Fluid's powers was another question to ask, particularly if Filthy Henry wanted any hope of figuring out how to undo the damage. Plus, among other questions, motive. Why was Milton running around collecting the memories out of people and leaving them empty afterwards?

But the fact that Milton was not a fairy creature meant that the ritual spell currently containing him was in doubt. Generally magical prisons only worked on magical beings. If you lacked that magical element you were essentially standing amongst some string and candles with chalk all over the floor. Holding a human in place required different magic entirely. A lot less complicated, but not something that could be cast over the containment spell. You could either restrain a human or a fairy in one place, but not both at the same time. The magics effectively cancelled each other out.

This meant that Filthy Henry would have to use the fact that Fluid was going to wake up in a basement, surrounded by people he had never seen before. The fairy detective would then explain the containment spell mechanics and, all going well, Fluid would just believe him and not try to escape. It was something of a long-shot, but Filthy Henry intended to lay it on thick about just how bad an idea it was to attempt to test the boundaries of the make-shift prison.

He held up his left hand and clicked his fingers three times at Milton.

In the wheelchair, Fluid slowly started to waken from his slumber. He sat upright in the seat, blinked twice, shook his head a few times, and opened his mouth. The facial expressions he ran through ranged from the deranged to the downright comedic.

"Dr. Milton? Doctor, can you hear me? Filthy Henry asked, leaning forward an inch and trying to catch the man's eye.

Fluid looked up at the fairy detective and blinked twice.

"Quinn...isn't it?" he said.

"He's going to play dumb? Really? Oh why don't they ever just confess?" Shelly said, moving her chair across the floor to get a better view of the prisoner.

"You know it isn't my name," Filthy Henry said, giving the doctor a half smile. "That's why you did your little mind mojo on me. I was onto you and needed to be taken out of the game. What better way to pull that off than to wipe my mind."

"Wipe your mind?" Milton said.

He sounded confused, as if still half asleep. Usually when people woke up in such situations they would do some shouting and screaming, maybe threaten to rip a person's head off and beat them to death with it. That last one was a personal favourite of Filthy Henry's, since surely the act of having your head ripped off meant being beaten to death was an impossible feat.

Rarely, though, did a person come to and sound like all they wanted to do was roll back over and continue sleeping.

Filthy Henry walked to a chair, picked it up and brought it over to the ritual circle. With little care, because it was the Druid's chair after all, he dropped it to the ground. It made a little thud sound as the legs landed on the thick rug. He positioned the chair so that its back was facing Fluid, then Filthy Henry sat down on it so he could rest his arms along the large wooden back.

Milton just stared at him, his eyes slowly moving back and forth. The fairy detective was beginning to think that his sleeping spell had been too powerful for the man. After all, despite using magic to steal people's memories, Fluid was still only a human. That was the risk of being able to cast a spell slowly, the magic required could be channelled with a finer level of control. Meaning the chances of overloading the spell were slightly higher than, say, being in the middle of a fight and lobbing fireballs back and forth.

Of course, this was not Filthy Henry's first rodeo. He had been involved with the Fairy World long enough to know that everything was not always as it seemed. Just because you had a man standing over a body with a fireball in his hand did not mean he had killed the guy. Likewise, if you seemed to be groggy after waking up that did not necessarily mean you were still sleepy.

"Shall we begin?" Filthy Henry asked.

Fluid's head lolled left and right as he tried, apparently, to focus on the man before him.

"Begin? Quinn…. where are we?"

Filthy Henry grinned. It looked like they were going to be playing a game

"Let's lay out the ground rules first," the fairy detective said. "You're currently in the middle of a holding circle. It will contain you both physically and spiritually. If you try any magic it will result in…let's say 'unpleasantness'. For you, by the way. Not me. Just to be clear. Shelly over there is going to be following our conversation and taking notes. You can ignore baldy and the leprechaun. For now, it's just us. Any questions?"

The bad doctor, head still not fully under the control of his brain clearly, stared blankly at Filthy Henry and said nothing.

"Fine," Filthy Henry said. "Question number one."

# Chapter Sixteen

He looked around the room, at all the faces, and wondered what was going on in each of their minds. Tiny, confined, fragile minds that never reached their full potential. In a way, he felt that his work, his Life's Work, was a service to humanity. Why allow a mind to be wasted, such a terrible thing to do, when another person could take that mind and put it to much better use? It was a safe bet no god, even if they paid attention, would question his flawless line of thinking. Skills that would have been lost when the owner of the mind died were being preserved instead. All those collected experiences, the memories and knowledge, taken so they could still be put to use in the world.

Making him, at the most basic level, a walking repository of human knowledge. Just because the knowledge was taken long before a person died was a moot point.

Yet in this room, right now, he could see faces looking at him. Wasted minds in their little heads, all with their stories at risk of being lost forever if he did not collect them.

"Shall we begin?"

The man sitting in front of him asked the question and everyone else in the room went silent. Like they were waiting for some sort of Earth shattering revelation. Rarely one to be lost for words, it was surprising to find none come to him. After all, such a simple question to be asked. How could a person not have a simple answer in response?

Then again, he had never expected to be in a room surrounded by such people. That had not been part of the plan. Ever. The plan had always been to collect stories, particularly from those who were on The List, and blend in. Draw little to no attention, avoiding any magically-gifted inquisitive sorts. The memories of his victims, for want of a better term, always helped with blending in. As new information was gathered you learned about more ways to hide in plain sight. It was, the memory thief felt, part of the reason he found himself in his current location. When you took a person's memories you were given a chance to relive their life, going to the places they had gone.

Literally getting a chance to walk in their shoes, or at least retrace their footsteps.

Everyone was still looking in his direction, not speaking. It was unsettling. The chair was starting to get uncomfortable underneath him, like it did not want his posterior to be at rest.

"Em?" the memory thief responded to his questioner.

It was the best response he could think of, particularly with everyone watching.

"Right. Let's try that again. Shall we begin?"

#

Shelly decided to just let Filthy Henry do his thing.

Doctor Milton kept on staring at each of them randomly, his gaze lingering for a second or two before moving to the next person in the room. The effects of the sleeping spell had obviously worn off at this stage. He rose slowly from the chair, made sure his legs were responding as expected, then stood up straight and looked at Filthy Henry. There was no malice in the stance he took, no threat implied. He appeared to be a man completely unsure of what was going on. Which was something Shelly could relate to. Most of her dealings with the Fairy World involved a crash course in what was going on and why, provided by the sarcasm of one ginger man with magical abilities and a penchant for winding people up. Generally, these information dumps happened five seconds after they were truly needed.

Elivin had taken position just to the right of the fairy

detective, her gloved hands closed into fists. Looking at the leprechaun with her fairy vision, Shelly could see little threads of magic swirling around the bounty hunter's hands. She did not have any spells prepared, but was definitely ready to start casting them if the situation arose.

That was good. Filthy Henry was skilled when it came to throwing fireballs around the place if required, but a backup spell caster never hurt.

Dru the Druid just stood near the ritual circle, silently observing the proceedings. There was not a whole lot he could bring to the situation. Druids lacked any sort of innate magic, according to Filthy Henry. Most of them could do some very basic spells, such as tracking or protection from paper-cuts, by borrowing magic from an actual fairy. Of course, the term 'borrowing' was loosely defined when describing how a druid performed magic. Either the fairy benefactor had been captured by the druid, essentially making them a magical servant until they were released, or the druid and fairy made some sort of deal in exchange for power. Nobody was sure which of the two camps Dru the Druid fell into. On only one occasion had he mentioned to Shelly that the pact with his magical patron was 'mutually beneficial' to both parties.

Regardless, when the destructive magic started flying about the place Dru was going to be diving to the floor just like Shelly.

"I'm sorry, Quinn," Dr. Milton said, drawing Shelly's attention back to the centre of the circle. "I really don't understand what is going on. Why am I standing in the middle of a Satanic circle?"

Dru snorted, crossing his arms and giving the doctor a look that somewhere between disbelief and mockery.

"Don't you know anything?" the druid said. "That's not a pentagram it's..."

"Shut up, you," Filthy Henry said, cutting him off. "Listen up, doc. If that is your real profession..."

"It is, I can assure you," Dr. Milton said, a quiver entering his voice. "I can help you...just let me try."

Filthy Henry narrowed his eyes.

"You're going to play it like this? Really?"

Elivin took a single step forward, her hands making a rubbery groan sound as she tightened her fists.

"I've been after you for a while," she said, her voice low and slightly terrifying. "Don't drag this out, because I don't need an excuse to deal with you."

Dr. Milton looked aghast at the leprechaun, lowering himself back into the wheelchair. He pulled a handkerchief out of his jacket pocket and started to dab gently at his forehead.

"They never warn you about this bit," the doctor said, half to himself. "You do the training, pass the course work, read up on the edge cases. But they never tell you that one day a patient could...Quinn, please let me help you. We can keep this our little secret. You'd like that, right? Nobody else needs to know what happened here today."

Shelly frowned and watched Dr. Milton, trying to gauge from his body language what he was up to. He seemed to be genuinely distressed with his current predicament, but that could also have been an act. Wiping your forehead did not mean you were definitely sweating, just that you wanted others to think you were. Likewise, sitting back down after a fairly innocuous threat of violence was a little on the dramatic side. But not if you wanted people to think you genuinely feared for your safety. It was the pleading Shelly felt was a little over the top.

Ham acting at its best.

"Milton," she said.

"Yes?"

"You do know why you are here, right?"

A slow, sad, shake of the head.

"I can only assume that when Quinn was in his session with me I was attacked and brought here. You people should not be encouraging this sort of behaviour. It only reinforces bad patterns. Making it harder for those of us in the medical profession to help our patients."

"You think we're allowing him to do this? You don't think it strange that you're sitting in the middle of a devil circle?"

"Of course, I do...but...I am keeping calm," the doctor said. "I'm using my training to not start screaming for help."

"But you haven't even tried screaming for help."

"Would it do any good?" Dr. Milton asked.

"Probably not, Fluid," Filthy Henry answered. "But luckily I've got all the time in the world to get answers to my questions."

"Likewise," Elivin added.

"I'm a little more constrained on time," Dru the Druid said. "One normal human life and all that."

The doctor lowered his head into his hands, then balanced his elbows atop his knees. Shelly was not sure, but it looked like he let out a shuddering sigh. She glanced over at Filthy Henry.

"You sure?" Shelly asked the fairy detective.

He nodded.

"Course I am," Filthy Henry said. "When am I ever wrong?"

"Well there was that time with the ghost bus..." Dru began to say.

"We said we wouldn't speak of that again," the fairy detective snapped. "Now, while I am in the middle of something, kindly shut your yapper."

349

Dru the Druid shrugged his shoulders, a cheeky grin on his face.

"I hate working with you two," Shelly said. To the doctor she asked. "Can you tell me the last thing you remember before today?"

"My head hurts," Dr. Milton said, the response muffled as he spoke from behind his hands. "I was trying to ignore it but this doesn't look like a great situation here. So why hide it from you?"

"Got any aspirin?" Shelly asked Dru.

"Yes," he replied, making no movement at all.

"He doesn't deserve help," Elivin said. "He's a monster!"

"Please, I haven't done...whatever it is you think I have done. I shouldn't be in this room. I try to help people like your friend."

"Whoa, let's not be too quick with the 'F' word," Shelly, Dru and Elivin all said at the same time.

Filthy Henry looked around at each of them.

"Well thanks guys! Way to make a fairy detective feel welcome."

"I generally do my utmost to make you feel unwelcome," Dru said. "Doesn't matter either way with you."

"Plus there is more than one fairy detective in the room," Shelly said. "I don't feel unwelcome."

"Oh it goes for you as well," the druid said, looking at Shelly. "More unwelcomeness for you as well, depending on how recently you punched me."

"Just go and get the bloody aspirin," Filthy Henry ordered Dru.

The druid turned and walked over to a small wooden chest. He flipped the lid, reached inside, and pulled out a small

350

medicine bag and a bottle of water. From within the bag he took out two tablets, before dropping the bag back into the chest. He brought the tablets and water over to the circle, stopping at the edge.

"How does this work?" he asked Filthy Henry. "Couldn't it be a ploy? You drop the holding spell and he escapes?"

Dr. Milton looked up at the druid.

"You people believe that magic is real? You're not enabling your friend at all. You all need help. I can help you. Let me help you!"

He stood up from the wheelchair, which rolled back a couple of centimetres as he pushed away from it, and walked towards the druid. With one hand outstretched, the doctor smiled at Dru and started nodding his head.

"Let me help you, I can help all of you. Shared delusions are not as uncommon as people think."

"I wouldn't get too close to the edge there," Filthy Henry said, pointing at the glowing circle on the ground.

The doctor ignored him, his eyes fixed on the druid. Shelly could tell what the man was thinking. One tact had not worked with Filthy Henry, so move onto possibly easier prey.

"Seriously, I'd listen to Filthy. Be careful," Shelly said as the doctor's hand came closer to the edge of the ritual circle.

On the ground, the soft light started to pulse, as if a proximity detector kicked in with each step the doctor took. His fingers were inches away from crossing over the line.

"Whatever you think I am, I can assure you I am not. I mean you no harm at all," Dr. Milton said, his fingers moving closer to Dru's hand. His eyes opened wide, pleading.

"Will you step back," Filthy Henry said, sternly.

The doctor's fingers passed over the ritual circle's edge and Shelly took a deep breath, holding it until the spell triggered.

Nothing happened.

"I just want to help you," Dr. Milton said, reaching out to grab the tablets from Dru's hand.

His entire arm had now crossed over the boundary of the containment spell, without any barrier of magic preventing him going further. As magical prisons went, Shelly thought this one sucked greatly. Prisons were not like impromptu plane landings, the prisons you could walk away from were generally considered bad.

Fluid's left foot came down on the yarn Filthy Henry had stretched out between the candles. There was a pulse of purple light and, for no apparent reason, Dr. Milton fell forward with his arms flailing wildly in the air. He crashed face first into the ground, banging his head on the one exposed bit of stone floor that a rug was not thrown over. The impact knocking him out.

Shelly looked to Filthy Henry.

"That's what the rope is for?"

The fairy detective was staring at the forlorn figure on the ground, tapping thoughtfully on his chin.

"Yea," he said. "The yarn is magically enforced tripwire, just in case he could get past the containment spell."

"How did he get past it?" Elivin asked, walking over and looking down at the unconscious doctor.

Filthy Henry did not say a word, a move so out of character that Shelly knew it could mean only one thing. That the fairy detective had no clue why events had just unfolded the way they did. She looked back at the ritual circle, slowly looking over the lines of chalk on the ground. There were no breaks in them anywhere, nor was there a section missing from the glowing circle on the ground. It was all as complete as complete could be, at least to her relatively trained eye.

"You've no clue, do you?" she asked the fairy detective.

He looked up at her and shook his head once.

"Not a bloody one," Filthy Henry said.

#

They picked Milton up off the ground and placed him back in the wheelchair. The 'they' in question had been Shelly and Dru, since Elivin and Filthy Henry would have triggered the containment circle if they crossed the border of it. What little magic flowed through Shelly's veins, allowing her to see the Fairy World, would barely have registered with the ritual magic. Dru the Druid was fully human, which meant no magic to worry about.

Not dissimilar to Dr. Milton, it seemed.

At the fairy detective's request, Elivin conjured up a set of handcuffs. Shelly used these to attach Milton's left wrist to the arm of the wheelchair, then clicked the wheelchair's lock into place to prevent the chair moving around any more. Once the bad doctor had been secured, she stepped back over the tripwire and took up her notepad again.

"So?" Shelly asked.

Filthy Henry shrugged his shoulders and glanced down at Elivin.

"You tell me," he said to the leprechaun. "But there is no magic in that guy at all, right?"

The bounty hunter frowned and stared at the unconscious doctor so intensely that Filthy Henry felt sure the man's head should have exploded from all the attention it was getting. She was chewing on her bottom lip.

353

"Right," Elivin answered. "He is mortal, all the way through."

"Maybe he is like me?" Shelly said. "A freak of nature?"

"You're hardly a freak of nature," Filthy Henry said.

"Yea, you're not a dirty half-breed," the leprechaun added.

Filthy Henry did his best impersonation of a bad stage actor and feigned hurt, placing the back of his left hand against his forehead and fluttering his eyelids quickly.

"Why do you wound me so?" the fairy detective asked, taking on a dreadful Southern accent. Turning to Shelly he said, in his normal voice. "You have trace amounts of magic, nothing more. The spell is aimed at containing powerful magic. It wouldn't affect Dru either, on account of his magic being provided from an external source."

Shelly slowly nodded her head as the fairy detective spoke.

"Maybe he had a friend bring him back from the dead and not tell him," she said, coolly.

Dru the Druid groaned.

"Are you still harping on about that? You'd think Filthy had done something terrible the way you go on. 'Oh no, my friend brought me back from the dead and didn't tell me because he wanted to spare my feelings.' Walk it off already."

Filthy Henry stopped himself just in time. He was about to agree with everything the druid had said and then add some of his own thoughts on the topic. It was one thing to be annoyed immediately after discovering you had been resurrected without knowing it, but to carry on the grudge for months was a bit much. In all the world, the fairy detective was pretty sure that nobody else had a friend capable of performing such a feat. Let alone giving up their one and only reality altering wish, granted by none other than the King of the Leprechauns himself, to make said feat happen.

The sad thing was that, knowing how it all would turn out, Filthy Henry knew he would do it exactly the same again. Changing absolutely nothing. Not telling her had been a kindness. How would a conversation like that even start? Did you just bring it up suddenly or make a joke about it? Everyone out for a nice night of food, drink and story telling, the opening line of one tale being 'Remember that time you died and were resurrected?'.

Shelly made a face at Dru, sticking out her tongue, and started to write in her notepad. A sign the fairy detective had seen enough to know that she was no longer interested in hearing about logic, particularly if it meant Shelly being in the wrong.

He turned his attention back to their guest.

Fluid had a slight bump forming on his forehead, a bit of purple discolouring on the skin. To the casual observer the candles should have just moved when the doctor's foot hit the yarn. The yarn certainly did not look like something that could have held a suspension bridge in place. But that was the wonders of magic. Turning the everyday into the what-the-hell. Some light healing magic would have reduced the swelling and left the doctor with nothing more than a headache, but Filthy Henry was not exactly sure if he wanted to help the man just yet. While Milton had not triggered the containment spell, being able to pass right over the border, that did not rule him out completely as the villain. There were, after all, other ways to employ magic if you did not have a natural affinity to it.

The fairy detective caught Dru moving out of the corner of his eye. He looked at the bald man and flicked on his fairy vision.

Dru's lack of an aura, since he was not a fairy creature by birth, was normal when it came to humans. The not-so-normal bit about the druid was the pink trail of smoke that came off his hairless head, curling on magical winds and drifting through a wall of the basement.

That meant that the Druid's magical sponsor, be they a captive fairy or a willing partner, was not in the building with him. Probably a wise move on Dru's part, since removing that fairy from wherever they where would deprive him of the small bit of magic available to him. Turning to examine Fluid with his fairy vision, Filthy Henry expected to see something similar. An external source that the doctor could employ in order to perform his dreadful magic.

Milton lacked greatly in the magical aura department. Even intensifying the amount of the Fairy World Filthy Henry could see revealed nothing.

"Hmm," he said, standing up and slowly walking around the perimeter of the ritual circle.

"Having trouble thinking?" Elivin asked him as he passed her.

"To have trouble thinking would require one has a brain first," Shelly said, without looking up from her notepad.

Both Elivin and Shelly laughed at the statement, with Dru trying and failing to hide a smile on his own face.

Filthy Henry ignored them all. They were prime examples of why all the good heroes in stories worked alone.

"Dru," he said, stopping after completing a circuit of the circle. "Could you check Milton here for any charms or trinkets. Wands, rings, chains. That sort of thing."

"Why don't you ask Shelly?"

The fairy detective did not bother turning around, keeping his gaze locked on Milton.

"There are a few reasons," he said. "Firstly, you would know better what I'm looking for since you do have a tendency to sell actual charms that work from time to time. Secondly, I'm not sexist and assumed that asking a man to do the job wouldn't have resulted in such a daft question. Thirdly, don't you think helping me would get rid of me sooner? Finally, I've ran out of things to say to keep you distracted so how about you just do it after your shoulder accidentally connects with Shelly's fist?"

"After my shoulder accidentally...what doOOOOOWWW!"

"Just get in there and check him," Shelly said, having silently moved across the room to thump the druid. "Before your nose accidentally meets my elbow."

Rubbing furiously at his left shoulder, the druid walked into the circle, stepping carefully over the yarn, and started to rummage around Milton's pockets. He examined the doctor's fingers, opened the man's shirt collar and checked around his neck. Even the earlobes were not spared an examination. Two minutes later, Dru looked over at Filthy Henry and shook his head in the negative.

"There's nothing here," he said. "It's all just mundane stuff."

"Nothing at all?" Filthy Henry asked, surprised that he was surprised by the result. "Then how is he doing it?"

Somewhere a cricket solo started, the fairy detective was sure of it. Dru the Druid walked back out of the ritual circle, stepping over the magically strengthened yarn, and leaned against the table. Shelly and Elivin simply stared at the unconscious doctor, as if the act of watching him would reveal all of his secrets with the smallest of efforts. But, at that moment, everyone in the room was clearly as stumped as Filthy Henry.

They had reached a dead end.

"Well, bugger me," the fairy detective said.

#

Falling asleep had always fascinated him. Not sleep itself, that was something else entirely. Nearly every living thing on the planet seemed to require sleep. A period of rest so that the body could recharge for the next day. Sometimes people pushed their body longer than they should, resulting in more rest being

357

required. That was fine, he supposed. Not entirely normal, considering that your body knew its own limitations regardless of how far you felt you could go. Falling asleep, however, the actual act of going from being awake to asleep, that was the interesting bit.

For some it was obviously a conscious choice. They lay down, found a place to get comfortable, closed their eyes and slept. Others struggled, tossing and turning, sleep evading them for hours on end. Then there was when the body itself decided that sleep was required and, without warning, you just nodded off into the land of slumber. As if the body knew about an override switch in the brain, one only it could trigger without warning because it needed to rest and clearly felt it knew better.

Waking up in the chair was a little like that. He could not clearly recall wanting to go asleep. A wave of exhaustion had been crashing over him for the last three hours, but then a lot of activity had happened in the last three hours. It made sense that his body, however young it seemed, would take the first opportune moment to make him fall asleep. Although the sore head was an unwarranted addition, he felt. Why, after a period of rest, should a person have to wake up with a headache?

There was also that strange moment of disorientation. When, for approximately five seconds, his host tried to reassert control of the body. A brief, ultimately pointless, battle of the minds until he took over fully once again.

His chair had been moved, over to the wall, so that it no longer sat in the centre of the room. This had obviously been done when he was asleep, because he had no memory of it happening. Somebody was holding a damp cloth against his forehead with one hand, while firmly holding his arm with another. Opening his left eye, he looked at the care giver.

"What happened?"

The old lady smiled at him.

"Oh, thank goodness. You gave us quite a fright, my dear," she said. "One minute we were about to start the play, you clearly finding it hard to remember your line. The next you passed out. Have you been working double shifts again without getting proper sleep? We talked about this last time."

He nodded his head, slowly. It caused less pain to do it that way. Control had been fully taken back now, the voices in his head reduced to whispers once more.

"That's it, exactly," he replied. "I guess I shouldn't have come along tonight."

"No, you should have gotten some sleep, Linda," the old lady said, gently patting his hand. "We know you don't want to let the others down, but the play is weeks away from starting yet. We'd understand."

The smile was on his face, her face, before she even realised it. Jumping bodies had always been a useful trick, one that Blacksmile complained he over-used. Not that she should care about it, at the end of the day Blacksmile provided the magic for one reason. So long as he, she, kept up her end of the bargain they would be happy and not care about anything else.

She.

This was the first time in centuries that the pronoun had been changed. Hopping from body to body had not been a regular occurrence, longevity being another benefit to when you were infused with magic. But on occasion it suited her needs to leave the old body in favour of another, so that The Work could carry on with a new face. Typically, such transfers had always been into other men, allowing the pronoun to be kept consistent across the years.

As she, Linda, slowly became fully accustomed to her new body a feeling of great tiredness started to come over her.

The hunger.

Moving bodies, complete with the collecting of memories, required a great amount of energy. Which would explain why she had passed out. A quick top up would fix that, not even a full collection. A snack of memories if anything.

"Sarah," the newly possessed Nurse Faul said to the old lady beside her, having pulled the name from her host's memories. "Why don't you tell me your story."

# Chapter Seventeen

Dr. Milton had woken up five minutes before, but said nothing all that time. Discreetly he tested the strength of the handcuffs which kept him attached to the wheelchair, or at least made a half-hearted attempt at freeing himself, then sat back in the seat and remained silent. Every couple of minutes the doctor would look at each of them in turn, then return his gaze to the candle in front of him. Something about his body language gave Shelly the impression that the man had given up. He made no attempt at communication. Nor did he bother to try and move the wheelchair as part of an escape attempt.

Even the obvious negotiation tactics of 'I am your friend, I can help you.' had stopped completely. There was just no fight left in him it seemed.

Shelly joined Elivin on the last step of the stairs. The leprechaun gave her a friendly nod of the head as she approached, sliding over so that Shelly did not obscure her view of Milton.

"I don't think we have the right person," Shelly said as she sat down.

"We have to," Elivin responded. "There was magic coming off him. Linda figured that he was up to something. All the patients under his care just happen to be ones who have had their minds wiped. That can't be all coincidence."

"There's no such thing..." Shelly mumbled to herself. To the leprechaun she said. "No, I don't think we have the right guy. If your magic combined with Filthy Henry's couldn't hold him, doesn't that sort of suggest Milton is a normal person. No magic in him, sorta thing."

"One possibility, sure. The other is he has an Artefact that is hidden somewhere and we know nothing about. Maybe he has a charm stored back in his office. You don't know."

"I know it isn't an Artefact," Shelly said with confidence.

The leprechaun arched her left eyebrow and gave Shelly a sideways look.

"Oh really?"

Shelly nodded.

"Yes, really," she said. "The last case me and Filthy worked together had a magical hurley, an Artefact. So I know a little about them and what they do."

Elivin raised both her eyebrows.

"Well look at you, you do get around," she said.

"For Dagda's sake stop that!"

Filthy Henry's little outburst drew their attention to the ritual circle. Dru the Druid was tapping on the purple yarn with his foot, much to the annoyance of the fairy detective. He was waving the druid away with wide sweeps of his arms.

"It could be, you don't know," Dru said.

"I know enough about magic to know that you can't cross the streams by having two casters conjure the same spell!"

"What are you idiots arguing about?" Shelly asked them.

Dru pointed down at the ritual circle.

"All I am saying is that you have leprechaun magic mixed with half-breed magic…"

"Hey! Racist much?!" Filthy Henry said, looking abashed.

"…so who knows if this containment spell was actually going to work in the first place," the druid finished, clearly ignoring the comment from Filthy Henry. "And in the movie they are adamant you shouldn't cross the streams or bad things happen, so there."

Elivin slowly stood up from her spot on the stairs, remaining on the last step for that added bit of height. She looked at Dru the Druid. Shelly tried very hard not to laugh when the bald man took a step backwards, trying to put Filthy Henry between himself and the leprechaun.

"Are you somehow insinuating that I, a full blood fairy from the most powerful leprechaun family in the country, somehow could not conjure a ritual holding circle on my own?" the bounty hunter asked, balling her hands into fists as she spoke.

"Take a deep breath before you start having another tantrum," Filthy Henry said, making calming motions with his hand towards both of them.

Elivin barely moved. One second she was staring down Dru, the next a blue fireball was flying through the air towards the fairy detective. Filthy Henry jumped back, raising both of his hands in front of him and spreading his fingers as wide as they could go. Around each hand Shelly could see the air shimmer slightly, like a mirage on a hot summer's day. The shimmer expanded around his two hands in a pair of circular shapes, each roughly the size of a car wheel, which the fairy detective used like a couple of shields. He brought them close together, protecting as much of his body as possible.

The little blue fireball halted an inch from his first shield, stopping completely in mid-air.

"I counted to ten," the leprechaun said, smiling.

The fireball winked out of existence.

"For Dagda's sake! You're meant to start counting *before* throwing a fireball. Do you know how much magic it costs me to make wards like this?"

A shrug of her padded shoulders was the only answer Filthy

Henry got.

"Maybe you should count past ten, just one number higher....," the fairy detective said.

"That's enough of that!" Shelly said, jumping up from her spot on the stairs and stepping between Elivin and the male morons. "We have a bigger problem to figure out and bickering like children with nuclear weapons isn't going to resolve that any time soon."

Shelly could see that Elivin had been ready to go straight to eleven, from the scale of one to ten, on how to make things worse. There was a warm, blue, glow coming from both of her hands. Anger shone in the leprechaun's eyes. Certain people were born with short fuses, some lovely long fuses. Shelly would never have guessed that you could have an extremely short fuse when you were, yourself, short.

It made her think that maybe fairy folk with tempers did not have a fuse, they were just grenades with the pin already pulled out. How all-out magical war had not spilled into the mortal world before now was a question Shelly would rather not worry about.

"Fine," Elivin half-snarled, the glow disappearing from her hands.

"What are you talking about?" Filthy Henry asked Shelly.

She pointed at the silent doctor in the wheelchair.

"We've basically kidnapped a man. Then made him think we were some sort of Satanic ritual group and he was about to be sacrificed. Not to mention haven't we broken like a dozen of The Rules by now?"

Elivin shook her head.

"Not really. Everyone else in the room is aware of magic. Fluid is involved in this whole situation, somehow. Once we get rid of him none of The Rules will be broken."

"Oh dear," Dr. Milton sobbed, drawing everyone's attention.

"Probably the wrong choice of words there," Filthy Henry said.

"I didn't mean in the 'sleeps with the fishes' use of the phrase," Elivin said, leaning to her left and trying to catch the doctor's eye.

"Regardless," Shelly said. "We need to figure out why Milton here seemed to be the most likely suspect when he clearly isn't."

Nobody spoke. It always seemed to go that way, particularly when they were working on a case. Once all the big ideas involving fireballs, magic and explosions were taken off the table, no one ever had a proper solution to work with. Hail Mary plans and one-in-a-million shots became the expected norm. Shelly was not entirely sure how Filthy Henry had solved cases in the past when he worked completely solo. There must have been a number of near misses, lucky escapes and miraculous breaks.

Either that or the jammy git just managed to blunder his way to success so many times that it made him think he was actually doing a good job.

Staring at Fluid, Shelly had a strange thought. An idea that, given her immediate access to a pair of spell-casters, was definitely worth saying out loud.

"Whatever the Big Bad is, they've been going around taking memories out of people. Right?"

"Yes," Elivin said.

"We think that it was Milton, but maybe it wasn't. Maybe it was just something inside of him."

"OK," the bounty hunter said, sounding a little unsure of where the conversation was headed.

"So, if Milton isn't the guy and is in fact just Milton again, what if the Big Bad left something behind?"

Filthy Henry walked around the circle, keeping his gaze fixed on the doctor.

"You mean...if whatever had been in Milton jumped out of him and left a memory or two behind?"

Shelly nodded, secretly delighted that nobody had shot her idea down straight away.

"Why not?" she asked the fairy detective. "Think about it. They have been going around, scooping out memories and personalities left, right and centre. For centuries. To do that a body was needed, a vessel. Like your soul container thingy. But Dr. Milton here still seems to have his personality, so what if the possession doesn't do a reset like it did with everyone else. Anything the creature did while in Milton's body..."

"Might have left a memory behind in Milton's brain, one that he didn't consciously make himself. Like the memories I have from when Quinn was using my body."

"You're all crazy," the doctor said, sounding extremely despondent.

Filthy Henry stopped beside Shelly, crossed his arms, and stared at Fluid.

"Crazy like a fox," the fairy detective said, smiling.

#

He...she...that was going to take some getting used to... walked through the apartment and smiled.

If this was to be her new home until Blacksmile's master plan kicked off, it could have been a lot worse. Linda Faul considered returning to that gods forsaken hospital every day, to keep her disguise intact. It would allow her to keep an eye on the Blank Slates, maybe siphon off a few of them every now and then as a top up. Not that the sponsors liked that, but they did not have to deal with the ever intensifying hunger. The need to collect a story or two from people, just to take the edge off until the next big Collection could be made.

She dropped down onto the sofa in the sitting room and put her feet up on the table.

It was taking her some time to adjust to the body. Jumps twice in one half-century were always tiring. Not to mention it cost a sizeable amount of energy from the collected stories. Every time a body hop was needed, Blacksmile complained about it. Which was hardly fair, when you considered he, she, had always gathered more energy afterwards to compensate. People not on The List, never intended for Collection. That was why so many of them, the Blank Slates, had appeared over the years, particularly around a body swap. Not that the sponsors ever cared, they had their own agenda and that was all that mattered to them.

Linda stretched out on the sofa and enjoyed the feeling of not having an ancient body. Milton had not exactly been a spring chicken when he was originally possessed and over the years the man had aged dreadfully. Poor fitness prior to becoming a host had resulted in a serious drop in vitality as he entered his later years. But the plan all along had been to use him to collect the last soul. Tick off the final name on The List and then enjoy the just rewards of a revenge plan executed to perfection.

"I guess this body will have to do for that," she said, looking over her new form.

The people at the amateur acting group had all been very concerned about Sarah. Once the ambulance had arrived Joe, the play director, asked Linda to go along with the old woman. Given that she was a nurse and they would probably bring her to St. Patrick's. Linda had politely declined, much to the surprise of everyone around the back of the emergency vehicle. She had patted the old woman's hand, wished her a speedy recovery, then headed home.

If it had meant that much to Joe, that somebody had gone along in the back of the ambulance, he should have volunteered himself. That was what was wrong with the current generation, Linda had found over the centuries. Nobody wanted to do the good deed, they all just wanted to say it out loud while volunteering somebody else to do the act itself. To seem wise and caring, but not actually care about being wise at the same time.

The only reason nurse Faul had even been at the acting hall was because of the body swap. It usually took a few hours to assert full control over a new host. During that time they still could slip into the driving seat, so to speak. Linda, the original owner of the body, had obviously thought going to her acting group might result in her being saved from the possession. All it had really meant was that the nurse was not missed by people. His, the current owner of Linda's body, would remain undercover for a while longer.

On the wall, just by the television, hung a small digital clock. It displayed the current time, a little after eight at night, and the date as well. It made sense for a nurse to have a clock like this, given how it was all shift work in their world. Linda, or rather the memories within, had seen the clock in a computer shop and instantly bought it. She smiled at the memory. While it served the original Linda, now it would act as a countdown to the final Collection.

Then Ireland, in fact the world, would remember his name for all time.

"That's the correct pronoun for that thought," Linda said out loud, smiling to herself.

#

Filthy Henry sat directly across from Fluid in the lotus position, one leg over the other, hands resting on his knees. With much cajoling and only a suggested hint of violence to speed the process up, Milton had taken a similar position on the floor. After being released from his handcuffs the doctor had seemingly decided that something bad was going to happen. His course of action on how best to avoid future badness was through lack of co-operation. In a way the fairy detective could not blame him. The man was not so much playing the victim as actually being one. But still, there were limits to how uncooperative a person could be before you just wanted to slap them in the face a few times.

They both had taken up their yoga-style places within the ritual circle. Filthy Henry was many things, but a fool was definitely not one of them. If Fluid had been acting all this time, somehow managing to trick the containment magic, there was no way in hell the fairy detective would try this outside of the circle. At least in it Filthy Henry stood a chance of keeping his memories, his soul, where it all belonged. You could extract all you wanted, the containment circle would render any such magical attack null and void.

Typically what they were about to try required a lot of magic. More than Filthy Henry would have on a good day, never mind one were he had been conjuring some spells without getting a proper meal into his stomach first. Thankfully, if such a word could be used in these circumstances, Elivin was on call to donate some more of her magic. After raiding Dru's shop once again for supplies, the leprechaun bounty hunter had started to create the required objects. Once completed, she would stand ready with a half dozen of her little blue fireballs. Just in case somebody tried something they should not.

Shelly, standing outside the circle, hunkered down and smiled at the fairy detective.

"You sure about this?"

He shook his head, slowly, then shrugged.

"Not really," Filthy Henry said. "Never done something like this before. I've got the theory of it all down, but you know how

369

that usually turns out."

"A theory is all well and good until somebody proves it," Dru the Druid said, his tone suggesting it was not the first time the line had been uttered.

Filthy Henry looked over at the druid, who was once again sitting in his armchair in the corner, and grinned.

"Exactly, baldy," the fairy detective said. He turned back to Shelly. "But we don't have any other options right now. There is something out there that we have to stop. You know how we operate."

"I know how you operate," Shelly said. "I've tried to be the type of fairy detective that doesn't keep crucial bits from their partner in order to get the job done."

The comment was probably meant to hurt, but it did not. Filthy Henry rarely filled everyone in on what his plans involved because, at least ninety percent of the time, he made said plans up as he went. If people found out that their survival depended on whatever random idea floated through your mind they tended to not react well. Plus, having luck factor in at ten percent of your plan was just crazy by anyone's standards.

Even though that had worked for the fairy detective so far.

Elivin walked over to the circle and tossed Filthy Henry two, glowing, fifty cent coins. On the tail side of each coin a crudely formed eye had been added, made from little bits of wire that had been fused to the metal. Both eyes were created so they appeared to be closed.

"You sure about this?" the leprechaun asked.

"Why does everyone keep asking me the same question?" the fairy detective said. "This was my bloody idea to begin with."

"Not entirely true," Dru chimed in, raising a finger into the air like he was a professor making a point. "I believe Shelly said something that gave you the idea. You merely fleshed out her initial idea into this new one."

Everyone ignored him.

Filthy Henry flicked one of the coins over at Fluid. It landed on his left leg. The doctor slowly looked up at the fairy detective and shrugged.

"What is this, pray tell?" Dr. Milton asked. "Yet another of your shared delusions? Something you will force me to..."

"Oh put a sock in it already," Filthy Henry said, cutting the doctor off.

He had started to get annoyed with the man. Yes, this was obviously not anyone's idea of a normal situation. Sure, technically they had kidnapped him and brought him here via magical means. Definitely, he had a reason to be complaining about his current lot in life. But, at the end of the day, Filthy Henry had a case to solve and Milton was his only real lead. Making him equal parts useful and irritating at the same time. None of which, the fairy detective felt, entitled Fluid to complain and bemoan his predicament every time they tried something. Something that would both help with the case and possibly speed up the doctor's return to the free world.

Filthy Henry held up his coin, turning it so the eye design faced Milton, and tilted his head to get a good look at the doctor.

"Now," Filthy Henry said, keeping his voice low and free from anger. "Listen to what I am about to tell you. I know you want out of here. We want you out of here. People who don't even know you're here want you out of here. But for that to become a reality you need to work with me. That means less crying like a baby and more just following some simple bloody instructions. Understood? Pick up the coin and hold it like I am."

Dr. Milton reached slowly down to the coin on his leg, took it up and held it as instructed.

"You know your bedside manner could use a little work," Fluid said.

"Not the first person to tell me that and more than likely won't be the last," Filthy Henry replied.

From the corner of his eye he caught Elivin looking over at Shelly. Shelly nodded her head and shrugged her shoulders.

"I'm serious, this is why Batman works alone," the fairy detective muttered under his breath.

"But Batman doesn't need Robin to make all the gadgets," Elivin said, walking back from the ritual circle.

"Whatever," Filthy Henry said. He pressed the coin against his forehead until it stuck, then slowly lowered his hand. "Now you, doctor."

Milton did the same with his coin. As soon as it stuck the coin began to glow brighter.

"Excellent," the fairy detective said. "This next bit is easy. Close your eyes and think a happy thought."

"Does not being in this God forsaken basement count as a happy thought?" Dr. Milton asked.

"If that floats your red balloon in the sewers of happiness who am I to judge," Filthy Henry said. "Just do it and keep the crying to a minimum. You're working on my last nerve."

Fluid took a deep breath, inhaling through his mouth and slowly exhaling from his nostrils, then closed his eyes. The glow around his coin lessened, flowing from the edges of the coin into the wire design eye until each part of the eye shone brightly. There was the barest of flutters and the eye on the coin suddenly opened. Instead of a metallic surface beneath it, there was a swirling orange ball of energy that darted back and forth. Like the normal pupil of an eye, except for not being in a normal eye.

Milton's Third Eye.

"What the hell is that?" Shelly said, leaning over the edge of the circle to get a better look.

"What the hell is what?!" Milton asked, panic in his voice.

"Nothing, nothing," Filthy Henry said to the doctor. "You just keep sitting there with your eyes closed and don't open them."

Shelly slowly worked her way around the edge of the circle so that she was behind Filthy Henry.

"What is it?" she asked, whispering.

"It's his Third Eye, the mind's eye," Filthy Henry said. "Elivin made these two, well let's call them charms. Basically if both of our Third Eyes are open at the same time it will allow me to sift around in his mind."

"Oh," Shelly said, pretending to understand when the fairy detective knew full well she did not. "Gotcha."

Coughing to clear his throat, Filthy Henry closed his own eyes.

The skin on his forehead beneath the coin tingled briefly as the magical energies within moved through the metal into the wires. A second later the fairy detective could see the room again, even with both his eyes firmly closed. His field of vision took on a more central, singular, point of view. Looking over at Dr. Milton, the fairy detective could see the man's Third Eye still darting around the place. For the doctor absolutely nothing would have happened. Without any magic in his body there was no conduit for his Third Eye to send information down. That was why it darted back and forth. The eye was open, seeing things, but not able to relay this back. Filthy Henry, on the other hand, had magic in his blood. Allowing his Third Eye to show him everything it saw.

"Milton," the fairy detective said.

The doctor's Third Eye moved to the centre and looked at

Filthy Henry, a subconscious act on the part of Fluid after hearing his name. It would remain there for only a second, but the fairy detective needed just that second to make a connection. Focusing his Third Eye on the doctor's locked their gazes and Filthy Henry lurched forward slightly.

It felt like somebody had just pulled him free from his body, an oddly familiar experience. This made sense, to a certain degree, since when his soul had been pulled into the container it had been, essentially, ripped out of his body. Now was different, thankfully. Instead of some outside force doing the ripping, Filthy Henry was in control. A connection had been established between himself and Dr. Milton, a bridge opened as they stared not-so-lovinginly into each other's Third Eye.

The fairy detective quickly travelled through the pathway and entered the mind of Dr. Brendan Milton.

#

Knocking always seemed a rude way to get the attention of someone, Linda felt. Without the knowledge of what the person was doing in the privacy of their home, people just came up and banged on the wooden surface to announce their presence. How many naps had been ruined in the course of human history all because of a knock?

Whatever the tally was, Linda knew the number had grown by one. All because of the knock on her apartment door, rudely waking her.

She pushed herself up off the sofa and trudged over to the door. Opening the door, Linda was surprised to see her sponsor standing in the hallway of the apartment building.

"How did you even know I would be here?"

Blacksmile looked up at her and smiled that horrid smile. Not a single tooth was left undamaged in the fairy's mouth. Then again the mouth had not exactly been home to an amazingly white set of gnashers all those years ago when Linda, in her original body, and Blacksmile first met.

"How?" Blacksmile asked. "Don't forget whose magic lets you do your little tricks, mortal."

Without waiting to be invited, the sponsor barged past Linda and sat down on the sofa. Linda got the feeling she should be offended at this act, but brushed it off as just a stray thought from her host. After all, the Linda currently in command of the body had no emotional attachments to the apartment one way or the other. She closed the door and walked over to the living room area, taking a seat in the chair opposite the sofa.

"Don't you have to be invited into a dwelling?" Linda asked, frowning. She closed the frontdoor and followed the fairy over to the sofa.

"Do I look like a bloody Stoker to you?"

"Stoker?"

"Modern slang term used by fairies to describe a vampire, primarily used when they are of Irish origin," Blacksmile said.

She dropped her ugly backpack to the ground, the bag falling over and opening up in the process. From inside the bag there came movement, followed by the rag doll crawling out. It stood up, looking at Linda's sponsor.

"That bag is not as big as you think," the rag doll said. "Also how much crap do you keep in there? I couldn't even shout to get your bloody attention. You should have given me some magical means of getting about the place."

Blacksmile looked incredulously from the rag doll to Linda and back again.

"Would somebody in this room please tell me when I started answering to mortals?"

Linda pointed at the doll.

375

"That's not mortal," she said.

"It's a magically animated doll with the soul of a mortal inside," Blacksmile said.

"Doesn't really count, does it?"

Pointing a gnarled finger with a hideous, cracked, nail on the end, Blacksmile glared at her from the one good eye she had.

"Listen here, smart-hole," she said. "If you want to see what fifteen hundred years will do to that new, pretty, little body of yours then just go right ahead. Continue to be a smart alec. Otherwise you can drop the act. Okay?"

Linda nodded.

Her sponsor's tone was slightly more serious than usual. Although this was the first time she had just shown up after a body swap. Usually they went months without contacting each other. For a while there, in the 1700's, they had gone the entire century with no communication at all. But the timeline of their grand plan was headed towards the final stretch. Only a matter of hours, when all was said and done, until the plan was completed.

"Got it," the possessed nurse said. "I didn't mean to overstep."

"Right," Blacksmile said. "Heard it all before. Just why did you swap bodies anyway? How much energy are we going to be short now?"

"I had to, he was onto me," Linda said.

"The bloody fairy detective," the rag doll chimed in.

It placed its hands on its hips. A stance that might have been intimidating had it been done by a regular sized person. Also if it had been performed by an actual person, not a magically animated doll.

"Filthy Henry," Linda confirmed. "He came back to the hospital, somehow managed to get his memories back. After my last Collection I felt something...happen. I just didn't realise that I couldn't hear his voice amongst all the other any longer."

The rag doll threw its hand up into the air and turned around to face Blacksmile.

"I told you we should have just killed him on the spot. Saved a lot of hassle. But no, you figured hide him in plain sight and nothing would go wrong."

"It was a sound plan, Medb," Blacksmile said. "What would you have rather we do? Risk getting the attention of his father? Last I checked, gods don't take kindly to their children being killed. Particularly when such a killing would benefit the forces of us."

"His father is a god?" Linda asked.

"Don't worry about that," Blacksmile said. "I told you to lay low, I warned you something like this would happen. But off you went, literally after we talked, and did another Collection out in public."

"He was waiting for me back at the hospital, the Collection didn't reveal me to him. He already knew. Still don't know why I didn't just possess him?" Linda asked, making a mental note about the rag doll's name.

It was strange to have gone all this time and never actually learn the creature's name.

"Do you think me daft? Why would I give you the power to possess fairies, even half-breeds? You could have just jumped around gaining more and more magical abilities and done away with me. Besides, his fairy side would have prevented your possession. The memory stealing was the smarter move. Still, this changes nothing. You've expended power we can't afford to lose so late in the game with yet another body jump. Milton was meant to be your last. At least you can stop wearing the stupid surgical gloves now I guess."

"The gloves ensured I never left prints behind," Linda said.

"You perform a Collection by using a verbal piece of magic and have changed bodies over the centuries. Fingerprints were never something to worry about," Medb said, sarcastically. "Now, what are we going to do about this lost energy?"

Linda leaned over and picked up her bag from the small coffee table in front of the sofa. Reaching in, she pulled out a flyer and tossed it towards her sponsor. It drifted through the air and, defying the Laws of Gravity entirely, floated just in front of Blacksmile's face.

"What is this?" her Blacksmile asked, keeping the page in the air with some hand gestures and magic.

"That is a gathering of story tellers," Linda explained. She settled back into her spot on the sofa, the cushions releasing a puff sound as air escaped from them. "I managed to grab it and my journal before leaving the hospital. To make sure nobody else found them. Look who is the headline act for the night."

Medb jumped up into the air and snatched the flyer in her hands.

"Tracey Fitzgerald," she said, reading the name from the page. "So?"

This was the part that Linda had enjoyed the most over the years. Most people, when they planned their revenge on those who wronged them, went for instant gratification. But a detailed revenge plan, particularly one executed perfectly, that was just better than waking up and finding out every day for the rest of your life was Christmas. The only thing which made it all the sweeter was when, even after explaining your plan, other people did not fully understand it.

"That," Linda said, pointing at the flyer in the rag doll's hands. "Is the last descendant from the banquet hall. The great granddaughter, many times over, of Cadán Ó Briain. The man

378

who ruined my life."

Linda only realized she had clenched her fist when the nails started digging into the palm of her hand. Long nails were not a common feature of her previous hosts. Little spots of blood appeared where her nails had broken the skin. She looked at them with a detached interest.

"Meaning you will have a full set, correct?" her sponsor asked. "Everyone who wronged you and all the descendants for a number of generations?"

The nurse nodded her head, smiling like a cat swimming in cream.

"Doesn't explain what we will do with the energy you wasted upgrading your body," the rag doll said, crumpling the flyer and tossing it to the ground.

Wiping the blood away from her hand, Linda looked down at the magically animated doll.

"I'll figure something out," Linda said. "Maybe I can do a load of smaller Collections between now and the event."

Blacksmile cackled, actually cackled like a witch, and nodded her head.

"Well if that isn't just the best thing I've heard all day," she said, sarcastically. "Now, since you obviously didn't listen to my advice about laying low before, we're going to stick with you until the story gathering happens."

"Looks like we're having a girls night in," Medb said, running towards the end of the coffee table and jumping down to the floor. "Let's make some popcorn."

# Chapter Eighteen

Sitting beside the ritual circle, on the ground with her legs crossed, Shelly alternated her gaze from Filthy Henry to Dr. Milton and back again every couple of seconds. Observing the spell and feeling well and truly...

"Bored," Shelly said to Elivin. "Bloody bored. That's how I feel right now."

"Yeah," the leprechaun said, once again sitting on the last step of the stairs. "It's a pretty boring spell for those not partaking in it."

Dru the Druid walked across the room to a large wooden chest set beside the back wall. Pulling a key out from one of the pockets in his robe, he knelt in front of the chest and unlocked it. The lid opened on creaky hinges. He returned the key to his pocket and started to rummage around inside the chest.

"What are you up to?" Shelly asked him.

"Think I put a kettle in here," the druid said. "It would be more entertaining to watch it boil than that mystically mundane affair over there. Plus, we can all have a cuppa afterwards."

Shelly looked over at Elivin. The leprechaun was staring at Dru, looking very confused. She raised her left hand in the air and clicked her fingers three times. A cup of tea appeared in front of Shelly on the ground and beside Elivin on the step. Over at the chest Dru moved something, then started cursing loudly as something made from porcelain could be heard breaking.

The bounty hunter snorted with laughter and picked up her cup of tea.

"Guess I should have conjured it on the floor *beside* the chest, instead of *in* it."

"You think?" Dru the Druid said, standing up and flapping his right hand in the air quickly. "That's going to leave a mark."

"I'll heal it for you, stop your crying," Elivin said.

Shelly picked up the cup of tea in front of her and took a sip. It was perfect. The best leaves had been used, no milk added and only a drop of lemon.

"Neat trick," she said, holding the cup in the air and toasting towards Elivin. "Spell does a quick mind-read before creating the tea? Allowing it to be made exactly as the person wants?"

"You're pretty quick for a non-magical type," the leprechaun said.

"Technically I am a magical type, just can't cast magic," Shelly said. "What's this spell actually do anyway? Other than have some animated coins on their foreheads, making them look like a couple of idiots in university playing a drinking game."

"It's actually pretty dangerous," Elivin said.

"Really?"

"Yep. Basically Filthy Henry is risking his own mind by entering Milton's. Even though all he is going to be doing is looking for information, he is relying on the doctor not trying to peak back inside *his* mind. If you thought having your soul ripped out was interesting, having your mind invaded by another person's is even more fun."

Shelly blew into her tea and took a sip, thoughtfully staring at the fairy detective.

"I don't think you're using that word, fun, the right way," she said.

Filthy Henry had not moved for the past twenty minutes, other

382

than breathing. The animated coin on his head stared straight at Dr. Milton, the orange of its pupil fixed in place. Completely stationary. Five minutes into the spell Shelly had asked Filthy Henry a question, but he never answered her. It was like the lights were on an automatic timer but nobody was home. Plus the timer had broken slightly and only worked on the first floor.

The possibility that Filthy Henry had just opened himself up to another attack was worrying.

"How long does this usually take?" Shelly asked the leprechaun.

"That all depends on any number of things. He might find what he is looking for immediately. Milton's mind may rebel against his presence and put up serious resistance. There is a chance that nothing at all happens and we've just wasted more time sitting around instead of trying to find the memory thief. Plus there is the rare, very rare, chance that Filthy Henry brings something along into Milton's mind. Something that causes problems for them both."

Dru the Druid came over and looked down at the two men in the ritual circle. He was wiping his left hand on his grey Druidic robe.

"Like what, exactly?" he asked.

#

Filthy Henry had read the theory about what he was attempting, but never put it into practise. It was crazy dangerous magic to try, half-breed or not. In order to gather information from the mind of another you first had to open your own. It was like preventing your house from being robbed by leaving the front door wide open. The insane logic being that if a passing thief saw this most opportune of moments they would think twice before entering. After all, why would a sane person leave their front door open? Surely something lay on the other side that would be detrimental to an honest thief's health.

Plus, the house right beside had all the doors and windows locked. Making them a much more logical target.

After opening your mind, assuming your target also opened their mind, you had to leave your body. Not literally, or spiritually. Not even like having your soul inserted into a spirit container. It was more a freeing of the mind, a projection of thoughts.

Apparently. At least that was what the spell books all implied.

What it actually felt like was having all of your consciousness sucked out your forehead by an industrial strength vacuum cleaner. Before being rudely deposited into a bag, the bag just happening to be the other person's mind. A second after leaving his body, Filthy Henry opened up his eyes and looked around.

The first thing he noticed was that he actually had eyes. Along with hands, feet, and all the other limbs and body parts that generally went with having a corporeal human form. Even his clothes had somehow come along for the ride, everything matching in perfect detail to what his body in the real world wore. Except that it was all, clothes and body, a shade of light blue. He held up his hands and could see through them, their translucency giving the fairy detective a ghostly appearance.

"Well this is interesting," Filthy Henry said, surprised that his voice echoed slightly.

"You can say that again."

Filthy Henry lowered his hands and turned to his left. His gaze fell upon another version of himself floating there. Everything was the same, in every minor detail. Even the shade of blue. Like a strange out of body experience, experienced while being out of his body. He frowned and pointed at the other him.

The other him smiled.

"It's me," he said to himself. "Quinn."

If he had been breathing, which apparently the ghostly body did not need to do, Filthy Henry would have gasped.

"I can sort of feel how your thoughts are going," Quinn said, tapping his right temple. "I think it might be easier if I just explain. No, I did not just vanish into thin air when you got your body back. No, I cannot do anything with your body without you being involved. Yes, all your dirty little secrets are safe, mainly because they are also mine. No, you're not in any danger of me taking back the driver seat."

"That's a horrible colour on you," Filthy Henry said.

Quinn stared at the fairy detective, mouth open with shock. He closed his eyes and gave his head a little shake. The movement started a swirl of colour which travelled down his body. It began in his hair and quickly moved towards his feet. The blue was replaced with a vibrant red, his entire colour scheme changing.

He pursed his lips and held up his hands, shrugging.

"Better?"

"Sure," Filthy Henry said. "Although I'm still not entirely happy that you're still here."

"Yeah," Quinn said. "I wouldn't be either if I had just gotten my body back. Look at it this way. At least you're not a murderer."

"First of all, you have to have a body that you aren't squatting in to be murdered," the fairy detective said. "Secondly, I've killed before and I'd do it again too. So, behave."

He felt his point had to be backed up by a display of power. With his right hand before him, Filthy Henry conjured a small fireball. At least that was what he attempted to do. The result was very much a failure in the grand scheme of fireball conjuring. Quinn tilted his head and looked at the fairy detective's empty hand.

"There going to be more to follow or am I getting a private showing of the worst hand puppet display ever?"

"I thought everyone said you were nicer than me?"

"They did," Quinn said. "To everyone else. You? I figure you deserve to get some snarky comments sent your way from time to time. Keep you on the straight and narrow."

Filthy Henry was not entirely sure how to take that statement. One theory he had been working on, shortly after learning that Quinn had been a fully formed personality, was that the alternate persona came from within. Some deep, maybe even repressed, memories that had gathered together and formed a little neurological club in the dark corners of the fairy detective's mind. Like an idea, once there impossible to shift. It had grown and, when nobody was actively driving the body any more, spread out. Taking control. So, to be speaking with this strange anthropomorphic memory cluster once again and have it tell him that manners were going to be taught, put Filthy Henry a little on the uneasy side of things.

On some level the question had to be asked: was Quinn an entity in his own right or was Filthy Henry just having a mild psychotic episode?

"So, you're what? My conscience? I'm pretty sure I have one of those already," the fairy detective said.

Quinn shrugged his shoulders and looked around at the vast whiteness they both stood in.

"If you have a conscience it is seriously neglected from under use. No, I'm not that. Maybe your very own cricket. Only much taller and definitely more ruggedly handsome."

The fairy detective was smiling before he could consciously stop it from happening. There was a comedic beauty to having one of your own lines thrown at you by a construct of your mind. He decided to worry about Quinn later and instead focus on the task at hand.

He looked at the infinite whiteness all around and put his hands into his pocket. There was nothing to see in any direction, not even something resembling a ground. Staring down at his feet, Filthy Henry wondered what he was standing on. There was obviously something underfoot, yet it appeared as if he was floating in thin air. As that thought crossed his mind somebody decided to throw the rules right out a window. Whatever had been acting as the 'ground' up until that point stopped doing so.

Filthy Henry suddenly dropped, falling into the endless white. Air, or something like air, whipped past him. He looked up and saw Quinn standing in the same spot as before, watching the fairy detective fall. It was as if the man, for want of a better term, was standing on a clear glass platform above Filthy Henry.

"Help!" Filthy Henry shouted, reaching up with his arms.

Quinn was rapidly becoming a tiny figure above as the fairy detective continued his descent into nothingness. Then, in the blink of an eye, Quinn was no longer there. He simply vanished. Filthy Henry swore under his breath and started to think of some magical way to put a halt to his drop.

Each attempt failed in a similar manner to when he tried to conjure the fireball. Nothing happened. Then, as suddenly as it had started, Filthy Henry stopped falling. The collar of his shirt snagged on something, pulling it up tight against his chin. He hung in the air and sighed with relief, twisting around to see what had caught him. Instead of a tree branch or some strange floating hook, Filthy Henry's gaze fell on a very familiar hand. Although it was a translucent red colour, much like the owner of said hand.

"Gotcha," Quinn said, smiling.

The fairy detective looked down at Quinn's feet. Feet which appeared to be on a flat surface yet were actually on nothing.

"Okay," Filthy Henry said. "What's the bloody story?"

"You're not playing by the rules of the mind," Quinn said. "We're guests in this place, don't try to enforce your logical thinking onto the mind of another person. Milton doesn't know about magic, that's why you can't do any. Likewise when you start questioning things your mind and his disagree, hence you falling. Now, think about standing on solid ground provided by the doctor."

Filthy Henry squinted out his left eye at his mental co-pilot.

"That's the dumbest thing I've ever heard," he said.

Quinn hoisted the fairy detective up in the air with one hand, twirling him around so that they faced each other.

"One thing I learned since giving up your body," Quinn said. "Is that when it comes to the mind-scape, I might know a bit more than you do. Exhibit F, for feet. Mine. Firmly in place and preventing me from dropping."

Through a series of complicated and highly impressive manoeuvres, Quinn spun Filthy Henry around a few times so that he was holding him under the arms. He pulled the fairy detective close, so that their translucent noses touched, and stared directly into his eyes.

"So, for once, stop being an idiot and listen to the advice of somebody else," Quinn snarled.

Filthy Henry was not used to people giving him advice, particularly when it came to magical matters. Then again, this was the first time the fairy detective had ever entered another person's mind. He would admit, although never out loud, that if anybody was going to know about the mind-scape it would most likely be his mental construct. Even if said construct was just some pale imitation of Filthy Henry that had come about because of a random sequence of events. Events which, somehow, were allowing the mental construct to continue existing.

The fairy detective closed his eyes tightly and stopped

thinking about the fact there was no obvious ground beneath him. Instead, Filthy Henry focused on the idea that they were both standing on a giant sheet of glass. One which stretched out in all directions, infinitely. A sheet which Milton was kindly providing for any guests in his mind. Then, slowly, the fairy detective lowered his feet.

Solid footing was his reward.

"Huh," Filthy Henry said, opening his eyes and looking down as he stood on nothing. "Well I'll be damned."

#

Quinn was feeling a mixture of emotions.

The one mainly being felt was happiness at once again having a body, even if the body was just a manifestation in another person's mind. After Filthy Henry had returned and decided that he wanted his body back, which was a fair request really, Quinn had felt a sense of finality to his existence. In all human history, there had never been a reported instance of one person having two distinct minds inhabiting their body. He had assumed the return of the fairy detective's consciousness would simply erase all traces of his own.

Making it a very pleasant surprise to find out that had not happened, at least not exactly. While control over the body had been completely relinquished, Quinn gained instant access to all of the fairy detective's memories. The flood of information had been too much to take, making him pass out. In so far as a person without a body could pass out.

All Quinn knew was there had been a definite period of time which he had no recollection of. Then he was back. Not so much awake, but certainly aware. Aware of what was going on outside his strange abode. When he discovered that Filthy Henry could sense his presence Quinn had been very amused. What had probably been intended as the final chapter in the story of Quinn's life instead turned into a strange sequel.

389

So, when Filthy Henry opened a conduit to join his mind with that of Dr. Milton's, Quinn saw the opportunity to stretch his legs. Legs which were his own, mentally speaking. It felt good, in fact it felt even better now that he had saved Filthy Henry from an act of fairy detective stupidity.

He smiled at the fairy detective, now mastering the art of not falling through the whiteness, and nodded with approval.

"There ya go," Quinn said. "You can follow instructions."

Filthy Henry looked at him, confused.

"I still don't understand how you are here," he said. "I'm back in my body, meaning you should have been expunged. I thought I heard you laughing back at the hospital. But I wasn't sure if that was real or just my imagination."

For no other reason than to show off, Quinn floated upwards slightly so that the fairy detective had to tilt his head back.

"No, that was me. I wasn't sure if you'd heard me or not to be honest."

The fairy detective looked around in a nonchalant manner.

"No, I heard you," he said. "I just didn't want to admit to myself that it was possible. I mean, is this going to be the new normal now? What exactly are you?"

Quinn stopped and considered the question.

In many ways there was no simple, straight-forward, answer. They were both in uncharted territory. For starters, neither of them knew how Quinn had come into existence in the first place. The other Blank Slates had just been empty people, still with communication abilities and random skills but no personal memories. Once Filthy Henry had been returned to his body everyone, Quinn included, had assumed that Quinn would simply cease to be.

Not hang around in the unused corners of the fairy detective's mind. Even with access to all of Filthy Henry's memories and knowledge about magic, Quinn was still unsure if he would eventually fade away into nothingness or continue to occupy the brain space he was squatting in.

"Dunno," was the best answer Quinn could come up with. "But let's do what you came here to do first."

"You know what I came for already though, don't you?"

"Sort of," Quinn said. "It's complicated. I don't have direct access to your short term memories. Just the long term stuff. But I don't just have all of those memories, I need to go looking for things. Like a big mental library that I can walk through. Even then you seem to have bits walled off...mentally speaking. How are you able to do that? What's in there?"

Filthy Henry took one quick step forward and jab his spectral blue finger into Quinn's ghostly red chest.

"Nothing that you need to concern yourself with, Afterthought," the fairy detective said. "Now, since you should, in theory, know more about mental matters than me, how about you make yourself useful? What is this place? I was expecting to see the doctor's memories, not a big white room."

"Well, I haven't exactly examined your mind using a similar technique as this so I don't know if it would look the same. At a guess, however, I'd imagine that since Milton is a doctor his mind would present itself to outside entities as a clean room. A place for him to mentally scrub up."

"That's not entirely on the weak side, as theories go," the fairy detective said. He turned around and looked about. "Then how do we get a look at his memories? We need to see if he was possessed or not."

Quinn pondered the problem, wondering at the same time if Filthy Henry was doing the actual thinking or were the thoughts his own. If he came up with a solution would the fairy detective

391

have arrived at it himself? Merely relaying it to Quinn.

It was a quandary tough enough to cause a person to split their personality, just to have more people looking at it.

He focused on the white room situation. If he was right and Milton's mind was presenting itself as a clean room, then maybe his mind operated under a lot of doctor practises. Most of the time, things that Filthy Henry did in order to solve a case clearly fell into the realm of chance. A thought that Quinn found comfort in, since his current idea was a lucky guess at best.

"The doctor will see you now," Quinn said out loud, looking at the whiteness around them.

Filthy Henry looked up at him.

"Are you kidding me? That's the best my subconscious can come up with?"

"Yes," he answered. "I didn't see you coming up with anything. Just standing there looking dumb."

"I look like you!"

"I'm thinking about bringing back the beard," Quinn said. "To look less dumb."

"Gentlemen, please," Dr. Milton's voice echoed around the white space. "I don't generally do group sessions, I'm not sure who made this appointment."

Quinn and Filthy Henry turned around and were greeted with the sight of a therapy couch placed in front of a large wooden desk. Behind the desk Dr. Milton sat, looking much younger than he did in the real world. His leather desk chair was currently home to the man's posterior. There was nothing on the desk itself. The doctor was tapping thoughtfully on his chin with a thin, silver, pen.

Both the ghostly detectives, because that was how Quinn now thought of himself, walked over to the couch. Quinn took two

392

steps down, walking on the same level as Filthy Henry. They stood in front of Milton's desk.

"You're serious?" Filthy Henry asked. "All we had to do was say some cheesy line and here he is?"

"Have you ever done this before?" Quinn asked.

The fairy detective gave him a sideways glare.

"You know I haven't," he said.

"Then let's just play by the rules of the man's mind, shall we?"

In a way it made a certain amount of sense. While Quinn existed in Filthy Henry's mind, he did not see things the same way. It was more like being a passenger in a car, one were the driver never spoke to anybody else in the vehicle. Upon entering Milton's mind neither of them had known what to expect. Seeing a white room made sense. Doctors would have to keep a lot of medical jargon stored away in their heads, obviously that meant a clean and orderly mind was required.

He looked at Filthy Henry and wondered what the fairy detective's mind looked like when viewed through a Third Eye. Probably a cross between Merlin's magical mystical laboratory and a sixteen year old boy's bedroom.

Milton stared at them both, one eyebrow arched.

Quinn found it funny that the doctor still mentally thought of himself as being a much younger man than he was. He looked a like a man in his mid-twenties. Then again, how many people looked in the mirror and were not surprised to see that the years had crept up on them? Age enjoyed a strange place in the human world. People physically grew older but could mentally feel the same forever.

"Can I help you gentlemen?" the doctor asked.

Filthy Henry leaned over to Quinn.

"Seems like the Third Eye has but him into a sleep-like state. He must think this is a dream."

"Guess that explains why he isn't freaking out that a pair of ghosts are talking to him," Quinn said. "What's the plan?"

"One of us has to get on the couch and ask questions while the other tries to look around for memories," he said, keeping his voice low. "Play into this whole therapy thing he has going on."

"Makes sense," Quinn said. "Just make sure to ask him questions that will make him think about what we want."

"Exactly," Filthy Henry agreed. "Try not to give him too much about yourself as well, primarily because I don't want you to share my dark secrets with him."

"So, on you go," they both said in unison.

Each of them turned and eyed the other one up.

"Em...you lie down!" they both yelled.

#

The most boring spectators event, next to the international 'Watch Grass Grow' competition, was still going on. A second cup of tea had been conjured, courtesy of Elivin. Neither Milton nor Filthy Henry had done anything in the least bit entertaining.

In the corner of the basement, stretched out on his wooden chair, Dru the Druid was snoring. Content in whatever dreams his baldy head came up with. Elivin had come over and joined Shelly on the ground beside the circle, her tea floating just above the floor.

Shelly nodded towards the cup.

"Why do you fairy folk do that?"

"Do what?" the leprechaun asked.

"That. The floating cup thing. The blatant display of magic."

Elivin looked over at the cup, then to Shelly and shrugged. She may as well have asked the leprechaun why the sun was yellow or how come water made things wet. There was no answer forthcoming because, apparently, it was a rhetorical question in the fairy's eyes.

"Go on then," Shelly said, her voice low. "Tell me how you got past Dru's wards."

The bounty hunter grinned and tapped her nose.

"Can't let all my secrets go," she said, keeping an eye on the druid. "But I like you, for some strange reason. So if you swear to not tell the half-wit or the baldy man I'll share the secret."

Shelly grinned. Having a secret from Filthy Henry felt like a rebalancing of the karma scales.

"You have my word on it, may Dagda himself strike me down."

"No need to go that serious," Elivin said, looking at Shelly. "But I like your commitment. When we were here earlier I hid a small stone, a beacon, inside the toadstool statue I was messing with. Wards are all well and good at keeping people out, but if you can get past them once and leave a beacon stone behind then the wards do nothing."

"Huh," Shelly said. "Like a magical backdoor, of sorts."

"Pretty much," the leprechaun said, lifting up her cup and taking a sip of tea. "Generally folk don't get a chance to use a beacon, but I figured putting one in here would be good. Just in case Dru ever made it onto my list."

Before them, Filthy Henry's left hand twitched. They both stared at it.

"Is that normal?" Shelly asked.

The leprechaun slowly shook her head.

"Nope," she said. "The way the spell works should stop that from happening. Both parties are meant to enter a dream state, their bodies basically asleep. Otherwise any memories that are being examined would be acted out. It would be as dangerous as a sleep walker moving about, they could really harm themselves."

Filthy Henry's hand twitched again, this time his right one. Like a fish out of water, it started to flop about on his knee. After a minute his left hand began to mimic the right, bouncing about in a strange rhythm to the right. The fairy detective's head started to twitch, short and quick motions left and right. It seemed to Shelly that Filthy Henry was having a nightmare.

She looked over at Milton. The doctor was totally still, the only movement being when he inhaled or exhaled. There were no twitches, starts or movements from Milton at all. His eyes were still closed, the magical one on the coin looking directly into Filthy Henry's matching magical eye.

The fairy detective, however, was now to mumbling to himself with each jolting movement. It was like somebody had attached a low-level electrical line to his body, the spasms twisting him in every direction. Both hands rose up from his knees and hung limply in the air beside his face, his arms rigid. He looked like a demented puppet.

As Shelly watched him, another spasm ran through Filthy Henry's body. Then, without any indication it was about to happen, the fairy detective slapped himself in the face with his right hand.

"Ouch," she said, leaning back in surprise. "That looked sore."

Filthy Henry never even opened his eyes. His entire body rocked to the left, before he swayed back into his yoga pose. The twitching in his neck increased. When the fingers on his left hand opened out Shelly knew what to expect. Even still, the slap was so hard that she was sure the fairy detective should have woken up. Instead he just wobbled back and forth on the spot, flexing the fingers on his right hand.

Elivin took another sip from her tea.

"My money is on Lefty," the leprechaun said.

"Shouldn't we wake them up or interfere or something?" Shelly asked. "What if Milton is attacking him? This can't be normal."

Slurping from her cup, the bounty hunter shook her head.

"No, you're right. It isn't normal. But let's not be too hasty here with the whole 'wake them up' plan. It is highly unlikely that Milton is doing this. You don't get control of a body when using the Third Eye, only access to the mind."

Shelly frowned.

"Even though you just said something is happening that shouldn't be you still want to wait and see?"

The leprechaun nodded and took another slurp of her tea, thoughtfully eyeing Filthy Henry's hands.

"Yep," she said. "Because I will give you good odds that Lefty wins."

Gambling was not exactly a new concept for Shelly. Everyone in Ireland had at least one uncle who was fond of 'a little flutter' when it came to horses or dogs. They would stroll into a betting shop, pick out the most unhealthy looking creature to ever grace a race-course, and slap down a week's wages on the off-chance it would come back a hundred fold. Friendly wagers were much more Shelly's thing. Two pals betting which of them would purchase a nice bottle of wine if a certain outcome happened. No risk, all fun.

But this was a bet with a fairy, a leprechaun nonetheless. All the books said to never make a deal or bet with a fairy creature. True, those books were actually sold in the fiction section of book-stores the world over and considered to be nothing more than tales. Only people like Shelly, those who knew such stories had a grain of truth in them, would take heed of such warnings. Betting with a fairy creature on the surface seemed like a harmless act, but that all depended on the sort of wager they expected you to make.

Plus there was the ethical quandary it put Shelly in. While Filthy Henry was still in her bad books, he was a friend. Of sorts. Betting on whether or not his left hand would slap him down to the ground before the right one managed it was, at the end of the day, not something a true friend would do.

"I'll give you two-to-one odds on," Elivin said, eyeing her over the lip of her mug. "Just taking money bets by the way. I'm not stupid enough to risk something like a boon or a wish."

"Oh," Shelly said, a little surprised. "In that case make it three-to-one, I'll throw down a tenner, and you're on."

# Chapter Nineteen

His face hurt. Not the one currently being used so others could easily identify him, that blue see-through face was completely fine. No, his actual face, back in the real world, hurt. Hurt like Hell, if anyone wanted to quantify the level of pain being felt. All because a mental construct, who lacked the common decency to fade away and become a distant memory, was failing to follow a simple instruction.

Filthy Henry ducked to the left and brought up his right fist in a hay-maker punch.

It connected with a very satisfying thud sound that echoed around the white-space. Quinn spiralled on the spot, then fell over rubbing his face.

"You do know you're only hurting yourself, right?" he asked from where the ground should have been.

"Just get up onto the bloody sofa already before I figure out how to suppress you," Filthy Henry said, pointing at the therapy couch. "Trust me, buddy, I'm really good at suppressing memories I don't want to bother with any more."

Quinn picked himself up, dusted off his clothes, and stood straight. Why the pantomime of clearing dirt off, Filthy Henry did not bother to ask. Neither of them were actually in any danger of getting dirty or even bruised while inside Milton's mind. The entire time they had been punching it out, the doctor's younger mental projection had just sat at the desk and watched. Passing no comment, not even paying any real interest in the fight.

The fairy detective walked around the strange little office setup and stood behind Fluid's desk.

Dr. Milton did not even acknowledge him.

"See," Filthy Henry said. "He doesn't know who I am. Ergo you are the better person to do some pretend session with him so we can get some answers."

"I'm you," Quinn said, stomping over to the therapy couch and dropping onto it like a child having a tantrum. "It wouldn't have mattered."

"Maybe not," the fairy detective said. "But I know what we are looking for so that means you get to be the distraction."

Quinn lay back on the couch and crossed his arms in front of his chest.

"I know what you know, don't forget," he said.

"Sure, for now..."

What the fairy detective had stopped himself from saying was how he intended to lock Quinn out completely.

But that was something to focus on when they were not both in Milton's mind. Assuming they both returned to Filthy Henry's mind, of course. Right now they needed to gather some information. Which meant making Milton reveal stuff.

Filthy Henry raised his eyebrows at Quinn. The mental construct let out a sigh.

"So, doc, I've been having these thoughts...about....puppies," Quinn said.

"Dog gone," Milton said, still tapping the pen on his chin. "Sorry, I meant to say 'do go on'.

Around them a stream of orange light appeared, travelling through the whiteness. It circled the trio like a lazy kite. At the front of the stream a rectangular shaped began to form, solidifying in a matter of seconds into a folder similar to the one used for keeping patient records together. It drifted through the air, the orange light coming off it like a strangely shaped comet tail. Filthy Henry looked up at it and smiled. Obviously the simple act of making Milton behave like a doctor was enough to trigger some sort of memory recall, assuming that was what the floating file was. The trick, now, would be to make Fluid remember what they needed him to. While at the same time figuring out a way to actually use the folder as it spiralled around them.

Filthy Henry walked around the desk and came over to the couch, leaning down close to Quinn's ear.

"You've to get him thinking about the last few months," the fairy detective said. "That thing up there is what I want to get my hands on."

"Considering I know how to fly in here and you don't, how about you get on the therapy sofa and I do the orange spiral chasing thing?"

"Just do it," Filthy Henry snarled. "We need him to start thinking about when he was possessed by the evil spirit."

Quinn shifted his position slightly and looked up at Filthy Henry with barely veiled contempt.

The fairy detective stood up straight and watched the folder spiral as it rose up into Milton's mind-scape. It did a little loop-the-loop then altered course, shooting straight into the nothingness and vanishing from sight.

"Keep him talking," Filthy Henry said. "But about stuff that we, you know, care about. Common memories with the pair of you should be easiest to get."

"Fine, fine. So, Doc, what have you been up to the past month?"

Milton stopped tapping the pen on his chin and stared at Quinn, his mouth wide open. He looked around his desk, then leaned back in the large leather armchair.

"It has been...interesting," Fluid said. "Although I fail to see

401

how my month is going to help you with your puppy fixation."

Filthy Henry motioned with his hands for Quinn to start talking.

"Yeah...because..em...if I hear about how you've been I will find it easier to talk about my crap," Quinn said. "Share problems and all that."

The doctor considered this for a moment. Filthy Henry half expected to see the white area become a hive of activity as Fluid used his mind to think things over. Instead, Milton carefully placed the pen down and steepled his fingers. He stared over his fingertips at Quinn, still not seeing Filthy Henry apparently.

"What if we did a sharing session," Dr. Milton said. "You tell me something and then I can give you a story of my own that will relate to it."

"Doc, you do know who I am? Right?" Quinn asked.

Dr. Milton shook his head.

"I don't believe so, no. However, I take my job very seriously and if a person comes to me looking for help I am going to try my best and help them. Although you do look familiar."

That was an odd thing for Milton to say. Assuming his tale was true, the doctor would possibly have no memories from his time dealing with Quinn. However he had been held in the basement of Dru the Druid's shop for the past couple of hours. With the face of one fairy detective right in front of him for most of that time. Either Milton had a dreadfully bad memory when it came to faces or this place, this representation of the doctor's mind, acted more like a dream for the subject being visited.

Filthy Henry knew he was using the term 'visited' extremely loosely.

This was why Filthy Henry disliked doing spells he had no familiarity with. Not only did it mean he was trying to figure out

402

how to solve the case, he also had to learn at the same time. Who could be bothered doing that?

Quinn was, also, proving to be less than useful. By now the conversation between him and the doctor should have been flowing. The air, or whatever was around them, filled with swirling folders giving off orange streams of light. Enough that Filthy Henry would be able to capture one and see how to interact with it. Shelly would have been more use than Quinn.

Presumably as part of the feedback loop that Quinn was privy to, the mental construct looked over at Filthy Henry.

"Fine, I'll try something else. But how about you dial back a little on the disapproving thoughts?"

The fairy detective smiled.

"This strange telepathy is becoming annoying," he said.

"Only when you focus on a topic for too long, otherwise I've to go digging," Quinn said.

"Good to know," Filthy Henry replied.

"Why didn't you just try telepathy anyway?" Quinn asked.

"Gee, I dunno, maybe because I am not telepathic," the fairy detective said. "Plus that is like healing magic, you really need to know what you're doing otherwise it can go all sorts of wrong. Now make with the talk-talk."

"Doc, I was thinking about the first time we met at the hospital," the mental construct said, turning back to look at Milton. "Remember that? Our first session?"

Above the doctor's head a folder appeared. It spun around him for an instant, growing in size with each circuit. Milton did not acknowledge the floating folder at all, but it was clearly visibly to both Filthy Henry and Quinn.

"I do...I think I do," Dr. Milton said, his voice sounding like he was busy recalling a dream. "Strange, it is like I both can and can't....recall."

The fairy detective watched as Milton's newly summoned floating folder began to make intricate patterns above the doctor's head. He reached out and patted Quinn firmly on the shoulder.

"Keep it up," Filthy Henry said. "I'm going to try and grab it."

"I think it was a Tuesday, right?" Quinn said, nodding at the fairy detective's instruction.

Dr. Milton drummed his fingers on the edge of the table.

"No, I believe it was a Wednesday."

"Was it raining? I'm fairly sure it was raining. Maybe snowing? The sun was splitting the trees, that was it."

Each request for clarity on detail caused the orange stream coming out of the folder to glow brighter, as if the act of Milton being made to remember more information fed energy into the flying folder. Without giving any indication at all it shot forward, shooting over the desk and heading towards Quinn.

Filthy Henry stepped onto the edge of the therapy couch, ignored the dirty look his mental construct fired at him for ruffling his imaginary coat, then reached out and grabbed the folder with both hands. It tingled slightly, like electricity.

Then things got very strange.

Even stranger than they had been up to this point.

#

Shelly held out her hand and smiled at Elivin.

"Pay up," she said.

"No way," the leprechaun replied. "We don't know if it isn't going to start again."

"That doesn't mean anything. He hasn't slapped himself in the face in the past fifteen minutes and the last hand to issue a slap was mine. Ergo, I win."

"How do you figure?"

"Who throws the last punch when a fighter gets knocked out in a boxing match?"

"The winner," Dru the Druid said, now feigning sleep in the wooden armchair.

"Thank you," Shelly said, gesturing towards him with both hands. "Therefore, by that definition, I won the bet. So, pay up."

Elivin shook her head.

"Nope, that's just Filthy Henry logic. You wait and see, my hand, so to speak, will make a comeback any minute now."

Milton's head twitched. Ever so slightly, but it still counted as a movement.

"Double or nothing on this one," Elivin said, indicating the doctor with a jerk of her thumb.

"Alright," Shelly said. "But only if he actually starts slapping himself in the face. Otherwise I want my cash. Real cash as well, none of your fairy fakery."

#

Filthy Henry never played video games. He had seen them over the years, it was hard not to when you had been alive for over eight decades. He watched as they evolved from two paddles and a little square to something that looked like a movie with extremely impressive special effects. Kids, teenagers, hell even a large number of adults, spent hours a week playing the things. Immersing themselves in the stories of other people.

It had never been something that appealed to Filthy Henry. He spent enough time running around the country, shooting fireballs out of his fingers while battling whatever crazy fairy creatures were trying to destroy the human world. The need to pretend he was doing the same during his downtime seemed pointless.

Even the one with the dragons did not appeal to him. Who wanted to come home from work and then play games that were like their job? With dragons?

Milton's magical memory folder was very much like playing one of those modern computer games. Instead of observing from the outside, Filthy Henry had been inserted into the doctor's own point of view. He was reliving, or living for the first time in his case, Dr. Milton's memory from the first person perspective. The fairy detective had no actual control over the doctor's actions. Whatever had happened before was happening now, exactly the same way. All that Filthy Henry could do was observe.

Luckily, all he wanted to do was observe. Take in every and any detail about this memory so that it became easier to extract the information they actually wanted from Fluid.

The edges of the memory were tinged with a faint orange light, no doubt the folder's comet-like-tail energy as it generated all the information being seen. All the colours were dulled a little, not as bright and vivid as they would be in the real world. Which sort of made sense. Memories faded over time, details became less clear. What mattered was that the primary information persisted throughout the years.

Sound was slightly muffled too, like listening to something underwater.

Filthy Henry tried to close his eyes, chuckled inwardly when he realised that blinking was now going to be part of Milton's memories, and began to look at what the memory was of.

Fluid was in his office, sitting behind that gaudy desk. To his left stood a stack of patient files and folders, on the right a computer that had clearly seen better days. Those days being during the 1980s, judging by the old style keyboard and green screen. Filthy Henry knew that the health service in Ireland had some funding issues, but he was fairly sure that the computers had been upgraded in the hospitals. At least moving them all closer to something with a colour screen.

Somewhere, out of sight, a clock was ticking. Slicing away the seconds of Milton's life as he jotted down some notes on the pad in front of him. This was strange, until the fairy detective realized that if Milton had in fact been possessed the entity would obviously try to blend in. Pretend to be a doctor so that nobody became suspicious.

It was a dastardly level of genius, one Filthy Henry had not factored into the case. He was not just dealing with something that could steal the memories of another person, but also steal their place in the world. Live as they did, with access to all of their memories so that the deception was perfect.

A magical chameleon.

There was a knock at the office door, which drew Milton's attention and shifted his gaze. Filthy Henry had a sudden feeling of motion sickness, like being on a roller-coaster as it went through a loop.

"Come in," the doctor said, loudly so as to be heard through the door.

When he spoke it was easier to hear, another detail saving aspect of how memory worked Filthy Henry assumed. Unimportant sounds and noises were muffled, just as colours were dulled.

Linda opened the door, stepped inside, then guided Filthy Henry into the room. Rather, guided Quinn in the fairy detective's body into the room. She closed the door behind them and nodded at Milton.

"This is Quinn," Nurse Faul said, indicating the man beside her by pointing to him. "He is the new Blank Slate that arrived the other day. Although, he could remember his name. Bit odd, considering how the rest of them come in."

A wave of emotion rushed through the fairy detective, but from an outside source. The memory, it seemed, was not just about what had been seen or heard. It was about feelings, what Milton experienced at that moment. Right then, upon seeing Quinn, the doctor felt a mixture of anger and interest. Emotions so strong that Filthy Henry was finding it hard to not let them railroad over his own.

*I'm an observer, I'm an observer,* the fairy detective started saying to himself.

This seemed to help. The emotions, while still there and being felt by Filthy Henry, became walled off slightly. He could tell they came from the doctor and not himself. Now the question was why? What about his, or Quinn's, arrival in the office had caused such contrasting and intense emotions to spring up within Milton.

Then he saw it, just on the edge of the doctor's field of vision. A sign that something else was there in the room too. The nurse, the patient, the doctor.

The other guy.

It was not a physical presence in the room, rather something that was unseen and caused the prickles on a person's neck to stand up. In fact Filthy Henry was almost certain that the only way to see it was by looking through Milton's eyes. It was a presence that not even the doctor himself was aware of.

Just on the edge of the orange haze, the shimmer that was part of the memory, Filthy Henry spotted a matching blood red coloured light. It ran around the entire field of vision, growing in size as each wave of emotion crashed over Filthy Henry.

Milton, it seemed, had been possessed for sure. Now the fairy detective just needed to figure out how to access the last memory Fluid had shared with the entity and see what more could be learned.

Unsure of how to proceed, Filthy Henry focused his thoughts on the whiteness of the mind-scape and willed himself to leave the memory. For once, this trip down somebody else's memory lane went exactly as desired.

#

Quinn had been rambling on for the past five minutes about his first meeting with Milton, poking the doctor every so often with a verbal queue to provide more details. Dr. Milton was only too happy to correct some facts or add in little bits of information. All the while the folder, with its orange fiery tail, raced around in random loops like a sentient kite high on drugs.

The fairy detective, a title Quinn decided to leave with Filthy Henry rather than take on himself, had grabbed hold of the folder as it sailed overhead. Through means unseen, Filthy Henry then entered it, vanishing from sight completely. Milton had not noticed this happen at all, which was a good thing Quinn figured.

Keeping an eye on the flying folder was easier said than done. Even though it could only race around the inside of Milton's mind, it had the infinite vastness of the mind-scape within which to travel. On its latest loop over the pair of them Quinn noticed that the colour of the streamer had changed. It was still a bright, sunburnt, orange colour but the edges of it looked more red. Red with a hint of black.

He tried to peek into Filthy Henry's memories, searching for anything that the fairy detective may have discovered while in Fluid's Flying Folder. Surprisingly, all of Filthy Henry's memories were now blocked off. Quinn was, for all intents and purposes, a single entity.

"Well that is a little unsettling," he said.

"What is?" Dr. Milton asked.

Before Quinn could answer the folder flew over his head,

making an odd popping sound. There was a brightly coloured puff of smoke, something that sounded like an elephant farting, and Filthy Henry appeared in the air. He dropped to the ground with the grace of a falling cannonball, landing in a painful pile beside the couch.

"Not my fault," Quinn said, leaning over the therapy couch and looking down at the fairy detective. "Milton started talking and then you just..."

"Shut up," Filthy Henry said, standing up and rubbing his neck. "He was possessed."

"You're sure?"

"Positive," the fairy detective said, looking up and turning until he spotted the folder. "See the dark red tint? Coming off its orange trail of sparks? That's whatever was in Milton. He has the memories, but he wasn't the driver. Whatever that red thing was, it's left traces behind."

"Meaning?"

"Meaning, my mental challenged construct, that if we get the last memory when the thing was in here we can figure out what it intends to do. I think. At least we can figure out why it isn't here any longer."

Quinn frowned.

"Don't you mean 'mentally challenged construct'?"

"Nope," Filthy Henry said.

"Whatever," Quinn said, ignoring the fairy detective's dig. "You think that's what we should be looking for?"

"I do," Filthy Henry said. "Right, get the doctor to talk about his last conversation with Linda. That has to be who it jumped into, if it is no longer in here."

Quinn looked over at Dr. Milton and nodded his head.

"Hey, doc. Isn't Linda just the best?"

Dr. Milton nodded his head.

"She is one of the better nurses at the hospital, yes."

"But, like, how she deals with the patients. It is a bit above and beyond, don't you think?"

"I suppose," Dr. Milton said. "I am not sure how that relates to our session now though."

"Oh, I was just thinking about the last time I was chatting to her. Right before she brought me down to you. For an emergency session."

Above Fluid's head a second floating folder appeared. This one looked different to the first, which was still spiralling around the trio in the whiteness. The new folder had a longer tail than its older counterpart, a tail with the dark red colour already present.

Filthy Henry pointed at it, smiling.

"If it's already got that colouring to it then this must be the last memory before the thing jumped ship," he said. "Or a memory that the entity was really active in."

The fairy detective did not wait for this new memory to start moving. He ran towards Milton's desk, jumping so as to land on the surface. Using his momentum, he jumped and grabbed onto the bottom corner of the folder, vanishing just as before.

Dr. Milton stared above his chair, shock clear on his face.

"I'm not sure I like that man," he said.

Quinn laughed.

#

Getting orientated this time was a lot easier. Like riding a bike, Filthy Henry guessed. He wondered, briefly, if jumping into the memory of Milton riding a bike would be the easiest memory

411

of all to access. After all it was a memory most people would have in common.

With that stray thought out of the way, the fairy detective returned his focus to the task at hand. He looked around Milton's memory, the orange haze at the edges already tinged with red, and saw they were once again in his office. The stack of folders were still in place, the ancient device that passed for a computer powered on. On the desk was an A4 pad with what looked like a family tree drawn out on the open page. Names had been crossed out in the upper branches, some had circles drawn around them and arrows pointing to other names on the page. None of the names looked familiar, but viewing them through the orange-tinted glasses of Milton's memory gave Filthy Henry a sense that this was not just any old list. It had been written out, numerous times, over the years. What he was looking at now merely fell into the category of 'Current Draft'.

The names had to be important though, which was a declaration of the obvious in practically every sense of the word. People did not generally write down complicated family trees for no reason, particularly those who had been going around the country stealing memories.

Filthy Henry tried to read the names at the base of the tree, but the doctor's left hand was resting on the page. What he did notice, however, was the amount of traditionally spelled names just above the root. Some of the branches were not straight lines, rather being little dotted ones, moving from an old style name to the more modern ones.

*This is definitely important,* the fairy detective thought. *Shame I can't write down notes while I'm in here.*

Milton looked up from his family-tree scribblings at the therapy sofa, to the forlorn figure of Bosco Burns. Streams of red light poured out of the man's mouth, drifting like smoke through the air towards Fluid's desk. The doctor nodded his head, then returned his attention to the notepad.

*Like he is having a snack while doing paperwork,* Filthy Henry thought.

A familiar knock at the door made Milton look up from the notepad again. He waved his hand towards Bosco, stopping the lights and pulling the last of it towards him. Before Fluid could call out to the knocker the office door swung open.

Linda stepped into the room again, giving the fairy detective an intense sense of déjà-vu. If such a thing was possible when hijacking another person's memories.

"Is he alright?" she asked, motioning towards the forlorn figure on the sofa with a nod of her head.

"Em, what? Yes, yes, of course he is," Dr. Milton said, shaking his head. "Didn't you see the sign on the door saying I was in session?"

"I did," Linda said, walking over to Bosco and checking his pulse. "But I didn't hear you talking so I figured it was alright to come in. Are you sure he is okay?"

Fluid started to shuffle papers around his desk while avoiding eye-contact.

"Oh he got into...a...fugue state, after telling me some....stories," Dr. Milton said. "Medical term, you can look it up later."

Linda helped Bosco to his feet. She slid an arm around his back, holding tightly onto his top, and started walking towards the door.

"I'll bring him back to his room," Nurse Faul said to Fluid. "But I was looking for you."

"Oh yes?"

"Yea. Quinn was wondering if he could have a session today. Said he was feeling a bit fuzzy and to be honest I don't think he is acting like himself."

413

For whatever reason Milton became suspicious at that seemingly innocent statement, Filthy Henry could feel it. Nothing about Linda's manner or speech gave away that she actually was trying to get Filthy Henry, pretending to be Quinn, into the office. Yet the doctor had picked up on something and then...

Once again Filthy Henry felt strong emotions coming from the doctor. This time it was fear, fear of being discovered by the fairy detective. It was strangely nice to know that the bad guy feared him. Filthy Henry was going to tell Elivin once he returned to his own body. The thing she had been chasing for centuries feared him and not her.

Fluid stopped moving the pages around his desk and looked directly at Linda.

"Quinn wants a session? He did miss his session yesterday for some reason, must have been those visitors you had him seeing. How exactly is he not like himself?"

Linda stopped by the door, leaning Bosco against the frame.

"Oh, you know," she said. "Saying stuff that doesn't make sense. Keeps talking about a fairy detective. To be honest I think he needs to see you."

The doctor's fear intensified, only to be replaced rather quickly by a feeling of calm. It was the strangest sensation the fairy detective had ever experienced, which was saying a lot for a person who dealt with magic on a daily basis. He, or rather Fluid, rapidly started to think up of an escape plan to avoid being caught.

*We're getting to the interesting bit,* Filthy Henry thought.

"Well then, bring him in," Dr. Milton said to Linda. "After all, the patients must come first."

"I'll bring him right down," Nurse Faul said.

"Excellent," Dr. Milton said. "Just wait a moment though. I

414

need to have a word with you about something."

Without saying anything else, everything went red and Filthy Henry felt like a thousand wood chippings thrown to the wind. There was a rush and energy built up just before the doctor. Red and swirling, like an angry balloon filled with electricity.

Linda stood still, a few feet in from the doorway, her face a mask of shock and fear. She was frozen to the spot, the office door closing slowly behind her.

The energy started to move away from Dr. Milton and Filthy Henry realised there were two distinct sets of memories now forming. Those within the doctor, his original personality taking control again, and those of his passenger as it moved into Linda. Without wasting a second, the fairy detective focused on the departing memories and felt his consciousness being pulled along with them like a leaf caught in the current of a river.

As the red ball of energy slowly travelled across the space between Milton and Linda, Filthy Henry thought about how he would have preferred if it had been possible to observe the memories from outside. Not have to simply relive them. There had to be some details he was missing, he was sure of it.

Without warning, Filthy Henry suddenly found himself standing in the room in his blue, slightly transparent, form. Everything around him was frozen in place. Linda stood like a scared statue, awaiting her impending doom. Her impending doom hung mid-air, red energy crackling around it. Milton remained behind his awful desk, a slightly sleepy look on his face. It seemed like the doctor was about to collapse from tiredness.

"Well this is all very interesting," the fairy detective said, looking around the memory.

Outside of Milton's point of view the details of the room became fuzzy, cloudy almost. Whatever he had not looked at during the memory clearly became unimportant to his

415

recollection of events. It gave the scene a strange, almost tranquil, feeling to it. There was an incompleteness to it all, like an unfinished three-dimensional painting. Whole sections of wall behind the doctor were missing, while the filing cabinet on his left, which had been just on the edge of Milton's vision, was missing all sides except the one he had seen.

Filthy Henry stepped forward, relieved that the movement worked, and examined the ball of red energy up close.

It was roughly the size of a football and left a trail of dark red mist in its wake. Magical energies ran around the outside of the sphere. This was no fairy creature, at least not one Filthy Henry had ever seen. Had it been slightly smaller, and made from a less blood coloured light, he would have guessed it was a wisp. But this, beyond a shadow of a doubt, was something very different to a wisp. The question was what the thing actually was? A new, malevolent, sort of wisp?

Filthy Henry looked over at Linda, seeing the fear in her eyes. He knew there was nothing to be done at that very moment, since the moment had happened already and was not currently taking place, but when he was back in the real world things would be different. Very different. Nobody was going to be emptied out on his watch. Not again.

The fairy detective turned back to the red menacing ball and stared at it.

This was the bad guy, in the flesh. So to speak. But everything currently being observed was a memory, contained inside the head of Dr. Milton. What Filthy Henry was looking at right now were fragments of whatever had gone into Linda and presumably taken her over.

Filthy Henry licked his lips, for no real reason considering it did nothing to moisten the mental representation of his mouth, and rubbed his hands together.

Contained inside the ball of energy were the last vestiges of information Milton remembered while possessed. Meaning it was a wealth of information on the Big Baddy they were chasing. Information needed to solve the case and save Linda, along with everyone else who had had their memories stolen.

"This should work," Filthy Henry said, looking over at the frozen figure of Fluid. "Memories within memories, why wouldn't it work..."

The fairy detective raised his hands, lining his fingers up with the red sphere before him, and steadied himself. Taking an imaginary deep breath, Filthy Henry pushed his hands forward and into the energy ball.

Which resulted in a world of pain like he had never experienced before.

# Chapter Twenty

"What happened?! What happened?!"

"If you give me a second I can figure it out."

"He just fell over. Should he just fall over? Is it part of the spell?"

"I don't know, we don't generally use this spell for a variety of reasons. Mainly because it is dangerous!"

"You're not much help then, he was right. God dammit, Filthy Henry was right."

Elivin shot up into the air on two bursts of magic and floated in front of Shelly so they were staring into each other's eyes. Something about the leprechaun's expression suggested that a fireball was about to be conjured and thrown around.

"Don't. Ever. Say. That. Again."

Shelly gulped.

"The 'not much help' bit or the..."

"The other bit!" Elivin snapped at her. "Now, shut up. Sit down. Let me do some basic healing magic to see what is happening."

Shelly did as she was told and took a step back from the circle. Since Filthy Henry had fallen over, a sense of dread and panic had been rising up inside her. Watching the fairy detective get knocked down during a magical duel was just an every day occurrence. A 'nothing to worry about, carry on with your daily business' sort of thing. You could see the destructive magic being thrown at him, allowing your brain to figure out the reason he fell over was because of an injury. Seeing him fall to the ground without anybody throwing so much as a tennis-ball at him was very worrying. Who knew what was going on inside the doctor's skull, or even if the fairy detective was able to protect himself?

When he hit the ground, Filthy Henry smacked his head so hard it actually woke Dru the Druid up from his nap. He snorted and shook his head around, the hood of his druid robe sliding down.

"Was going on?" the druid asked, his voice a little slurred and his sentence syntax obviously playing catchup.

Shelly waved wildly at the forlorn figure of Filthy Henry.

"He's dead!" she near screeched.

"He's dead?" Dru said, jumping to his feet and running over to the ritual circle. "Dead? Like dead dead or just fake dead?"

"What the hell is fake dead?" Shelly asked, the panic rising higher.

"You know...when you..." the druid began to say.

"He's not dead!" Elivin snapped. "For the love of Dagda would you pair of mortals go and make yourself useful by annoying some other fairy. The one here is trying to figure out what is going on."

"Then why aren't you doing something?" Shelly demanded. "Take down the circle and do something!"

The leprechaun took a deep breath, her chest rising and falling slowly. With her fists clenched, she turned and looked up at Shelly.

"I'm going to try and explain this, so listen carefully. The ritual circle is the only thing keeping their minds in this basement. The Third Eye opens up the connection, but if something has gone wrong with that then right now their minds could be floating in the air between their bodies. We drop the circle, we risk those minds just racing away. Maybe even leaving the building."

"Leaving me with two bodies to get rid of?" Dru the Druid asked. "Keep that bloody thing up. No circle dropping. They can free their minds in their own basements. I haven't the time to get rid of bodies, or the bags of lye..."

"You're all heart," Elivin said to the druid. "But yes, it would mean we have two bodies left behind. Right now the spell still seems to be working, otherwise the Third Eyes would have closed and severed the connection. So, it looks like whatever has happened is as a result of the spell. Now, let me check him over will you?"

She waited for Shelly to give her a nod of acknowledgement that what had been said was heard, then nodded her head twice. Elivin knelt down and gently touched the ritual circle. Slowly she stepped over the border of the circle, ensuring her fingers kept in contact with the design on the floor.

"My magic powering the thing," the leprechaun explained to Shelly and Dru. "Means I can pass through if required. Just don't ever tell Filthy that."

Making sure not to touch him, Elivin knelt down beside Filthy Henry and held her hands over his head.

A faint yellow light enclosed both her hands, pulsing ever so slightly as Shelly watched. She moved them slowly over his head, starting at Filthy Henry's forehead before moving around to his temples. The examination could not have taken more than ten minutes, during which time Elivin kept her eyes closed and head tilted ever so slightly as if listening to something only she could hear. To Shelly, however, those ten minutes felt like years. Each second dragged out forever, while Dru the Druid did his very best impersonation of a useless idiot. Saying and doing nothing to help calm the ever rising tide of worry she felt.

"Why would you have lye?" Shelly asked Dru, trying to

421

distract herself.

"Makes decomposing a body that bit quicker," the druid said. "Not that I know for a fact or anything..."

Elivin opened her her eyes, the glow around her hands remaining in place, and looked directly at Shelly.

"Physically he's fine," the leprechaun said. "There isn't anything wrong, no damage at all. Whatever is going on it's in his head. Or rather in Milton's."

"Then break the connection," Shelly said, amazed that she had to say it out loud.

Stating the obvious to fairy detectives and fairy folk was rapidly becoming Shelly's most undesired, newest, hobby of all time.

"We can't," Elivin said. "Didn't I say that already? I feel I said that already. If we break the connection without knowing for sure that Filthy Henry is back in his body we could kill him."

"Not the worst outcome," Dru said, an ill timed smirk on his face.

Shelly took a swing at the druid with her right fist. Dru moved with all the grace of a catatonic ballet dancer, taking the brunt of the assault on his shoulder. He spun on the spot, reached up to rub at the injured shoulder, then tumbled to the ground. It was all overly cartoonish, but Shelly felt a small amount of satisfaction from it.

"Show some respect, " she said to Dru. "He's spent most of his life saving two worlds that don't want anything to do with him."

"It was just a joke," the druid said, his voice full of regret.

"Poor taste," Elivin chimed in. "That's coming from a fairy that has a lot more reason to dislike this half-breed than most."

"Fine!" Dru the Druid said, walking back towards his chair.

"Filthy would have appreciated it."

Shelly watched the druid walk away and wondered what went on in his extremely bald head. While it was true Filthy Henry did very little to ingratiate himself with other people, nobody deserved to be spoken about like that. It was, however, a little surprising that Elivin had come to his defence.

Looking down at the fairy detective, Shelly wondered what was going on in both his and Milton's head.

#

The memory folder had started to make more intricate patterns in the whatever-passed-for-air of the mind-scape. Loops, swirls, the stuff of roller-coaster nightmares. Basically whatever controlled the route the folder took had given it carte blanche with an extra side of crazy. The tail colour was now almost completely red, only the barest edges of it still showing any shade of orange. Even the folder itself sported a reddish-hue.

From his spot on the therapy couch, Quinn watched the folder fly erratically about the place while he kept Fluid in ideal chit-chat mode. It was a lot harder than one would have assumed. The trick, he discovered, was phrasing your responses in the form of a question. At least half-question, half-answer. A hook, so that when Milton gave his psychologist expected response there was something left over for him to reply to. It was simultaneously mentally challenging and mind-numbingly boring. But it seemed to keep the floating folder in flight, which was the main thing.

Quinn found it an interesting situation to be in. On one hand he was trying his very best to prove that he was his own entity, not just a strange by-product from Filthy Henry's body. Hand number two, however, had him doing everything in his power to make the fairy detective happy.

An odd replacement-abandoned-father complex being worked out in the mind of a psychologist. All very Freudian.

"Ooh, ooh no," Milton said to himself.

Quinn rolled onto his side and looked over at the doctor.

"Everything alright?" he asked.

"You're making me remember something I would rather not. I think we should change the topic."

This was bad, you did not need to be the mental construct of a fairy detective to figure that out. If the doctor decided to no longer think about the memory within which Filthy Henry now resided then they would not get the information they sought. Plus, Quinn was not completely sure what would happen if the memory folder stopped being a thing whizzing around the place while the fairy detective was still inside. They were in uncharted territory and any theories that Quinn could come up with were wild at worst, insanely out there at best. Regardless, he was not willing to take the risk in order to prove any of the theories. Something told him letting Filthy Henry vanish inside the memory of their kidnap victim would reflect badly on Quinn.

He jumped up from the therapy couch and ran over to the desk.

"Nope," Quinn said, shaking his head quickly from side to side. "We aren't changing topics at all, doc. I need you to tell me everything that happened."

Dr. Milton leaned back in his chair, pushing away from the table to put some distance between himself and Quinn.

"You're a bit close," he said. "I think you should return to the couch and we can continue this session."

Quinn punched the desk so hard it hurt, which made no sense since he technically did not have a body inside Milton's head. The act had the desired effect on Fluid. He stared at the fist being pressed into his desk, eyes opened wide, and started breathing quickly.

"We're not doing anything like that, I want to hear all about..."

Three columns of swirling mist formed behind Fluid's chair. Thick and black, with thin bases and wide tops. Each moved toward Milton's seat, one remaining directly behind the chair and the others taking up position on either side of it. The doctor tilted his head a little to the left and looked at Quinn.

"I don't think you understand," he said. "I want you to sit back down on the couch or leave."

Eyeing the three swirling mists, Quinn wondered what exactly was about to go down. They looked both menacing and intriguing at the same time, which was a very dangerous combination. He looked around for the memory folder and spotted it coming towards the desk, the red colour looking oddly threatening.

It raced through the air and took a low pass over them, pulsing brightly in the process.

Filthy Henry was deposited onto the desk, appearing out of thin air, landing with a painful thud on the wooden surface. His eyes were closed and it looked like he had been through some sort of battle or fight. One hand, the right, was closed tightly around something while the other hung limply off the edge of the desk.

Both Quinn and Milton looked at the forlorn fairy detective for a moment, then at each other.

"You can take him with you," Fluid said, indicating Filthy Henry with a nod of his head.

Filthy Henry's survival was paramount to Quinn's own continued existence, regardless of what that existence actually entailed. He figured taking Fluid's advice was the wisest course of action and reached down to grab the fairy detective by his coat.

Milton raised up his hand, motioning for Quinn to stop.

"Please," he said. "Allow me."

The doctor gestured to each of the swirling mists, then pointed at Quinn and Filthy Henry.

"Show them out."

Quinn watched as the mists increased their rotational speed and moved towards him and the fairy detective. He decided against fighting them and just went limp, figuring it would be easier. Like a peaceful protest. As the first tendril of mist gripped his arm like a vice he realised it made no difference.

Milton wanted them out of his mind, quickly.

#

Shelly watched Filthy Henry so intensely she felt sure her eyeballs would pop right out of their sockets.

Elivin had given up trying to coax him back awake using magic about twenty minutes before, opting instead to just monitor him. Dru the Druid had suggested they go and get Bunty Doolay, but as the *Sidhé* never left her bar it was something of a non-runner. Teleporting to the bar was also out of the question, much to Shelly's annoyance. The way Elivin explained it, the fact both men's minds were interlinked at the minute added a whole bunch of complexity to the teleportation spell. The sudden destruction and reconstruction that made up the very essence of a teleport spell sort of assumed things were not magically linked together. Doing a teleport with two minds housed in the same body was a sure fire way to discover if the right mind wound up in the correct body on the other end, assuming it arrived at all.

With a high percentage on the 'not completely sure what will happen' scale.

Although something about how the bounty hunter had explained it all gave Shelly the feeling that she was over complicating things. Almost as if Elivin wanted to make the task sound nigh-on-impossible to do, so that she did not even have to attempt it.

This left them with the 'wait and see' plan. The one plan which Shelly truly despised, as it felt like nothing productive was happening and the longer things stayed that way the worse they would get.

Since the bounty hunter ceased performing any magical healing, Filthy Henry had remained stationary. If he was under some horrific mental assault, nothing on the outside showed it. Likewise if he had already been killed his body seemed fine, unharmed. At least he was still breathing, generally considered a good indication by people both in and out of the medical profession that a person was alive.

"Can you send me in?" Shelly asked Elivin.

"Huh?" both the druid and the leprechaun said at the same time.

"Can you send me in? Make one of those coins and let me jump into the spell. In case Filthy Henry needs help."

"No," Elivin said. "It doesn't work like that. You can't have three Third Eyes in the same connection. It's highly likely you'd not find the correct body to return to."

"Well we have to do something!" Shelly said, a feeling of desperation rising up in her.

Dru the Druid took a step towards her, his arms stretched out.

"I swear to Dagda if you try and hug me I will punch you so hard your eyebrows will be relocated to the back of your head."

The druid continued walking, arms still held out before him, but adjusted his course slightly and walked around Shelly. Once safely on the other side he kept moving, heading over to a bookshelf. There he began to search for something, not looking back at Shelly.

"He gets that treatment a lot?" the leprechaun asked.

"Sort of the only defining characteristic he has in these

stories," Shelly replied.

"That and the comedic value," Filthy Henry said.

"Filthy!" Shelly said with delight.

He was still lying on his side, eyes closed, but the fairy detective had definitely spoken. Across from him, Dr. Milton slowly tumbled backwards and lay on the ground. Both of their coins stopped being so animated and slid off their foreheads. When they touched the ground each coin melted into little metal puddles.

Shelly glanced over at Milton, who seemed to be asleep but still breathing, then turned back to Filthy Henry. He had not moved.

"You heard him talk, right?" she asked Elivin, pointing at Filthy Henry.

The leprechaun nodded.

"Technically you heard him talk," Filthy Henry said, eyes still firmly shut. "But I'm not really able to do much else."

Shelly and Elivin both stood beside the fairy detective and looked down at him, frowning. Sometimes people talked in their sleep, she was fairly certain that everyone did at some point in their lives. But the rules always changed when you brought magic into the equation. Whatever had happened to knock Filthy Henry over may have put him asleep, or it could have done something much worse.

Such as freeze his body and make it a permanent prison, one which would allow him to communicate and nothing more.

Although there was something about how Filthy Henry was talking that sounded off.

"Em...Quinn?" Shelly asked.

"Hey," Quinn said, using the fairy detective's mouth. "I could

428

use a hand getting up. I could also use a hand opening my eyes."

#

The rag doll was creepy. Spending more and more time around it only helped to hammer home how unnatural a thing it was. Sure, there was a soul of some sort inhabiting the tatty creation, but that did not make it any less creepy. It was an animated object which generally should not be animated, moving around. Complete with free will and an attitude problem. Although that was only one of many problems the grumpy rag doll had.

Right now it was indulging in another of its problems; having a glass of wine.

This was as entertaining to watch as it was strange. A large glass of red wine was being held between two hands, which resembled sausages made from wool given the lack of fingers, and slowly sipped from. Considering the doll had no stomach for the fluid to go into, a pool of red wine was seeping out from the doll's backside. Even so, it appeared like the rag doll was drunk.

Meaning Linda was now in an apartment with a hideous fairy creature, one that definitely belonged under a bridge somewhere, and a drunk doll. If she had not spent the last few centuries jumping from body to body, collecting stories, her current situation might have seemed crazy. Instead they were having a girl's night in, followed by a day in and most of the next night. At least up until the writers event started. Then they had to be out of the apartment in order to do some collecting. But that was part of the plan, to keep a low profile and remain hidden so that no fairy detective found them before the Big Event.

The doorbell rang, drawing everyone's attention.

"Who is it?" Medb asked Linda, slurring her words slightly.

"I'd have to open the door to find out," she answered.

"Stop bickering," Blacksmile said. "I decided to order some

429

food for us while we wait. I'm not sure what abilities the half-breed has at his disposal and I was hungry. Didn't want to risk conjuring up anything, in case the magic gave away our location."

It made sense, except for one minor detail.

"I don't have any money," Linda said.

"Paid for with your card," Blacksmile said, smiling the black toothed smile. "Just because I am a magical creature doesn't mean I am totally oblivious to the ways of mortals."

Linda had to hand it to her, the ugly creature was certainly cunning. Then again, you would have to be in order to survive for as long as Blacksmile had. Neither the rag doll nor her partner had divulged to Linda, back when they first met, how they came to be in their present states. As near as Linda was able to figure out Medb had died but wanted to live on in order to witness vengeance, while their sponsor had been ousted by her own fairy people. Cursed to forever live in the mortal world and not be able to jump back and forth.

Over the years Linda had tried to see more and more of the fairy creatures in Ireland. At first it was difficult. One thing the fairy folk were good at was hiding from mortals. They had once ruled the land, then they did a little magic and hid from everything not a fairy. But if you watched, paid real close attention, learned, it was possibly to see them even when hidden.

The doorbell rang once more. Linda got up from the sofa and answered the front door. Outside stood a small, wiry, teenager with a plastic bag held before him. A delicious aroma hit her nostrils, wafting through the small opening in the bag. She reached out and took the plastic handles from him, smiling.

"Thanks," she said.

"You're welcome," the teenager replied.

He coughed and rubbed his thumb and index finger together, just under his chin. Linda brought the bag down to her left hand-side and looked at the gesture being made by the boy.

"Tip?," Linda said. "Yeah, here's a tip. If you want to keep being able to do that with your thumb and finger get the hell out of my sight."

This wise advice seemed to offend the youth. He looked at her, slightly shocked.

"I just climbed up three flights of stairs you old pox bag," he said. "You couldn't throw me five Euro for bringing you your food? Some sort of religious freak, is it? Wants to keep the black man down?"

Linda frowned.

"I'm not even forty yet, you little jerk. Also you're not black," she said. "You're a pasty white Dubliner who needs a good kick up the backside. Now scram."

The door to the apartment opened slightly wider and Blacksmile stepped into view. She looked up at the teenager, her expression hard to read. One eye, the good one, was focused on him. Her other, oddly sized, eye squinted at him.

"Empty him out," she said. "Ingrate."

Linda shrugged.

"Fair enough," she said, turning to look at the boy. "Why don't you tell me your story."

#

Not being in control of one's body can be a terrifying and irritating experience. A prison without walls. Your own limbs failing to do as instructed, when you knew they followed instructions before. It was as if an unruly two-year-old had gone dead weight in the middle of a shopping centre, except the two-year-old was really your own body. The only thing that could make this a more unbearable experience was having to rely on other people to move you about. To lift, angle and bend your

431

body into position.

Positions you used to be able to get into yourself.

Asking for help to move always caused the same problem for people, at least initially, as they accepted the new order of things. It meant swallowing your ego and being humble in the face of limitations beyond your control. Most people mastered this the first-time round, making all follow-up requests easier to make. Others took a little longer.

Quinn could feel the rug rub against his, or rather Filthy Henry's, left cheek. It was rough, cheap spun, wool and literally meant to cover a floor and take damage. If the thread count reached double digits he would have been impressed. Only able to see out of his right eye, on account of the left being pressed into the rug, Quinn peered up at Shelly and Elivin, watching both of them try their best to contain their laughter.

Neither was doing a particularly good job at it. In fact, they were poster women for how not to contain your laughter when a situation called for it. Between the inward snorts and the tightly closed eyes, there was a sense that neither was putting any real effort into not laughing.

"Little help?" he asked.

Shelly broke first, tittering away like a school girl who had just read about male genitals for the first time. She covered her eyes with her hand, barely concealing the tears streaming down her face.

"Lost cause," Quinn said to her, turning his gaze to Elivin. "Come on, leprechaun. Magic me into a proper seating position."

Elivin snorted, her smile stretching from ear to ear.

"But this one looks so comfortable," the bounty hunter said. "I'd no idea that the fairy detective was into yoga. Downward facing half-breed."

That sent Shelly over the edge. She fell to the floor, guffawing loudly, while clutching her stomach. Quinn was annoyingly amused to see that she started kicking, actually kicking, her legs in the air. He thought that was something that only happened in silly comedy novels.

"Stop," she said, between gasp of air. "That isn't nice. But still so funny!"

"Seriously," Dru the Druid said. "This is not funny. Help us out!"

The source of mirth for both ladies was Dru the Druid's miserable attempt at moving the fairy detective. He had hoisted Quinn up, wobbled backwards on unsteady feet, and crashed into the rug covered floor. Quinn had landed on top of the druid, his backside pointed towards the ceiling while his face and knees embraced the rugs.

With absolutely no way to rectify the situation on his own, Quinn remained in that awkward position.

Every attempt at moving a body part other than the fairy detective's mouth and eyes had been met with resounding failure. Thankfully, breathing was a reflex action performed by the body. Otherwise Quinn was sure he would have suffocated by now.

"Shelly!" Dru shouted, pushing with all his might at the fairy detective's ribs. "I can't move him. Come on, I don't want to die with him lying on me. Two minutes ago you were panicking that Filthy Henry was in trouble, now you have a fit of the giggles!"

"Okay, okay," Elivin said, wiping tears from her eyes. "I'll do it. You got him out of the circle, so I can use magic now without lowering the holding spell. Just move the chair when you can get out from under him."

The bounty hunter held up her left hand and pointed at Quinn. He felt her magic wrap around Filthy Henry's body, lifting him two feet into the air. Below, Dru the Druid shuffled backwards and, once clear of the floating detective, stood up. With an over the top dusting down of his robes, the druid looked at Elivin, frowning.

"Couldn't have just done that earlier, no?"

The leprechaun shrugged.

"You need to make yourself useful if you plan on continuing your meddling in the magical world," Elivin said. "Making me laugh, that counts as being useful."

Something about her tone gave Quinn the impression this was an opinion held deeply by the fairy. At the start, when Filthy Henry's memories had been accessible to Quinn, there had been a moment of information overload. Now, after everything settled down, he found that not everything could be recalled easily. But Elivin not being happy with how Dru the Druid operated was a certainty.

With a wave of her hand, Quinn tumbled through the air and reorientated so that everything was the right way up. Dru dragged a chair beneath the fairy detective and Elivin magically lowered him into it, ensuring that he could remain in a seated position without any help. Once the manoeuvrer had been successfully completed, the leprechaun ended her spell. Quinn felt Filthy Henry's body slump into the chair, his head hanging limply to the left, but not dropping down like a sleeping commuter on the bus. It allowed Quinn to look at Shelly and Elivin, even though he had no control over the fairy detective's body.

Shelly had, finally, stopped laughing and got back to her feet. Her cheeks were wet with tears and she started to massage the bottom of her jaws underneath her ears.

"Oh that was too funny," she said. "I wish we'd taken some pictures."

"I can put them back if you want," Elivin said, a mischievous smirk on her face.

434

"Are neither of you concerned that Filthy Henry is not in charge of his own body?" Quinn asked them.

This had the desired effect. Both ladies sobered up, their expressions serious once more.

"He's right," Shelly said. "I was freaking out when Filthy Henry fell over and yet found it hilarious when himself and Dru got tangled up on the floor."

"Adrenaline...nerves...stress," Elivin said. "Any of those could have flooded your body. The second something happened you were not expecting you simply over compensated. That's what I'm telling myself."

Dru walked around from behind Quinn's seat and stood between Shelly and Elivin.

"So," he said. "Should we be worried that Filthy Henry isn't here giving us some snide insults as he tries to prove he is the smartest person in the room?"

Elivin nodded towards Milton, still unconscious in the ritual circle.

"What happened in there? What's the deal with the doc?"

Quinn coughed, or attempted to. It seemed that while controlling Filthy Henry's mouth was allowed, clearing the fairy detective's throat for dramatic effect was out of the question. He tried to look over at Fluid, failed miserably when his field of vision reached its limit, then just looked back at the three people before him.

"It was...strange," he said. "I'm not sure if Filthy Henry could have managed it on his own. Milton's mind was all set up for therapy sessions.. We had to ask him questions in a round about way to get memories to appear. Then Filthy Henry would enter the memory while I kept the doctor talking."

"Sounds like a simple enough plan," Dru said.

Quinn looked up and down, the best imitation of nodding he could manage at that moment, and hoped that they got what was being implied.

"Exactly. Thing is I don't know what went on inside the memories."

"I think we're also overlooking something big here," Shelly said. "How are you...you know...back?"

"Not entirely sure on that subject myself. I didn't exactly disappear once Filthy Henry returned to his body, just became a memory. Of sorts. When he jumped over into Milton's mind I was able to follow him and...well...here I am."

He knew how it sounded. Even in a world were the norm consisted of fairies and magic, being a memory that could take over a person's body was still a little far fetched on the sanity scale.

"So...where's Filthy?" Elivin asked.

"In here," Quinn said, going to point with his hand and remembering at the last instant that he had no control over it. Instead he settled for sticking out his tongue and pointing at his nose. "We had to get out of Milton's head pretty quickly."

"Why?" Shelly said.

"The last memory we made him recall was when whatever was in him left his body. Filthy spent a lot of time in there, relatively I guess. It made the memory change colours and then it...dumped him out. The doctor created these swirling misty things, they acted like bouncers. We weren't welcome any more, so they turfed us out."

Shelly crossed her arms and looked at him.

"Then how do you know he made it back and isn't trapped inside Milton's mind?"

"I carried him," Quinn said, flatly. "I'm not looking to take

436

over his body again. I've accepted that I'm not a real boy."

"Go easy on yourself there, Pinocchio," the leprechaun said.

Quinn ignored her, but did find the comment funny.

"If he didn't make it back in here, I'd be gone as well. I think...maybe. But he's definitely in here."

"Then what did he find?" Dru asked. "It must have been something good if Milton got all defensive about it."

"No idea," Quinn said. "You'll have to ask him that."

Shelly looked down at Elivin.

"How exactly are we going to do that?"

# Chapter Twenty-One

The sky was read.

No red.

Read? Red...

Both words made sense, seemed appropriate, yet he knew one was wrong. It was just really hard to remember which one. Even thinking about it, debating internally if the sky was red or read, raised up another question.

Should the sky be that colour?

It was normally a colour of some sort and right now it was definitely a colour, of that he was sure. Which meant that it had to be red. Even though red was the wrong colour for any sky. At least he thought it was. There was something about shepherds giving warnings...taking warnings. Maybe they read the sky? Was that it?

Like a fortune-teller and tea-leaves. The sky was read.

No, red. Red like his hair. Except he was ginger, not red. People dyed their hair red. Redheads were really ginger, just a brighter shade of it. Carrot-top. That was what the kids in school had called him. But they had not called him that, because he was a dark haired boy and always had been. His entire clan had been dark haired, it added an air of mystery to him. When he had gone off to The College everyone in the village had agreed he would do well.

The dark haired boy, not the read haired one. Red?

College? He had just about finished school. College was what some people went to, along with their friends. He had no friends, friendships never took. Names like Carrot-top did little to endear a person to the name-caller. Yet there was another name, it was important. He knew it was important. It had been given to him, meant to hurt his feelings. But he had used it, in spite of what the name meant. Kept it, made it his own. You did not grow up being called Carrot-top without knowing that names meant to hurt did nothing if you accepted them.

If he could grasp at it now, this name, the confusion currently felt would disappear.

Half-breed. Filthy.

That was it! Filthy!

Like being gently slapped in the face with a house, Filthy Henry's sense of self returned with a bang. It knocked him off his feet so that he landed on his back in the grass and looked up at red sky. Actually being able to pick the correct word to describe the colour was more satisfying than the fairy detective would have guessed. He looked at it and felt logical thinking return.

There was something very wrong with the sky and it had nothing to do with the colour. Instead of clouds there appeared to be hexagon shaped tiles drifting over the land, black as night but with bright, white, edges.

Filthy Henry slowly stood up and checked his surroundings. The only thing worse than waking up and not knowing who you were was doing it when you had no idea of your location. If something was waiting for the opportune moment to take revenge, while the person was utterly confused would be the perfect situation.

It appeared he had woken up in a field, with no memory of having gotten there. Thankfully the grass and plants had missed the memo about being the wrong colour, all of the flora being reassuring shades of green. There was nothing really of note to see in any direction, aside from a small wooded area nearby, while overhead the hexagon tiles drifted past. The area was eerily quiet, not even the sound of wind blowing could be heard.

He turned around, looking for Quinn, but was met with only more empty field.

"Hello?" Filthy Henry called out.

Nobody answered.

Off to his left, just under some trees, the fairy detective thought he saw some movement. Something about the trees looked oddly familiar, which made no sense to Filthy Henry. He was fairly certain that if people were asked to describe the fairy detective's interests, horticulture would not even be on the secondary list of things. But there it was, a bunch of trees that gave him a sense of déjà hedge-vu.

With no better options presenting themselves, Filthy Henry started walking towards the treeline. Being blessed with a healthy dose of paranoia, the fairy detective kept his eyes peeled for any movement around him. He cupped his right hand behind his back and began to slowly create a fireball, just in case.

Except the spell failed to start. No magic at all came to his request.

"I'm still in a memory," Filthy Henry said, as much to himself as anyone else.

This thought helped to solidify things once more for him, pulling tighter the threads of self that made him who he was.

They had been inside Milton's mind, looking for information on whatever may have been in the doctor's body. The entity that allowed him to steal memories. One memory was filled with intel on how the spirit jumped bodies. Filthy Henry had managed to leave the doctor's head and step into the entity's memory, getting a glimpse at the thing as it jumped into Linda's body. He had reached out, touched it...

Then woke up in this mystical hell with the red sky and black

441

clouds of doom.

No Quinn. No mental representation of Dr. Milton, sitting behind his pretentious desk and looking a couple of decades younger than he actually was. With hexagon tiles of evilness, because why would clouds suddenly be pitch black and dangerous looking otherwise, floating through the sky.

The red sky.

"I'm in the memory of the spirit from the Fluid's memory," Filthy Henry said out-loud, purely from habit at this stage. "This is some serious trippy Inception-style stuff going on."

Being in Milton's memories had been strange enough, reliving events as seen from the doctor's point of view. In a way, the fairy detective figured being able to enter the memory of a spirit who could possess you made some sense. The entire reason he had gone into Milton's mind was to make the doctor remember things his possessor may have left behind. This, however, was not exactly how Filthy Henry expected those memories to present themselves.

Whatever they were presenting.

Approaching the treeline, Filthy Henry moved as quietly as possible and ducked behind the nearest tree. There had been flickers of movement amongst the rest of the trees, but just that. Flickers. Like watching a video with two scenes merging briefly. Images of people there one second and gone the next. Their outlines only. Yet the trees still reminded him of some place, somewhere he had been.

Jumping from memory to memory had clearly scrambled his own memories. It was possible the trees looked familiar because of a memory Milton had, not the fairy detective.

Something scurried by his feet, small and running on two legs. It was not a distinct shape, more like a three dimensional shadow with lines of white crossing it horizontally. Whatever it was vanished three feet away, passing into the roots of a tree. Filthy Henry was not sure if it had actually gone into the tree or just stopped being visible at that point.

"I really don't like this place," he said, peering around the trunk of the tree.

Another of the hexagon tiles floated on by, passing briefly in front of what Filthy Henry considered the 'sun' in this place. As it obscured the glowing orb, the fairy detective noticed something extremely interesting. The blackness of the tile changed, making it act like a sort of window. On the other side of the tile he could just about make out Dru the Druid's basement. Then, as the tile continued drifting onwards, the blackness returned.

Everything clicked into place right then, all the holes of his Swiss cheese recollection filled in. He was once again running with a solid wheel of cheddar. Thankfully nobody was around to make any smart alec remarks about his epiphany.

This place of redness was not a magical realm. Filthy Henry remembered being ejected from one of Milton's memories and passing out, or at least not making new memories. It was hard to be knocked unconscious when you were not actually conscious. Regardless of the semantics, he and Quinn had been returned to the fairy detective's body safely. But not before Filthy Henry managed to bring along some fragmented memories of what had possessed Fluid.

That was why this place was all disjointed, beings flickering rather than appearing as they normally would. Filthy Henry was inside a memory fragment. He had managed to grab some bits, but not a lot. The raw energy of the spirit had frazzled his own memories, which at least explained the disorientation at the start.

Filthy Henry looked up at the tiles floating over head. Another one passed before the sun, revealing Dru's basement once again. At a guess, the fairy detective figured the tiles were his own memories or at least the ones being made by his body at that moment. If Quinn had managed to get them back safely into his body, then this was all presumably happening inside his mind. Filthy Henry could not figure out what other organ might be able to replay memories, particularly ones brought in from outside.

As a current working hypotheses, it was not a bad one.

"So, I am actually inside the memory fragments I brought along with me," the fairy detective said. "Plus I am talking out loud for no reason other than I am not enjoying the silence at all. Now that we've figured that out, let's see what we can actually see."

He stepped out from behind his cover and started to slowly walk through the forest. Behind him the little three dimensional shadow thing appeared again, running along the same path as before. From this angle it looked like a tiny person. Not one of the fairy folk, although there were some fairies roughly the same size, but definitely humanoid in shape.

The silence of the place was very unsettling. Filthy Henry felt that at any minute a murderous mime could jump out at him and silently stab him to death.

Up ahead three shapes flicked into existence, one of them the same size as the small figure running around on a loop behind the tree. Filthy Henry cautiously made his way towards them, keeping close to the trees as best he could. Even if this was just a memory, he had no idea how dangerous it could be. Yet another problem when working with unfamiliar magic. If something happened, the poor spell-caster had no baseline to act as reference. Making it impossible to know if you should panic or not worry about your pants requiring a long soak before laundry day.

Just like the small flickering figure, the three figures ahead vanished from sight after performing some actions. It gave Filthy Henry just enough time to observe them without revealing himself. Looking around the base of the tree, the fairy detective found a small stone. He picked it up and waited for the figures to reappear. It was hard to gauge the passage of time, but roughly a minute went by before they flickered into being once more. He took aim and tossed the rock directly at the tallest of the figures. It went straight through but did not distract any of them. They each played out the same sequence as before and vanished again.

This allowed Filthy Henry to relax. If the beings were unaware of a stone thrown at them, it was safe to assume they would pay him no attention as well. At his foot, the fairy detective noticed the stone had reappeared in the same place as before.

Overhead the number of black tiles had increased slightly. Some of them appeared to be tinged with a golden light along the edge. Filthy Henry had no idea what it meant, but it was a change in what passed for normal around here. That could only mean it was not good, considering this place was the fragmented memories of a malicious spirit.

He walked over to the spot where the three figures appeared and took two steps back. The last thing he wanted was for them to appear with him smack bang in the middle. As Filthy Henry stood there, counting down the seconds before the show started, the sense that he had been in this place before was growing. Not in the memory, because that was obviously a crazy thought, but the location.

Wherever it was out in the real world, he had definitely been there.

"What is it about here...?" Filthy Henry said, just as the three figures appeared.

From the way each of them stood it was clear they were holding a meeting, having a conversation about something. Since it was happening so far into a forest, away from the eyes of others, the fairy detective guessed it was a meeting nobody else was meant to know about. The smallest of the flickering figures

445

stood with its hands on its hips, looking up at the other two. It stood beside a squat, slightly tubby, flickering figure. For a brief second, Filthy Henry thought he could see some details on the squat figure, as if the memory was sharpening before him.

The last flickering figure was standing beside Filthy Henry and nearly matched him in height. It was a little leaner than he was, but broader in the shoulders. As what passed for sunlight broke through the canopy of the forest, some details briefly passed across the third flicker.

"I'm going to have to name you three," the fairy detective said. "Otherwise referring to you each as a flickering figure will make me go crazy. More crazy, maybe. Crazier. Sure, I'm talking to myself. That's a fairly good indication the crazy has started to creep in."

He decided to call the small one Tiny, the squat one Tubs and the remaining one Stringbean. It was a safe bet none of them would mind that the names were not actual names, considering none of them knew he was even there.

The scene reset and Filthy Henry walked around so that when the players returned he would be standing behind Tubs. As they appeared, he leaned over Tubs' shoulder and tried to make out what was happening in the little silent play.

Stringbean seemed to be leading the discussion, waving their arms around in the air as if the topic of conversation was extremely important. Once or twice they pounded their right fist into their left open hand, hammering home whatever point was being made. Tubs nodded along, then raised an arm and pointed it directly at Stringbean's chest.

They vanished again. Filthy Henry moved so that he was standing by Tiny, squatting down beside it.

Tiny did not seem to add anything to the scene. While Tubs and Stringbean had their conversation, complete with gesticulating, Tiny just nodded along. Only once did the small arm come away from the right hip, to point up at Tubs.

So, whatever Tubs and Stringbean were discussing, Tiny obviously felt like it needed to add something. Clarification? Reinforcement, maybe? Tubs and Tiny were definitely on the same side of the conversation. Another ray of sunlight shone through the trees, Filthy Henry noticing for the first time that even it was on a repeating pattern. Where it hit Tiny some details formed over the flickering body. Filthy Henry could just about make out the skin on the creature's arm.

Skin that looked strangely like tatty wool or some sort of material that belonged on a doll. An ancient and old doll, back before plastic and mass production had swooped in.

The scene reset once more.

Filthy Henry stood up and moved to stand behind Stringbean.

Each of the flickering actors took to the stage and repeated the performance without missing a beat. From this angle it definitely looked like Stringbean was either demanding something from the pair, or possibly just relaying information with a dramatic flair for the sake of it. For the first time since waking up in this memory fragment, Filthy Henry found himself wishing for a little sound to go along with the amateur theatrics. At least then it might have been easier to figure out what exactly was going on.

Stringbean finished with his fist slam and all three vanished again.

"If this is going to be some sort of a 'solve the riddle in order to leave' deal I'm going to be here forever," Filthy Henry said.

He had gotten nothing new from the performance. Judging from how all three stood, it at least appeared like they knew each other or had planned to be here. It was not a surprise meeting. But that did not tell the fairy detective anything of worth. Looking down at the spot of grass the three figures stood on, Filthy Henry tried to figure out if there was some significance to the area. At

447

least then the unwavering sensation of having been amongst these trees before would have made a little sense. A magical focal point would mess with any fairy's mind, half-breed or not.

While looking at the grass Filthy Henry had a sudden, possibly crazy, idea.

When he had been viewing Milton's memories it had been from the point of view of the doctor. Seeing the world through Fluid's eyes and no more than that. After somehow managing to step out from the doctor's head things had taken on a more generic appearance. Maybe repeating the act, but in reverse, would yield some results.

The fairy detective carefully stepped forward, placing his feet roughly where Stringbean's would appear. Either this crazy idea would work or not, but at least picking a similar sized body had to help in some way.

To say the experience was unnerving would have been an understatement. As the figures returned, Stringbean materialised around the fairy detective. Filthy Henry watched as bands of black and white light formed around his legs, slowly working up towards his head. It felt like snow was being poured over his body, a wet coldness seeping into his bones in a very unpleasant manner. Once his neck grew cold the fairy detective prepared himself.

His mind was flooded with emotions and thoughts coming from an outside source. It was easy to tell they were not his own because of the overpowering desire for revenge. A revenge in response to some sort of public humiliation. Filthy Henry focused on the rush of information coming from Stringbean, trying to store it away somewhere for analysis later. Compartmentalise it for future examination. Right now he felt any interaction with the emotions would be too much. They were so raw, filled with a pure fiery hatred, that whoever Stringbean was he certainly felt aggrieved.

"I.....make.......deal," Stringbean said, his voice skipping.

Filthy Henry paid attention to what Stringbean said and saw, feeling sure that some clue would just present itself to him.

Tubs and Tiny remained flickering shapes in front of Stringbean, going through the same motions as before. Whatever they said, if they even spoke, was not part of the possession experience. Hardly an ideal situation to be in, but Filthy Henry was pretty sure nothing about his current predicament was ideal.

".......collect.......random.......tenth...least," Stringbean said in his stuttering voice.

Listening was not exactly proving useful. The entire scene was as broken as the rest of the memory and Filthy Henry could feel the cold starting to fade, which presumably meant the flickering figures were about to disappear once more. More wasted time in the memory of a malevolent spirit, with nothing to show for it.

Then it happened.

Just as before, the branches above the trio swayed on unfelt winds and allowed sunlight to shine down from above. It passed over Tubs and, like it had with Tiny three iterations back, caused some of her details to appear in place of the flickering lines. Not something useful like her entire face, or even half her face, because that would have made Filthy Henry's job easy. But what did appear, for the briefest of moments, was enough to point the fairy detective in the right direction.

A smile filled with hideous, black, rotten teeth.

All three figures vanished, leaving the fairy detective alone once again. He could feel the grin on his face.

"I'm ready to come back now!" Filthy Henry shouted up into the trees. "I know who the bad guy is!"

#

"You're sure he is okay?"

"I'm certain, relax. I can...feel him, if we can use that term, in here. Somewhere."

"I can't relax! As annoying as he is, Filthy Henry just happens to be one of my closest friends these days."

"You need to invest in other friends."

"Don't you think I know that?!"

The only thing worse than being told you needed a better friend, Shelly figured, was being told you needed a better friend by the person you counted as the friend who needed bettering. Of course, there was the technicality that currently it was only her bad friend's body. A shiny, much nicer, personality was behind the wheel. Shelly wondered if Elivin could do some magic to merge Filthy Henry with Quinn and keep the best of both men. All the smarts of the fairy detective with the actual humanity of Quinn.

If nothing else, it might help raise the fairy detective's standing in the country. Filthy Henry seemed to take it as a personal challenge to annoy the maximum number of people, human or fairy, in a single day.

Shelly guessed that such a request might be in direct violation of The Rules. But then Rules were meant to be broken. At least that was how the saying went.

Elivin had spent the last twenty minutes trying to come up with a spell that would allow them to bring Filthy Henry back. She tried summoning spells, séance magic and at one point resorted to just shouting into the fairy detective's ear. Shelly felt like the bounty hunter should have had a few more spells up her sleeve, given that she was a leprechaun, but did not press the matter. Whatever Elivin was doing was above and beyond any magic Shelly could do.

Nothing seemed to work though. Quinn remained in control, with Filthy Henry being homo defuit.

Dru the Druid had pulled some books out of his collection at the back of basement and was searching through them, coming across nothing of use.

Time was running out, Shelly could feel it. If Milton was not the person they were looking for then they had to get back out onto the streets. To find the real culprit before it was too late. But to do that Filthy Henry needed to be back in his body, more importantly in the driver seat.

As Elivin began to cast another spell, Shelly started to think about how she could help.

Quinn was watching her.

"You're planning something," he said.

"You can't know that," Shelly replied. "You barely know me."

"I know what he does...sort of," Quinn said.

"What do you mean by 'sort of'?"

In place of shrugging his shoulders, Quinn rolled his eyes before returning his gaze to Shelly.

"Filthy Henry has managed to block of parts of his memory," he said. "Not sure how, to be honest. I guess that was the first thing he managed to hide from me. But, before that, I had access to bits. So, I know what your face looks like when you're planning something."

Shelly smiled.

"Well you solved your first case then," she said. "Elivin."

The leprechaun looked over at her, while continuing to make intricate patterns in the air around Filthy Henry's head. As her fingers moved they left trials of light swirling around his head.

"I need you to make another pair of those coins," Shelly said.

#

It had been an interesting experience the first time, being hauled along for the trip into Milton's mind. On the receiving end, having another mind enter your head, was something else entirely. Quinn had expected there to be a moment were it felt like his Third Eye was being pried open, but that never happened. Elivin placed the newly made coin on his forehead and suddenly he could see things with a clarity not present before. Once Shelly's coin was put in place, their Third Eyes lining up, everything became very bright.

They were standing in an empty space. Similar to how Milton's mind had presented itself, yet different at the same time.

Shelly's mental form was completely purple, while Quinn had once again taken on the shades of red from before. They stood beside each other, Shelly looking around the whiteness with a confused look on her face.

"Em," she said. "What the hell is this?"

Quinn frowned.

"The inside of our head," he answered. "Mine and Filthy Henry's. Maybe just Filthy Henry's, I'm not entirely sure on the ownership aspect of things. What were you expecting? Some sort of rolling landscape and beautiful structures?"

She nodded.

"Yeah, or, you know, something more than just white. Why are we not watching a bunch of memories play out like some old, grainy, films? Where's the ground?" Shelly asked.

He felt a guilty pleasure growing inside. At any minute now Shelly was going to repeat the same mistake made by Filthy Henry and start tumbling through the mental-air. When Shelly knelt down and placed her hand beside her foot, carefully going on past the sole of her shoe, Quinn was disappointed.

"You're doing better than Filthy Henry did," he said. "Last time he fell for a while until he managed to grasp the concept of 'ground'."

Shelly looked up at him, slowly standing back up.

"Yeah, well I am better at not taking things for granted," she said. "But seriously, this is disappointing. Is this what Fluid's head-space looked like?"

Quinn looked around at the blank canvas of Filthy Henry's mind and nodded his head.

"Mind-scape, we called it a mind-scape. Yeah, it was," he said. "Which is sorta weird. I figured that was because he was a doctor and kept his mind in order. Filthy Henry isn't exactly known for being the cleanest of people."

"You've seen his apartment," Shelly said, tapping her foot on the nothingness they stood upon.

"Not in the flesh, but I know what you mean."

Quinn turned around, not entirely sure what he expected to see. Something a bit more...detailed. Maybe that was the right term? At least a few mental trappings. A projection of the office, perhaps a representation of the apartment. Even a collection of oddly shaped seats that had at one time or another caught the fairy detective's attention.

This total lack of anything spoke of a man with no imagination. Quinn had spent a lot of his existence, since learning he had no actual body, wondering what caused his creation. It was disconcerting to think that Filthy Henry's mind seemed to have little to do with it.

Unless, as a result of being locked out of the fairy detective's memories, this was exactly the mind-scape he should have expected to see.

Even worse, Quinn had no idea where they should go from here. He had never been in this place before. The trip with Filthy Henry into Milton's mind had been an experience, one heavily

453

relying on luck. Milton had mentally appeared right when they needed him to, in order to forward the plot along. That stroke of luck was apparently not going to happen this time.

Shelly tapped him on his left shoulder.

"This is sort of your area of expertise," she said. "What do we do now?"

Shrugging felt like the worst response to that question, but it was the only one he had. So, Quinn shrugged his shoulders and took two steps back to stand beside her.

"I have no...hey! What's that?"

Out in the middle of the whiteness, if such a destination existed considering the blank canvas spread out infinitely in all directions, an object had appeared. It looked like some sort of modern art sculpture, a random bit of red plastic twisted and contorted into a strange shape. A shape that had no basis in reality or usefulness. Something that most definitely did not look like the struggles of the modern woman in a male dominated world, no matter what the young, male, hipster, artist tried to tell you. As they watched it, the red object slowly began to revolve in the air like it was on an invisible turn table.

Shelly pointed towards it.

"I guess we go take a look," she said.

Quinn nodded.

Walking to the object was interesting. It was hard to tell if they were moving through the whiteness or if the object came towards them. The distance between definitely decreased, but without any other landmarks to work from movement was just an illusion. A state of mind, even.

After an indeterminate amount of time they stood in front of the revolving red object.

Up close the mental modern art installation held more details.

Hexagon shaped tiles covered its surface, red in colour but with a few of them black. Some sections were missing tiles completely. It was not just spinning around but also twirling in the air, reminding Quinn of an animation Filthy Henry had once seen about a DNA strand. Now that they were standing beside the object it was easier to take a guess at the size of the thing, even though the object apparently had other ideas. On one rotation entire sections of it moved around, sliding down the length of the thing before merging with a different part completely. Even still, Quinn figured it was four foot squared in size. At least if you ignored sections jumbling around, intent on making any size calculations hard.

Shelly leaned in closer to the red thing and watched it rotating.

"What the hell is this?"

Looking at it, Quinn could feel an energy coming from the object. No, that was not the right word. More like a tug or pull. As if he was a magnet of the Northern kind and this was a Southern variety magnet. Without saying a word to Shelly, he reached out with his left hand and touch the red object. The tiles beneath continued to move along its surface, like pages flipping in the wind. When one of the sections with missing tiles came by Quinn did the only dumb thing he could think of.

He stuck his head into the hole.

#

In days long since past, prisoners would mark off on the wall how much time they spent in a cell. Chalk or charcoal lines were drawn, each stroke representing a day. It was a penal tradition as old as the concept of being in jail itself. Something that was passed from prisoner to prisoner through a strange sort of osmosis.

Either that or the guards figured giving prisoners a way to count out their term would keep them occupied for a few minutes each day, helping maintain some peace.

Whatever the reason, it was a good way to track how long you were confined to a location you would rather not be in. The only problem was it required the location to not reset every couple of minutes. Counting with markers was hard if the marker went back to the starting position each time.

Filthy Henry lay on his back and watched the black tiles travelling across the red sky.

He had observed the little flickering figures perform about twenty times, gleaned as much information as was possible from them, and then left the wooded area. While everything else in the memory fragment reset every couple of minutes, Filthy Henry was left to his own devices. Presumably because he was not an original part of the memory. Whatever the reason, it was a relief to be left alone. Even if only to stare up at the sky while trying to figure out how to escape.

Not having magic was definitely hampering any plans. Even if he had known what magic was required to get out of the fragment. The fairy detective was so far off the map at this point he felt like taking up cartography as a new hobby. Explore the unknown and be the first person to do it.

If things had remained in place for longer than a few minutes he would have tried building something. Breaking a few branches off the trees and lashing them together.

But that would have meant knowing where the exit was.

From his spot on the ground, Filthy Henry had no idea where the boundaries of the memory fragment were. Either it stretched on forever in every direction or stopped at what was visible.

All of this made plan forming extremely difficult. The more data a person lacked, the more variables they required to plan for. Factoring in not only the known unknowns but also the unknown unknowns.

"Dagda be damned," Filthy Henry swore, staring at the tile about to pass before the 'sun'.

Right as the 'sun' was obscured by the hexagon shaped floater it did something none of them had done before. It wobbled. Like a leaf floating on the surface of a pond, disturbed from below. Filthy Henry frowned and stared at it, pursing his lips together.

Change was good, assuming you knew what the change was about or its cause.

The tile ceased trekking across the sky, blocking out the 'sun' completely, and wobbled a couple more times. Something sparkled on its black surface, like a tiny star, before shooting down towards the ground. It landed a few feet from Filthy Henry

He got up and ran over to the crash site.

"What the hell are you doing here?"

"I'm...looking for you," Quinn said.

"How'd you even get in?"

Quinn looked at his body, or rather what constituted his body at that moment, and stared up at the fairy detective.

"I'm not sure I got in properly."

The mental construct's head was on the ground, upside down. His neck stretched back up into the sky, disappearing into the wobbling tile.

"You got in, that's the main thing," Filthy Henry said, following Quinn's elongated neck upwards. "Can you move your body back out there?"

Quinn went silent, his face full of concentration, then quickly nodded his upside-down head.

"Yup," he said. "I reckon I can even bring my head back."

"Do that," Filthy Henry said. "Right now. As fast as human-shaped-split-personality possible."

"Alright."

Quinn's head started to travel up, his neck drawing back like a thick fishing line. Right as his head was level with the fairy detective's, Filthy Henry jumped up and wrapped his arms around Quinn's head. He held on tightly, gripping the mental construct's chin.

"Here, get off!" Quinn said as they were pulled up into the sky.

"Shut your moaning and get your head out of this ass of a memory," Filthy Henry said, looking up as the tile above grew bigger.

As his neck wound up, Quinn's face was a mask of strained effort.

"You're heavier than you look," he said.

"We weigh the same you unwanted thought process," the fairy detective said. "Are we there yet?"

Before Quinn could answer, they slammed into the tile. The force caused Filthy Henry to let go of Quinn's head, but something prevented him from falling back to the memory of the ground. An energy from the tile gripped his body, pulling him into it. Quinn's head was already gone, having entered the black tile and disappeared.

As he went into the darkness, Filthy Henry felt his body contort. First it was stretched, then squeezed, then flattened. His passage through the tile lasted forever and a second simultaneously. He lost control of everything, other than a sense which told him what was happening to his body. Then, up ahead, a tiny pin prick of white light appeared. Whatever force was moving Filthy Henry through the tile altered course, pushing him directly towards the light.

His nose touched it first, or at least the part of his face usually home to his nose. With all the stretching and flattening it was hard to be sure what parts were still in the right place. From behind there came a rushing sensation as the fairy detective's body was gathered up and squeezed through the pin prick. Filthy Henry had a fleeting moment were he could relate to how sausages were made, then there was a blur and the fairy detective was dumped out.

He landed face first on the ground, groaned and, with great effort, rolled over onto his back.

Shelly and Quinn were looking down at him.

"Hey," Filthy Henry said to them both. "What the hell are you doing in my brain?"

# Chapter Twenty-Two

"I've been doing the maths," Blacksmile said. "You've screwed this up. Big time!"

Linda took great umbrage at this. For centuries she, or rather 'he' since this was the first gender transfer performed, had gone around collecting the memories and stories from the people of Ireland. Entire family trees had been visited multiple times over the years, to ensure the best stories were collected. Strangely, if a family tree was visited more than once the collected power seemed to have a subtle difference to it. As if the family story itself was being enhanced by having earlier victims. This made sense, in a way. People would talk about how dear old Uncle Jim lost his marbles and went walking down the road with no trousers on. If the great-nephew of Uncle Jim was also targeted for collection then the historical story would be stronger.

Compound stories.

The deal they had struck, Linda and Blacksmile, all those years ago was that he, or now she, could work on her List and exact a full and complete vengeance. So long as the required amount of power was collected in time, no supervision would be required. That had meant some random people, ones in no way related to The List, getting collected. But such was life. You could not write a great story without having a few throw-away characters.

There was a similar saying involving omelets and eggs, but cooking had never been a thing that interested her.

While it was true that the act of body jumping consumed some of the collected power, it in no way could have justified such a slanderous statement from Blacksmile. Thankfully the rag doll had discovered that lying in the pool of red wine somehow kept her intoxicated. She had been silent for over five hours now, otherwise her two cents on the topic would certainly be given.

"I'm telling you, we're fine," Linda said. "I will just take one or two people along the way before collecting Tracey's stories. No problem."

Linda's sponsor tapped on the sheet of paper in front of her. She was seated at the kitchen table with a cup of black, cold, tea beside her.

"I'm telling you, you've messed up. Here, hold this," Blacksmile said.

With a flick of the wrist she tossed a small piece of red stone towards Linda. The nurse caught it with her left hand and held it up in front of her face. It was a piece of marble, smooth on all sides.

"And?" Linda asked.

"Just give it a minute," Blacksmile said. "There."

From within the stone a pale light started to shine, beginning at the bottom and slowly working up to the top. The piece of marble was roughly the size of a two Euro coin. After a little under ten seconds it started glowing. Except, not entirely. The top quarter of the stone was still just marble, the rest of it pulsing with a soft light from within.

"Em...," Linda said, not entirely sure what the glowing piece of marble meant.

"It's a measure of how much power you have inside your fragile mortal form right now," Blacksmile said, picking up the cup of cold tea. She took a sip and, disgustingly, seemed to enjoy it. "You have either been lying about the numbers or not been feeding off the right sort of people."

"I was collecting from the fairy detective almost daily," Linda said, throwing the stone towards her sponsor.

It landed on the table, sliding across the surface of the wood before stopping beside the sheet of paper.

"I told you I didn't think that was a good idea. Now I'm sure of it. Whatever personality you were taking memories from while Filthy Henry was in the hospital was not rich in story or history. In fact, he wasn't rich in anything. Your numbers are way off and we have a little under a day before the ritual. We'll never make up the difference between now and then."

Linda walked over to the kitchenette area and started rummaging around the cupboards for some coffee. Even the instant muck would suffice for now.

This was bad, not horrific but far from ideal. She, or rather he, had always prided himself on completing a task once set. You did not get to walk out of the Bard's College and travel the land because you had a pretty face and a lovely sounding voice. You needed to meet requirements, achieve goals. Never fail. Even though those days were long gone, the thoughts of failing a task now still struck a chord deep within. It would be a shame to live longer than any man before, in order to complete an intricate a plan as they had been working on, only to fail at the last hurdle.

Centuries of work effectively wasted as Blacksmile had assured Linda that the time for the ritual came around once every fifteen hundred years or so. They could always try again, she supposed. Given that longevity was something Blacksmile seemed to have no issues with. How long the rag doll could survive was another thing, but her interests in this entire affair had revolved around revenge against Filthy Henry. There was history there, between the fairy detective and the animated freak. A story that Linda would love to not only hear but consume as well.

Not that she wanted to try and take a story from a talking rag doll. Who knew what messed up things would come along in the process.

Suggesting that everyone just relax and they try again in a few hundred years was going to go down about as well as a butcher showing up at a vegan birthday with burgers for everyone. The final name on The List would contain a lot of stored up historical stories but, if Blacksmile was right, not enough to balance out the difference.

Unless...

"What if I took the entire venue?"

"How do you mean?"

"The storyteller gathering. My final victim will be there, but also hundreds of other storytellers. Possibly ones with a long-standing tradition of telling tales, maybe even a few who are generational storytellers. I could take them all in one go."

"That...isn't a horrible idea," Blacksmile said, tapping her chin thoughtfully. "But how? You can only kick it off if you are asking that phrase to your intended target."

"I enter the event?"

"This late in the day? Hardly an easy task. We may have to make a free spot and hope the missing person doesn't cause too much concern."

Linda heard what her sponsor had said, but was staring at the slumbering rag doll in the wine puddle. It moved, rolling over and landing on its back with a wet splat.

"These things always have a Q&A session at them," the nurse said. "That's when I will use my power, mix magic and modern technology together. Ask the question over the speaker system. Everyone will hear me."

Both of them looked as the doll struggled to sit upright on the table. She looked from one to the other with her head tilted to the side, the only indication that she was drunk considering the lack of a real face.

"Might work," Blacksmile said, leaning back in her seat and

sipping at the cold tea. "If it works great. If not we get rid of somebody. You take everyone at the same time and we might still be able to pull this off."

The rag doll started to wring the wine out of her left arm by squeezing it with her right.

"What did I miss?"

#

Filthy Henry had asked Shelly to leave his head, but not remove the coin from his forehead, in stereotypical Filthy Henry way.

"Get the hell out of here!"

"Are you serious? I just risked my neck coming into this bucket of madness you call a skull!"

"Thanks for that. Now. Kindly get the hell out. Just don't take the coin off, I'll do that when I get back."

She had looked at Filthy Henry with unbridled rage, threw a quick smile Quinn's way, then vanished from sight. It was safe to assume that was how people departed from the mind-scape of another person. But that left Filthy Henry and Quinn alone, inside the skull of the fairy detective. Technically it was home turf for both of them, but he knew deep down that Filthy Henry would see things a little differently.

"We don't have much time," Filthy Henry said, sitting down on an invisible chair.

"You're getting good at that," Quinn said, following the fairy detective's lead.

"Well, when you're kicked out of your body twice in the same year you either pick up some tricks or deserve to not have the body," he said to Quinn. "Which brings me to you."

Quinn frowned.

465

"Me? What did I do?"

"You're here, that's what you did."

"But you've sealed off your memories from me," Quinn said. "I am just in your head. In fact, I can't even start to figure out how to get around your memory lock because you've hidden that from me too."

"Once I was sure it worked I pretty much moved everything behind it," Filthy Henry said. "Fool me once, shame on you. Fool me twice and clearly I have some sort of learning deficiency."

"Not sure that's exactly how that goes," Quinn said.

"My head," Filthy Henry replied, pointing all around them with a wave of both hands. "My incorrect saying. But, you're still here."

A nod seemed the appropriate response, so Quinn did just that.

"My grandfather used to have a saying," Filthy Henry said.

"'There's no flies on him and if there was he'd charge them rent," Quinn quoted. "I remember that much, at least."

Some memories were not just stored as signals in the brain, to be accessed by thinking about them and causing all the neurons to realign in the correct sequence. Some memories were ingrained in a person. People sometimes called this muscle memory, but that was slightly different. Muscle memory meant if you put your hands on a keyboard they automatically would type in your password with very little guidance. It was not the same as your fingers being aware of the world, nor was it the fact they acted like extensions to the brain. Rather it was the brain recalling the exact sequence of steps the fingers had to move in order to type in the correct password, whether a person was attempting to recall their password or not.

But some memories, the ones with great emotional attachments, were embedded in a person. Deep down, right in the chambers of their heart. Happy memories, sad ones, all the ones in between. Things that brought up great emotions for a person. The birth of a child always ranked highly or, in the case of Filthy Henry, conversations had with his grandfather decades ago when the man was still alive.

Quinn found he was pleasantly surprised that those memories had not been locked away from him. If nothing else they could keep him company once Filthy Henry went back to running his body.

"Exactly," the fairy detective said, pointing at Quinn and winking. "Well, buddy, you're my fly. Until we figure out what you are and how to make you not be a thing in my head, you have to earn your keep."

"It sounds like you are talking to a teenager still living at home and telling them to get a job," Quinn said.

"Oh no, I'm not that bad," Filthy Henry replied. "I'm talking to a two-month old and telling them to get a job."

"By doing what? Not exactly like I can clear out the cobwebs in here so you become super intelligent."

"Really? Damn," Filthy Henry said. "Plan B then. If I give you access to stuff you can spend your time looking over it for me. Sifting through the data and then putting it into my conscious mind so I don't have to try and work through it."

Quinn frowned.

"You want me to be your interactive subconscious?" he asked.

"More than anything in the world," the fairy detective answered, smiling. "Mainly because I have been playing catch-up on this case for too long now and we need to get it solved before the bad guys win."

It was not a totally absurd request. If you woke up and discovered your brain had created a backup personality that was able to think independently, why not put that resource to use? Particularly if there was a problem that required some deep thinking to get solved. After all, what better way to exercise the frontal lobe than with a little mental construct spotting your effort?

But Quinn knew he was a product of Filthy Henry's personality, to some degree at least. Which meant he knew to make sure this deal was not one-sided.

"Or what?" he said.

Filthy Henry smiled, that smile which Quinn knew annoyed the hell out of everyone who saw it.

"Or I spend the rest of my waking days figuring out how to expunge you completely from my mind without a trace. I'll bring in every trick I know, call in every favour I've out there. Bunty Dooley will get rid of me from her bar for life if she can wiggle her fingers and get rid of you. You wouldn't even be left as a memory in here. Gone."

As ultimatums went, Quinn had never heard anything more terrifying.

"Okay," he said. "No need to get your pants in a knot."

"These are mental representations of my real world pants, they can't get in a knot," Filthy Henry said. "But, wise move on your part. Now, what I need you to do is very simple."

He raised his right hand so that it was half-way between Quinn and himself. Out of thin air a small red cube appeared, floating an inch over his open palm. It rotated around on every axis it could, slowly.

"I need you to look into this," Filthy Henry said.

#

Shelly pulled the coin off her forehead and flung it, with every ounce of strength she had, across the room. Without intending to,

468

she hit Dru the Druid on the side of his head.

"OUCH!" he shouted, rubbing furiously at his temple. "What is it with you fairy detectives assaulting poor druids? Can you not go and get a bloody hobby doing something less violent? Like cage fighting!"

"Walk it off," Elivin said.

The druid scowled at them both and walked over to the stairs. As he climbed up them, going back to the shop, he muttered something under his breath. Shelly thought it sounded a lot like 'You walk it off.' but decided not to question him. If a grown man wanted to throw a temper tantrum and strop about like a spoilt child that was all on him. Accidentally being hit in the face with a coin did not warrant a reaction of that level and Shelly had bigger fish to be annoyed by.

Namely the silent detective seated before her.

"Did you get him back?" Elivin asked, staring up at the shop door as Dru closed it behind him.

"Yeah, I did," Shelly said. "The bloody ingrate just told me to get out of his head so he could talk with...himself."

"Himself? You mean Quinn? I don't think that is him at all," the leprechaun said, coming over to stand beside Shelly. "I think that is something...new. Could be because he's a half-breed. Maybe it is what happens if a mortal has magic in their blood for too long, they go a little crazy in the head. Split personality."

That caught Shelly's undivided attention.

"I've got magic in my blood," she said.

"Not enough to be dangerous," Elivin replied, winking.

"I keep telling her that as well," Filthy Henry said. "But nobody listens to the wise and handsome ginger one."

They both turned to look at the fairy detective as he rose from

469

the seat, moving his head back and forth so that the muscles cracked with an audible popping sound. He interlocked his fingers and stretched his arms in front of him.

"You're back?" Elivin asked him.

"I'm back," he answered, complete with the trademark smirk that Shelly wanted to punch off his face.

"Goody gum drops," Shelly said.

He reached up and took the coin off his forehead, looking over at the still slumbering figure of Dr. Milton.

"What's going on there?" Filthy Henry asked, nodding with a quick movement of his head in the doctor's direction.

"Kept him asleep," the bounty hunter said. "Didn't want to have to listen to him moaning and pleading while you were having your little sabbatical."

Filthy Henry nodded, his forehead creased slightly.

"Makes sense. How about you bring him back to the hospital and do a mind wipe on him. Let's make him think this entire thing was just some sort of stupid dream he had."

Elivin did not respond. She clicked her fingers twice and both the leprechaun and Fluid vanished from sight in a shower of multi-coloured sparks. Shelly could not help herself from reaching out and trying to swirl them around with her hand, like smoke over a fire.

"Linda is, currently, the Big Bad," Filthy Henry said as the sparks faded from sight.

"What?" Shelly asked, surprised.

"I seen it with Milton's own eyes," the fairy detective said. "Whatever was inside the doctor was not just a spirit. It was an actual thinking thing, a person, that made a deal with a fairy to gain some powers they had no right to. When Linda brought me

470

back to the hospital it made a jump into her. To throw us of the scent, I guess."

"You got all that from the red thing you were inside?"

Filthy Henry shook his head.

"No," he said. "That was some sort of memory fragment, belonging to the spirit, that I managed to pull out of Fluid's brain before we got evicted. When it was in my head I got sucked inside. It is not an experience I want to repeat any time soon."

"But you're sure that Linda is now possessed by whatever this thing is that has been stealing people's memories?"

The fairy detective held a finger up in the air and assumed the stance of an uppity college professor about to dispense knowledge.

"Not memories," he said with a haughty tone of voice. "Stories. He has been going around stealing stories."

Another shower of magical multi-coloured sparks announced Elivin's return. She looked tired, like somebody just back from an extremely long run.

"That guy is going to give up drink for life," the leprechaun said, panting slightly. "Wiped his mind, left a few bottles of whiskey around the office. Empty, of course. Then placed him at his desk, still asleep, with the door locked. The perfect cover story. What's going on here?"

"You okay?" Shelly asked her.

"Yeah," Elivin replied. "Just catching my breath."

"You'll like this," Filthy Henry said, ignoring that last remark completely. "I found out how our story stealer gained his powers."

Elivin looked at him, eyes wide with curiosity.

471

"Oh yeah?"

"Yup" the fairy detective said, nodding. "Ever hear of a haig called The Crone McGarry?"

The leprechaun bounty hunter's eyes remained wide open, but Shelly could tell that something in them changed. Curiosity had left them, replaced with anger.

"You can't be serious!"

"As a heart-attack on an airplane," Filthy Henry said.

"Wait, you mean the fairy that we dealt with in Carlingford?" Shelly asked.

"The very same. Turns out she is involved in this, or at least I think it is her. There can't be many fairies knocking around the world with teeth so black you could mistake them for chunks of coal."

Elivin said nothing, staring at the floor of the basement.

"You both have already crossed paths?" Shelly asked her.

The bounty hunter shook her head once.

"No," the leprechaun said. "But I have heard what she has done to other bounty hunters that have gone after her. She is the living embodiment of a bad fairy. When your own race kicks you out of the Fairy World, restricting you to being a witch in some gods forsaken hovel, well that just can't be viewed as a character endorsement. I've heard over the years she has been working on some pretty dark stuff as well."

"Really?" Shelly and Filthy Henry asked at the same time.

"Yeah," Elivin said. "The whole being cast out thing didn't sit so well with her. She has been using every trick in the book she can think of to get revenge. Goes around with a mascot as well, the spirit of some old queen that worked with her once. Has it animating a horrible rag doll."

472

Filthy Henry scratched underneath his left eye, his face making the usual expression which meant thinking was being done.

"That would explain the small figure I couldn't see properly," he said. "But surely she wouldn't be crazy enough to...never mind. Right, so the plan as it now stands..."

Before she could stop herself, Shelly held up her hand and motioned for him to stop talking.

"You don't get to make any plans," she said. "This is still our case, mine and Elivin's, and we are working it together. So, suggest the next move and we will decide what needs to be done."

In the Game of Life people spoke about 'little victories'. Things that helped you get through the day. Events that gave maximum reward for minimum effort. Making Filthy Henry look like a chastised school boy was definitely a little victory. He stared at Shelly for five seconds, then shrugged.

"I was going to suggest that you both go over to Linda's, pretend I am still in the hospital, and see if the thing is still inside her. Make sure it didn't jump again while we wasted time here. I am going to research how to do a little exorcism of a story stealing spirit."

Elivin looked up at Shelly.

"Not exactly the worst plan in the world," the leprechaun said. "Unless you've got something better?"

Shelly did not want to admit that Filthy Henry was right, so instead she decided to say nothing at all.

"We have an accord then," he said, grinning. "Perfect. Now, if you'll excuse me. I have some research to do."

He walked pass them both and climbed up the stairs towards the shop door.

"All the useful books are down here," Elivin said.

"He's going to steal hazelnuts from Dru's display by the cash register," Shelly said with a sigh. "But dammit if that isn't a good plan."

"It is a good one," Elivin agreed. "I might do the same and get some nuts."

"Fine, whatever," Shelly said, walking towards the stairs.

When a fairy thought Filthy Henry had done something good, you knew the world was going crazy.

#

"What do you mean I don't have a tab?"

"You don't have a tab. You've never had a tab. Nobody has a bloody tab! This is a shop not a bar or pub you can just drop in and enjoy the facilities without paying."

"You've got facilities?"

"I've got free Wi-Fi."

Filthy Henry rested his arms on the counter top, leaning over so that his nose nearly touched Dru the Druid's hooked nose.

"Dru," he said. "The free Wi-Fi is because the coffee shop next door put up the blinky box on your adjoining wall."

"It's still free Wi-Fi in this shop," the druid said, defensively. "Just as long as you are browsing the shelves along that wall."

"What happens when they change the password?"

Dru smiled and tapped his left temple in the universal gesture meant to indicate smarts were being used.

"I get a coffee every morning from them before opening the store. They hand out the password as part of the order."

Filthy Henry had to admit, it was a pretty clever scam. Right up there with how college students acquired mounds of free toilet paper from fast food restaurants. In, order some grub, eat, raid the paper dispensers and run before the security guards copped onto the con.

With Dru still staring at him, the fairy detective snatched a packet of yoghurt covered hazelnuts and tore it open before anything could be said. He tipped several out into his left hand and popped them in his mouth.

"I'm going to get Elivin to do me up a ward that keeps you out," the druid said.

"Sure," Filthy Henry replied, munching on the hazelnuts and savouring the taste. "Get the bounty hunter, who has you on her hit list, to help protect your little shop."

Dru the Druid went to reply, apparently heard what had just been said, then thought better of speaking.

Filthy Henry winked at him and turned around, heading down the aisles. He focused on his thoughts, trying to see if it was possible to communicate with Quinn.

If interaction always required a Third Eye and Shelly to be the bridge, then the little partnership was not going to go far. But how else did you talk with your imaginary friend. Back at the hospital Filthy Henry had heard Quinn's laughter, but that had just been a sound. When a question had been asked no reply came back.

The fairy detective was not sure how to take that.

Either Quinn had not been able to respond, even though his laugh had been easily heard, or the mental passenger decided not to. It was a new and strange world Filthy Henry found himself in, which was a funny thought in itself. For a man that could conjure fireballs with a flick of the wrist, a self-aware voice in the head ranked highly on the weird scale.

Quinn's task had been a simple one and Filthy Henry figured he should have completed it by now. Mainly because the mental construct should have had no problem extracting information from a memory. It was not like Quinn had anything better to be doing with his time. Hanging out with his friends would have required a body of his own. Along with friends.

Minor details in the grand scheme of things.

Right then, Filthy Henry's head exploded with intense pain. It was contained to just the left side of his brain, like a migraine appearing to ruin his day. He dropped the packet of hazelnuts to the ground and clutched his head.

There was a strange sensation as information rushed around his mind. Sorted and catalogued with blindingly fast speed. It felt like every part of his brain was being exercised at the same time. What seemed like hours passed by in a couple of seconds, the pain fading away as quickly as it appeared.

"Next time let's go a bit easier on the data dump," Filthy Henry said, still holding onto his head.

Quinn either had the good manners not to laugh at the request or made no response at all.

Filthy Henry walked over to a pile of books, the cheap knock-off magical tomes that Dru the Druid sold daily, and sat down on them.

Whatever the mental construct had done had been super effective. The fairy detective could almost visualise a small stack of newly created memories in his mind. Although they were not memories, because that would have required Filthy Henry to somehow have been involved in their creation. These were files, extracted from the memory fragment of a man who had made a deal with the crone.

He began trying to sort through the newly acquired information.

It was a painful experience. Like trying to do complex quantum mechanics while horrifically hungover and balancing on your head. Every thought brought with it a concentrated burst of pain in the brain pan. Worse, there was no order to the information that Quinn had managed to extract. Some of it appeared, at first glance, to be utterly useless. A favourite smell or fleeting image of a red-haired woman. Nothing that could be used to solve the case.

Then, through the fog of pain and recollection, Filthy Henry latched onto a useful piece of intel.

A name. One with a great amount of emotion attached to it. The sort of emotions that usually indicated bad things happening to the owner of the name would not be the worst in the world. Which could only lead the fairy detective to one, somewhat obvious, conclusion.

"The next victim," he mumbled, rubbing at his temples to try and ease the pain.

A hand was gently placed on his shoulder, another on his knee. Filthy Henry looked up, squinting to reduce the amount of light hitting his optical nerve, to see Shelly and Elivin standing before him. The leprechaun's hand on his knee, Shelly's on his shoulder.

It felt good to have people caring for his well being.

"I've got the name," he said to Shelly and the bounty hunter. "We need to protect her from Linda."

"We've got this half-breed," Elivin said. "Maybe you sit this one out."

He shook his head, regretting each and every movement as it caused more throbbing in his skull.

"You need to find this person. Tracey something. Tracey Fitzgerald. I've to go and talk with Bunty Doolay," Filthy Henry said. "There are some bits in here that I need to research and she has the best books in the business. "

From his shop counter, Dru the Druid let out an exaggerated cough.

"Don't even acknowledge him," Shelly said to Elivin. "He's just going to say that half of the teenie bopper Wiccan books he sells here are the best magic books in town."

"You know it wouldn't hurt if you lot bought something from time to time," the druid said.

"Would hurt my wallet," Filthy Henry said, smirking.

"My pride," Shelly chimed in.

"And I think I'd be the laughing stock of the Fairy World if I purchased anything out of this hovel," Elivin added in.

"You know what, get the hell out," Dru said, gesturing towards the front door. "I'm barring the lot of you!"

# Chapter Twenty-Three

The great thing about being a fairy detective who worked *for* the people, as oppose to constantly *berating* the people, was it meant you took notes. Small, little, scraps of information that you assumed would be useful later in the case. It could be anything from a single word, to the address of your client. What this meant, in the simplest way possible, was that Shelly had details Filthy Henry generally did not bother with.

Like the address of her clients, such as one Nurse Linda Faul.

When Shelly and Filthy Henry had worked on their second big case the fairy detective had shown up in her apartment. Not *at* her apartment, but *in* it. There was an important difference between those two terms. People showed up *at* a place when they came to the door and knocked on it, seeking admittance to the premises. They showed up *in* a place by teleporting inside using magic and scaring the hell out of the resident.

Particularly when said resident was butt naked in the shower.

It had been the first time Filthy Henry ever stepped foot, magically or otherwise, into her apartment. The only way he had even known its location was because of a magical coin given to him by Dagda, Chief of the Celtic Gods. Otherwise, the fairy detective would have presumably spent his days wandering the streets of Dublin city calling out 'Shelly' until he stumbled across her apartment.

All because he had never written down her address, when she had been his client, over a year before.

Whereas Shelly, being a more approachable fairy detective, had not followed in his bad footsteps. Hence being able to head directly to Linda's apartment in the city.

"How do you want to go about this?" Elivin asked, once again under an illusion spell and appearing like a little girl.

Shelly found that very considerate of the bounty hunter. She had cast the spell without being asked, all so Shelly did not look like a nutter walking around talking to her invisible friend.

They were standing at the end of Parnell Street, looking up towards Linda's apartment building. It was late enough in the day that the street lights were on, casting their yellow tinted glow on the world. In the apartment building a number of windows were lit up, like square pimples on a flat face.

Approaching this was going to require a little planning, usually something that Filthy Henry loved to get involved in. He would concoct some sort of magical madness, then go into the situation on a hope and a prayer. Shelly, however, was going to use a different tact.

"I'm going to go up, have a chat with Linda. See if Filthy Henry is right and whatever has been running around is now actually inside her," Shelly said.

"You think he is wrong?" Elivin asked.

"It wouldn't be the first time. But we don't know if it stayed in Linda. The smart money would have been to use Linda as a means of escape from Filthy Henry back at the hospital. Then change bodies again, throw us off the scent"

"That's making the assumption that we would learn it was Linda who now hosted the thing."

"True," Shelly said with a sage like nod of her head. "But this thing has been around for centuries, so obviously it knows how to survive."

"Valid point."

"So, what I think we do is this. I go in solo, check if Linda is acting differently to how she did before, then leave. Try my best not to spook her. Maybe grab some evidence if I can, a clue or something. Once we know more we regroup with Filthy and see if he has any ideas from the research. You stay out here, in case Linda bolts."

Elivin frowned at her part in the plan. It was a very serious expression to see on the face of a small child.

"You want to go in without any magical backup?"

"Not exactly," Shelly said. "But if we go in and Linda is possessed, the presence of a leprechaun might have a bad effect on how things play out. We don't know if she could see you normally. The less magic in the room, the better. Why would anyone suspect a little old mortal like me of being a threat?"

"That has to be the dumbest plan I've ever heard," Elivin said.

"Look, just watch the exit. If you see Linda sneaking away, grab her. If you see me running, set fire to whatever is following me."

Shelly did not wait for any further conversation to take place. As soon as Elivin nodded her head, Shelly started walking down the street towards Linda's apartment building. The street level door was one of the older models, no security buzzer to get inside. She pulled the handle and entered the lobby. Linda's apartment was on the second floor, so Shelly opted to be lazy and take the lift up. It any form of running, particular for dear life, was in her future the smart move was to conserve as much energy as possible.

The floor looked like any of the numerous apartment building floors in Dublin. A bland hallway with doors along either wall, very much like your standard hotel floor. Linda's apartment was the forth door down. Shelly stood outside it for a moment to compose herself.

This part was going to be very important. She had to be careful not to tip Linda off, while at the same time try and figure out if the nurse was possessed.

With a deep breath to calm herself, Shelly reached up and knocked on the door.

#

"Tomorrow can't come quick enough," Linda said, leafing through a magazine that she had found in the apartment.

What passed for literature these days was downright terrifying. The art of story-telling had apparently gone by the wayside in favour of less important skills. Any two-bit journeyman could now write a string of words together and publish them online or in some glossy magazines. It was no wonder that women in this Age constantly seemed to have concerns over how they looked. They picked up trashy collections in magazines and read articles that told them they should have issues with their appearance, with guides on how to get the "perfect" look. Regardless of whether or not the ladies had "issues" to begin with.

It was slightly infuriating. Linda wondered if her newfound gender change was influencing her outrage or not.

The entire 'laying low to avoid any further encounters with Filthy Henry' plan had seemed good at the time. But after years of being able to go and do as she pleased, being confined to the apartment was giving Linda a strange view into what jail must be like. A very wealthy jail, catering to an elite kind of prisoner.

But a jail nonetheless.

"You better hope it doesn't come round before we're ready," Blacksmile said.

"Are you still going on about that?"

"Listen up you dope," Medb said, standing over by the kitchen sink. "You're the one that put this all at risk. Couldn't have just climbed out a window and ran away like your typical male when faced with a difficult situation?"

482

Linda watched the rag doll filling up the sink with hot water, adding in some of the liquid dish washing soap so that it bubbled up. She climbed in and rested her woolly head against the metal edge of the sink. A tiny, impromptu, bath. Secretly Linda was happy to see the rag doll cleaning herself. Before, she had smelled like a moving compost heap. After sleeping in the puddle of wine the smell had taken on an even more pungent aroma. A soak in her sink might help remove the bad smell.

"We will be fine," Linda said to the rag doll. "Nobody knows where we are and we've already got a new plan. You just remember your part on the night and we will be fine."

Medb looked over at her and smiled the sock puppet smile.

"Why do you think I am freshening myself up in the sink? It isn't because I wanted to see what taking a miniature bath was like."

Linda's response was interrupted by a knock at the door. She looked over at her sponsor.

"You order food again?"

"No. Whoever it is get rid of them, I'll hide out in the bedroom. Leave the doll in the kitchen sink, just in case. Medb, play dead."

Gathering up her things, Blacksmile stood up from the table and shuffled off to bedroom, closing the door slightly behind her. Linda could see her outline behind the door, peering through the gap. The light in the bedroom went out, making everything behind the door dark.

Linda stood up from the sofa and went over to the apartment door, looking through the peep-hole. Working through the nurse's memories she was able to identify the woman as Shelly, although there was no last name to be found for some reason.

Shelly stood in the hallway, looking left and right.

The nurse opened the door, enough to see out but not so much that Shelly could get past her.

"Hey," Linda said. "How's it going?"

Shelly looked at her and smiled.

"Oh, you know," she said. "Just thought I'd drop around and give you an update on the case...our case...the case you hired me to work on."

Linda quickly reached into her current body's memories. Thankfully they were relatively new, allowing for easy retrieval. She tried really hard to keep the smile from her face. It appeared that the nurse had hired Shelly to investigate herself, or rather Milton. Particularly around the number of people showing up at the hospital with no memories. The irony of this was not lost on Linda.

She leaned against the door, going for a nonchalant pose.

"Yeah?" Linda said. "So, you went and had a chat with him? Fluid? Got the bastard to admit that he was stealing stories?"

Shelly looked at her strangely for the briefest of moments, but shook it off.

"We went and caught him at the hospital," she said. "Just after you went home actually. Then we didn't hear from you for a while. Figured I'd check in, give my client an update on her case. Everything alright?"

A lie was required now, that much was obvious. If Linda wanted to get rid of Shelly and also make sure she did not continue digging it had to be a small but believable one.

"Oh, that. Felt...sick. Been coming down with something for a while, I think. All the excitement from the last few days, along with a few double shifts. Guess it all just got to me."

"To the point that you left right as we were about to solve the case?"

484

"Medical training kicked in," Linda said, tightening her grip on the door. "Get home, into bed, have a cup of tea with honey. You know, that sort of thing."

This was not going smoothly. Shelly was either genuinely concerned for Linda or she was up to something. Erring on the side of caution was the best course of action. Wrapping up the conversation now would prevent anything accidentally being revealed.

Linda coughed, loudly.

"Still not fully over it. Took today off as well. Should be alright by tomorrow."

"Well at least let me make you my gran's patent pending garlic tea with lemon juice," Shelly said, barging forward and catching Linda off balance. "Although I'm not sure if you can still have a pending patent when you're dead. Who knows, right?"

The door was shoved open, Linda nearly getting knocked to the floor in the process, as Shelly marched in and walked around the sofa towards the kitchen. She stopped at the sight of the rag doll in the sink and looked back at Linda.

"Some sort of restoration project? Found it in a knick-knack shop and are going to sell it on the Internet?"

Linda followed her into the apartment and stood by the breakfast bar on the edge of the kitchen area. She leaned on it and tried to remain calm and in control of the situation.

"That's it, exactly," she said. "Don't ever get time to work on it. Thing is ratty and smells of cat pee."

Rather than play along, the idiotic rag doll turned quickly in the sink and splashed water all over the floor. Luckily Shelly did not notice Medb moving, otherwise they would have had a situation on their hands. One that Linda would have left up to the talking doll and her black toothed associate to clean up.

485

Shelly looked down at the pool of soapy water gathering on the kitchen tiles, then stepped over it and lifted the kettle. She popped the lid and started to fill it from the cold tap at the sink, the base of the kettle pressing down on the rag doll's head. Linda took a great pleasure in seeing its raggedy head caught between the bottom of the electric kettle and the edge of the sink.

"Have you been resting?" Shelly asked. "I hope you've been resting. You hear horror stories about the health service giving a nurse a sick day but really it is just a normal working day with less contact with patients."

"No, I've been resting. I haven't even been entertaining guests," Linda said, hoping her tone would be picked up and the hint taken.

It turned out Shelly was tone deaf, in a non-musical sense of the word. She just carried on with her tea making, putting the kettle back on its base and flicking the switch. Medb moved smoothly in the sink, turning to stare directly at Linda. If buttons could have a look of death in them then those buttons were managing it perfectly.

Linda winked at the doll. The doll stared back with even more murder-death-kill in her button eyes.

"How have you been feeling? Aside from the cold, of course," Shelly said.

"Oh, you know," the nurse said. "Just lying about the place, catching up on my reading. It's great getting some time to work through the list of books you've wanted to read."

Shelly stopped searching around the herb rack and looked at Linda.

"Yeah," she said. "I guess you're right..."

Presses were now being searched for whatever poxy ingredients Shelly needed to put in her grandmother's magic tea. Not magic tea, plain old boring human tea passed down through generations. Tea that seemed to be taking longer than necessary to make as far as Linda was concerned. It was almost as if Shelly knew something was up, that Linda was not the same Linda she had known a few days before.

Something had to be done. Being discovered this close to the end was not an option.

"Shelly," Linda said. "Why don't you tell me your..."

The bedroom door slammed shut. Linda and Shelly both turned around to look at it.

"Oh," Shelly said. "I'm sorry. You've got company?"

"Cat," Linda replied, quickly. "Just going to check it, Lauren, the cat, didn't hurt itself. "

"Lauren...nice name for a cat. Go check, I will keep making this tea. You've got lemon juice...that should do. Oh a writing event, I keep meaning to go to ones of these..."

Linda ignored her and walked to the bedroom, opening the door slowly and stepping in. The darkness was not absolute once inside the room, light from the street casting an orange glow over everything. Including the furious expression on her sponsor's face.

"Lauren? Really. The best fake name for your imaginary cat you could come up with was my actual name?"

"Lauren is your actual name? Did I know that?"

"I told it to you centuries ago! I swear to Dagda, you mortals are infuriating to work with," Lauren hissed at her.

"Ah," Linda said, grimacing at her stupidity. "Yeah, didn't think about that. But Lauren isn't that rare a name. It isn't like she will run back to Filthy Henry with it."

"You better hope not. Although if you went and emptied her out how would she have gone back to the half-breed? What were you thinking?"

"If we had her stories then it would keep Filthy Henry busy trying to figure out where she was."

"Not how he works," Lauren whispered. "He uses attacks on her as a strange fuel to drive him. His one and only friend, if you were to believe it. If we'd harmed her in any way he would not have rested until we were all destroyed."

"While she wandered around the streets of Dublin with no memories?"

Lauren nodded.

"He's got a strange sense of honour. It's what makes him the most dangerous. He once burnt a vampire into nothing, all because the blood-sucker killed Shelly. Can you imagine that sort of reaction over something so small? Now just get back out there, don't take her stories, and get her to leave before she figures out Linda isn't in the driving seat any more."

"Got to run, will call you later!" Shelly shouted from the main room. "Something cropped up....about the case."

There was a loud splash, followed by the sound of wet socks being slapped against tiles. Linda opened the bedroom door and looked back out into the apartment. The rag doll, dripping water with every move she made, was running towards them.

"She left," Medb said, from the half-way point of the floor. "Just now."

Linda stepped out of the bedroom and looked around the corner, down the small hallway, to see the front door ajar. Of Shelly, there was no sign.

"Did she say or do anything?" Linda asked the rag doll.

"Finished making that gods awful sounding tea, then just left. Not a lot I could see while pretending to not be able to move."

Linda looked around the apartment to see if anything was missing. Everything seemed to be as it had been.

"Wonder what that was about?"

Lauren quickly came out of the bedroom.

"We've a leprechaun watching the apartment, seen her out the bedroom window. They're onto us. We need to move now, before they try something."

#

Filthy Henry's head was splitting.

Headaches were something he had had before, even the occasional migraine. It more or less was part of being alive. Any person that claimed to go through their entire life without ever having a headache were liars, he figured. Migraines were the worst, by a long shot. Usually they followed some seriously heavy bouts of spell casting and magic use. As the fairy detective pushed his body to the limits a migraine would appear, like a biological warning that things were getting risky.

But this was an entirely new sort of head splitting event.

All the information Quinn had uncovered was now sitting just under the surface of Filthy Henry's thoughts, the source of his headache. His brain was processing it all as best it could, but this was still information that had been inserted from an outside source.

Technically an inside source, Filthy Henry supposed.

Bunty Doolay tapping her nails on the bar counter did nothing to help matters either.

"You couldn't do a healing spell before playing your drum solo?" Filthy Henry asked her.

The *Sidhé* smiled.

489

"Nope," she said. "You came to me, asking for my books. I get to enjoy your suffering while you're here."

"You're a strange sort of friend," the fairy detective said.

"Thought you didn't have friends?"

Filthy Henry pressed against his left temple and groaned. Life was unfair, particularly when you had people in it that both helped and hindered you in equal measure. Nobody needed a paradoxical support network like that.

"I'm just here for the solitude, the book and the sparkling personality. Plus, silence. That bit is very important. The silence is required over everything else."

Bunty Doolay reached over and slowly started to pull the book away from Filthy Henry.

"Guess you won't be needing my history book," she said. "Since silence is required over everything else."

"Whoa! Whoa! Whoa!" the fairy detective said, wincing as the sound of his own voice caused more pain in his head. He clawed at the bottom of the book and dragged it away from her.

"You are one sorry excuse these days," Bunty said, smiling as she released the book. "What are you looking for anyway?"

"I'm trying to figure out what was done to this guy, see how he has been pulling stories out of people," Filthy Henry said, relieved that she had not been serious about taking the book away.

As a general rule, in fact one of The Rules, the fairy folk rarely let humans read their books. Even using the term 'rarely' was being kind to how infrequently mortals laid eyes on an actual fairy tome. Sure, there were magic shops and two-bit druids dotted around the country purporting to sell such tomes, but these were just knock-offs. Not even decent knock-offs, as the authors of such tomes were typically some mystic wannabe sitting in a

490

cave, pretending to commune with nature. Really all they were communing with was a big bank balance as they kept up a convincing charade.

This made researching things slightly tricky. You either had to use the books readily available to a human, the old fairy tales, and sift through the crud until you found a kernel of truth. During a particularly boring and basically case free summer, Filthy Henry spent hours combing through each and every Celtic fairy tale he could lay his hands on. He had compiled a small reference book, his very own Magnus Opus, detailing the true, common, elements found in most of these tales. Those that he had not been able to verify with absolute certainty were whittled down to a 'best guess' category. But that was only useful if the case involved creatures or stories that the fairy detective had come up against before.

An ageless bad guy without form, capable of jumping from person to person. That sort of thing required better reference resources than something cobbled together during a lazy season. It needed books from the Fairy World itself. Which meant having a friend, who was also a fairy, give you access to such a book.

If that combination of things could not happen then a fairy who at least tolerated you would do.

Bunty Doolay had an extensive library hidden away in her bar. It was actually a thing of legendary status. Nobody had ever seen the inside of it. Rumour had it the library moved location each night so that it never stayed in the same place twice. The rumours even suggested that the library was not even in the same world from one day to the next. In order to access it you needed Bunty's reference book, a sort of magical search engine. Except instead of searching the Internet for the latest and greatest place to watch movies in a totally illegal manner, it searched through her books.

"There is no mention of her anywhere," Filthy Henry said, rubbing his eyes.

"Who?"

"The Crone McGarry," he said.

Bunty Doolay straightened up and folded her arms before her.

"You told me that Cathal obliterated her, with that beam of raw magical energy. Wiped out everything it hit and then some."

"It did," he said. "All I found afterwards was her cauldron and shoes. Nothing else. But I know she is involved in this whole thing. I have the memories to prove it. Sorta."

"How can you be sure she survived Carlingford?" Bunty Doolay asked. "Think about it. You are working off the memories of the bad guy. They could be from before she struck her deal with Medb. You're possibly chasing shadows."

Bunty Doolay had a point. The Crone McGarry, first name Lauren, had been a haig working with a mortal queen from Celtic Ireland called Medb. Together the pair had tried to capture a powerful, magical, bull in the present day in order to reign over Ireland like a pair of demented witch-goddesses. Only forFilthy Henry's timely interference, coupled with some sheer dumb luck, had a magical disaster been diverted.

Afterwards there had been no sign of Lauren and Medb.

The memory fragment from Milton's mind, however, had clearly shown the haig interacting with the memory thief. It seemed that Lauren made a habit of breaking The Rules when it suited her needs. Nothing about the scene locked down the 'when' of it happening, but Filthy Henry knew that it had taken place after the events at Carlingford. It was why the forest had looked so familiar, he had been in it before.

Even still, there was something about the memory that felt like it had taken place centuries ago.

"Time travel makes my brain hurt," the fairy detective said, lowering his head and resting it on the bar counter.

"It's why nobody tries to do it, even with magic," Bunty Doolay said. "I've heard that the gods have managed it on occasion, but only to observe. When they've gone back to change things it gets all kinds of messy."

Something flickered in Filthy Henry's pained brain; an idea.

"What if that's why there are no references to her for ages?" he said.

"I don't follow."

"So, Lauren gets kicked out of The Veil for doing something pretty heinous. Bad enough that her own people force her to look like a disgusting witch and be seen by mortals everywhere. She goes to ground for a bit, resurfacing out of necessity to survive and earn a living as a witch that mortals can deal with. A chance encounter puts her in connection with Medb and they form a little plan to steal the bull, by sending the queen of madness through time until she arrives in the present day."

"I feel like you're doing a summary for people who hadn't read a book series chronologically."

Filthy Henry shrugged.

"I think better out loud. Anyway, in order for that spell to work Lauren will have to be sure she is around all those centuries. She goes to ground again, doing nothing that causes her to interact with the Fairy World and risk the plan. Everything happens as it did and the pair of them get destroyed by Cathal's raw magical energy beam from the hurley stick. Except the spell used to bring Medb forward in time is still in play. It recalls her to the past, the whole point being she was meant to be all powerful in modern times. Lauren, attached to the spell, is dragged back with her."

It was hard to tell, given that Bunty Doolay's eyes lacked pupils and were just one solid shade of blue, but the *Sidhé's* eyes spun around slightly.

493

"I'm sort of following you."

"Great, because I might need you explain this back to me. This headache is excruciating. Anyway, Medb and Lauren are sent back in time. The problem is now there are two Lauren's. The one that is waiting for time to go by and the one who has been dragged back with the queen. Modern-Version-Lauren doesn't want to risk a paradox by revealing herself and jeopardising the bull plan so herself and Medb lay low. Come up with a new plan, one that they can let fester and grow, nurture along the way, until the moment in time when they are past what happened last year in Carlingford."

"You're saying, I think," Bunty said, tapping thoughtfully on her perfect chin. "That Lauren McGarry survived Carlingford, went back in time, and came up with a revenge plan that would take longer to implement than her original plan? All because you can't find any mention of her in the books?"

When it was said back, using those words and a tone of utter disbelief, Filthy Henry had to admit it sounded beyond far-fetched. It was outright ludicrous with extra crazy flakes thrown on top for good measure. Madmen would look upon such a thought process and balk at it.

"You're damn right that's what I am saying," the fairy detective said, with added confidence for good measure.

"You do realise how crazy that sounds, right?"

Filthy Henry shrugged his shoulders.

"No crazier than a human running around seeing fairy folk and casting fireballs."

He tilted back on his bar stool, balancing with practised ease on the two rear legs, and started to think.

There was an angle in all this that Filthy Henry was simply not seeing. That annoyed him. Working cases was part and parcel of being a detective. You were hired to solve something using a

494

skill-set other folk did not have. But that meant you should be able to see things quicker. Figure problems out faster and get the solution before anybody else.

A fact that would be made infinitely easier if his brain had not been currently trying to split open his skull and go for a stroll.

The best way to approach this case was to break down the components. Motive was simple enough: revenge. It was not Lauren's revenge though, that could have been done in a different way entirely. Fairy folk had extremely long-life spans. She could have easily waited for Filthy Henry to be old and decrepit, then smother him with a pillow when he was too weak to fight back. Getting a mortal involved meant this was more complicated than simple revenge.

Revenge was still a strong motive, however. One that the story stealing entity obviously was partaking in as well. Just because it had teamed up with the crone meant nothing. They were just allies of circumstance.

Not it, he. Filthy Henry had that information from what Quinn had gathered for him. The entity had been a man once, a simple mortal. He had struck a deal with Lauren and that was where his power came from. Power to steal the stories that people gathered up during the course of their lives.

Random people, though? That did not make much sense.

"The victims," he said, out loud.

"Huh?" Bunty Doolay asked.

Rocking forward so that all four legs of the stool were back on the floor, Filthy Henry tapped the book on the bar counter.

"Can this thing do family trees?"

"What? Like who gave birth to whom?"

He nodded.

"I guess so, why?" Bunty said. "What fairy are you looking to find?"

"Not fairy," Filthy Henry said, holding a finger up in the air. "I'm looking for people. If I get you the list of people that have had their stories stolen can we work back through their family trees? That's the connection, it has to be. You don't pick victims at random. You pick them based on something. Wronged lovers. Blue eyes. People that pick their nose on the train and rub it into the cushions. He's been taking stories for centuries but there has to be a reason, a method behind it. Otherwise he is just bonkers and it was all random. Can't be dealing with random. It isn't fun with serial killers and it is doubly not fun with mystical memory takers."

Bunty Doolay pulled the book over to her side of the bar counter and placed both hands down on it, one on either blank page.

"Get me the list and let's see what we can do."

# Chapter Twenty-Four

After leaving Linda's apartment, Shelly and Elivin headed straight for Bunty Doolay's bar as fast as they could. Elivin complained, a lot, along the way. The bounty hunter felt like they were running away from a fight. Even worse, she kept insisting that they had just given up on their opportune moment to capture Linda.

"Look," Shelly said. "We were just meant to go and get intel. Not capture them. Spooking them was bad, Filthy Henry said so. He needs to figure out how to reverse what the story stealer has done, not just stop it. Plus I needed to get out, quickly."

"Why?" the bounty hunter asked.

"There was somebody else in there with her," she said. "Hiding in the bedroom. Linda tried to tell me it was her cat, but there was no cat stuff in the apartment."

"So?"

Shelly smiled, recalling her own cat. Not only her cat, the first fairy creature she had ever met.

"Trust me on this," Shelly said. "I know what a cat lady's apartment should look like. Somebody was in there and I needed to get out before Linda tried to steal my memories. There was also a hideous doll in the kitchen sink. Can't do dolls. I got the intel and ran."

Turning onto D'Olier Street they picked up the pace a little. Around them the streets of Dublin were crowded with city folk toing and froing. Elivin opted to use The Veil and walk a step ahead of Shelly. This had the enjoyable side effect of parting the crowd like the Red Sea did for Moses. As people approached the hidden leprechaun their minds spotted something was not right, adjusting their course so that they continued on around the pair.

While it was a great way to get through the crush of the crowd, Shelly still felt like people were looking at her as she seemingly spoke to herself.

"You couldn't cast an illusion so people don't see me moving my mouth, could you?" she asked the bounty hunter.

Elivin clicked her fingers and Shelly's vision momentarily shimmered.

"Done," the leprechaun said. "Everyone will just see your head, not the movement of your lips. Although I think it stops them seeing you blink as well, so if you get funny looks for that it's all on you. Not much I can do about that. Bit on the tired side."

"Well you can't win them all I suppose," Shelly said. "I still don't get why you didn't just keep up the little girl disguise."

"Just need to go back behind The Veil for a bit," the leprechaun said, quickly. "Nothing to worry about. A breather of the magical persuasion, if you will."

Shelly patted her left jacket pocket, making sure her little bit of intel was still secure, and continued walking. It was rare that Filthy Henry sent her out on a recon mission were he actually wanted her to acquire information. Usually the fairy detective, through some misguided sense of honour, sent Shelly away to protect her. On one occasion he had done it to prevent her from finding out about her untimely death. Even though Shelly did not actually need it, she felt this recently collected bit of information would get his approval for a job well done. If nothing else, it showed that Shelly was just as capable at working cases as Filthy Henry was.

When this case was solved, the bad guy stopped from doing whatever nefarious plans they had in play, Filthy Henry would have to agree that he and Shelly work together in the future as partners. Otherwise...

"I wish Bunty would let people teleport inside her bloody bar," Elivin said, as they neared the illusion of the run-down building that hid Bunty Doolay's Bar from the mortal world.

"I suppose it makes it easier to remain neutral and protect those within if you prevent that sort of thing," Shelly said. "Although I'm pretty sure Filthy Henry teleported us inside once, when I'd been stabbed in the stomach."

Elivin looked up at her, an eyebrow arched with clear surprise.

"Really?" she said. "You sure nothing is going on between the pair of them? That's a fairly specific loophole to leave in your barrier."

"Well, Filthy did have a coin from Dagda that allowed him to teleport anywhere inside the god's Realm," Shelly said. "That might have had something to do with it."

"Maybe," Elivin said, walking up to the door and opening it. "Still, it's a bit of a tell. No?"

Shelly had thought about it once or twice since the incident occurred. The relationship between Filthy Henry and Bunty Doolay was strange, even if you ignored the fact they were completely different species. When in the same room longer than thirty minutes, Filthy Henry invariably did or said something to annoy, offend or both. He was in a perpetual state of 'being barred' from Bunty's and Shelly could only recall a handful of times when he was on the *Sidhé's* good side.

If there was anything, even a spark of something, between Bunty and Filthy Henry it had to be on epic levels of the love-hate relationship scale.

Shelly walked into the bar behind Elivin, spotting the fairy detective up at the counter. Every other stool and table in the place was empty. She had never seen it so deserted.

"You closed for general trade?"

499

"No," Bunty said, pointing towards Filthy Henry with her left thumb. "People see this guy and turn around. He is like one of those Chinese good custom cats, only in reverse."

"But he drinks in here all the time," Shelly said.

"True, but I usually have customers *before* he shows up," the *Sidhé* said. "If the place is empty and they see him, well he drives them away."

"You know I'm here trying to save the world, right?" Filthy Henry said. "The least you could do is not insult me."

Bunty Doolay smiled at him, then gestured towards two empty stools for Shelly and Elivin to sit in. Shelly pulled one out and sat down, offering Elivin a hand up.

"Oh you're so polite," the leprechaun said, climbing up the stool with Shelly's assistance.

"Find anything useful?" Filthy Henry asked as he turned back and continued reading the book on the bar counter.

"This," Shelly said, pulling out her intel and sliding it across towards the fairy detective.

He reached over and picked up the folded sheet of paper, unfolding it to make reading easier. After a couple of seconds he flipped the page over, saw the back was blank, then turned it again and read everything once more. Finally, Filthy Henry folded the page back up and held it up between his fingers.

"You call this intel?"

"It is," Shelly answered.

"Told you it wasn't," Elivin said.

"It's not," Filthy Henry said.

Shelly reached over and snatched it back from him.

"This is where the next attack is going to take place."

500

"At a gathering of story tellers?" Filthy Henry asked.

"Yes!"

"How can you be so sure? Just because it was in Linda's apartment? That's a fairly weak argument. Did you even confirm that she is currently host to a magical presence?"

"This," Shelly said, waving the page in front of the fairy detective's face. "This is evidence. Linda doesn't read. She hates it. Reads social media and the odd article online, but that is it. Finds books and story telling to be drivel. Movies she can get behind, but reading for fun bores her to tears. Attributes it to her short attention span on things not interesting."

"So?" everyone else asked.

Shelly wondered for a moment if this was how Filthy Henry felt when he explained his theories to other people. They were all speaking the same language, they were all intelligent folk. Yet it was like they were from completely different worlds. What was staring her right in the face appeared to be hiding from everyone else.

An overpowering desire to smile smugly was rising up inside. She fought it down, not wanting to go full Filthy Henry.

"This is a gathering of storytellers from all over Ireland. Our guy is stealing the stories from people. Basically it is a buffet for him and his odd tastes. A whole group of people that literally just tell stories. But, more important than that, you clearly didn't read this leaflet fully. What's the name of the person headlining?"

Filthy Henry plucked the page out of her hand as she continued to waggle it in front of his face, opened it up once more, and read.

Slowly he looked up from the page and over at Shelly.

"Well?" Bunty Doolay asked.

"Well I'll be damned," he said, looking up at the *Sidhé*. "She gone done good."

Shelly could not help it. She smiled smugly.

#

Filthy Henry put the leaflet back down and looked at Bunty Doolay's book. It had been working away like a magical computer for the past twenty minutes, building multiple family trees at the same time. The algorithm they had come up with required some tweaking, which the fairy detective left entirely up to Bunty Doolay. After all it was her library they were accessing, why would he be expected to waste his magic on her stuff?

The idea had been simple enough. Each of the known victims back at the hospital was the root of a tree, the spell then worked back through their parents and grandparents and so on. If, at any point, families left Ireland they were discarded straight away. A return to the Emerald Isle brought them, or their ancestors to be precise, back into the equation. While these trees were being constructed a second search spell worked with the results of the first, the family trees, and tried to find links between them. Anything common at all that was shared across all the trees. This second spell was more complicated as it processed a vast amount of data. It still worked quicker than any computer would currently be able to, but it was not exactly instantaneous.

With a pencil, Filthy Henry carefully wrote down the name of the headline act, Tracey Fitzgerald, onto the page of Bunty Doolay's book. As the last letter was written the magic of the book selected it and began to create her family tree.

Shelly and Elivin watched the pages of the book with great interest. Filthy Henry decided to not follow his standard modus operandi, explaining nothing to anybody so that his results appeared all the more impressive. Instead he explained exactly what was happening on the pages, complete with his thought process behind it all. They nodded along, either understanding completely or feigning to do so. Possibly even a combination of both.

"That's not a bad idea, for a half-breed," Elivin said.

"Knock that crap on the head, right now," Bunty Doolay hissed at the leprechaun, her face a mask of annoyance and anger.

Elivin glanced over her shoulder at Shelly, smiled, then turned back in her seat.

"Sorry," she said. "No offence meant."

Filthy Henry wondered what the little smile between the bounty hunter and Shelly had been about. Some sort of inside joke? Maybe Elivin just being Elivin and putting the knife in whenever she could. Considering how her dear old dad behaved, particularly towards the fairy detective, it would be hardly out of character for a member of her family.

He watched as Tracey's family tree was sketched out on the page, enjoying the visual effects of the spell. It was nothing he had not seen before, but still beautiful to watch. The book behaved like a computer screen, ink tracing out patterns and words on the page. When the design reached the bottom everything shifted downwards, the old information moving to make way for new stuff.

Bunty Doolay spells worked using two distinct colour patterns, making it easier to see how the magical search was performing. Family trees were drawn in black ink, both names and branches, while the spell to match interlinks between the trees showed up as deep red lines. Around the names little clouds of tiny words appeared, each too small for the fairy detective to read. It was these words that the spell tried to find a common match. If the line failed to match all the trees before everything shifted, they vanished. So far, the red lines kept on disappearing. Not that this was an indication that there was no connection to be found, just that so far nothing common had been matched across all the trees.

503

Filthy Henry knew that this was a gambit, a Hail Mary theory. But sometimes those theories just happened to be the ones that proved things perfectly.

"This could take some time, right?" Shelly asked, nodding at the book.

"Yeah," the fairy detective said.

"Do we have a deadline in play?"

He tapped the leaflet.

"Either it finishes before this thing starts tomorrow night or we show up with no information and just go down the old fireball route."

"Fireballs? Nothing more elegant than that?" Elivin said.

"Sure, I was going to call you some height-related insulting name and see how quickly you lost your temper. But not all plans have to be perfect."

Elivin grinned, showing a little bit more teeth than Filthy Henry figured belonged in a non-threatening facial expression.

"You don't think you can stop him with fireballs, do you?" Bunty Doolay asked. "That's why you're working with the book. You need to find out how he is doing what he does. You want to reverse it, don't you?"

Not for the first time, Filthy Henry realised the dangers of having a friend in his life who knew him so well. Bunty Doolay could probably read a person's mind with her levels of magic, but with the fairy detective she had no need to use mystical means. Just by working the case with him she could tease out his motives for doing something.

She was right, as well. He was using her books to find out how and why the stories were being stolen. With that knowledge Filthy Henry figured he stood a chance at returning all the story stealer's victims back to normal. Plus, the bad guy was able to jump bodies. A trick that made the simple act of destroying its host utterly useless. Add in a large crowd of potential new hosts, with no discernible way to track who was possessed, and that made the game very one sided.

One sided and completely in favour of the other team.

Filthy Henry was not about to let that stand. The Rules had to be adhered to; honoured and protected. A human infused with some magic from a rouge fairy was ticking all the wrong boxes. There was also the small matter of what exactly they were doing with all those stolen stories.

Stokers, fairy slang for Irish vampires, required blood to live. All vampires did, in fact. They needed the life-force contained within the crimson fluid to sustain themselves. Thankfully, in this day and age, vampires had become a lot more civilized about the whole blood thing. Instead of going after fair maidens and handsome gentlemen for a little fatal hickey creation they went to blood banks. Withdrawing their favourite blend of A+ or O- without the inconvenience of having to dispose of a body. Even still, using this new mortal friendly method of blood drinking, it meant Stokers were collecting power. Energy to keep them alive or heal their bodies from injury.

So what did people's stories get you?

Stories were just tales told throughout time. Originally, they were passed on verbally, then along came the written word. A person's stories, however, were different. You did not just take what was said, you took emotions. Everything that a person had done, all the things experienced, pulled out.

To what end? What could you possibly need centuries of stories for?

There were ancient tales that spoke about the power that could be harnessed by learning a person's name. Their true name. Apparently the one your parents gave you was just the name everyone could use, no harm no foul. But there was a second name, a hidden one, everyone was born with. A name that most people these days never even knew about. When these special names, if known, were given between friends it was a sign of trust. If these names were acquired by enemies it was 'pucker up and kiss your ass goodbye' time.

Filthy Henry guessed that taking a person's stories yielded a result similar to learning their name, but with magnitudes more power. Not only did you take everything that made up a person, but you took all their potential as well. Whatever the future held for them was stolen along with their history. Without your history how could you work towards something? Taking used energy from a person's life was one thing, but tapping into the unknown possibilities of their future was something different.

A mad theory suddenly presented itself in the fairy detective's mind.

"He's a battery," Filthy Henry said out loud.

The other three looked at him, their frowns a clear indication that nothing had been said for the past few minutes and his sudden declaration was confusing.

"Who is? Shelly asked.

"The guy, the thing that is stealing the stories. He's a battery. Collecting energy all this time."

"For centuries? Seriously?"

"Why not?" Filthy Henry said. "I have limits to the amount of magic I can cast. Fairy folk do as well, just a much larger limit. Bunty Doolay would eventually tire if she had to cast magic for an extended period of time or was put under a lot of pressure during a magical battle. But if you plan on casting a big spell you can store up the power."

"Like you do when you binge eat?" Shelly said.

"Not sure that's how it works for you, half.... Filthy," Elivin said, glancing at the *Sidhé* behind the bar to see if the slip was noticed.

"It is," Filthy Henry said, patting his slightly flat stomach. "This body hasn't been inside a gym and follows a strict diet of eating whatever the hell I want."

"Still," Bunty Doolay said. "Your theory is that the stories are being collected to do what? Power some big magical..."

Everyone looked at the *Sidhé* as she stopped mid-sentence.

"There's a penny dropping in that head," Filthy Henry said, leaning towards Shelly as he spoke.

Bunty did not say another word. She walked out from behind the bar and headed towards the back rooms, opening a door and stepping inside. All three of them stared after her, then Filthy Henry turned back to Shelly and Elivin.

"I've no idea what is going on there," he said, pointing at the door Bunty had walked through.

"How's the book doing?" Elivin asked, gesturing towards it with a nod of her head.

He looked at it, the latest leaves on the various trees moving along the pages. The red line of commonality had stayed in place now on four of the trees, while the last tree was still working down through various ancestors. When the final leaf appeared, Filthy Henry was pleased to see the red line extend towards it, joining up all the nodes.

"Well now," the fairy detective declared, pulling the book closer.

With his finger, Filthy Henry tapped the red line twice and watched as it drew a box around the nodes on each tree. The rest of the words faded away, leaving behind blank paper. Underneath the red box words began to appear, forming as if ink had been spilled and the sheet was soaking it up. A paragraph quickly appeared, then another and another. Filling all the empty space with information about the names in the red boxes.

Filthy Henry started reading, scanning through for any interesting facts that jumped out at him. While he read Bunty Doolay returned from the back rooms, carrying a large leather-bound tome. She dropped it onto the counter in front of Shelly.

"This is a book that in some way isn't linked to the Magic Book of Everything over there?" Elivin asked.

"It is," the *Sidhé* replied. "This book contains powerful rituals and incantations that you don't want to get into the wrong person's hands. Plus, I'm not an idiot. Books that I'm going to let Filthy Henry get his grubby mitts on won't be dangerous. He'd get ideas and try something."

"That's not true," the fairy detective said, looking up from his information dump. "I try dangerous stuff all the time without needing to read up on it first."

He returned to the report and read the last paragraph as it appeared.

"Anything?" Shelly asked him.

"Yeah," Filthy Henry said. "But I'm not entirely sure how it explains what is going on. As connections between victims go it is pretty lame. Apparently, way back down the family tree of all the Blank Slates we had names for, their great-times-some-stupid-number grandparents were at the same fort for a meal. A banquet, celebrating some big battle between two minor kings in Celtic Times. It was held by a Low King called Cadán Ó Briain."

"That's the best connection that could be worked out between them? Looks like the *Sidhé's* records are not as magically useful as advertised."

"The records are fine," Bunty Doolay said, coldly. "A shoddy craftsperson blames their tools."

"Shoddy tools make a bad craftsman as well," the leprechaun said. "Although, the name of that king does sound familiar for some reason."

"Would you two pack it in. We need to figure out why that connection is important. Going back to Celtic Times means we at least know things are lining up logically," Shelly said. "Even if it is questionable logic."

"What makes you say that?" Filthy Henry asked her, genuinely interested to hear her theory.

Right then he had absolutely nothing to go on, so if somebody else was able to make sense of the worst clue in the history of crime solving the fairy detective was all ears.

"If the crone was somehow sent back in time after we defeated her and Medb, and Medb had been a queen catapulted forward in time from Celtic Ireland, then it stands to reason that this connection is important. Whatever happened at that dinner led to somebody going to her and making a deal in exchange for power. Meaning we can at least place Lauren at, or somewhere near, the banquet. Now, can the book tell us anything about the banquet? We might be able to come up with a suspect at least."

Filthy Henry shook his head.

"Nothing, just names of those who attended and why it was held. Bunty, the least your records could do is keep track of what was served as the main course. Maybe it was enough to annoy people into seeking revenge over the centuries."

"This isn't a cheap knock-off of Dracula you're reading," Bunty Doolay said. "Besides, we've got bigger problems."

"Oh?" Filthy Henry said.

Bunty Doolay had been flicking through the pages of the large tome on the counter while the discussions had been going on. One page was being tapped on with her left index finger, landing on the cursive script along the top. It was written in a language that Filthy Henry had never seen before. He was having trouble even figuring out if the words contained letters or was it all written in an ancient dialect of the fairy folk that used nothing but emojis.

There was definitely one symbol that looked like a frowning smiley face.

"This," the *Sidhé said*. "Is the Ritual of *Sióg Rí a Ghairm*."

"Elf King Summon," Shelly said, slowly as she thought about the translation. "That's pretty straightforward, in terms of the bad Irish syntax fairy spells usual follow."

"Sounds pleasant enough," Filthy Henry said.

"It isn't," Bunty Doolay said, staring at him. "It is very, very bad. If Lauren has been collecting stories, power, to perform a big ritual then this is it and we have a huge problem on our hands."

"Such as?" Shelly asked, staring at the tome.

"Basically, this ritual requires a lot of magical energy, more than any one fairy creature would have. More than even Dagda would have on his own and he is basically a god. It was used only once, long before mortals stepped foot onto Irish shores, and even then it took about two hundred, very powerful, fairies. One of them was casting the ritual, the rest supplying the energy and power. It opens a gateway, a portal, between this world and another. Allowing things to step through into our Realm or be sent over to the other side, into a very Hellish world. In fact the Hell described in all the various mortal religious texts would seem like a child's amusement park when compared to the world this gateway connected to."

That, Filthy Henry had to admit, sounded bad.

"You think that Lauren is after coming up with a way to do the same ritual on her own and use centuries of collected stories as the power source?"

Bunty nodded.

"Worse, the ritual can only be cast once every fifteen hundred years."

"Let me guess," Filthy Henry said. "That's coming up really soon."

"See, you are a great detective," Bunty Doolay said, her voice dripping with sarcasm.

"It was more a lucky guess, I reckon," Shelly said. "Seems to me that we always get dangerously tight deadlines when working cases like this."

"True," Filthy Henry said. "Just once it would be nice if somebody hired us and said that the deadline was ten years from now. A nice, easy, case that we could take our time solving."

"Crap," Shelly said.

"What?" Filthy Henry asked her.

"I don't know why I didn't put two and two together sooner. Lauren! Evil Linda said her cat, which was just an excuse to cover up the fact somebody was in her bedroom, was called Lauren."

"The crone was at Linda's apartment," the fairy detective said. "At least we know three things now. A, that this story thief is really bad at coming up with character names. Two, you made the right call running out of there before things got serious. And D, that The Crone McGarry is definitely the fairy we're looking for."

Elivin had been silent during the entire exchange, staring off into the distance as if mulling something over. Filthy Henry nudged her gently on a padded shoulder.

"What's got you so quiet?"

She shook her head, slowly, but kept staring at the mirrors behind the bar counter.

"Nothing," the leprechaun said. "Just, I think I can get us some information on what happened at that banquet. I know somebody who was at it. Since I am guessing we need to find that out in order to come up with a way to stop the story stealer. Right?"

"Right," Filthy Henry said, looking at her with slight confusion. "Are you going to say what I think you're going to say?"

"Yep," Elivin said, turning to look at the fairy detective. "We've to go chat with my father."

#

"You're sure this will work?" Linda asked the crone.

"Of course," she replied. "I've kept you alive this long, haven't I? Trust my magic."

"It isn't a lack of magical trust that I have. It is the fact that I have a possessed doll giving me the old 'stink-button' while we keep a low profile."

Medb shrugged her shoulders.

"Excuse me, but they didn't have those fancy pants self-closing eyes back when the doll was made. You get your spirit put into whatever container is close to hand."

They had moved shortly after Shelly left, rather when she basically ran from, the apartment. Lauren had watched through a slit in the curtains and seen the leprechaun leave with Shelly. This was a suspicious event, considering a leprechaun would have, apparently, been enough of a match on a magical level to keep the crone busy. But the haig had decided not to look an opportune gift horse in the perfectly timed mouth. She had bolted out of the bedroom as fast as her crooked legs could carry her, grabbed the rag doll up in one hand, and headed straight for the apartment door. Linda followed close behind. Nothing had been taken with them, aside from the crone's bag of odds and ends. They ran along the hallway, towards the fire escape, and climbed down the rusty ladder. Once in the back alley the crone had cast a Spell of Disinterest over the three of them, meaning people could see and hear them but just not really find them that interesting to pay attention to, and motioned for Linda to walk towards the mouth of the alley.

The streets of Dublin city were rarely empty. At any time of day there would be somebody walking along or at least visible. Crowds, like the tides, came and went at specific times. Right then the streets were thronged with people going about their lives. Linda had looked back at the crone and waved her hand, gesturing for the fairy to come forward. She had waddled up and peered out from behind Linda.

"This spell isn't going to hide us, just make it less likely for somebody to see us directly," the crone said. "If that leprechaun is lurking around still she will spot us. But any monitoring magic left behind will be confused."

"Okay," Linda had said. "So, what is the plan? They are onto us, otherwise Shelly wouldn't have left so quickly. That means we need to hide."

"Correct," Lauren had said. "In the least obvious place anybody would think of."

"You have a place in mind?"

"It just so happens that I do," Lauren said, smiling her hideous smile.

Which was how, in a very short space of time, Linda had gone from hiding in a comfortable apartment to sitting on an upturned crate in the storage room of The Leprechaun Museum on Jervis Street.

If somebody had asked Linda to come up with a list of the top one hundred places to hide out in, this museum would have been number three hundred and sixty-nine. She, or rather her current

513

body, had never even stepped foot inside it. None of her previous hosts had entered through its bright red doors either. It was the very definition of a tourist attraction aimed at children, with very little to keep an adult mind entertained.

They had breezed through the front doors, past most of the exhibitions, and completely ignored the large fibre glass tree that was meant to be 'the home of a leprechaun'. As they passed the giant piece of art Lauren had let out a derisive snort.

"If a leprechaun was living in something even close to that they'd have fallen on hard times," the crone said, walking around it and opening a storeroom door just to the left of the trunk.

"How did you know this was even here?" Linda asked.

"Where do you think we've been staying when not checking up on you?"

"You've been staying in the store room of a museum about fairy folk? It hasn't been here longer than five years."

"True," Lauren said. "But before that it was a run-down building and nobody was paying it any heed. Besides, it's just for a few hours. Once that gathering begins tomorrow night we can get out and head straight to it."

"Is it not a bit obvious a place to hide?"

"No," the rag doll had said. "Seems like the other fairy creatures find this place highly insulting. They don't like being made out to be cartoon figures. They avoid it. Plus Lauren has cast a number of wards on either side of the door. Makes people ignore it and any sounds they hear from it. Perfect hiding spot."

Linda just accepted this and entered the store room.

It was obvious that the crone had been staying her for some time. There was a small cot set up in the far corner of the room, an old clock ticking away on the floor beside it, and a tiny cat basket. The nurse figured that Medb was not the sort of thing you

514

cuddled up to after a long day and assumed the cat basket was her bed. Something about the odd little creature gave off more of a stabby feeling than a friendly one.

A single bulb hung down from the ceiling, no shade on it at all. The walls of the room were painted in a beige that would have screamed boring if the simple act of screaming had not been too exciting. Otherwise there was nothing remarkable or noteworthy about the room.

The room they ended up just waiting in, hiding from the world.

The rag doll lay in her cat bed, seemingly sleeping although Linda was not completely sure how such a thing would be possible. Sleep required your eyes to be closed and buttons lacked greatly in the eyelid department. On the cot bed the crone sat, reading from a battered book that had been stored in box at the end of the cot. It looked to be ancient and smelled faintly of rotten leaves.

Linda kept these observations to herself. It was because of these two that her planned revenge had been possible and now, so close to the end, she was not going to upset either of them. At least not too greatly. The proposed idea to balance the amount of energy it had taken to jump out of Milton would work, of that Linda was sure. All they had to do was wait.

After what felt like an age, the sounds outside the room lessened. An indication the last of the museum patrons had long since left, the staff following shortly after them. Silence had reigned for the past few hours. Yet still the three of them remained in the store room.

She tried to nap, but the rag doll's buttons made her feel as if the thing was watching her. Even though it had started snoring, Linda was not going to take that on face value from a thing that got drunk by absorbing wine into it's body by sitting in it.

"What's the book?" Linda asked the crone.

"Rituals," Lauren said, without looking up from the pages.

"Rituals on...?"

Lauren took a deep breath and slowly raised her head, her one good eye staring at Linda while the other squinted.

"Tonight, if you manage to collect the last of the power we need, will be the first night of the Cruatan Equinox. I need to be sure I have everything in place before the moon is at its zenith. Otherwise this entire thing will have been for naught."

"Why do you lot use words like 'zenith' so much? Can't you just say at the 'peak'? Everyone would understand what you mean."

The crone smiled, her hideously black and crooked teeth making the smile about as affectionate as a stampeding rhino.

"Then fairy folk wouldn't sound mystical, would we?" she said.

"Alright," Linda said. "But you're going to share the plan, right? At the minute, it seems to be just sitting around in this storage room. I'm going to die of boredom. You know, if you hadn't done the magic mumbo jumbo on me that basically made me immortal."

"It's simple," Lauren said, closing the book and placing it on the cot beside her. "You take Medb there with you to the gathering. When you get the collected stories is not important, just that you get it before midnight. I will be preparing the ritual and then, when I get the signal from Medb, open the portal and bring forth He-Who-Has-Been-Exiled. After that you can stick around with us if you want, but the magic will be out of your system. You'll be mortal and trapped in that body."

Linda looked down at her legs, held out her arms and flexed the fingers on her hands.

"Fair enough," she said.

516

Medb snorted in the cat bed, impressive due to the lack of a nose and all the internal plumbing that made snorting possible, and rolled over. Beside the crone the clock ticked away.

# Chapter Twenty-Five

Filthy Henry had one rule about the chair in his office: it was his chair. A fairly basic rule, as rules went.

He had it positioned behind his desk so that the window was always at his back, leaving a good view of the office door. The room lacked any other chairs because Filthy Henry felt more seats would encourage people to stay around longer than required. His idea of an efficient client was one who came into the office, hired him, gave some details on the case, then departed so he could work the case. Chit-chat was to be left at the door.

If the clients could hire him by just sending in a letter, even better.

One thing the fairy detective needed to do was enter the digital age. Being able to use magic was all well and good, provided you did not look upon modern technology as magic that could never be understood.

Elivin stood just inside the doorway to the office, her arms crossed in front of her chest. Shelly could have sworn that the leprechaun was trying a macho stance while glaring at the person in Filthy Henry's seat.

"Can we skip the staring contest and get down to business?" the occupant asked.

"Sure thing, Lé Precon," Filthy Henry said. "Just as soon as you get out of my seat."

Shelly tried her best not to smile at that line. Filthy Henry being annoyed by other people was becoming her guilty pleasure in life.

"But there are no other chairs in the room and you need my assistance, at least that is what Elivin led me to believe. Why should I stand when I am the one here to help you?"

"You could just magic up another chair while I sit in my one," the fairy detective snarled.

"True," Lé Precon said, placing his hands behind his head and tilting the chair back slightly from the desk. "But I did that already, on my last visit. The chair was obviously something you didn't want, hence it clearly being thrown out and replaced with this horrible one. Why expend my magic again?"

Shelly looked at Lé Precon and was amazed that somebody so small, with a stereotypical fashion sense, could get under Filthy Henry's skin with ease. He was dressed in a bright green suit, sort of in the style of a tuxedo, with a green bowler hat to match. Resting against the edge of the desk was a solid gold walking-cane. To round out the entire stereotype of what a leprechaun looked like, he had a neatly trimmed ginger beard.

Lé Precon was the most powerful of the leprechauns in Ireland and, as a result of his abilities, their current king. He had previously hired Filthy Henry to find his crock of gold. The King of the Leprechauns was also the reason Shelly's mild case of deadness had failed to take. In one way she probably owed the him a debt. Thankfully, that debt had been paid in full by the fairy detective when he had given up his one wish in order to resurrect her.

She glanced over at Filthy Henry.

For whatever reason, them all being in this room made Shelly realise just what the fairy detective had sacrificed in order to keep her alive. Possibly his one chance at being made a full blood fairy, removing the half-breed label he had carried his entire life. That was not the act of a selfish person, even if Filthy Henry had kept this all from her for well over a year. It was something that a decent person would do for somebody they considered a true friend, maybe even thought of as family.

Filthy Henry caught her looking at him and returned her gaze with a quizzical stare.

Shelly shook her head, to indicate he did not need to ask any questions, and turned back to look at Lé Precon.

"Listen, dad," Elivin said. "We need information, okay? That's it. No talks about stuff, no bringing up old grudges. Just some information."

Lé Precon shifted in his seat and looked at the bounty hunter.

"Do they know?" he asked her.

Both Filthy Henry and Shelly looked down at Elivin.

"Know what?" Shelly asked.

"Know what she threw away in order to pursue this ridiculous life as a bounty hunter. A fairy bounty hunter. As if that is actually a thing!"

"People said there was no need for a fairy detective," Filthy Henry said. "Nobody seems to be complaining now."

"That's not true," Lé Precon said. "We've been complaining for decades. Just your father is somebody too important to ignore. But my daughter chose to become a bounty hunter. Chasing down rouge fairy creatures to protect the mortal world from their influence. Long before you appeared with your unique parentage."

"He knows who your father is?" Shelly asked.

"Don't worry about it," the fairy detective replied. "It's common knowledge, apparently. Something of an open secret. Maybe the worst kept one, who can tell for sure? What did you give up, pint size?"

Elivin looked annoyed at the cute nickname, but kept her anger in check.

"I gave up seventy percent of my magical powers and turned

my back completely on the leprechaun people."

The room fell silent. Nobody knew where to look or who to look at. Elivin's gaze was fixed on the floor. Filthy Henry had picked a spot on the wall beside him and was examining a small crack with great interest. Shelly sucked on her bottom lip and focused on the corner of the desk.

"Well, since nobody else is saying it," Lé Precon said, breaking the silence. "I will. She basically turned her back on her birthright, completely and totally. She sacrificed most of her powers to become a glorified tracker, hunting down fairies that were doing nothing more than embracing their powers."

"Is that why you can't do as much magic as other leprechauns?" Filthy Henry asked her.

"Oh it is even better than that," the King of the Leprechauns said. "Her powers tire her out after a short while or a big burst of magic."

"That's why you looked so tired after teleporting Milton back to the hospital," Shelly said.

Elivin nodded her head, not saying a word.

"Teleporting tires you out, Dagda above even the half-breed can do a bit of teleportation without getting tired. See what turning your back on your family gets you?"

"Fairies that were trying to destroy the world," Elivin said. "Fairies that were a danger to both human and fairy!"

Filthy Henry placed a hand on her padded shoulder, gently. She did not shake it off.

"Listen up you glorified Power Ranger wannabe," the fairy detective said to Lé Precon. "Humans have as much right to live in this world as fairies. Should we be able to co-exist? Yes. But we can't, so tough. But if one of the fairy folk wanted to go into the business of protecting the human world before I showed up, well then that's just peachy in my books."

Lé Precon pulled the chair in close to the desk and rested his elbows on the edge of it, clasping his hands before him. He looked up at Filthy Henry.

"You want information from me," the King of the Leprechaun's said, his tone cold and unfeeling. "I need payment. Nothing for free in this world. Either world."

"Name the price, then cough up," Shelly said, stepping in to take control of the situation before it became another mystical-macho-man contest.

Elivin and Filthy Henry both slowly turned their heads towards her, a not so subtle indication that what Shelly had just done was possibly the wrong course of action. Both of them stared at her, mouths open wide, and blinked twice. From the desk, Lé Precon started to chuckle.

"This is why mortals don't belong in the Fairy World," he said. "You do not understand The Rules."

A painful realisation dawned on Shelly.

Every fairy story that involved deal making always contained the same common theme. Whenever a deal was struck between a human and fairy, the fairy came off the better. All the time. It was all the clever word play they used when making the deal, giving the poor human very little time to play the mental gymnastics required to tease out the double meaning of what had been said.

Telling a leprechaun to name his price in order to provide information was probably a cardinal no-no when it came to fairy-human bargaining. Having been so careful before when Elivin wanted to bet on Filthy Henry slapping himself in the face, Shelly felt like kicking herself for making such a rookie mistake now.

With no better idea presenting itself, Shelly looked over at Filthy Henry for help.

He rolled his eyes and let out a sigh.

"Oh, I am the big fairy detective. I can solve cases on my own. I don't need you to be doing your stuff on my cases. Blah blah blah," Filthy Henry said, doing a strange sort of dance while waving his hands about in the air.

"Whatever floats your boat," Lé Precon said, smiling at the little outburst. "But that doesn't change the fact that your partner over there has agreed to the terms. Payment for information."

The fairy detective paused mid-dance and faced the leprechaun in his seat.

"Let's get this over with," Filthy Henry said, standing up straight and putting his hands in his trouser pockets. "What are you looking for."

Lé Precon looked from Elivin to Shelly, then finally back at the fairy detective.

"I want you to talk to my wayward daughter and convince her to come back to the family business," he said, a hint of a smile on his face.

"That's it?" the fairy detective asked, looking quizzically at Lé Precon.

"I'm a grown leprechaun!" Elivin practically shouted, stamping her booted foot on the ground.

"That's it," her father replied. "You have to convince my daughter to stop being a bounty hunter and reclaim her powers. Convince, not just have a chat and hope for the best. Actually make her see the error of her ways can come back, permanently, to the family business. Understood?"

"You will tell me all the information we are after and my payment is that I have to convince your daughter to step down from her life's work? I'm guessing once we agree to this there is no way for me to get out of it? Such as dying?"

524

"Can you people not hear me?" the bounty hunter asked, looking around at everyone. "Am I under a spell of silence or something?"

Lé Precon, still looking at the fairy detective, nodded his head in agreement at what had just been said.

Filthy Henry stepped towards the desk quicker than Shelly would have anticipated, his right hand out for a shake, and reached towards Lé Precon. The King of the Leprechauns grinned and took the fairy detective's hand, shaking it firmly three times. Two little green sparks appeared over both their hands, rising up into the air and joining together before vanishing. A sign that they had both entered into a pact that was now magically binding.

The fairy detective grinned and stepped back from the desk, hands once again in his pockets.

"Spill," he said.

Lé Precon leaned back in the chair, the leather creaking, and stared at Filthy Henry.

"Em...you do know how pacts work, right? You have to convince her first, then you get the information."

The fairy detective held up a finger in the air and wiggled it back and forth, as if telling off a naughty child. Shelly saw the smile on his face and knew immediately that he had just done one of his patented 'Filthy Henry fairy scams'.

"See, the problem with fairy folk is this," the fairy detective said. "You lot are usually the ones making deals with mortals that don't pay attention to what is being said. Then you get more and more power, stop meddling with mortals as much, and forget how to make these deals go completely in your favour."

He stopped talking, looked back at Elivin and Shelly to wink at them, then sat down on the edge of the desk.

"I will convince your daughter to give up on her bounty

hunter work," Filthy Henry continued speaking. "But you forgot to say which order these events were to happen in. In fact you agreed to my wording of the pact which has you give me the information first, then I talk with Elivin. You even failed to say when I had to convince her by. So, we're both in a magically sealed pact. One of us has to convince somebody of something and the other needs to give the information. I mean we can take this further up the magical food chain if you want, but I'm pretty sure we both know what will happen if they get involved."

Shelly had no idea who the 'they' he was referring to were. Some sort of committee made up of magically powerful creatures that ranked above a leprechaun king? A panel of judges, completely made up of floating heads that spoke without moving their lips? Whatever this next level of magical dispute settling was, it clearly gave Lé Precon something to ponder.

The smile on his face slowly faded.

"Sometimes I really wish that we had managed to swap you with a Changeling before your first birthday," Lé Precon said.

"Yeah," Filthy Henry said. "But then things would be boring as hell for you all."

#

Linda woke from her dream in a cold sweat.

She was back there, back *then.*

Back when her body had been more male than female. Back when it all happened. When the people had laughed and mocked, treating her like nothing. Back when her desire for revenge had been born.

In the good old days of Celtic Ireland, the term used by modern society to describe what had just been Linda's Ireland, storytelling was considered a craft. Not just somebody with the ability to spin a good yarn after his son had gotten their head stuck in a ditch. Although being able to turn what could have been a disastrous event into a humorous one did require some level of skill. True storytelling, however, involved years of dedication and training. Without the novelty of the Internet and an education system that favoured sword prowess over reading and writing, storytellers were given the task of carrying knowledge around with them. Primarily in their heads. While the druids were known to write things down in an attempt at preserving knowledge, a storyteller would have needed an entourage to carry around all the books required for their trade.

Instead, they went to the Bard College. A place of learning for those who not only sought knowledge, but had a flair for retelling it as well. Years of study were required, rote learning the old tales so that you could seamlessly blend them into each other. More than that, the storyteller had to learn the morale of each tale. Just because the dragon was slain by a hero did not, in any way, lessen the fact he had done so with good manners and upright posture.

After their initial training, a storyteller had to leave the college and spend a number of years travelling Ireland as a journeyman. They would take shelter only where it was offered, paying for it by reciting a tale of their hosts choosing. If the storyteller was unable to recall the tale requested they could try using another. Failing that it was possible to work off their bed and board by doing labour around the homestead. No more than three nights in the same place was permitted, to ensure the storyteller did not get too comfortable and forget his true purpose in life.

A purpose which was to spread knowledge, wisdom and the history of Ireland to all her people.

Linda had enjoyed this part of her training, it gave her a freedom that did not really exist in the College itself. Every day there had been a copy of the one before, right down to the meals they ate. It was designed that way, so that the storyteller's mind and body could easily adapt to its new role. The days blurred together, all the while the story fragments built up in the young trainee's mind. Being able to have different food each night, while travelling and sleeping under the stars, was like visiting another world.

Then, through a sequence of fortunate events, Linda happened upon a grand master from the College who had been summoned to a great feast. Their paths had crossed in the fields of Galway. The Grand Master was old, much older than any who had come before him, and was making the trek to do that which all storyteller's aspired to.

Be involved in the creation of a story.

No longer reciting words and deeds performed by other men, but to be the one to craft the tale and give it back to the land. He had insisted that Linda accompanied him on the journey, mainly so her then young male body could carry the Grand Master's things.

When they reached the fort of the Low King Cadán Ó Briain, the Grand Master had introduced Linda as his apprentice. A title not technically true, since an apprentice never left the College, but the guard on the gate did not seem to know that. They were ushered through and shown to a small hut, just outside the grand lodge.

Shortly after arriving a young boy, no older than nine or ten, came to the hut and related the events of some battle which had been fought by the Low King and his men. All of this was told over and over to the Grand Master until, at last, he nodded his head in thanks and instructed the young boy to leave them.

"This is why I was summoned," the Grand Master explained to male-Linda. "I must create an epic to honour the men who lost their lives during this battle. It will make me immortal as you, young journeyman, and others from the College retell it until the end of time. Bear witness to what your craft can lead you to, should you stay true to the cause."

Linda had thought the speech a little pretentious, but back

then she was still only a journeyman. Disagreeing with a Grand Master would have been, in today's vernacular, career suicide. She would never have told another story, for money, again.

So, under the pretending to be his apprentice, Linda had watched and learned from the Grand Master on how a story was created. The young boy had supplied them with names and identifiable traits for the main people King Cadán wanted in the tale. This was a great honour, to have your name added into the deeds and adventures of another man's story, because it meant those names never died. Each telling would keep them alive in the memories of those who heard it.

It took the better part of two days to flesh out tale and another three before the Grand Master was happy with it. Once done, the Grand Master instructed Linda to inform the king. This news had been met with great joy, mainly because King Cadán was very fond of roast pig and had been waiting for a feast to justify cooking one over the fire. Now that the epic was ready there could be celebrations at once, the food prepared, the guests seated and, when everyone had drunk and ate their fill, the Grand Master would tell his tale.

The main event to close out the night.

Linda was given a seat beside the Grand Master, on the platform to the left of the king's own throne. Such a position placed her above basically all the assembled guests of the king in both physical and social standing.

At last, after all the plates had been cleared from the tables, the time came for the Grand Master to tell his tale. To begin what would be his masterpiece and add his name to the great storytellers of Ireland. All eyes in the room looked up at him.

He stared blankly back at them all.

This was one of the first lessons taught at the College for Bards: dramatics. You did not just rise up when the people expected you to. You let them wait, allowed the anticipation to build in the audience. Then, just before anxious joy became anxious 'need to smash somebody's head in because I'm sick of waiting', you jumped up with a flourish and started to talk. It was a difficult skill to truly master. Most journeyman lost several teeth as they perfected their timings, learning that each crowd had a subtly different point in time when they flipped from being your adoring public to your bored enemies.

Seconds crept past, then minutes. At the back of the hall somebody coughed. Loudly.

Linda nudged the Grand Master in the side, hard. Hard enough that it caused him to topple forward from his seat and hit the ground. Dead as the wooden floor he fell onto.

Without missing a beat, the king turned to face Linda's manly form and pointed at her.

"Did he recite the story in front of you?" the king demanded.

She had nodded her boyish head.

"Then get up there and tell it. We shall have the guards look after the old man. My guests need to hear of the heroic deeds from the battle."

There had been no arguing with the king. Linda tried to explain that she was a journeyman, that the Grand Master had been the true creator of the epic story which was to be told. That there was no way she could possibly fill the shoes of the man currently lying dead on the floor, even if they did swap shoes. Low King Cadán dismissed all her points and ordered her to get up and tell the story or join the Grand Master on the ground in a similar state of not-being-alive. To hammer home that point one of the king's guards gripped the handle of his sword and smiled at her.

Linda had slowly risen from her seat and stepped forward, standing in front of the throne and facing the guests in the hall. This was a defining moment in her storytelling career. Word would spread that an original tale had been first recited by her, technically him. Sure, it had been crafted by the dead Grand Master, but the first performance would still get her enough recognition to join the ranks of Master faster than anyone else in the College had ever done.

She opened her mouth and, from memory, recited the first line.

To the rapturous laughter of everyone in the hall.

A laughter that Linda kept hearing every time she had the nightmare.

Back in the storage room, Linda looked over at the crone, sleeping away in her travel cot bed, and at Medb in the cat bed, then decided to roll over and try to get back to sleep. With the faint, horrible, laughter still echoing in her mind.

#

Filthy Henry burst out laughing.

"You're kidding me," he said.

"Swear to the Old Gods," Lé Precon replied. "That's what happened."

"He got up on stage and mixed up the name of the king's first-born son with the horse that ran into a tree? In front of everyone?"

Lé Precon nodded his head, smiling.

"It was brilliant," he said. "If it hadn't been a pair of storytellers to begin with you would have thought some storyteller made it up for a laugh. Like a bad joke."

"Where did this happen?" Filthy Henry asked Lé Precon. "I'm pretty sure I would have heard about something like this by now."

"Around where Carlingford is today," the King of the

Leprechauns replied.

"Huh", the fairy detective said. "Guess that explains why the forest in the memory fragment was so familiar. We must have passed by it or something last year when we were in Carlingford helping Cathal."

"Totally not fascinating. I don't get it though, this storyteller at the feast was insulted that everyone laughed after he made a mistake?" Shelly asked.

"Pretty much," the Lé Precon said. "You lot, mortals, tend to get easily offended, I've noticed. Anyway, he never finished telling the story. The low king kicked him out for insulting his first-born. Then the College removed him completely from their books. He was exiled and left wandering the land without any marketable skills. Sad story when you think about it, pun slightly intended."

Filthy Henry had heard of worse reasons to go seeking revenge, but this was definitely in the top ten. Maybe the bottom ten, it all depended on how you rated things when they were bad. Either way, top or bottom, it was obviously why the spirit had been stealing stories all these years. Except...

"Wait, that doesn't add up at all," the fairy detective said. "What is the reason for stealing stories over centuries? I made a guess at it being energy, but it is a shot in the dark on my part really."

Lé Precon frowned at Filthy Henry.

"Just how much information am I meant to divulge here for a deal that you managed to pull one of your clever word plays on?"

"Dad," Elivin said, not looking directly at her father. "Just help us out, please. We need to stop this guy before whatever they are planning happens."

He scratched the tip of his nose, staring across the desk at his daughter. Filthy Henry had had many dealings with the King of the Leprechauns over the years. Most of them revolved around favour trading. Since Lé Precon was the most powerful of his people that also made him the wealthiest. The Rules stated that magically created money could not be used to influence the mortal world in a noticeable manner. Creating the odd twenty Euro in order to pay for dinner or get a taxi somewhere was one thing, since they faded away later anyway. Magically making a couple of million appear in your bank account would be a direct violation of The Rules, bringing some unwanted attention from the Fairy World your way.

As such, Filthy Henry had sometimes treated Lé Precon like a bank. Borrowing from him when things were a bit quiet in the detective business, then paying him back when his finances improved. The end result being he spent as much time in Lé Precon's debt as out of it, with the leprechaun very rarely owing Filthy Henry anything. It did mean, however, that over the decades he had tried numerous ways to curry favour with the leprechaun, failing each and every time.

Elivin, as Lé Precon's daughter, presumably would be able to pull at the short arse's heart strings and make him cough up more intel without payment.

Unless the King of the Leprechauns was in the running for 'Worst Father of the Year' award. If your daughter ran away from the family trade to become a bounty hunter, then something had to be rotten in the homestead.

"Fine," Lé Precon said. "But call your mother when this is all done. She worries and no matter what I say she still seems to think you need help wiping your backside after making number two."

Shelly tittered. Actually tittered. A titter that stopped quickly after Elivin shot her a glare.

"I'll drop around for dinner later this week," the bounty hunter said, eyes still locked onto Shelly. "Promise. Now can you tell us what we need to know?"

"What I am going to tell you is just what I heard," Lé Precon said. "After the feast ended and he became a complete laughing stock, the young storyteller decided to take revenge. But revenge of the kind that only a true student of the dramatics could conceive of. Not content to just take it out on those at the feast he swore, to every and any powerful being and deity listening, to take revenge on all in the hall and their descendants tenfold."

Filthy Henry stood up from the desk and started pacing back and forth in front of it. If a mortal swore revenge on somebody that was nothing strange or unusual. Generally, it was just something said in the heat of the moment, forgotten about in the cold light of sobriety the following morning. Other, more serious, people would follow through on their stated desire for revenge. But never something along the lines of the people you dislike and a bunch of their family later on through the years.

For starters, a mortal would never be able to carry out such a plan. Owing, largely, to how stunted the human lifespan was.

"How?" was all the fairy detective could say. "I mean, how? We're talking about a mortal here, right? Not another half-breed you lot let slip through your fingers."

"No," Lé Precon said, slowly shaking his head and giving Filthy Henry an almost sarcastic look. "You're the only one of those that's survived long enough to be a pain. He was a mortal, a storyteller. Nothing special about him."

"Until he met Medb and the Crone McGarry," the fairy detective pointed out.

The look on Lé Precon's face made up for the fact he was sitting in Filthy Henry's office chair. The fairy detective had obviously just said something, revealed a bit of information, that the King of the Leprechauns figured was not general knowledge. Nothing was more satisfying than showing the fairy folk, particularly those in extremely powerful positions, that they were not the smartest in the room.

Lé Precon cleared his through with a cough, then inclined his head slightly towards Filthy Henry.

"Maybe you do have some skills," he said. "Yes, the storyteller met Lauren. Turns out she was walking around harvesting mushrooms or whatever that crazy haig gets up to in the middle of the night."

"Then that's where the magic comes from," Shelly blurted out.

Filthy Henry, Lé Precon and Elivin all slowly turned around and looked at her. She immediately blushed.

"Just...you know...figuring things...out...loud...," she said, clearly embarrassed.

But, she was right. Lauren had done something to the storyteller allowing him live through the centuries and enact his revenge on everyone who had, seemingly, wronged him. The ability to take the stories of his victims, converting that into power stored in his spirit form. Energy which could be used to change bodies when the time was right. Such a thing, though, was not a spell. There were no rituals or incantations that turned a mortal into a magically powered thief who did not die.

Which meant it had to be something else. Lé Precon would know, of that Filthy Henry had no doubt. Whether the pint-sized pain in his ass would reveal this was another thing entirely.

So, Filthy Henry had to figure it out and then just get the King of the Leprechauns to confirm it. He started more pacing back and forth, thinking.

Most of the stories, the old Celtic fairy tales and legends, that involved humans with magic in their lives had a sponsor of some description. An object, a Relic or Artefact, that empowered them to be the champion needed by the Forces of Magic. But, sometimes, on rare occasions, the hero of the tale agreed to a request from a fairy creature in return for power. They would take on something similar to a curse, but one that had positive and negative aspects to it. The positive allowed them to use the power gifted by the fairy, the negative was meant as a fail-safe in case they strayed from the path the fairy desired.

After all, if you were going to raise up a lowly mortal into the magical playing field it did not hurt to have a switch that put them back on the bench after half-time.

"A Geis," Filthy Henry said, stopping his pacing and looking at Lé Precon.

"A Geis," the King of the Leprechauns replied after a minute. "Now, I've fulfilled my end of the bargain. Make sure you get around to keeping up your end."

One second he was there, the next Lé Precon had vacated the seat and taken his cane with him. Two little shamrocks spiralled in the air where his head had been, before falling to the ground.

"Geese? Is that another Leerling thing?" Shelly asked.

Filthy Henry walked around his desk, pulled out his chair, and dusted it down with a few slaps from his hand. Making sure that no leprechaun molecules remained, he sat down and leaned back. The creak of the leather was a much more enjoyable sound than he expected it to be.

"No, not geese as in the birds," the fairy detective said to Shelly. "Geis, as in a magical vow or curse. Most of them are nothing special. You just agreed you wouldn't eat after six or you'd forever have a runny nose, that sort of thing. But a few humans were given a double Geis by a fairy, a public and private one. The public was what you used as your power and everyone in the world could know about. The private was never to be shared with anybody other than the person who put you under the Geis. It was a fail-safe. Right?"

This last bit was directed to Elivin. The bounty hunter nodded her head.

"Yep, that's about the simplest explanation I've ever heard for them. But, yes. That's what a Geis is."

"Still not entirely sure I follow," Shelly said. "It's a curse that you volunteer for? Doesn't that sort of make it the opposite to what a curse is? Like the Wicked Queen in Snow White didn't put a curse on her for poops and giggles, just so they could have a funny story years later over a glass of wine."

"That's because you're mixing up a Geis and a curse," Elivin said. "If you wrong a witch, they will go and curse you so bad stuff will happen. A Geis, however, is something that two parties enter into willingly. More like what the fairy godmother does in Sleeping Beauty. Uses her gift to work against the curse. Make sense?"

Filthy Henry could tell that Shelly was only partially following. It tended to happen when she first heard about something new in the Fairy World. Her mortal mind tried to align what made sense to humans with what was common knowledge to fairies, failing miserably on both counts. It was possible that Filthy Henry and Elivin had explained it using poor terminology. Once the word 'curse' was used it would have set Shelly's thoughts down negative curses, not leaving a lot of room to grasp the subtle differences with a Geis, which were positive curses.

He watched as she began to form her next question and decided, rather then head it off, to let her say it out loud. That way at least, Elivin would see what Filthy Henry had to deal with on a regular basis.

"So," Shelly began, her brow creased slightly in deep thought. "Does that mean that not only Celtic fairy tales are re..."

"Nope!" Filthy Henry said, cutting her off before she asked the rest of the daft question. "Well...maybe. I don't know and neither will Elivin. We deal with the fairy stuff only. Now, back to Geis. We need to figure out the private part, that will allow us to halt Lauren and her tool in the middle of whatever they are doing."

Shelly stuck her tongue out at the fairy detective and crossed her arms, taking her annoyed stance.

Elivin hid her smile behind a gloved hand.

The fairy detective started to think about how a Geis worked.

Typically, the private part of a Geis was tied closely with the public part. It was how they were designed, although Filthy Henry had always considered it to be a bit on the risky side. If people wanted to stop you or put a halt to your nefarious schemes, assuming you were up to no good, then it just meant they had to think a bit harder than normal. Tying the parts of a Geis so close together did not make it an impossible task. Although, for some strange reason, in the stories it was always an impressive feat when somebody found out the private part of a Geis.

"Like Cú Chulainn," Filthy Henry said out loud.

"Huh?" Shelly asked.

"Cú Chulainn, he had a Geis on him," the fairy detective explained. "It was part of the legend. It was placed on him and gifted him with incredible levels of stamina or something like that."

"What was it?"

"It was based around hospitality, if I remember correctly. Right, Elivin?"

The leprechaun nodded her head.

"Yep. The public part was that he could never refuse refreshment when offered it."

"Not exactly the worst curse to be under," Shelly said.

Filthy Henry groaned at her continued misunderstanding of a

Geis, but said nothing.

"The private part, though, was that he could never eat dog meat," the bounty hunter said, her eyebrows raised.

"Em," Shelly said. "I'm not entirely sure what to say to that."

"Usually people just say 'yuck' and move on," Filthy Henry said, smiling.

"Wait a second," Shelly said. "We met his descendant, Cathal. There is no way he was going around with that sort of curse on him."

"Geis are not hereditary," the fairy detective said. "What time is it?"

Shelly checked her watched.

"Coming up on two in the afternoon," she told him.

He nodded thoughtfully.

"Right," Filthy Henry said. "We need to work the brain cells between now and seven this evening to figure this out. Elivin, brew up some magical, strong, coffee there while us mortals start firing around a few neurons. It's late and time is against us."

# Chapter Twenty-Six

The rest of the night had passed uneventfully. Once or twice Medb shifted in her basket, like a demented puppy. Linda's dreams had remained in the category of the fanciful and not nightmarish, never returning to the long-hall of guests laughing at her old body. Her first body. Lauren had probably slept as well, it was difficult to tell with the crone. She existed in a perpetual state of looking energetic and exhausted, like some kinda of insomniac energiser bunny.

It was a paradoxical appearance to maintain.

Breakfast had been sourced from the museum canteen. Medb climbed up into the ceiling space, taking full advantage of being small, and ran across the roof tiles. She returned with coffee and toast, dragging jams along behind her in a small plastic bag. Lauren had taken a coffee and left the toast for Linda to eat. Since there was no way of making the food into a puddle which the rag doll could soak up, Medb did not bother partaking.

"I do miss having a stomach," the rag doll said, climbing back into her dog basket

"Well how else did you expect to be kept alive all this time?" Lauren asked, sipping from her coffee.

"You managed it with him," the rag doll said, pointing at Linda. "Why couldn't we do the same with me?"

"Firstly, he is under a Geis," the crone said, her tone suggesting that this was not the first time the matter had been discussed. "Secondly, I did offer to put you under a similar setup but pointed out that I can only maintain it for one person at a time. Especially one as complex as what he is currently under. Don't forget I was kicked out by my own race. I don't have the full raft of powers I used to. We work with what is available to us.

541

Also, remember, that you were literally about to die and our plan for revenge sort of needed that not to happen."

"You were about to die?" Linda asked Medb.

Medb waved the statement off as if it was nothing.

"I got transported back in time to the point of my death is all," she said.

"That's all?" Lauren said, leaning over the edge of the cot. "That was the entire purpose of the spell in the first place. You only travelled forward in time because you were about to die. If I saved your body at that moment then you would have caused a paradox. Which we're meant to avoid!"

If button eyes could have rolled, Linda felt sure the rag doll would have rolled hers.

"Yes, yes. A universe destroying paradox all because I didn't die when I was meant to. What use is magic if that sort of thing is something queens have to worry about?"

The crone made a noise, dismissive in nature and nasal in origin, then shifted on the cot into a more comfortable position. Beside her the big tome was opened on the same page Linda had seen the previous day.

Listening to the pair of fairy creatures speak, she realised just how little humans knew or understood about the magical world. They, Lauren and Medb, spoke about time travel like it was a common occurrence. Humans, mortals, knew about the concept purely from science fiction stories. Things that destroyed the universe being another topic that did not get brought up on a regular basis in human circles.

She decided to change the subject. The gathering of writers was tonight. Their planning session, such as it had been, had involved very little actually planning. There was a rough idea, the guideline to something, but nothing set in stone. Linda would show up at the event, with Medb in tow, and somehow get up on the main stage in order to extract her revenge.

Fully and completely.

The crone, however, was not going to be with them. That was the part Linda was very unsure about. If she had been a bit more sceptical, the timing of both events being so close together would have raised some alarms. It had the hallmarks of a badly written detective story. One that required the two villains to be separated so the hero could only resolve one problem, while the other was developed into a plot for a later novel.

Linda would have written a much more self contained story.

"How will you know when I've taken enough power for the ritual?" she asked Lauren.

"The grotesque doll of affection over there will be my eyes during tonight's performance," the crone explained. "You get up, do your thing, and then I will know through her that we're ready."

Something had been bothering Linda since the modified plan's inception. Before, all her story stealing had been one-on-one. Generally in isolated locations, away from the prying eyes of others. There had been one or two over the years that had taken place in public, but even they had been semi-private matters. The transference from her victim usually caused a bit of air to blow around them, but nothing that would have raised eyebrows really.

Tonight she planned on stealing a lot more than just one person's stories. In all her centuries, Linda had never attempted a multi-steal. It brought up a number of unknown elements to the entire affair. Could her body handle that influx of power at the same time? Would the effects on a crowd of people cause a noticeable outpouring of magic?

She asked the crone these questions.

"I suppose, in theory, it might," Lauren said, frowning as she spoke. "But don't worry, I will be safe up on my hill doing the ritual and Medb there can't really be injured. What with her being a rag doll and everything."

"Thanks," Linda said, sarcastically. "That's so reassuring. It's like a big, comfy, hug."

"We don't hug," Medb chimed in. "Just keep your eye on the prize. You wipe out entire family trees in the most elaborate revenge plan ever known and we summon somebody who can sort out the fairy detective once and for all."

Linda nodded.

"I know," she said. "I'm just getting impatient."

"Not long now," the crone said.

Her black toothed smile was very unsettling. Linda decided to try and sleep. Tonight was going to be a big night, she wanted to be as fresh as possible for her final performance.

The performance of many lifetimes.

#

Filthy Henry woke with a creak in his neck. The sort that felt like body parts had merged seamlessly with sofa arms, before forgetting they should not do that. He groaned, stretched, felt a number of other body parts crack and snap, showing the signs of age, and slowly sat up.

The sweet aroma of freshly brewed coffee wafted out from the kitchen. After the night they had had, it was as if the gods themselves had decided to make breakfast.

One of the reason's Filthy Henry loved his apartment was the proximity it shared with his office. A lot of people in Ireland shared a common interest in 'The Commute'. The journey that took place during the working week between home and a person's place of employment. It was both feared and loved. Those who commuted for over an hour 'had it rough', while folk who managed it in under an hour were 'jammy gits'. The dream was to have a commute so short it basically was an effort to make it longer. Living over your office qualified for that in spades.

Then again, being your own boss sort of made the whole 'showing up to work on time' thing a moot point.

After Lé Precon's 'share and disappear' show, the three of them had worked the problem. Researching the Geis was tricky for a number of reasons. Mainly, they were going off what had been observed over the past few hundred years. People were showing up with their stories taken, giving the rest of the world the impression that they had gone crazy and lost their mind. That part had been pretty easy to figure out when all was said and done. In order to steal a story the thief-in-Linda's-clothing used a phrase. A simple string of words that, on some conscious level, caused people to offload. They just happened to offload everything until no more offloading could be done. Logically, the problem was none of the victims could tell them what the phrase was, as they would have all forgotten it. Luckily, Filthy Henry had been popped back into his body. Meaning he now possessed two sets of memories to shift through in order to figure out the phrase.

"'Tell me your story.'. That's what he said to me, right before I was flung into my soul container for safe keeping," Filthy Henry told Shelly and Elivin.

"It's so innocent a phrase," Shelly said. "Nobody would think something bad was about to happen. But, doesn't that mean we're at risk?"

Elivin shook her head.

"Nah," she said. "I will cast a spell on us just before we go to the writer's thing. It will add a small delay into how fast your brain hears things. If that phrase is said, the brain will completely ignore it. Replace the word. Should make us immune."

"Should?" Shelly asked.

"Will. Will, okay?"

545

Shelly shrugged.

"It will have to do I guess."

"This still doesn't solve the problem of what the private part of the Geis is," Filthy Henry said.

This had started a hardcore research session. They pulled down every book the fairy detective had on the topic of Geis and curses. Pages and pages of stories, tales and yarns, none of which explained how to figure out what a Geis required. If the private part was something that only the caster and recipient were meant to know, then chances were no private element had ever been documented. It was like trying to solve a fifty piece jigsaw puzzle after somebody hid twenty of the pieces.

The problem was they had a limited amount of time to figure all this out in. Taking a nap so late in the day was not helping them solve the case. Even worse, the fairy detective did not remember falling asleep to begin with.

Groaning, Filthy Henry rose from the sofa and plodded down the small hallway between kitchen and living room. Shelly was brewing the coffee over by the sink, Elivin watching as she sat at the table. For the first time the bounty hunter was out of her padded armour. It made her look a lot smaller.

"Sleep well?" Elivin asked, smiling over a cup of tea.

"Yea," he said, rubbing at his stiff neck. "I feel like an old man."

"Don't you mean a 'new man'?" Shelly asked, pouring out two mugs of coffee.

"I meant what I said," he replied, gruffly. "How long was I out?"

He took the nearest mug of coffee and started drinking from it, enjoying the bitter taste immensely.

"Just forty minutes," the bounty hunter said. "After jumping around between Milton's head and your own, not to mention the whole returning to your body thing, you were due a crash. You haven't slept since getting back into your own body."

"We are sort of working to a deadline," he said. "I shouldn't be sleeping."

"There is that," Shelly agreed. "But you also need to be ready for tonight. A little nap while we continued the research didn't seem like such a bad idea."

The fairy detective decided not to argue. A nap to recharge the batteries, both magical and physical, had helped. Plus, he was sleeping for two at the minute. At least until they figured out what to do with Quinn.

"We need a game plan," Filthy Henry said. "For tonight. Maybe even before. We've only two hours until the writers thingy kicks off and no clue where Linda and co are hiding out."

"Reckon they've gone to ground?" Shelly asked. "We could go back to Linda's apartment, capture her there."

"No, they went to ground for sure," he said. "They must have known Elivin was with you when you went around to Linda's apartment. The crone is many things, but I don't think she is stupid. I'd love to know who her accomplice is though. The doll was giving off magical energy when you were in the apartment?"

"Definitely," Shelly said. "But not a trail, like it was being powered somewhere else. It was more like power had been put into it. At least that's what I could see with my fairy vision. "

Filthy Henry took another sip from his coffee and thought about the doll.

Charms came in all shapes and sizes. The size of the object generally reflected how much power it was capable of storing. Little stone charms, for example, could be used to contain at most three small charges or one big charge. Typically stone charms were all aimed at protection. The stone acted as reinforcement for the spell within, protecting the wearer. You could, of course, put other spells into stone charms but fairy folk were big on keep things traditional.

A rag doll, however, was a new one. The fairy detective had no idea what sort of spell you would put inside something like that. Maybe if it was being carried around by a child, some sort of ward from danger or evil. But the crone and Linda were not exactly children. So why have a doll with magical energies stored in it? He was regretting sending Shelly now. While she had a head for figuring things out, her only magical ability made understanding the spells in an area totally beyond her.

"What the hell was that doll?" he said to himself. "Wonder if that was the thing I saw in the memory fragment..."

"I've been thinking about later," Elivin said. "We need to be clever."

"Hmm?" Filthy Henry mumbled through another sip of coffee.

"I know I've been chasing this guy for a while, but there is obviously something bigger going on too," the leprechaun bounty hunter said. "While we have to capture him, we also need to know what the others are up to. From what I've heard about The Crone McGarry, she isn't exactly known for getting involved in something that did not, in some way, suit her needs."

"What are you suggesting?" Shelly asked.

Elivin smiled.

"I think we can let him, or her... - whatever the correct pronoun for a body swapping mortal is! -, we let them get up and nearly complete their plan. 'Nearly' being the operative word. Right to the point they think that it is all in the bag and they are going to win. Then we take them down and, in the process, maybe figure out what McGarry's bigger plan actually is."

It was not a completely horrible idea. In fact it was a fairly good one. The bad guys, at least in Filthy Henry's experience, always seemed to get overly cocky when things came to the dramatic climax. As if they were thinking about their roast chicken dinner on Sunday before the egg containing that very chicken had even dropped from the hen. Letting Linda believe she was about to steal Tracey Fitzgerald's stories might give them an edge on stopping the crone, permanently. At the very least they would stop Linda from causing any more harm and, assuming they figured out the private element to the Geis, undo all her bad work.

Plus, something about Elivin's cheeky grin suggested she had a Filthy Henry style plan up her sleeve.

"That's very controlled of you," he said, waiting to see if show rose to the bait.

Disappointingly, she did not. Which meant that whatever Elivin had come up with was enough to keep all of her attention on not getting angry.

"It is," the leprechaun said. "What's more, I've a plan."

#

Events organised in Ireland generally fall into a few categories.

There are the ones organised by people who have absolutely no interest in the event itself or what is being hosted. They purely want to make some cash selling tickets and overpriced street meat to a bunch of people willing to part with hard earned money. Such events, generally, get held in fields that nothing really big or important was happening in anyway. Meaning it was free and needed filling. These events are ran once, maybe twice, then word spreads about the shoddy organisational skills and everyone starts to avoid them. Not that the organisers really care. By then profit has been made, the fees covered, and they have bought a second home somewhere.

Then you have events that the government get involved in.

Ireland, like most countries in the world, has a government that could not organise a group walk through a hedge maze with a map and GPS. Events ran by the government are typically outsourced to an event management company. In swoops a bunch of professionals who will, with almost military precession, provide an event that people will be impressed by. They will have agendas, timelines, and, if patrons are lucky, goodie bags containing any number of business branded paraphernalia. People will say the experience was not half bad and it will become a fixed event on the calendar. The government, being like any mass collection of talentless politicians, will claim all the credit for an event well run and pat themselves on the back. While the event management company will frown from the wings but ensure that the contract for running the event is very lucrative for a number of years to come.

The final type of event typically found in Ireland is one ran by people who want the event to be a success. For the attendees to enjoy it and the organisers to feel like it is just one big party. If some money is made at the end it gets funnelled back into the event so that the following year is better than before. An event ran for the fans, by the fans, and typically one that lasts for years and draws numbers that only grow and grow.

In The Irish Writers Centre at the top of Parnell Square, the gathering of storytellers was an event clearly being ran by other writers. No event management sorts could be seen organising in the background, nor were there any people looking bored at the patrons but happy with the amount building up in the collection box. This was an event being ran by writers and storytellers for writers and storytellers. Anyone not falling into those brackets but attending had decided to come for some wholesome entertainment.

As Linda entered through the main door of the building she felt a momentary pang of guilt. These people were, technically, her family. Ireland had a rich tradition when it came to storytelling. It was almost something that made up the very genetic nature of the Irish people. They seemingly could not help themselves. Those who did not turn it into a full time career were considered 'the life and soul' of any party they attended by being able to entertain with funny yarns. Coupled with the urge to travel, to explore the world and visit lands foreign, it was no wonder that the Irish had a reputation for being entertaining people. But, as quickly as it came on her, the guilt left Linda the minute her eyes locked on Tracey's face.

She was sitting just to the left of a little platform in the main room. Chairs had been arranged in rows, all facing the stage, most of them occupied by eager attendees. Some people had opted to watch the night's performance by standing at the back of the room or standing along the walls. On the stage there was a microphone stand, one of those fancy wireless mics sitting in it, and two chairs. One empty, one with Tracey, the last name on Linda's List, sitting in it.

A small bag hanging over Linda's left shoulder contained Medb. The rag doll had opened the flap partially and was looking around the room. Despite being an animated doll, Medb did a good job of not drawing attention to herself. Nobody else in the room seemed to even notice that Linda's bag had a small head checking the place out. Spying a solo chair along the left wall of the room, Linda headed towards it and sat down. She placed the bag on her lap, adjusting the flap slightly so that Medb could see her, then made sure nobody was paying them any heed. Around them the room was filled with voices, dozens of little conversations going on in the build up to the night's event.

"We're good," Linda said. "He isn't here."

"Doesn't look like it," Medb whispered, peering around the room slowly. "Leave me under the chair, in the bag. When nobody is looking I will slip out and move through the room. Those book shelves over there look like a good spot to watch out for the ginger haired moron."

Linda nodded in agreement, trying not to seem like she was

551

talking to herself. A young girl came walking through the crowd, a bundle of programmes in her arms. She handed one to Linda, smiled, and carried on passing them out to anybody without one. Linda opened it up and scanned over the line-up for the night. The first entry caught her eye. She folded over the page and angled it so that Medb could easily read the writing.

"This is just the introduction to the performance?" the rag doll whispered. "It is moving to a bigger venue?"

"Seems that way," Linda said, talking the page up and pretending to read it. "Due to demand for space they are doing a quick intro here, then moving it outside so more people can attend."

"More people to give us their stories," Medb said.

"Exactly. With any luck we may even avoid bumping into the fairy detective, because it looks like we're moving now and the flier I had from the hospital did not list an outdoor venue for the event."

It was hard to tell with the sock style face, but Medb appeared to be smiling.

"Guess we're going for a little jaunt then."

#

One of the big problems with Ireland was that everyone who thought they were anyone looked upon Dublin as the 'be all and end all'. Sure, as a county, it was not all that bad. But it was not the centre of the island. It was not even just off centre. For a coastal county to even consider itself the centre would have raised many questions about what the country looked like on a map.

It would have had to be a lot smaller, for starters.

This thinking did have some benefits. One being that The Midlands were more or less unmolested by the advance of civilization as Dublin forever was favoured for improvements. Whole fields stood as they had for hundreds of years, untouched by the trappings of mortal man. Roads were nowhere to be seen, buildings completely missing, the only sounds being those of nature.

As it should be.

The Crone McGarry detested how humans had spread across Ireland like a virus. Leaving their mark on the land in concrete, glass and stone. It showed how far they had moved away from the Old Ways, the traditions. There was no respect shown to the land any more. If a man wanted to build a gaudy construct that marred the beauty of nature all they had to do was pay another man some money. At no point was The Land asked about the transaction, or if it even wanted to be sold.

Mortals needed to be put back in their place, especially if Lauren had anything to do with it. They would be wiped clean from Ireland and the fairy folk could take their rightful position in the world once more. No longer hidden away, seen only by accident. They would be back in power for the good of the country.

A direct result of the mortals spreading across Ireland was the destruction of the fairy forts. A name used by all fairy folk to describe the little rings of stone that were found out in the middle of nowhere. Small stones, pebbles really, were arranged on the ground to form a little circle, with long blades of grass spread over the stones to give the impression of a ring. While no proper sized fairy would actually be involved in their construction, pixies were not proper sized fairies. They were little bigger than flies, glowing brightly as they flew around the world doing absolutely nothing worthwhile.

Nothing, save for one useful thing. Something all pixies did without consciously knowing it, Lauren reckoned.

Pixies built the little fairy forts at the intersections of ley lines, invisible sources of magical energies that criss-crossed the country. The larger the ring, the more ley lines intersected at that point. Nobody, not even the fairy folk, truly understood where the lines came from or what governed their creation. They could not be directly tapped into in order to boost one's own magic levels and, occasionally, simple spells performed near them could have unexpected consequences. But at these ley line intersections, on the right day of the year, at the right point in time, there were benefits to be found.

Right then, Lauren stood in the middle of a fairy fort roughly the size of a three-bedroom mortal house. Some of the grass over the stones was fresh, having only been placed there in the last few days, and even now a pixie, purple in colour, was racing around the circle and fixing the stones. The creature probably did not even know why it was doing this, only that a compunction to ensure the circle was maintained had to be obeyed.

It did not matter. What mattered was that the crone was in a spot of great power and shortly more energy would be coming.

Then a revenge that made the storyteller's plan seem like a petty child's squabble would be taken out on a world that deserved to be taught a serious lesson.

Lauren waited a heartbeat, then lashed out with her good leg and stamped down on the pixie as it flew close by. She smiled, reached into her bag, and began to lay out the ritualistic objects.

#

"Run that one past me again?"

"It isn't here, it moved."

"Moved how?"

"Moved, as in moved. Everyone got up and left."

"To where?"

"I don't know."

"Why not?"

"Because that isn't part of my job. I'm just meant to look after the building when everyone is away."

"Away? Away where?"

"Lady, you really need to get your ears checked. I just told you, I don't know. That was the whole point of this event. They left about thirty minutes ago I reckon, best I can do for you."

Shelly glared at the young man behind the counter, turned sharply on her heel, and marched back out of the writer's centre. At the bottom of the steps outside stood Filthy Henry and Elivin.

"Well?" Filthy Henry asked.

"Don't," she said, annoyed. "Just don't."

"I thought we sent her in because she is the people person," Elivin said.

"I am the people person!" Shelly snapped. "The guy in there is either a moron or the most annoying idiot on the planet."

"First time I haven't been called that," the fairy detective said, grinning.

"You rapidly moved back into first place," Shelly said.

"Knew we should have come earlier," Filthy Henry said. "Shouldn't have taken that nap. Damn I hate working a case when I am not at my best."

"You must hate working all the time then," the leprechaun bounty hunter said to him, smiling.

"You're better than that," the fairy detective replied.

"What did you find out? How come we're not just going inside?" Elivin asked.

Shelly could feel the headache building already, right above her eyes. She pinched the bridge of her nose and started to take some deep, calming, breaths.

"Apparently tonight's event was mainly organised by Tracey Fitzgerald. The only thing that happened here was a staging area for some of the local writers to gather in. But the actual event is taking place somewhere else."

"Where else?" Filthy Henry asked.

"He didn't know," Shelly said. "Because the man, as I've already pointed out, was clearly a moron. He never thought to ask for the sake of any late comers to the event. Super late comers, might I add, since they left thirty minutes ago. Supposedly it was all organised online through Tracey's fan site, which you have to be a member of. Anyone who just showed up was escorted, with Tracey leading the horde, to the super secret location for the event to kick off properly. Apparently more people will be meeting them at the new location because it was sold out for here and they didn't want to disappoint folk. Even the starting time on the flier is wrong. Sme mix-up when they printed and distributed them. Tracey's website had the correct time on it. Meaning we are even later than we thought."

Filthy Henry stared at her, clearly surprised at this burst of information.

"You've got to be kidding me," he said after nearly thirty seconds of staring at her. "They could be anywhere!"

Shelly nodded, pinching the bridge of her nose even tighter.

"Yep," she said. "Basically we're boned."

The three of them stood at the end of the stone steps and said nothing. There really was nothing to say. All their information had led them to the Writer's Centre and now that was a dead-end. Complete with a dead-end idiot sitting behind the desk with about as much useful intel as a blank page. Shelly knew, without even asking, that magic was not a solution to the problem. Neither

Filthy Henry nor Elivin would be able to track down Linda without some sort of hair sample. Even suggesting they teleport around the city was a bad idea. It would be taxing on the fairy detective and the bounty hunter, and that was if they could take it in turns. Plus they would just spend the night bouncing around, checking places that might, possibly, be suited for a gathering of writers.

For the first time ever, Shelly really hoped that Filthy Henry would be able to pull off one of his near trademarked insane plans. The kind of plan that began as a Hail Mary idea and ultimately saved the day. Last time it had involved kissing a girl in the middle of a battle. Surely something similar could pop into his head now.

Although, thinking about it, Shelly was not sure how that could be possible. They had all been working the case together and nothing so far had even suggested that a random cheeky kiss would save the day.

She mulled over what options they had open to them. Options that clearly Filthy Henry and Elivin were overlooking, as neither had said a word for the past few minutes. As she thought about things a young couple walked towards them down the path. The man on the left had a soul patch and was carrying what honestly looked like a typewriter under his arm. His boyfriend was clean shaven and, to Shelly's eye, looked almost embarrassed to be seen in public with a typewriter. At the steps the soul-patched man stopped, handed his typewriter to his boyfriend, and quickly ran up the stairs and entered the writer's centre.

"Please don't," the clean shaven man said.

"Don't say your boyfriend looks like the king of the hipsters?" Filthy Henry asked, staring after the man.

"Yeah," the clean shaven man replied, walking a few steps away from their little party and trying to not draw attention to the fact he was holding a typewriter.

Filthy Henry slowly shook his head.

"I wonder if sometimes I shouldn't just let the evil fairy sorts take over," he said. "Come on, Shelly. You're an arty-farty type. Where would your people congregate for something like this?"

"My people?" she asked. "I'm an artist, not a writer. How the hell would I know where they would meet up for something like this. Aside from here?"

"Potato, tomato," the fairy detective said, waving his hands in a dismissive way. "You free spirits are all the same."

Behind them, the door to the centre opened and Soul-patch stepped out. He ran down the steps with his phone out, furiously typing into it. Spying where his boyfriend stood, Soul-patch ran over to him and showed something on the phone screen. He took back his typewriter and they both headed off down the street.

"What if we go to Linda's apartment, get some of her hair. Do a tracking spell?" Shelly asked.

"No point," Elivin said just as Filthy Henry answered with "Not a bad idea."

The fairy detective and Shelly both looked at Elivin.

"Why is there no point?" Shelly asked her.

The leprechaun indicated with a nod of her head at the two men as they turned the corner.

"No point," she said. "Because it looks like those guys figured out with their smart phone where everyone else is."

Filthy Henry watched as the men rounded the corner and were gone from view.

"How come you didn't think of that?" he asked Shelly.

The irony of this question was not lost on her. Thankfully the desire to continue such a conversation held no appeal. Without

saying a word, Shelly marched down the street after the two men
with Elivin and Filthy Henry close behind.

# Chapter Twenty-Seven

The ritual preparations were complete. All the candles placed correctly and lit. Sheep's blood had been poured in an intricate pattern within the fairy fort. A number of pixies had come by to do some minor repairs on the stone circle. Each had been caught and killed, their little glowing bodies incorporated into the design on the ground.

"Waste not want not," Lauren said, sprinkling some bone meal around the outside of the fairy fort.

Everything was ready. The hour slowly approached. All that she required now was an infusion of power and finally her plan would be kicked into full swing. Lauren, standing outside the stone circle, dropped her bag to the ground, tossed aside her walking stick, then removed all her clothing.

Undressing was not really needed in order to perform the ritual, it was just a hot evening. Chances were all the dancing around would cause a bit of a sweat to be worked up. Nobody wanted to have that happen while fully dressed. Plus, part of the crone's exile meant she could no longer use the *Caillí Mór,* The Big Veil, to hide from human sight. If any mortals did happen to stumble by, a haggard old woman dancing buck naked in the middle of a field would dissuade them from being too nosy about affairs that were none of their business.

Mainly, though, Lauren just did not want to have to wash her clothes afterwards.

Dipping her hands into the last of the sheep's blood, she drew three red lines on either cheek and then dabbed a single spot on her forehead. Stepping back inside the fairy fort, Lauren began calling upon her own magic and slowly started to perform the ritual.

The ritual that would right all the wrongs in her world.

#

Linda smiled the entire walk from the writer's centre. It was almost as if Fate had gotten involved and decided to make her revenge all the better. Moving the venue to a location with even more people in attendance just sweetened the entire affair.

When nobody was looking she reached into the bag and lifted Medb out. The rag doll did a good job of looking inanimate when in the possessed nurse's hand. Linda brought her up, close to her head, and started whispering to Medb.

"Anything to worry about?"

Medb's button eyes looked back over Linda's shoulder.

"Can't see if the ginger one is following us. I think this group left just at the right moment. Stick to the plan though, right?"

Linda nodded.

"Of course," she said. "I was reading over the schedule for the night. Right before Tracey gets up and does her thing there is an audience Q and A session. With a microphone being passed through the crowd so that everyone can hear the questions being asked. Supposedly it was a sign up sheet she held on her website. People all put in a question, along with their name, and then folk voted on the top ten."

"Okay," Medb said, going limp in her hand. "How does that help us?"

"This lot appear to be traditionalists when it comes to writing," Linda said. "There is bound to be a hard copy of that question sheet floating around. All we need to do is alter the list. I get to be a person in the crowd asking a question, meaning we don't have to come up with some other idea to get my hand on a microphone. Everything comes up on the side of evil."

Medb's rag doll mouth opened in that twisted little smile she did.

"Oh," the rag doll said. "That is fantastic. Once we get to the new venue, I'll jump out of this bag and change the list. You're not bad at improv when it comes to plans, you know that?"

Linda shrugged.

"Maybe it's all the decades of making up lies on the spot. Either way, this lot will not know what happens to them."

She began to wonder just where this gathering of writers were headed. It was a lovely summer's night, not too cold and with a sky full of stars instead of clouds. In fact, for Ireland, this was practically the best definition of summer weather. Irish people, in general, did not do well when the weather got very hot. It was a strange condition the entire country had been afflicted with, running all the way back to the first person ever to step foot on Irish shores. Something about extremely hot weather made the Irish people lose their minds slightly. They would either complain ad infinitum about how hot the day was and could it not just rain for a few minutes to cool things down or, surprisingly, complain that it was raining and that the heat made it unbearable. Failing that they would, en masse, flock to parks and beaches or back gardens and proceed to drink copious amounts of alcoholic beverages. Disregarding the fact that heat tended to make people need proper hydration and booze did a great job of dehydrating people.

Linda had observed this during her extended time alive and found it most entertaining. You could almost work out the country average for sick days by seeing what the temperature was like during the months of summer. Hot days would always lead to 'sick days' directly afterwards. It had gotten to the point that she wondered if the Irish Government would not be better served bringing in official hangover days. A legally supplied day that could be used during gainful employment to prevent wasting sick days on hangovers.

563

The group continued walking down Gardiner Place, a herd of writers and lovers of the written word, without veering at all. Linda guessed that the final destination would be Mountjoy Square Park. If they had decided to take the event outdoors and enjoy the rare good weather, while also having enough space for extra attendees, then the park was the logical choice. Crossing at Mountjoy Square West validated her thinking. Everyone filed through the small gate in the wrought iron fence that surrounded the park, moving down the path to the recently installed event area.

She smiled.

"What's so funny?" Medb asked.

"Nothing," Linda replied. "I'm just so happy to finally finish this. Let's get a seat in the middle. I want to see everyone as they are emptied out."

#

Filthy Henry was annoyed.

Once again the modern world had made a mockery of the magical one. It was like a horrible joke at this point. A leprechaun, a half-breed and a human who could see the Fairy World are working on a case and hit a brick wall. How did they resolve this blocker? They followed a pair of humans with a smartphone and a social media account.

The internal laughter was as bad as if the world had started laughing at him. For a second he wondered if Quinn was actually laughing. He sent the query inwards, to the corners of his mind, but got back no response.

Ahead of them, by about twenty feet to avoid spooking the pair, the young couple walked. Every few feet the clean shaven one would point at the typewriter his boyfriend was carrying and say something. The hipster-boyfriend would respond, there would be a lot of head shaking, and on they continued.

"We sure these guys know where they are going?" Shelly asked.

"Positive," Elivin said, completely invisible to humans. "You don't let your partner keep carrying that stupid glorified paperweight around if you aren't going to meet a bunch of writers. Besides, I saw the phonescreen when he walked down the steps and they had that app open that only let's short status updates. So it is trending, as the kids say. Humans and their need to tell everyone in the world what is going on in their tiny little lives. Using less than one-hundred and fifty characters."

"Hey!" Filthy Henry said, looking down at the bounty hunter. "If it wasn't for that stupid trait we would be still standing at the bottom of those stairs and the world would be screwed. Plus, you'd never get a chance to catch this guy. Humans aren't nearly as bad or useless as fairies would have you believe."

"Whatever," the leprechaun said. "Looks like we're going into that park."

"Huh," Shelly said. "That makes sense. Lovely night, you want to sell a bunch of tickets, you host it in a park. I'd read somewhere that they were trying to make Mountjoy Square Park more event friendly. Something about it being overlooked and the council wanting to rejuvenate the area."

"Didn't think to mention this earlier?" Filthy Henry asked. "Considering we were standing around with no clue or hunch?"

He did not wait for Shelly to answer, put quickened his pace and closed the distance between himself and the young couple. Together the three of them, Filthy Henry and the young men, crossed the road and entered the park, falling in behind other attendees for the event. Once through the gate Filthy Henry detached himself from the bickering pair, an argument that had escalated slightly when the clean-shaven one had bumped the typewriter with his elbow.

On the other side of the gate a large crowd had gathered.

Everybody from budding writers to avid readers, with a healthy mix of people strong in the belief that they were working on the next best seller. They milled around the park in small groups or as individuals, clutching what they no doubt believed were works of amazing literary feats.

Of Linda there was no sign.

Filthy Henry slowly scratched his left cheek and scanned the assorted faces before him.

"Well this is going to be like finding a Pulitzer amongst the slush pile of a publishing house. On the first go," he said.

Shelly and Elivin had caught up with him.

"Oh crap," Shelly said, looking around at the crowd of people.

"Exactly!" he said. "We've to find Linda before she kicks off her little party trick and this place is completely bunged. Who knew Dublin had so many budding wastes of space interested in something like this."

"Budding writers," Shelly said. "Everyone here is a budding writer."

"Right," Filthy Henry said. "That's what I said. Isn't it?"

"You called them wastes of space," Elivin told him.

The fairy detective looked down at her.

"Don't you have somewhere else to be?"

Elivin smiled and walked away from them, the crowd moving so she was able to weave between people with practised fairy ease.

"Fairy vision," Shelly blurted out.

Several nearby people, with what appeared to be screenplays in their arms, looked over at her. When nothing further appeared to happen they returned to their stimulating conversation about naval gazing or whatever they had been talking about. Filthy Henry was sure the topic of conversation would not have interested him in the least.

"You do get that we've to keep the whole fairy thing to ourselves, right?" the fairy detective asked Shelly, keeping his voice low so that none of the soon-to-be-rejected Spielbergs could hear.

"I'm just saying," she whispered. "We could use our fairy vision to find Linda. It would make sense. She'll be the only thing with magic in the crowd."

"Won't work," Filthy Henry said. "She's really human, just under a Geis. Even the fact that her body is currently possessed won't work in our favour. Only way we would find her that way is if we catch her using her magic. It's the spirit that would give off magic and it is covered in a handy human body camouflage."

"The doll," Shelly said.

Filthy Henry looked back over the crowd and felt like his needle was in a haystack with hay that looked like needles.

"Okay," he said. "Let's give it a shot. You swing left, I'll go right, and we work our way towards the middle."

Shelly nodded, closed her eyes, then opened them with the tell-tale blue glow of her fairy vision.

"Try not to blow anything up while we're out there," she said. "Plus, you know, if you could figure out what the private part of that curse is so we can use it to stop her. That would be awesome."

"For the last time it's not a curse!" Filthy Henry said, stopping when he heard a chuckle.

There was a chuckle, followed by a whoop of delight, coupled with the sense that a fist had been punched into the air. None of which happened outside the confines of the fairy detective's head.

Shelly walked off into the crowd, leaving Filthy Henry alone with his thoughts.

Thoughts which he was not fully alone with in a cranial capacity.

#

The crowd had steadily grown for the past twenty minutes, more and more of the writing community filling every inch of the park. All of the seats on Linda's row, plus the ones behind and in front, were occupied. Some of the occupants were chatting amongst themselves, others were reading the itinerary or making adjustments to their manuscripts with pens.

Nowhere could she see any of the old style storytellers, the vocal traditionalists. The Keepers of Oral Tales. It seemed that, of all the storytelling arts, these were the only ones not represented. Another sign that Ireland had lost the run of herself. Everyone just cared about information in digital format. Being able to read it on a device that could be kept in your pocket. Stories no longer than a hundred or so characters. Bite-sized tales. The Age of Epics had long since passed.

Even printed books were dying out and they had been the most amazing thing to happen since druids copied text by hand.

Although, judging from the hefty tomes some of those around Linda carried, there were still some fanatics of the printed word. One young woman appeared to have cut down an entire forest to print her work. Linda even caught a glimpse of the title page and was surprised to see it contained the words 'Part One'. Given that the first part required a small trailer to transport it, Linda dreaded to think how big the next part was. Parts, even.

She had lost sight of Tracey Fitzgerald when the crowd had left the Writer's Centre, but that was not exactly cause for alarm. Everyone had been heading in the same direction and Tracey was the main attraction for the event. Somewhere in the park Tracey was wandering around, unaware that her last creative thoughts were rattling through her head. While, elsewhere in the park, a little demented rag doll was moving through the crowd, searching for a list to alter so that Linda's name was on it.

The thrill of anticipation was like a drug in her system.

Nothing could spoil a night like this. Not even Shelly walking along the outskirts of the crowd.

Linda did a double take and frowned, staring at Shelly walked through the crowd. There were enough people in the park to have little groups moving about, strolling around the seats. They kept Linda hidden one second, then left large gaps the next. She looked to her left and right, cursing the popularity of the event. She was boxed in. Standing up and moving along the row of seats risked drawing attention to herself.

On the back of the chair in front of her a young man had left his hooded jacket. Quickly, while nobody was watching, she tugged it slowly down to the ground from the seat. Waiting no more than two seconds, Linda bent down and picked the jacket up off the grass. She pulled it on and flipped the hood up, tugging it forward so that it covered most of her head and face.

One thing that always happened in situations like this was the person would run. They would get up from their seat, bring undue attention on themselves, and try to make a break for it. Linda had read enough stories, told enough of them and stolen just as many, to learn a thing or two from them. Running right now, while Shelly was just looking around, was the worst thing to do. Changing bodies was also off the table. Even with the extra energy in the area waiting to be collected, mortals would notice a red mist floating out of Linda towards her next body. Again, attention that she could do without. Not to mention the drop in power would be a problem, coupled with the distinct possibility that once Linda was back to herself she would remember who the next host was.

No, the best plan at that very moment was to remain in her

569

seat. Appear aloof, uninterested, in what was going on around her. Maybe even pretend to be asleep. Two rows up a student looking type was doing exactly that. Linda slouched in her seat, head resting on her chest and tilted forward. She hugged her stomach with her left arm, while using her right hand to both prop up her face and cover one side of it. It was not the best disguise in the world, but it should be enough to pass the casual examination Shelly was currently doing.

Linda glanced at the watch on her left arm and saw that the event was about to kick off, opening with the Q&A session. Ten minutes, all she had to do was stay uninteresting for ten minutes.

Then she spotted Filthy Henry walking along the other side of seating area.

"I just can't catch a bloody break," Linda mumbled into her hand.

#

With her fairy vision turned up to maximum, Shelly slowly worked her way through the crowd.

In her former life she had lived for events like this. A gathering of like-minded individuals to share ideas with, collaborate together and maybe even form friendships. Although that last one had never really happened for Shelly. Neither had the collaborations, come to think of it. She never knew why that had been the case. Her eccentric years were ahead of her, wandering around some nursing home with dollops of paint all over her face muttering about invisible creatures. True, she had tried to convince a lot of people that her cat really did speak with her. But that was hardly something a person should be judged by and promptly shunned afterwards, was it? Just because everyone else did not know that Cat Síths existed was not Shelly's fault.

After a while she had stopped going to the gatherings, retreating in on herself at the expense of finding 'workmates'. Shelly had a few good friends in her life, ones she grew up with, and did not need the approval of her peers.

But it would have been nice to get all the same.

This event, for the writers of Ireland, seemed to basically be the same as the old painting jams. Some had come to share their projects, others to pawn their wares in the hopes of striking a lucrative deal. A select few, the wisest of folks, tried to impart their wisdom on the younger generation. Just because said wisdom had not actually worked and was probably the scribblings of a mad man, on the back of a beer mat nonetheless, did not mean it should not be shared.

Strangely, there were some fairy folk in the crowd. Not just the usual random ones you would see around the city from time to time, fairies simply going about their business and generally ignoring mortals. These seemed to be fairies genuinely interested in the event. Some carried books, written by humans, clutching them tightly to their chests while others even appeared to be carrying manuscripts themselves. As if they were here for advice on how to succeed in the human publishing world.

Shelly was not sure if they were in violation of The Rules or not. Mainly because she was not completely sure of all The Rules. They mostly seemed to govern magical acts involving the fairy and human world. It was highly unlikely they would prevent a fairy trying to become a published author or attending a writers event for some tips on the trade. Maybe if they tried to use magic in order to succeed with their book, like a certain author-turned-vampire had, it would be different. Otherwise, Shelly figured it was all fair game.

Of Linda, however, there was no sign. Shelly had worked her way through most of the standing crowd, looking at people with her fairy vision, and seen nothing out of the ordinary.

Her hope had been that Linda would be giving off an aura that could easily be spotted, even though Filthy Henry had said that would not be the case. All the fairy races, when viewed with the full blast of her fairy vision, displayed some sort of aura. But obviously the Geis did not alter the host body, just as the fairy detective had said. Annoyingly, this made him right once more. Meaning the age old eyeball approach to searching would be needed.

She spotted Filthy Henry on the far side of the seating area and walked over to him, weaving through the crowd.

"Any luck?" Shelly asked him.

He shook his head and looked at a lady walking past, the blue glow around his eyes indicating his fairy vision was also currently in use.

"Nothing," Filthy Henry said. "There are a lot of fairy folk around here though. Did you notice that?"

"Yeah," she said. "Didn't think they would be interested in something like this."

"Maybe they want to get a little culture in their lives. Either that or fairies can be just as hipsterish as humans when it comes to going against the norm. 'Oh I was reading human sci-fi before it was cool.'," Filthy Henry said, putting on a real nasal voice for the last part. "It's like how, suddenly, everyone loves comic-book movies. Go back ten years and they would have been the stuff of nerds only."

Shelly smiled and started to check the people up on stage. None of them had any magical energies coming off them either. While fairies seemed to be interested in attending the event, organising it was something they clearly wanted left to the humans.

"Elivin is doing what exactly?"

"She's doing what any useful leprechaun would do," the fairy detective said. "Staying out of sight and working in the background. It has to be in the seats, right?"

"It?"

"Linda," Filthy Henry said. "I can't use the pronoun for it, just doesn't feel right. The body is female, the mind is male. Who has time to be working out what is the politically correct way to address such a person?"

"I'm sure a lot of transgender people will feel delighted by that logical leap," Shelly said.

"No! That's not the same thing at all. They know they are a man in a woman's body, or vice versa. They make a choice to change the outside so it correctly matches the inside. That makes perfect sense. This thing, Linda, is a woman with a woman's body currently possessed by a man who had a male body. Don't go coming at me with your apples and oranges comparison."

"Whatever," Shelly said, secretly chuffed that she had made the fairy detective feel the need to justify his words for once.

In the rows of seats Shelly spotted something interesting. While most of the attendees were sitting around, conversing amongst themselves or just reading the programme for the night, one person was apparently asleep. At least that was what anybody just glancing at them would have assumed. They had their hood pulled up and forward, obscuring the top part of their face. They were resting their cheek on a hand. All in, it seemed like a person just catching a sneaky nap. Unless you were searching for somebody, then they looked like a person trying very hard not to be identified.

She nudged Filthy Henry in the ribs, nodding towards the sleeper. He followed her eyeline and frowned, then took a step forward.

"Might be," he said. "Let's be those annoying people who arrive late to the cinema and work through the seats."

Before he could ask the first person to move, something ran past his feet. It was roughly the size of a small cat, and jumped up

573

into the air. It clung to the side of his coat, climbed quickly up to stand on his shoulder, then, with a round and pudgy, hand punched him in the nose. As the thing, which Shelly now saw was the horrible rag doll from Linda's kitchen sink, landed another punch to Filthy Henry's cheek it jumped at her. She tried to bat the rag doll away as it flew through the air but failed miserably. The thing landed on her chest, scrambled up her coat, using the zipper like some sort of mountain climbing line, then hauled itself up onto her shoulder.

"This will teach you both not to meddle in the affairs of a queen! One who just wanted to get a matching set of bulls!" the rag doll shouted, grabbing onto Shelly's hair and pulling herself up until she was on top of her head.

"OUCH!" Shelly screeched as the rag doll grabbed two tiny fistfuls of hair and started to pull. It felt like the hairs were coming out at the roots.

Shelly reached up and tried to pull the doll off her head, but the animated nightmare had a firm grip. Around them the other writers and attendees were watching events unfold. Nobody seemed to be taking the attack seriously. Some even had their phones out and were recording the whole thing, like it was some sort of performance piece. Which, Shelly thought during painful pulls on her hair, it would probably look like to people unaware of the magical world.

Filthy Henry had staggered backwards after the initial attack on his face. He straightened up, holding his nose, and looked at the rag doll as blood poured out his left nostril.

"Medb?" he mumbled through his hand. "You are in the doll?"

The rag doll decided not to answer. Instead it pulled so hard on Shelly's hair that she had no other option but to turn in the direction to try and mitigate the pain.

"Hiya, bull!" the rag doll shouted. "Hiya! Mush!"

More hair pulling caused Shelly to move forward through the crowd of people, desperately trying to free herself of the tiny terror on her head.

While all around them people cheered, clearly enjoying what they did not fully understand.

#

Linda lost track of where Shelly was after the woman had walked past the front of the stage and over to the other side of the seating area. Pulling down the hood and taking a quick look would have been the smart move, but also the most risky. Chances were that the minute the hood was pulled down Shelly would be looking directly at Linda's seat. Putting everything in jeopardy and risking the wrath of Lauren was not worth it.

Her heart started to pound. At that very moment she could be safe or have a fairy detective standing directly behind her ready to pounce. When something brushed against her feet, it took all of Linda's self control to not jump from her seat. She moved her head slightly, looking at at the grass, and saw Medb's rag doll face staring back up at her. The doll remained on the ground, standing underneath the chair in front of Linda in an effort to remain hidden from anyone nearby.

Neither of Linda's neighbouring chairs seemed to be paying her any attention. She motioned with her finger for Medb to come up. The rag doll did so, quickly, climbing inside the hoodie and moving up towards Linda's left shoulder.

"You're on the list," Medb said. "Thankfully they did this entire thing old school. All I had to do was pull out a blank page, scribble your name onto it, then leave it at the top of the pile. Even managed to pop on and off the paper-clip. I think I should have gone into this sorta crime much earlier."

"Great," Linda said, keeping her chin on her chest and aiming her mouth in Medb's direction. "But Shelly and Filthy Henry are here. Shelly just walked past."

Medb pushed down a fold of material that was blocking her view from inside the hoodie.

"Over the other side? I see them. Crap, what are they doing here? Okay, play it cool."

"Cool?" Linda asked. "I've been sitting like this for nearly five minutes to avoid them seeing me."

"Double crap!" Medb hissed.

Linda's heart started beating faster. She really wanted to move and have a look at whatever the rag doll was seeing, but knew it was a sure fire way to disaster. Instead she decided to let Medb be her eyes.

"What?" she asked.

Medb peered around the bit of hoodie that was concealing her, looking at the sleeping man two rows up.

"They've spotted that dude," she said to Linda. "Which means they are going to start checking people in the seats. I'm going to run interference."

Before the nurse could ask what that meant, Medb shimmed back down her torso, using Lnda's left leg to slide to the ground. She stepped underneath the seat in front of Linda again, then ran between the chair legs towards the right. Without moving, Linda knew that the ensuing commotion had to be because of the rag doll.

Linda slowly, carefully, turned her head in the direction of the shouting and saw Medb had climbed up onto Shelly's head and was pulling the woman's hair. Filthy Henry was holding his nose, stemming the flow of blood from his nostrils by the looks of it.

Then Shelly, batting at Medb, ran off into the crowd and away from the seats.

Linda took a deep breath, steadied her nerves as best she could, then checked her watch. Five more minutes.

It felt like an eternity to wait.

#

The Crone McGarry had worked up quite a sweat and was glad to be buck naked.

There was a reason that rituals of this nature required so much dancing and cavorting. While the magic requirement, the sheer insane levels of energy needed, was one impediment to put people off doing it, the physical exercise was definitely another factor to consider. It made all those work out videos that humans loved seem like a lazy Sunday on the sofa watching repeats of boring television shows.

Sweat was dripping from her body as she went through the intricate movements of the ritual. Each time an arm was flung out the movement filled the air with sweat droplets. Lauren was happy that nobody else was doing this little performance with her. It was bad enough spraying the land with salty goodness without the risk of a fellow practitioner dousing you with sweat.

The clear night sky was full of stars, a full moon lazily rising upwards. Lauren had started to channel some of the magic stored in Linda through her own body, pumping it into the ritual spell. Already it was beginning to take effect. Some of the stones that made up the fairy fort had started to glow with a bright white light, like stars that had fallen to earth but continued to shine.

In the centre of the fort Lauren had place a large flat stone earlier, covered in some sheep blood. This was the pedestal, the central point for the ritual spell. Her last circuit around the fort would either begin to take effect, assuming everything had been done correctly, or show nothing at all. Relief washed over the haig as she spotted the purple crack appear in the air directly above the stone.

No larger than a child's hand, the crack started to cast a purple hue over the pedestal. Sparks of energy came off it, spiking out into the empty air before vanishing. With each new movement

577

more magic was channelled through Lauren into this crack, slowly but surely causing it to grow in size and widen.

The crone could not wait to show all the other haigs what she had achieved on her own. Right before she wiped each and every one of them from the face of the Earth.

She continued dancing, the crack steadily growing.

Overhead some clouds began to gather, out of nowhere.

Clouds dark in both colour and nature.

# Chapter Twenty-Eight

Filthy Henry felt sure that there was an argument to be made about the stupidity of people. Particularly the kind that saw a woman running through a crowd, clearly in distress, and took out their phones in order to record the proceedings rather than help her. When your sole aim in life was to capture fifteen seconds of footage in an attempt to go viral, you had to stop and take a long hard look at yourself.

Even more baffling was how nobody batted an eye in his direction. With a bloody nose, the fairy detective definitely did not look alright. The fact he was, technically, chasing after Shelly could only make the entire situation worse. How many stories involved a man with a bloody nose running after a woman ending well for all parties involved? Although everyone's attention was focused on Shelly, as she furiously hit the doll on top of her head, so that might have explained nobody even paying him any heed.

Shelly's screeches of pain were a handy way to track her through the crowd, not that following her was a problem. Most of the attendees were stepping aside to let her run past, nobody wanting to risk interrupting what they all seemed to think was a performance piece. Why they all thought she was acting was beyond him, but then not many people would have assumed the doll on Shelly's head was actually alive.

Alive and, if Filthy Henry was correct, currently home to the soul of Queen Medb. An historical figure from legend whom the fairy detective had thwarted not so long ago. The sort of thwarting that could really make a person hold a grudge.

As he ran behind Shelly, Filthy Henry was struck by the brilliance of the rag doll as a spirit container. Nothing ever said that your container had to be a solid object or a lovely urn, just all of the stories implied it needed to be. Any research he had done

579

on the topic suggested that urns and pots were the usual choice, but presumably that had something to do with a lack of imagination. Using a doll, complete with a mouth, as a container for your spirit when your body was otherwise indisposed was actually a stroke of genius. While inside such a container you could still move about and communicate with others.

Filthy Henry cursed himself for not coming up with the idea. He had spent nearly six weeks inside a plastic toy on his desk. Worse, if Shelly had not seen the toy fall over he could have been stuck in it forever.

*Then I'd still be in the driving seat.*

The thought ran through his mind so quick that it caught Filthy Henry off-guard. He stopped running and turned around, expecting to see Quinn somewhere in the crowd.

*Get back after Shelly,* Quinn's inner voice told Filthy Henry. *Also, I've figured out the private curse. I think. Oh, I've also figured out how we can talk when I am in your head, apparently. Man I am on a roll at figuring stuff out tonight.*

Shelly screeched again, drawing Filthy Henry's attention back to the problem at hand. He started running once more, weaving through the crowd. By now they had ran clear across the park, to an area that the event was not being held in. It was dark, lit only by the street lamps on the other side of the railings. The fairy detective spotted Shelly over by a tree, attempting to bang her tiny jockey off by headbutting the trunk.

"GET OFF!" she roared, running at the trunk again with her head lowered.

Just before the doll was flattened against bark it jumped off Shelly's head, holding onto her long dark hair, and swung in the air. Shelly's head connected with the tree, hard enough to cause the leaves above to shake. She wobbled on her feet and fell backwards, landing on the ground in a heap. Medb climbed up on her face and started to punch her.

"God dammit what is in those arms!" Shelly said, desperately trying to grab the doll.

Medb hopped around on her chest, avoiding Shelly's hands and landing a blow each time.

"Rocks," the rag-doll said. "The better to hit you with, my dear."

Filthy Henry raised his left hand into the air, spread his fingers out wide, and called upon his magic.

"*Rud atá*" he said.

A small, circular, net made from thin beams of white light sprang forth from his hand towards Medb. Generally a spell like this was used to hold something much larger than a doll, but Filthy Henry was limited by how much power he could pump into such a spell. A full blood fairy could, probably, use it to hold an elephant in place. The fairy detective would have passed out from the drain on his body if he tried such a feat. But a doll not much bigger than a small cat, that was no problem.

The magical net wrapped around Medb right as she raised her arm to hit Shelly again. It enveloped her, forming a bright hammock style cover over her doll body. With the wonders of physics behind the spell, it knocked Medb off Shelly's chest to the ground. She went down cursing and swearing, squirming against the magical bonds.

"I swear to Dagda, you magical freak, I will make you pay for this," the rag doll snarled.

"Magical freak?" Filthy Henry said, running over to Shelly and helping her back to her feet. "That's a bit rich isn't it? Pot calling the kettle a dark colour and all that."

"Thanks," Shelly said, taking the fairy detective's hand and climbing back to an upright position. "That's the Medb you obliterated in Carlingford?"

Filthy Henry nodded.

"One and the same. She's lost a few pounds though."

"I mean it, let me out of here!"

The fairy detective reached down and lifted Medb up, hauling her up by one of the magical beams of light that surrounded her. He brought the doll level with his face, hanging it upside down, and twirled the net around so that they could look at each other.

"What's McGarry up to?" he asked her.

If buttons could glare, these were doing a very good glare.

"As if I would tell you. I owe you. You and that halfwit with the hurley stick. Revenge is a dish best served over centuries. Do you have ANY idea what it has been like for me?"

"Do I look like I care?" Filthy Henry said, shrugging. "My job is to stop bad magical crap happening. You are up to bad magical crap. You should be dead, this whole living in a doll thing. That's on you. Make better life choices ... don't do drugs."

"I CAN'T EAT!" Medb shouted.

"This isn't exactly getting us anywhere," Shelly said, looking back at the crowd. "Plus, it sounds like the show is about to kick off."

Medb started to laugh. Laugh like a villain in a movie. The slow, throaty, laugh that gave the impression the bad guy actually had won and the hero was left with no options. Considering the rag doll lacked a throat, it was an impressive laugh.

"You can't stop us," she said, wiggling her body so that the magical net began twirling in his hand. "We've won."

Filthy Henry looked back at the stage. The crowds had gathered from all the little spots of the park and formed a full-on-mob just at the back of the seating area. Everyone stood close together, a wall of writers and readers staring ahead at the stage.

Somewhere, somebody unseen ran through the standard mic check loved and hated by everyone the world over. It involved the tapping of the mic so that a gravel-like sound came through the speakers, followed by the repeated count from one to three.

Speakers, unseen, howled with a little feedback as the person holding the mic brought it up to their mouth.

"Ladies and gentlemen, readers of all ages. Welcome to tonight's entertainment. We have a very special guest for you this evening. One who has agreed to take questions at the start of our little get together. Now, the lucky few are already on this list I am holding here..."

This was met with a resounding 'boo' from the crowd, followed by a smattering of 'awws'.

"I know, I know," the speaker said over the PA system. "But if we didn't have a list we would be here all night. Now, without further ado, I have the pleasure to introduce the author of Ireland's best crime novels. Tracey Fitzgerald!"

The crowd erupted into cheers and applauds.

Medb's laughter increased, getting on the fairy detective's last nerve. Which was when he clocked what was going on.

"Oh crap," he said to Shelly.

"What?"

"Medb wasn't attacking you out of payback. She was a bloody distraction!"

#

The minute hand finally moved into the right position on her watch and, like clockwork, the speaker system turned on. There was that annoying feedback loop to grab everyone's attention, then a lovely young lady stepped out onto the stage and started addressing the crowd.

583

Linda glanced over her shoulder to see if Filthy Henry or Shelly were anywhere to be seen. Medb had done a good job of running interference, but there was only so much that a small, magically possessed, rag doll could do. If they managed to stop Medb, then chances were they both had returned to the seats and everything was about to get chaotic. Reassuringly, this did not seem to be the case. The crowd that had been mingling around the park now formed a near solid wall behind the seating area. Everyone was here for one reason and that reason was about to walk out on stage to start talking.

All she needed now was for the microphone to be passed over before Filthy Henry did anything to derail things.

Staring at the young lady explaining how the event would proceed, Linda willed her to hurry up. Questions and answers was the first thing and, if Medb had done her job right, Linda was going to be lucky number one on the list in the young lady's hand.

Finally she stopped talking, introduced Tracey, and handed over the microphone as the author walked towards the centre of tthe stage.

At the sight of Tracey stepping out onto the stage Linda felt her mouth break into a wide smile of its own volition. The author had no idea how dramatically her life was about to change, or even why. Linda found that just made the entire affair all the more enjoyable.

Tracey Fitzgerald waved to the assembled masses, smiling like some sort of superstar. She motioned for them to calm down, the yells of joy slowly dying, and then smiled some more.

"Hello everybody," Tracey said into the microphone, her voice coming out of the speakers set around the park. "And can I just say a big thank you to the organisers of tonight's event."

The crowd cheered and clapped some more.

"I mean things like this are what makes the love of the written word so strong in Ireland," Tracey continued. "Thankfully the writing gods smiled on us, the weather is great tonight. Otherwise this whole outdoor thing was definitely not going to work."

This was met with some laughter and even a genuine titter from the man seated next to Linda.

If this was what passed for The Craft in modern Ireland, Linda felt she was doing the world a great service working with Lauren. After tonight, The Craft would be much better respected again. She made a mental note to talk with the crone later about getting some sort of promotion in the ranking system. An Overlord of Writing, maybe.

"Now," Tracey said, once the laughter had died down. "I know we have a packed agenda to get through tonight. Let's dive right into it, yes?"

The young lady who had acted as the announcer ran up, handed the Tracey a sheet, then ran back off stage. Tracey held the page up before her and read from it.

"So," she said into the mic. "First up we have Linda Faul, a poet. Seems we wrote te wrong name down originally. Lucky for you Linda somebody spotted the mistake and...scrawled, I suppose is the right word, your name over incorrect one. Well, let's see if we can't help you out a little. Fiona, if you wouldn't mind getting a microphone down to Linda. Linda, could you make yourself known to our lovely assistant."

Linda stood up, tried to act as coy as possible, and held her hand in the air. Fiona jumped down from the stage, a second microphone in her hand, and started to run down along the sides of the seats. At Linda's row she tapped the man in the end seat and handed him the microphone, pointing towards Linda. He dutifully passed the mic to the person beside him and slowly it made its way down to her.

Taking the mic from her row neighbour, Linda felt a thrill of excitement run through her entire body. She brought the microphone slowly up to her mouth, cleared her throat and closed her eyes.

Savouring this moment was wasting time, but Linda did not care. There was nothing that could stop her now. She opened her eyes and focused on Tracey.

"Hi," Linda said. "I was just wondering if you, if everybody here actually, would do me one little favour."

Tracey tilted her head slightly, looked confused, then smiled.

"But of course, my dear," she said. "What favour do you want us to do?"

"How about you all tell me your story?" Linda said.

#

A rumble of thunder broke the silence in the field. To the casual observer it was just thunder, the sign that a storm was about to hit and ruin somebody's lovely night-time stroll. For the crone, it meant the ritual was nearing completion. The last of her available magic had been tapped, pumped into the fairy fort and channelled back towards the pedestal stone. She was going to need to start channeling the energy stored in Linda, the walking magical battery.

Proving, once and for all, that she, The Crone McGarry, was the smartest of the haigs to ever live.

Twirling past the pedestal stone, Lauren looked at the streak of purple energy floating in the air. It now appeared like a tear in fabric, a little over seven-foot-long and widening inch by inch as the ritual continued. Like one of those paintings with the eyes that followed you around the room, the tear always faced Lauren so that she could see into the opening. A bright, purple, light shone from the tear now, illuminating everything within the fairy fort.

Lauren glanced into the tear on her current pass, glimpsing the world beyond.

586

Part of what the ritual did was break down the walls between this world and the one beside it. Similar to how fairy folk could use The Veil to hide themselves from mortals, other worlds did the same with magical barriers. What the stories forgot to mention, though, was that behind the barriers the other worlds moved. Like planets orbiting each other in a solar system. That was why magical capable people did not go around opening gateways whenever they wanted. Sure, you might know the right incantations and have a collection of like-minded powerful individuals. But if you opened a doorway into space all that happened was you destroyed your own world, by having it sucked through an inter-dimensional gateway. That was why timing played such a hugely important role in these things. Before you started the ritual you had to know that both worlds were in alignment with each other. The bigger the solar system the more complicated the maths.

This did not even factor in things like time differences. Some dimensions moved slower or faster than the one Earth occupied. Which was why alignments could take centuries to happen.

With awe, Lauren stared through the gateway at the world beyond. It was hard to make out exact details with the purple lighting, but she could clearly see something standing on the other side. Something, or rather someone.

Standing and waiting to cross over. To return. After an unintended exile from this world he would once again walk the Earth and aide her in her plans for revenge.

A small price to pay to the person who helped you return from a hellish dimension.

Lauren spun away from the gateway and continued dancing, accompanied by the music of thunder in the clouds.

#

Shelly and Filthy Henry tried to push through the crowd, but it was like asking the tide not to come in. Everyone was sure they had the best seat in the house, with nobody having any intentions of giving their spot up. Even if it meant saving the world from magical doom. Using elbows and arms to move people around felt like being in a bouncy castle. One that could fight back when pushed, while also being able to swear at you too. Filthy Henry was using his patented 'bad manners' approach to the affair, shoving people out of the way who did not move immediately after being politely asked to.

The fairy detective's idea of polite involved shouting the word 'move', then immediately pushing his way through. Still, they were only making their way through the crowd at a snail's pace. If Linda kicked off and managed to do her mojo on Tracey there was nothing Shelly or Filthy Henry could do to stop her.

The fairy detective reached out and grabbed Shelly's shoulder.

"Make your way up to the stage, go around the outside of the crowd. Get to Tracey and stay close to her," Filthy Henry said. "I'm going to make my way to the seats and head for that sleeper we seen. It had to be Linda. Either that or the one sitting two rows behind."

"Then what?"

The fairy detective tapped his forehead.

"I think I have an idea," he said.

"You think?" Shelly asked him.

That had to be one of the daftest things he had ever said. A person either knew they had a plan or they did not. They knew winging it was in their future or they were going into battle with a Hail Mary of an idea. You did not think you had an idea. An idea was what happened after some thinking.

"Yeah," he said. "I'll explain later. Now get up on that stage. Stay close to Tracey. Real close, got it?"

588

He let her go and turned, forcing his way through the crowd again. Up on stage the announcer had finished her introductions, bringing out Tracey Fitzgerald to the stage. The author took the microphone in her hand and addressed the crowd. Shelly turned left and started to work her way to the edge of the assembled masses, taking a leaf out of the fairy detective's book and just forcing people aside with a subtle elbow prod. She made it through, helped along the last few feet by people pushing her out of their way, then started to run along the edge of the grass towards the stage.

Three event organiser-types were standing around, clipboards in hand, watching Tracey as she talked to the people. Shelly fell in behind one of them, spotting an identification badge poking out from his jacket pocket. With nimble fingers, she plucked it out of his pocket and hung it around her neck by its lanyard.

Without saying anything, she stepped past the three of them and headed towards the stairs that led up to the stage.

"Sorry," one of them call after her.

Shelly did not turn around or stop walking. She held up the stolen badge so they could see it.

"Grand so," came the response.

Shelly was delighted that her little stunt worked so smoothly. Climbing up the small set of wooden steps, she walked across the stage towards Tracey.

"But of course, my dear," she said. "What favour do you want us to do?"

Looking out at the crowd, Shelly saw Linda standing up in the centre of the seats. She was holding a microphone up to her mouth.

"How about you all tell me your marshmallow?" Linda said, her voice coming out of every speaker in the area.

Shelly dove towards Tracey, arms outstretched, and crashed into her. They both fell to the floor in painful unison, but not before Shelly managed to cover the woman's ears with her hands. The theory they had all been working on was that if you did not hear the question Linda asked it prevented her powers working. So far that theory had held true for Shelly, all thanks to Elivin's spell which made the word 'story' be randomly replaced with another one. It meant her brain never heard the question correctly and, thus, put a halt to Linda's main means of attack.

By covering Tracey's ears, Shelly hoped that she had gotten there in time to stop the magic from sucking out the writer's memories. Filthy Henry had seemed sure that once the last person on Linda's list was taken she would be at full power. Something about the desire for revenge making the energy stolen all the more potent.

"I'm here to help you!" Shelly mouthed at Tracey.

"Get off me you bloody energetic human," Tracey said.

Shelly, hands still firmly clasped over Tracey's ears, leaned up from her and frowned.

"You're a fairy?"

Tracey shimmered beneath Shelly, transforming into Elivin.

"Yes," the leprechaun said. "What gave it away?"

"But what are you doing pretending to be Tracey? Were you really her all the time? Like a second life?"

"No, idiot," Elivin said, wiggling out from beneath her. "The real Tracey is knocked out in some bushes by the fence. This is part of the plan. Did you even listen when we came up with this plan back in Filthy's?"

Shelly stood up.

"Oh," she said. "I was writing something into my notepad when you both talked, so I was only half listening to you. So you acted as a decoy in case we didn't stop Linda in time. That's actually a good plan."

"I know," Elivin said, getting to her feet also. She frowned and looked out at Linda. "Except it seems to have backfired a little."

Before Shelly could ask what she meant an invisible force crashed into the pair of them, sending both Shelly and Elivin hurtling across the stage. They slammed into the back wall, falling to the floor. From the stage floor Shelly saw Linda, floating a good two feet above her chair, as around the nurse all-Hell seemed to have broke loose.

#

Linda said the words and waited for the rush of power as she absorbed all the stories around her, particularly Tracey's.

An immense feeling of satisfaction washed over her as her revenge plot finally came to fruition. Made all the sweeter by the fact that Tracey Fitzgerald had no idea her memories, her stories, were being stolen all because of something her ridiculous-amount-of-greats grandfather had done centuries before. To add to the overpowering sense of joy, Linda felt a rush from all the other stories she was collecting. Never before had she performed the magical theft on a crowd of people. Even taking two at the same time had been an experiment left undone. But as she uttered the phrase, that most simple and basic of sentences, those nearest her immediately fell under the spell.

It was almost as if she was a meteor hitting the earth from up on high, her seat the epicentre for an area of destruction. Working out in circular waves, all the people began to fall over. One by one. Some leaned back in their seats, heads angled towards her, others toppled forwards. Each and every one of them now sporting a stylish white and black stream of smoke, spiralling out from their mouths and working through the air towards Linda.

She never tired seeing this happen. If you looked closely at

591

the mist you could see that the black parts were actually letters, elongated and skewed out of shape by the movement of the white smoke. The words that made up each person's story, visually displayed for the world to see. Linda had always enjoyed this part of a story steal, but up until now it had always been a very private affair. Even when taking a person's story in a coffee shop, it happened so quickly and cleanly that nobody around noticed. She wondered if, in their final moments of making new memories, anyone else in the crowd would see what she saw.

The circle of chaos spread out further and further, people amazed at what was going on and too overpowered to do anything about it. Each of them dropped to the ground as the spell encompassed the entire seating area and moved to the folk standing around the park. Up on stage Shelly was running towards Tracey, clearly making a desperate attempt to halt something that was way beyond her mortal means to prevent.

Linda smiled at the sight of the would-be hero. In a matter of seconds the spell would reach Shelly and, like everyone else, she would give up her stories to a greater cause. A fitting end for any hero.

Then, inexplicably, Linda felt a tugging sensation in her shoulders. Like a giant, invisible, hand was lifting her up from the ground. The story-streams started to swirl around her, growing in intensity and causing a strong wind to surround her. This, it seemed, was lifting her up from the ground so that she floated above the chairs. There was no way to control the effect, it just lifted Linda up a couple of feet and kept her stationary. While the stories continued to gathered, worming their way through the air to her.

She leaned back into the invisible force, spreading her arms, and smiled some more.

The last few people, too shocked to move, were hit by the spell. As their stories mingled with the rest there was an audible boom, a rush of air spreading out from Linda, and everyone in the park was knocked to the ground. Up on stage Shelly and Tracey flew backwards, slamming into the rear wall before falling to the ground.

*Good job,* Lauren's voice said inside Linda's mind.

"What?"

*Don't worry about it,* the crone said, in her head. *I'm performing the ritual and you've just kicked in with the power we needed to continue at the perfect moment. I've to go and concentrate now. Enjoy.*

With a physical force that none of the previous story-steals had involved, Linda was struck by the first of the black-and-white mists. It hit her in the stomach, not as painful as being punched but definitely on the same levels of discomfort. Briefly, she wondered if it was true about the female of the species having a much higher pain threshold than the male. There was no way to repeat the experience now in another body, but if it was true then Linda thanked the Gods of Chance she had taken over a woman's body before tonight.

Floating freely above her seat, Linda looked around at the scene of chaos and destruction. The swirling mists from each of the attendees and event staff had gathered together, like a smokey swarm of snake like bees. As the swirling mist moved around her the wind it generated built up, growing ever more powerful. Chairs, complete with their comatose occupants, were pushed back or knocked over. It was not the gentle breeze ideal for professional kite flyers, this was a powerful gale. Meant to alert all that the area was experiencing something and to either stay away or make sure all your affairs were in order.

Linda tracked a story-mist, selecting it at random from among the dozens swirling, and focused her attention on it. Never before had there been so many to pick and she wanted to try something. Concentrating on the story-mist, Linda directed it to leave the swarm and come towards her. It broke free without any

593

resistance, spiralling through the air for a moment before slamming into her shoulder. As she consumed the mist Linda realised something. The selection, while random, had not been entirely without some subtle details. The instant Linda had selected the mist she had known its source, the slumbering man two rows in front of her.

This raised an interesting quandary. She could continue to select the stories, whittling them away until only Tracey's was left, the best for last, or she could consume Tracey's now and look upon the rest as a bonus.

Despite having waited hundreds of years for this precise moment, Linda opted to take Tracey's stories up front. She began to search through the swarm, looking for the one mist that belonged to the object of her revenge. It was a quick process, merely looking at the same spot allowed for numerous story-mists to spin by. But after thirty seconds her search yielded nothing.

The story-mists began to lap each other. Linda was looking at the same ones for a second and even third time. But none of them belonged to Tracey. None at all.

"It has to be here!" she snarled, twisting in the air to see if any of the mists were not in the spherical formation yet. "IT MUST BE HERE!"

The winds began to whip up dust and leaves now, becoming a localised hurricane in the park. Linda narrowed her eyes and peered through the gale. Up on stage Shelly and Tracey were slowly getting back to their feet, complete with their stories still inside them.

Except it was not Tracey standing beside Shelly on the stage. The author was nowhere to be seen. Instead there was a small child in green body armour.

"WHAT?!" Linda roared, raising the microphone back up to her mouth. "TELL ME YOUR STORY!"

They both shielded their faces from the debris being thrown around, looking at Linda through their fingers. Looking, but not succumbing to her power. Neither of them even seemed to have heard what she said. Which was impossible because, even above all the noise of the swirling stories and wind, Linda was able to hear her own voice coming out of the speakers. She knew the magic was still working because a few extra story-snakes had entered the park from over the railings. Presumably people passing by who had heard her words. Yet still Shelly and and the child remained unaffected as they scrambled towards an upturned table to use as cover.

Presumably Tracey was already hiding behind the table.

"TELL ME YOUR STORY!!!" Linda screeched into the microphone, her voice causing tremendous feedback over the speaker system

Still nothing.

Without Tracey the plan would fail. The Geis had been specific and only people on Linda's List counted as valid stories with the right kind of power the crone required. Everyone else had just been a top-up, a snack to curb the ever growing desire to steal more stories. If she was denied Tracey, Linda would have to figure out how to get enough power before the end of the night. All while being unable to move as the swirling wind held her aloft.

She looked at the microphone in her hand, then watched the fresh story-snakes mingle in with the swarm. It gave Linda an idea, one which was basic but held some merit. If Linda continued saying her line over and over then anybody outside the park would fall under her spell. It would mean a few more mindless idiots roaming the streets of Dublin, but before anybody really cared about that the ritual would be completed. All she had to do was keep gathering stories, collecting power, to offset the lack of Tracey's stories.

595

Linda spotted Filthy Henry making his way towards the stage, struggling against the wind created by the swarm. He looked up at her, covering his face with his left hand and ducking just before a chair smacked him in the head. The addition of the extra stories to the swarm had increased the force of the wind. Making Linda's plan to acquire stragglers even more important now. She could gather more power, hopefully enough to cover the loss of Tracey, while at the same time raining down destruction all around her. Maybe even, if everything worked as expected, killing Tracey, Shelly and Filthy Henry in the process.

Something flew through the air towards her, coming from the direction of the stage. A small sphere of fire. It crashed into the story streams and exploded. Linda did not feel a thing, the winds protecting her completely.

With the microphone held before her mouth, Linda started to say the line over and over again.

"TELL ME YOUR STORY!"

#

Filthy Henry grabbed onto the edge of the stage and hauled himself up the steps. Shelly and Elivin were at the back, cowering behind an upturned table. The wind was incredibly strong now, lifting up anything not nailed down and even some things that were. Random objects sailed through the air, flying about in chaotic patterns before dropping to the ground. It made every step he took a struggle, some physical effort mixed with a small risk of personal harm for good measure.

The fairy detective made it onto the stage platform at last and, keeping as low to the ground as possible, headed over to Shelly and Elivin. They moved over to make room for him behind their makeshift protection.

"Status report?" he asked.

They both looked at him blankly.

"Are you serious?" Shelly said. "We're in the middle of a magical war-zone with some sort of all-powerful super possessed weapon of magical destruction and only a collapsible table to protect our very precious behinds. That's the status report."

"You think I have a precious behind?"

"She meant us, idiot," Elivin said, craning her neck to look over the table. "That...that was not expected."

Filthy Henry slowly peered around the edge of the table to get a better look at their impending doom.

Linda was floating a good ten feet off the ground, surrounded by streams of black and white mist. They were obviously the source of the strong winds, given the speed they circled her. All of the swirling air and streamers made it look like the nurse was floating in the middle of a white sphere.

"Screw it," the fairy detective said, leaping out from behind the table. He called upon some magic and took aim. "PEILE DÓITEÁIN!"

A ball of fire shot forth from his hands, growing to the size of a football as it raced towards Linda. Not that it actually got anywhere near the nurse. The sphere of air caught the fireball, deflecting it off its course and sending it straight up into the night sky where it blew up like a firework. Filthy Henry grinned like a maniac and dove back behind the table as a bin headed for him. He bumped into Elivin, knocking the leprechaun against Shelly.

"Didn't think we tried that already?" Shelly asked him.

"You with the no magic? No, I didn't think you tried that already. Although the leprechaun, maybe."

Elivin nodded at him.

"First thing we tried, she didn't even seem to notice it because of those winds surrounding her. Come on, you're meant to be the big smart fairy detective. Detect a way out of this."

Linda's voice started booming out of the speakers again, repeating the same phrase over and over. Thanks to Elivin's spell, Filthy Henry was not able to hear the exact phrase and thus avoided falling under Linda's spell.

"Tell me your bum bum?" Filthy Henry asked Elivin. "That was the substitution you gave us?"

Shelly tittered.

"Not what I hear. I get the word 'marshmallow' instead of 'story'. She made you hear 'bum bum'? Brilliant."

Elivin started chuckling.

"I'm glad that we all are taking a break from the impending doom to enjoy some adult comedy," Filthy Henry said. "Plan? Anyone got a plan? I'd even listen to one of Shelly's at this stage."

A chair crashed into the stage floor behind the table, causing the platform thing to shudder.

"She's getting more powerful out there," Elivin said. "I didn't know this would happen. You wouldn't think that stories from mortals warranted so much magical energy."

"They sorta make the world go round," the fairy detective said.

He spotted more of the magical streams coming in over the railings, merging with the growing sphere in the park. Linda seemed to point at random streams and consume them. But for every one that was removed from the sphere two more took its place. A display like this was visible to everyone, regardless of having fairy vision or not. That meant more people being drawn to the park out of morbid curiosity as to what was going on. More stories to be stolen, more power to be gained. Stopping her from getting Tracey's stories had been a simple and straightforward plan.

But a plan built upon missing information.

With the sphere of power protecting her, they had no way to get at Linda and stop her. Even if they could stop her. Any second now the Garda would be showing up. More victims for Linda, more power for her sphere of destruction. At the rate new streams were appearing, Linda would probably be able to compensate for Tracey's missing stories.

"I've got it," Filthy Henry said.

"Got what?" Elivin asked him.

"Huh?"

"You said you've got it," Shelly said. "What is it? A way to stop her?"

"I never said anything," the fairy detective said, frowning at them. "You're hearing things over that swirling vortex out there. The whirlwind of words. A wordwi..."

"Don't even finish that bum-bum," the leprechaun warned him, pointing at his face with her fist. "Nobody here wants to give a pun-name to that thing out there. But you did, just now, say you had 'it'. What's 'it'?"

Filthy Henry stared at the expectant faces of Shelly and Elivin, wondering if they had been hit on the head by flying debris. Then the mental light bulb went off.

*Did you just say something?* he mentally asked Quinn.

*Yeah,* came the mental reply. *Wasn't sure if you heard me shouting in here. Dunno how I got control of the speech centre. But, anyway, I have it.*

*Have what?*

*The private part of the Geis,* Quinn said. *Or at least the best guess at it. Since they always are somehow linked and we all know what her public part is because it is on loop at the minute.*

*Okay, what do you think it is?*

599

Filthy Henry listened as his imaginary friend explained the answer to the fairy detective, complete with an idea of how to get the upper hand against Linda. It was a horrible plan, but at that minute it was also the only plan they had on offer.

He peered around the edge of the table and looked at Linda amassing more streamers.

"OK," Filthy Henry said to Shelly and Elivin. "We're going to all die anyway if we don't stop her, so here's the plan."

# Chapter Twenty-Nine

The crone was getting tired. Rituals like this, even if they did require a group of fairies, were meant for much younger magical creatures. A single haig, well into her sixteenth century, simply lacked the stamina to do all the dancing and cavorting. Enacting your grand revenge on the world generally required that you did not die of a heart-attack in the process.

Evil plans to use magic in order to enslave the world of mortals was definitely a young fairy's game.

If only the youth of today had the will to use their magical powers for the betterment of all fairy kind.

Lauren looked at the purple gateway as it shimmered in the air. It was still growing with each circuit of the fairy fort, but the increase in size had noticeably slowed down. This was not a bad thing, the gateway did not have to be much larger than it currently was. The power that Linda had been gathering was meant to keep the gateway open, a metaphysical doorstop of sorts. Any excess would then be funnelled into the opening itself, the power transferring to the inhabitants on the other side. Strengthening them for the transition into this world.

After all, that was were all other evil plans involving dimensional doorways fell apart. Sure, the evil doer would manage to open up a rift between worlds, but then the big, powerful, creature on the other side would come across and collapse from exhaustion. Stepping through a gateway from one world to the next was no trivial act, even if somebody else opened the gateway for you. It took a tremendous amount of power, both will and magic, to step through and come out the other side still holding all your mental marbles. But in the stories a hero always showed up just as the traveller arrived, in a weakened state, and defeated them.

Meaning all the dancing, sweating and tiredness wound up being for naught.

Unless you factored this in with your power requirements. Then you could pump that excess energy through the gateway so the traveller arrived powered up, or close to it. Any hero showing up at Lauren's gateway right as her traveller stepped through would be in for a nasty surprise.

Just as it should be.

She felt a surge of magic coming into her from Linda and smiled. With a twirl on the spot, she channelled this into the gateway and started the second part of the ritual. The little human's crazy idea had proven to be a stroke of genius. Gather up multiple stories at once and take all that potential and historical power. The crone mentally communicated with Linda to tell her well done. Her response was one of a spoilt child. Tracey, the target of her vengeance, had been unaffected by Linda's Geis. The sad, small minded, mortal seemed to think this mattered. Her plan of a crowd-collection meant they had enough power for the ritual without Tracey's stories.

Not that Lauren even cared about Linda being upset. It would be like wondering if the battery in a mobile phone got sad when not fully charged. You did not care so long as it did the job, right down to the last drop of energy.

Linda was just a walking, talking, magical battery. Once emptied of energy she would end up like all used batteries. She would be discarded.

That was why fairy kind deserved to rule the world, not hide from mortals. Mortals took things for granted and accepted words without fully understanding the meaning. Such gullible creatures did not deserve the world. They were barely worthy of being ruled.

But, so long as Linda kept applying magical energy, she was useful to Lauren and the crone could continue with the ritual.

602

Prancing and dancing out in the middle of nowhere with nobody to try and stop her. A twinge of disappointment ran through the crone as she realised she would not see the look on Filthy Henry's face when he failed.

Failed to save the world.

Not that it mattered. Sometimes it was just nice to have a cherry on top of your victory cake.

#

"That's your plan?" Shelly asked.

"Yep," Filthy Henry answered.

"That's a fairly crap plan," Elivin said. "I mean should you even call that a plan? It is more the idea that might become a plan with more time to actually, you know ... plan."

"I didn't say it was a great plan," the fairy detective said, looking offended. "I also don't see either of you coming up with anything better."

Shelly nodded in agreement. What he said was true. Neither of them had offered an alternative to his plan. Then again they also had not proposed a plan that bordered on the insane and sounded downright suicidal. Which, in the grand scheme of things, meant they were both doing better than Filthy Henry in the planning department.

Any non-plan that you could walk away from was, by definition, a good plan.

"Just what makes you think it will even work the way you say it will?" Shelly asked him.

Filthy Henry pointed at the bounty hunter sitting between them.

"Her dad, basically," he said. "That guy isn't going to let me go back on a deal. Particularly one that we have sealed with a magical handshake. Ever since he had to grant that wish as payment he has been dying to pull one over on me. This deal is that. At least he thinks it is."

"I dunno half-breed," Elivin said. "I mean sure, technically you could say it will play out like you think. But I think you might be really twisting the words used in the deal."

"How am I twisting them?"

"You made him forget about an agreed time limit," Shelly said. "That does not, in any way, make you immortal or invulnerable."

"Sure it does," the fairy detective said. "It's all there in the wording of the deal."

"I really don't think that's how it is going to work," Elivin said. "Why would you think that you are totally impervious to harm all of a sudden?"

"It's simple," Filthy Henry said. "I need to have a chat with you about giving up your work as a bounty hunter. That talk must happen before I die. If I come to grievous bodily harm while attempting to save the world, your dear old dad's magic will kick in and prevent me from dying. Ergo, invulnerable and immortal."

"Yeah," the bounty hunter said, slowly shaking her head. "That isn't how that would work at all. You might be right on the whole 'not dying' part, but protecting you from harm? Let's just say you'd be surprised what you can live through."

He shrugged and peered back around the table at Linda.

"We are running out of options," Filthy Henry said. "Either of you want to suggest something better, I'm all ears."

Shelly craned her neck and looked over the side of the table, out into the scene of chaos and destruction that was the middle of the park. Some Garda had shown up, running into the park all ready for action. That is until Linda repeated her simple, yet sinister, line and pulled all their stories from them too. A few people in the chairs nearest Linda had started to come around. They looked dazed and confused, at least the lucky ones did. Those on the edge of the swirling sphere were lifted from their seats and flung out into night, banging off whatever objects happened to be in their path.

It was absolute carnage. There was no earthly way for them to get near Linda. Meanwhile the nurse could continue to capture stories and store the energy.

"It's crazy," Shelly said. "You're not going to get near her."

Filthy Henry took a deep breath and sighed. The final gasp of a man right before he rushed head first into danger.

"Quinn came up with this plan and you're just going to do it?" Elivin asked him.

"Yeah," the fairy detective said. "I know it is him putting my body on the line, but..."

"Sure," the leprechaun said, slowly nodding her head. "That makes sense."

"Right," Filthy Henry said, shifting position so that he was crouched like a runner on the starting line. "Time to get this over with. If I'm not back in five minutes, avenge me."

"I'll be running as fast as I can and dragging Shelly along with me," Elivin said. "In the complete opposite direction, by the way. Just to clear up any ambiguity on that."

Filthy Henry looked at her and grinned.

"That's the spirit," the fairy detective said.

"OK," Shelly said. "I guess we just go with this and hope for the best. Pray for a miracle that this works."

"I don't pray for miracles," Filthy Henry said. "I bully gods!"

He stepped out from behind the table and started running across the stage at a very unimpressive pace. Right at the edge of the stage, Filthy Henry jumped into the air. Shelly watched as Elivin lean around the table and cast a spell, flicking it towards the fairy detective. A small sphere of yellow energy connected with his back, propelling him forward quickly as he jumped. He easily covered the distance between the stage and Linda, thanks to Elivin's magical assist.

The fairy detective looked like he was about to pass through the swirling sphere when a fresh wave of streamers came in and joined the swarm. Instead of moving through the sphere, Filthy Henry was caught like his fireball had been. Streamers locked him onto the outside of the sphere and carried him around. He spun quickly as the sphere moved.

"HEEEEELLLLLLPPP!!!" Filthy Henry shouted.

"Em," Shelly said.

"I got it," Elivin responded, conjuring another spell in her hand.

The bounty hunter took careful aim and started to track Filthy Henry's rotations around the sphere. On his fourth pass-by she threw the spell. It flew forward, little crackles of energy flickering from it, and as the fairy detective spun past the ball of magic smashed into his feet. There was a small explosion on the surface of the swirling sphere and Filthy Henry was knocked free. He spiralled through the air, limbs akimbo, and vanished behind the sound-deck.

"Em, that's not good," Shelly said.

Elivin, hand still outstretched, nodded in agreement while staring at the sound-deck.

"Yeah, we need a new plan."

#

Linda had to admit, she was enjoying herself immensely. Not being able to move from her position in the air was annoying, but collecting more and more stories was exhilarating. There was no way to tell if the extras were compensating for the lack of Tracey's, but it did not matter. All that mattered now was keeping the energy supply going and the good people of Dublin seemed more than happy to oblige with that.

Since she had started to repeat the line, story-streams were coming in from all over the park. The Garda had arrived and fallen victim just like everyone else. Some of the boys in blue decided to set up a perimeter, attempting to keep people away, but it was ineffective. One thing that could always be said about the people of Dublin was this: if there was something happening that they should stay away from a Dubliner would be where they should not be. Watching things unfold.

Up on the stage Filthy Henry, Shelly and the tiny person wearing green body armour, were still hiding behind the table. Tracey had somehow managed to get off the stage without Linda seeing her leave.

Another reason to ensure she was killed before the night was over.

Linda had discovered that she could use the story streamers as whips, but only when she decided to consume that stream. As it wormed its way towards her, Linda could guide it towards something and then cause it to throw the object at the stage. It was not exactly accurate, but enough of a danger to make the three of them remain behind the table. So long as they stayed there it meant they could not interfere with her.

Which was exactly how it should be.

Filthy Henry had tried to attack her with a fireball a few minutes earlier. It hit the swirling vortex and carried on up into the sky, harmlessly exploding in the air. Now, it seemed, the fairy detective wanted to try another tact. By becoming the projectile himself. He ran across the stage, directly towards her, and jumped into the air. Somehow, presumably due to magic, Filthy Henry made the distance between them with ease. He slammed into the swarm, some newcomers twining around him and holding him in place.

"Well, well," Linda said, lowering the microphone. "I expected more from you. Something along the lines of brimstone and wrath. But it looks like you can't stop me at all. You're pathetic."

As he spun around on the sphere, Linda smiled. Filthy Henry's face was being pressed into the story-streamers by the force of the wind and the spinning momentum.

"Oh, looks like you're little buddy is going to help," she said.

The person-in-green threw a spell at Linda's sphere. It smashed into some streamers, caused a little explosion, and sent Filthy Henry spinning away into the night. He vanished behind a table covered in cables and sound engineering gear off to the right.

An annoyance Linda no longer needed to concern herself with.

While in the sphere she was protected. Untouchable.

Nothing could stop her now. She raised up the microphone and started to say her line again.

"Everyone, tell me your story!"

#

There is a lot to be said about waking up in your own bed. For starters, you are waking up in your own bed. You do not need to figure out where you are nor do you risk having to walk back home from a stranger's house, possibly missing a shoe. The comfort factor is definitely not something to overlook, as your body relaxes fully.

Waking up face-down in the dirt with a tangle of cables around one arm and a collapsible chair on your head, this is generally considered a bad way to wake up. If you felt like a rhino had used your body as a ping-pong ball for the last hour, that only compounded the levels of badness associated with such an awakening. Parts of Filthy Henry ached, parts that he had forgotten he even had. There was also something running out of his nose. He moved, regretting it instantly as pain ran through his body, and wiped his upper lip. The back of his hand came away with blood on it.

"Well that's just great," the fairy detective said. "Looks like it is possible to be surprised by what you can live through."

He shifted, pushing the chair and other debris away, and slowly got up to his feet.

Everything hurt.

Linda's sphere continued to spin, her body now glowing. You did not have to be a magical genius to tell that this meant she was reaching critical mass. All that stored energy could only be contained in a human vessel for so long. Either the crone tapped into it soon and used it all up quickly or Linda, most likely, was going to explode.

A magical time-bomb, one with a nuclear radius of destruction.

Filthy Henry checked where he had landed, searching for inspiration. Something had to be done, now, and that meant he was going to have to do it. He tugged the cables off his arm and examined them. They looked important, with little coloured tags on each one. Following them with his hands, tracing each through the twisted loops they had been collected in, led the fairy detective to a large sound board.

It looked like the dashboard of a spaceship. Dials, levers, knobs along with lights, gauges, and little screens with coloured bars moving up and down. All very impressive looking and, no doubt, easy to understand if you were a sound engineer.

Filthy Henry was many things, a sound engineer was not one. He looked at the soundboard, examining the cables plugged into it, and tried to figure out what random bits could be pulled out to stop the speakers working. That, at least, would stop Linda from getting more story snakes.

*Don't.*

Quinn's voice intruded on the fairy detective's thoughts.

*Don't what?*

*Don't just smash it up to stop it working.*

*Why? She is ready to pop and Dubliners are flocking to the scene, adding to her power. That's bad.*

*Stick with the plan, but use the speakers. We're not going to get through the vortex around her.*

*And not destroying her sound system is bad because?*

Laughter in your head is disconcerting to hear, especially when it is not you laughing but the laugh is your own.

*Because we can use the speakers for our plan,* Quinn said.

The fairy detective rummaged around the table, moving cables and pages, eventually finding a small plastic box with a number of microphones in it. He picked one up and spied a label on it with the number ten. Looking over the soundboard he saw similar handwritten labels by a group of sliding levers. Some levers were pushed up near the top of the board, others were all down.

Looking from microphone to soundboard and back again, Filthy Henry slid all the levers down.

Linda's voice stopped coming out of the speakers.

He looked up at her. She was staring at the microphone,

banging it with her hand. The nurse looked around quickly, saw the fairy detective, and glared at him.

"Who can't be stopped now," Filthy Henry said, smiling at her.

He moved the slide-lever up for microphone ten, then tapped the top of the mic in his hand.

A bang echoed out from the speakers around the park.

*See what happens when you stop and think.*

"Shut up, you," Filthy Henry said. "You better hope this works."

*I don't hope for things,* Quinn mentally said. *I bully fairy detectives.*

Bringing the microphone up to his mouth, Filthy Henry stared at Linda.

"You've heard everyone's stories," the fairy detective said. "Now, why don't you tell us about…yourself. Séan Chaí, tell me your story."

For a moment, nothing happened at all. Linda continued to float in the air. Then her back arched and she went completely rigid.

#

Nothing can ruin your day more than when somebody interferes with your plans. Particularly revenge plans. Filthy Henry had decided to be a thorn in her side and now, irritatingly, had turned off the microphone. Limiting any new story acquisitions to within her vocal range. She flung the microphone at the swarm, where it was picked up and carried away on the winds.

The swirling swarm prevented Filthy Henry from getting close to her. Which meant that all the stored magical power was still out of his pesky reach. He had no way of coming in, casting his fancy spells, and ruining things even further.

A boom came out of all the speakers around the park.

Linda looked over at the fairy detective. He was smiling at her, a microphone in his hand.

"You've heard everyone's stories," Filthy Henry said, his voice coming out from the speakers. "Now, why don't you tell us about…yourself. Séan Chaí, tell me your story."

The pain was sharp and sudden, every muscle in her possessed body spasmed as an electrical jolt coursed through it. Limbs went rigid, unresponsive to her instruction. A white-hot fire burned within, agony at an unimaginable level. Filthy Henry, uttering that line, complete with her birth-name, had weakened her. Worse, it had locked her in place. She looked at the swarm moving around her and focused on one of the streamers, willing it to come towards her.

The white-black mist ignored Linda completely. Instead it broke free of the formation, moving through the air and out of the park. Like a flock of birds disturbed from the ground, rising back into the sky, all the other streamers did the same. Detached from their siblings and spreading outwards, moving away from Linda.

"No. No! NOOOOO!!!" she roared after them, unable to move.

Unable to do anything to stop them.

Around her people started waking up. The streamers swirled in the air, a large section of them breaking off and zoning in on the event attendees and staff. Returning to the people they had been stolen from, restoring them completely. Undoing all of her good work and, more importantly, stealing all the magical energy that had been gathered.

Linda saw Filthy Henry step around from the sound table, walking down through the chair aisles until he stood directly in front of her.

"Howdy," he said, smirking. "Didn't think I would figure that one out, did you? Such an obvious private Geis, nobody would think of it. It was a long shot, sure, but then that's sorta my forte when it comes to saving the day."

She looked down at him, gritting her teeth through the pain.

"Oh, I know. You're probably writhing up there in agony. That's what would happen when you have hundreds of personalities all trying to get out at the same time. Didn't know that bit, did you? Right now you've just lost control of the swarm around here. But all the ones you had taken up to now, the ones you've been carrying around with you. They are all just bursting to get out."

What the fairy detective said made absolutely no sense. Stories that had been prepared for consumption returning to their owners, that was impossible. The ones that had been brought in, added to the collection, they were her's forever. No two bit con-artist magician was going to be able to reverse that, even if he had guessed the private Geis correctly.

Except there was a strange sensation, deep inside, and Linda could not figure out what it was. It felt like somebody had turned her into a coffee machine and flipped the switched.

Something was percolating.

"You're lying," Linda said through clenched teeth as even more agony ripped through her entire body.

"Let's wait a few seconds," the fairy detective said, pulling back his sleeve and looking at his watch. "I won't insult you by suggesting we make a bet."

#

Right when an infusion of power was needed, Lauren felt a tug on the magical side of things. A worrying tug. A suggestion that something was happening which should not be. Something along the lines of her battery being rapidly drained. Which could only mean that Filthy Henry, once again, had interfered with her plans.

"I should have just killed him, paradox be damned!" the crone snarled into the empty night.

She stopped dancing and looked at the gateway. It was still crackling with raw, magical, power but there was a translucency to the edges of it now. A sign that it was no longer stable, that the ritual was basically dead in the water. Using her link back to Linda, the crone checked out how much power was still available. There was some, possibly enough, to keep the gateway open for a few seconds more. A minute at most.

The shadowy figure on the other side of the gateway stepped closer.

"Get through now before it's too late," Lauren said, channelling as much magic as she could from Linda and sending it towards the gateway.

Like something out of a nightmare, the shadowy figure poured through the opening in the air. There was no elegant stepping between the worlds. One second the figure was standing inside the purple crack, the next it was oozing out and spilling down onto the grass around the base of the gateway. It made a dark, humanoid shape, on the ground that slowly started to inflate like a disturbing bouncy castle. Meanwhile, the gateway began to collapse in on itself, flickering in and out of sight as the power sustaining it began to evaporate.

The crone cursed Filthy Henry, his assistants, Medb, Linda, the storyteller and basically everyone and everything that had ruined this ritual. She stopped dancing and turned to face the flickering gateway.

Whatever was on the ground looked like it was stabilizing, becoming a part of this world. Above the pedestal the tear between worlds flickered a few more times before vanishing completely.

"I am going to cook up a revenge plan that will make Filthy Henry wish he was never born," Lauren said to herself, walking over to the new arrival.

"Let me know if you want any help on that front," the figure on the ground mumbled, slowly pushing up from the ground with their hands. "I owe him a crispy death. Also you are very naked, did you know that?"

#

Shelly and Elivin went down to join Filthy Henry as he secured Linda to her seat. Since the whirlwind had stopped, the nurse was no longer floating in the air. As they reached him, Elivin cast a binding spell of some sort on Linda. Glowing bands of yellow light criss-crossed her and held her to the chair.

"Thanks," Filthy Henry said. "But I was going to do that myself."

"I've been after this guy for centuries," the leprechaun said. "I didn't want to take any chances with your half-assed magic."

Surprisingly, the fairy detective allowed that one to slide.

"How did you know the guy's name?" Shelly asked Filthy Henry.

He tapped his right temple.

"Turns out Quinn found it inside the memory we pulled from Milton's head. It wasn't anywhere I'd have been able to find it, so without Quinn we wouldn't have figured it out. The private part of the Geis was very precise, we needed his original name in order to shut him down. That was why the body hopping made him so tricky to catch all this time."

"But Séan Chaí?" Elivin said, keep her gaze firmly locked on Linda. "If you put those words together it is literally 'story teller' in Irish. What are the chances of that happening?"

"Same as somebody with the surname 'Moneymaker' winning

the poker world series," the fairy detective said.

"What's the plan?" Shelly asked them. "We need to get it out of Linda so that we can mark the day off as a win. Right?"

Filthy Henry had been staring at his watch the entire time, watching the seconds pass with keen interest. He looked up from it and winked at Linda.

"Times up," the fairy detective said.

Linda began straining against the light beams holding her in place, shaking in the seat. Her head whipped back, facing the night sky above, and she screamed. The sound lasted merely a second before, disgustingly, streams of smoke spewed out from her open mouth. Like the ones that had been swirling around earlier, they rose up into the air and snaked outwards into the night. Going this way and that with no obvious reason to their flight paths. Random ones even just carried on upwards, flying towards the clouds and leaving the world behind.

It was the stuff of nightmares to watch and Shelly felt sure that her next few disturbed nights of sleep would feature vomit-snakes.

"What's happening?" Shelly asked, looking away from Linda as streamers continued flowing out of her mouth.

"All the stories she has stolen over the years are returning to their owners," Filthy Henry said. "Last in, first out."

"But Linda wasn't involved in it all along."

"Yeah, but the thing inside her was," Elivin said, staring at the display before them. "It has carried them around, through every body hop made. The ones that still have bodies are returning, making the people whole again. The others...well I don't know what's going on with them."

That put a sour note on what was their victory. All along they had intended to find out who had been stealing people's stories, their souls, but Shelly never considered what would happen to people who were no longer alive. All the families that had had to deal with their loved ones forgetting them completely, passing from this world into the next like strangers.

She caught Filthy Henry looking at her.

"Don't think about it too much," the fairy detective said, as if reading her mind. "Sometimes you save who you can and hope the rest just works out."

"But..."

He shook his head.

"There is no 'but'," Filthy Henry said. "If there was do you think I'd honestly have been doing this for sixty odd years?"

"He's right," Elivin said. "And that's me agreeing with the half-breed for the second time this century. We save who we can. If you tried to save everyone you'd risk saving no one. The earliest souls collected...they will be lost forever. Chances any that were converted into magical energy are gone as well, sadly. I'd say we have at least prevented souls from the last eighty years being used up by the crone. That is a win, no matter what way you cut it."

The leprechaun opened her left hand, fingers spread wide, and with her right started to make circular motions above it. In her padded palm a golden sphere formed, roughly the size of a large apple. She continued to conjure it while watching Linda. As the number of streamers began to dwindle, Filthy Henry looked at the bounty hunter.

"You ready?" he asked her.

She nodded once, eyes fixed on Linda's mouth.

"Want me to stay out of this one?"

Another nod, now with an added look of such intensity that Shelly was fairly sure nobody would disagree with the leprechaun at that moment. Shelly could not blame the bounty hunter. Spending a few centuries chasing after something that could change bodies when the heat was applied, that would make anybody go a little super serious. Filthy Henry had even read the situation correctly, foregoing his usual sarcasm.

On the chair, Linda clamped her mouth shut and lowered her head. The streamers had stopped spewing from her, but it looked like she was holding her mouth closed on purpose. She glared at Filthy Henry, glancing at Elivin and Shelly, but not saying a word. Linda whipped her head to the left, her jaw firmly clenched, then flicked it right.

It almost looked like she was having trouble swallowing something. A child being forced to eat their vegetables.

"What's going on?" she asked.

Elivin readied her spell, a small sphere of magic hovering over her right hand.

"It's trying to stay in," the leprechaun said. "Everything else has been emptied out, it's the last thing in Linda. It's still in control of her, keeping her mouth closed."

Linda shook her head furiously fast.

"Oh, I can sort that out," Filthy Henry said, stepping towards the nurse.

Shelly expected him to do one of his little magical stunts. A spell to force Linda's mouth open, or a bolt of electricity to shock her into unclenching. What she did not expect the fairy detective to do was reach over and, with two fingers, pinch the nurse's nose.

"What good is that going to do?" Shelly asked him.

"You can't kill yourself by holding your breath," Filthy Henry said. "The body doesn't allow it. You either pass out, and continue to breath, or your mouth opens up. Science."

Linda was looking at the two fingers closing her nose, her face turning purple.

"Ready?" Filthy Henry asked Elivin.

"Ready!" she replied, taking aim.

In the chair Linda was trying to break free from the fairy detective's nostril pinch, mumbling through her closed mouth. It seemed that her plan almost worked, until Filthy Henry closed his left hand around his right, firmly keeping everything in place and preventing any nasal breathing at all. Linda's eyes started to roll back into her head and, before passing out, she opened her mouth.

A bright red streamer escaped flowed past her lips, gathering in front of her face much unlike the others. Elivin did not wait. She flung the sphere at the red mist. It opened up, like a ball cut in half. The bottom section sucked in the mist quickly, giving it no chance to move. Once completely full the top part joined the lower half, reforming the sphere. It dropped to the ground with a strangely metallic sound for something landing on grass, wobbled back and forth on the spot, before changing both colour and material. The golden hue was replaced with a coppery colour and instead of being made from translucent magical energy the sphere became metal. Once the transformation was complete a little hiss escaped from the sphere, followed by a tiny wisp of steam.

Everyone stared down at it, then slowly at each other.

"That it?" Shelly asked.

"Depends on whether or not Linda gives us the right answer to this question," Filthy Henry said.

Linda arched an eyebrow and looked up at him, then back down at the bands of light holding her tightly to the chair.

"Am I being held by magic?"

The fairy detective shrugged his shoulders and nodded.

"Not going to be the weirdest part of your day. Now, ask me

619

what your previous back-seat driver was asking people."

"You mean the thing he used to steal memories?"

"Yep"

"Tell me your story," Linda said.

Shelly was surprised. She had heard the sentence correctly, without any magical word substitution taking place. Before she could ask, Elivin spoke up.

"The spell only replaced it when spoken as part of a Geis," the bounty hunter explained. "Means Linda is Linda once again and that copper ball on the ground contains one of the most dangerous and irritating creatures I've ever had to track down."

Elivin walked over to the sphere, bending down slightly to pick it up, then smiled at the three of them.

"I am very appreciative for all the help you both gave me in catching this thing," the leprechaun said. "Although I was managing just fine before you all bungled into it."

"Whatever," Filthy Henry said. "Release Linda here so she can pay Shelly and we can all go home."

The bands of light faded away, freeing Linda from the chair. She remained seated.

"Not sure I can risk standing up just yet," she said.

"You going to put that in the drop off?" Shelly asked Elivin.

"No," the leprechaun said, shaking her head and staring at the copper sphere. "There is a rainbow with this thing's name written all over it."

"Will dear old daddy let you use his rainbow in that manner? Considering we still have to talk about your choice of career?" Filthy Henry said.

"Everyone has two parents, don't forget," the bounty hunter

said, smiling. "Dad did say I had to call my mother. You can try and track me down for that stupid conversation some other time."

Before anyone else could say a word, Elivin disappeared from sight. Not in a shower of shamrocks like Lé Precon did, but she was still nowhere to be seen. Filthy Henry let out a little laugh and looked around as the people who had attended the event started to slowly come to their senses.

"Her dad is going to kill me," he said to Shelly. "Or at least I will be surprised to learn what else I can live through."

#

Bosco Burns woke up with a start, whipping the blanket off his body and throwing it to the floor. He slowly sat up, turned, and moved over to the edge of his bed. Placing his bare feet on the cold tiles of the floor, he stood up. His heart was pounding in his chest, the nightmare that had woken him still fresh in his mind.

He looked around the room, a room that was both familiar and not in equal measures, and down at the bed.

"What the hell is going on?" Bosco asked the empty room.

Bosco walked over to the bedroom door and opened it, stepping out into a hallway that smelled like a hospital. A hospital, which he knew it was and yet had no idea why he was in it. Up ahead the light from a nurse station shone, illuminating the hallway a little. Bosco headed towards it, trying to sort out in his head why there were some memories he had no memory of making.

The young nurse at the station looked up from her book and smiled at him.

"What can I do for you this evening?" she asked him.

"Em, you could show me where I go to get discharged," Bosco said. "I don't belong here."

"Ah," the young lady said. "Having one of those moments are we?"

Bosco shook his head, looking down the corridor at another person walking towards them.

"No," he said. "Not one of those moments. I don't remember why I am here, but I do remember that I shouldn't be in a hospital. Now, if you wouldn't mind."

"I'm afraid I can't do that without a doctor approving it," the nurse said.

By now they had been joined by another woman, wearing similar pyjamas to Bosco.

"Terribly sorry to interrupt you both," the woman said. "But I'd like to know why I am in hospital and where I go to get discharged."

They both looked at the young nurse who was staring back at them, her mouth slightly ajar.

"I think you're going to be pretty busy in the paperwork department tonight, judging by how many doors are opening around us," Bosco said, helpfully. "This is the part where you run off to get a doctor."

# Chapter Thirty

The next day they stood outside the gate of the hospital, watching as the patients whose memories had been restored walked through the doors and returned to their lives. Some got into waiting cars, reunited with beloved family members, others just ordered a taxi or simply walked away. Not one of them gave any impression that they were missing a few marbles. In one case a lady looked to be so clued in that she was helping other people get sorted with transportation.

Filthy Henry leaned against a wall, arms crossed in front of his chest, and watched it all.

"Bringing back memories?" Shelly asked him.

"Not really," he said. "Don't forget, you lot came and took me out before I was back in my body. It's just nice to see they are all back to normal."

"That's true," Shelly said. "Imagine how it must have been for their families. Loved ones just losing their minds but no medical reason to explain it. Worse than knowing what the problem is has to be not knowing."

Earlier, the fairy detective had rang the hospital, pretending to be from a local newspaper. He fed the doctor who took the call a line about writing an article, one based on the reported miraculous cure of several dementia patients. Not being slow off the mark, the doctor was quick to say that some experimental therapy she had developed was proving to be very useful. One Dr. Milton had also been instrumental in assessing the improvements, giving each and every patient a clean bill of health. Whatever the story-thief had done, Shelly and Filthy Henry had successfully undone it. Everyone's memories were restored and the hospital was only too glad to release people back into the world.

A win, by any stretch of the imagination.

Linda had settled her accounts with Shelly shortly after the events of the previous night. She had thanked them both for helping her, then said she wanted nothing more to do with their magical world. The whole possession thing had been an experience she could have lived without, apparently. Filthy Henry performed a slight mind-wipe on her, to speed up the process of her forgetting magic was a thing in the world, and then flagged her a passing taxi.

Everyone else at the writing event had slowly come back to their senses, in equal parts praising and questioning the display that had happened. Many of them just wondered if the event was going to be rescheduled. The real Tracey Fitzgerald had wandered in, looking like somebody returning from a solid day of heavy drinking. The effects of Elivin's sleep spell still in her system. Without waiting for an explanation, Tracey had climbed up on stage and proceeded to give her talk as if the scene of chaos and destruction in the park was not there.

It had turned into a nice night in the end. Filthy Henry had left Shelly alone, saying they would meet up the following morning. She had not stayed for the entire show, but it was nice to see that a little 'End of the World' situation was not enough to deter writers from having a bit of fun.

"Listen," Filthy Henry said, snapping Shelly out of her memory. "I've been doing some thinking."

"You know when I say that line you'd come up with a quip about hurting my brain," Shelly said.

"And you'd deserve it. But, for once, I am being sincere."

He handed her a photograph. A genuine, printed, physical picture. In the age of digital photography and devices that could carry images of all of Da Vinci's works in your pocket, an actual photo was a novelty item. She took it from him and looked at it.

Filthy Henry had handed her a picture of his closed office door. It was not an artistically stunning shot, nor was it the sort of picture that a person would frame or have fond memories of. In fact, if Shelly was being honest, it was the oddest photograph anybody had ever handed her.

She looked at him.

"This meant to mean something?"

"Well, yeah," Filthy Henry said, nodding his head. "That is a genuine gesture right there. See this is why I don't bother making an effort with people. It always, somehow, comes back to bite me in the ass or they just don't understand what I am trying to do."

Shelly frowned and looked back at the photograph.

"What are you talking about?" she asked him. "You just handed me a picture of your office door. How is that remotely meant to be a nice gesture?"

"Read the door," he said, tapping the picture in her hand.

Bringing the photograph up a little closer, Shelly read the letters on the door. Filthy Henry's office was modelled after the old-school detective movies. A wooden door with a frosted glass pane set in it, his name and title emblazoned on the surface in gold lettering. But the words on this door were different. Instead of reading 'Filthy Henry – The Fairy Detective' they read 'Shelly – The Other Detective'. Looking at the door more closely, Shelly could see that this was not, in fact, the door into Filthy Henry's office. It had a slightly different handle on it, one which looked brand new.

"Huh?" was all she could say, trying to process what the photograph was showing her.

"I cleared out the spare office on the ground floor," Filthy Henry said, turning back to watch more patients leave the hospital. "It had just been a dumping ground for crap anyway, can't remember the last time I even stepped foot inside it. Figured it could be put to better use if you had it as an office of your own. You know, if you want to. If not then I am sure Bunty will be happy to keep letting you use her back room."

"What office on the ground floor?"

"It had a load of boxes stacked up in front of it," the fairy detective said. "Part of my important and complicated filing system. Might have blocked the door from view, now I come to think of it. People would have thought that the front door opened up to a stairs and nothing else."

"Are you serious?"

"Of course I am," he said. "Otherwise it would be like trying to retcon a change into some established backstory, like they do with comic-books."

"I meant about the door, idiot," Shelly said.

Filthy Henry let out a small chuckle.

"We've worked enough cases now," he said. "You seemed to be doing fine without me."

She looked back at the photograph.

"Why doesn't it say 'fairy detective'?"

"That's my brand," Filthy Henry said. "You can't use it and technically I should sue you for copyright infringement. Besides 'Other' has a mystical edge to it as well."

"Or it means there is one detective in the building and this office belongs to the other one," Shelly pointed out.

"Nah, mystical. It's all about how you present it. The Other Detective. Otherworldly? Other side? Who knows. A brand you can build on. Full of mystery. Maybe even a title of a spin-off novel series, if you played your cards right. I'm sure as hell intrigued as to what the title means and I came up with it. Just no more using my title."

Shelly smiled.

"How come it only has my first name up on it?"

"Dagda above what part of 'mystery' are you not getting here? If you don't want it..." Filthy Henry said, reaching over and snatching the photograph out of her hand.

"No, no," she said, smiling more. "I love it. Thanks."

Filthy Henry did not say anything else. He gave her a quick nod of the head, turned around, and started walking down the path towards the city.

"See you tomorrow? Partner?" Shelly called after him.

"Don't push it," the fairy detective replied, not breaking his stride.

Shelly laughed. She knew before asking that would be his response and was glad that he had not disappointed her. Maybe, given a little time, things between them would be completely back to normal.

#

After they had captured Séan Chaí, ensured that everyone in the area forgot they had witnessed a genuine magical event and gotten paid by Linda, Filthy Henry had gone back to the corner of the park where they left Medb in the magical net. Somehow the slippery little rag doll of evil had broken out of her magical bonds. All that was left behind were some glowing strands of his spell and what looked her arm.

It was like a magical reproduction of *127 Hours.*

There was no sign of the devil doll anywhere nearby, meaning Medb was long gone. Looking at her arm with his fairy vision revealed nothing, no trace of magic coming from it at all. Which meant that whatever was animating the doll, keeping her essence inside it, did not get mixed into the material of the doll. At least not in a way that could be used in a tracking spell. Still, Filthy

627

Henry picked up the arm, dropped it into his pocket, and destroyed the remains of his little cage spell with a wave of his hand.

Shelly had not seen him take the arm, which was testament to how bad her detective skills actually were. But once they checked in on the patients at St. Patrick's the following morning it meant he could go back to his apartment and examine the arm further, without the risk of being interrupted.

In a way the fairy detective was jealous that Medb, a maniac from the past with a grudge, had come up with such an ingenious spirit container. Something with movable parts and created out of cloth and stuffing, making it durable to boot. Again, Filthy Henry cursed his stupid attachment to the toy detective. But those with limited magical skills could not be picky and Bunty Dooley was hardly going to assist him in the creation of a spirit container.

The arm, though, did raise an interesting possibility. A pet project of the magical persuasion that would solve one problem while presenting a benefit too.

Filthy Henry looked at the full length mirror he had placed on the opposite end of the sofa, wedged between the cushions to keep it from falling, and waved his hand.

"*Scáthán comhrá scáthán*" Filthy Henry said.

Bright blue sparks came off his fingertips, moved through the air, and hit the surface of the mirror. It rippled like water and the fairy detective's reflection changed. The mirror still showed Filthy Henry, but it was not showing him as he currently sat.

"Well that's a neat trick," the reflected fairy detective said.

"Yeah," Filthy Henry replied. "As much as I enjoy talking to voices in my head, I figured a little waste of magic would make this conversation a bit more enjoyable."

"Sure," the reflection said. "I can see that. Oh I am so punny."

Filthy Henry held up Medb's arm.

"This contained the spirit of somebody human. You're, technically, a spirit of some description. We just don't know what. I'd really like to have my head back without a lodger in it, so we need to come up with a plan."

"A timeshare out of the question?" Quinn asked, smiling from within the mirror.

"Dagda above, that smile really would grate on the nerves. Here's the deal. You could be useful for a bit. I want to offer payment. Let's come to an accord."

The reflection settled back into the sofa and pondered what had just been said.

"What's the deal?" Quinn asked.

"A few years ago I tapped into some secondary source of magic," Filthy Henry said. "You figure out how I did and why I can't any more, I will make you an animated spirit container to the best of my abilities. Meaning you get your own body."

"That's the best you can do? Make me into a living dolly? I'm alright, thanks."

Now it was the fairy detective's time to smile.

"It is either the doll or I work on a spell to expel you completely from my skull. Shine a light on the darkest corners of my mind, leaving you nowhere to hide."

Quinn was as smart as his host gave him credit for.

"Alright," he said, quickly. "You have a deal!"

#

Medb was thinking up new and unusual ways to kill Filthy Henry. Each more painful and graphic than the previous. Ages ago she had decided to use the combined power of The Bulls to

629

kill, resurrect, then kill again everyone who even slightly wronged her. It would have been the sweetest form of revenge known to any woman alive. Complete and utter control over the world and the very Laws of Nature. What more could a person want? But now, now she was concocting entirely new ways to torture the fairy detective.

They involved limbs being removed. Parts fed to animals. Limbs reattached, but in the wrong location or facing a different way. If the crone's guest had made it across, from whatever magical backwater realm it had inhabited, there would be even more choices. Entire avenues of pain to walk down. Maybe even a few body transferences.

After all, it was because of Filthy Henry that she, Queen Medb, now existed inside a rag doll. A rag doll missing an arm because, once again, the fairy detective had gotten involved in things not his concern.

She made her way through the streets of Dublin as quickly as possible. It was somewhat easy to avoid people due to the late hour, mainly because they were all back home and tucked up in bed. Keeping low, out of sight, close to the buildings, Medb ran without being seen. The joys of Dublin city meant there were very few animals, generally more attentive than people, to steer clear of. The lack of an arm made it easier to hide behind things on the street, because there was less to be hidden.

After what felt like a day, but was really under two hours, Medb returned to the Leprechaun Museum. She headed around to the rear of the building. There she spotted a little window by the office door. With two arms, Medb would have jumped and climbed up onto the sill. One hand made it a harder task. Thankfully you only needed one hand to throw things.

Medb picked up a pebble and threw it at the window. It hit the glass with a plink sound, falling back to the ground. She repeated this four more times before a light was turned on inside the building. The office window opened out and Lauren's head appeared, looking around.

"Down here," Medb said, jumping up and down on the spot.

The crone looked down at her, then passed her cane through the window down to Medb. Climbing onto it, Lauren hauled the cane back inside the building.

"What happened to you?" the crone asked, dropping Medb to the ground and closing the window.

"The fairy bloody detective, that's what happened," Medb said, padding down the hallway to the storage room. "You alone?"

Lauren, walking behind the rag doll, coughed.

"Not exactly," she said.

That was good news. It meant that the plan had worked, even with Filthy Henry getting involved at the worst possible moment.

"Great," Medb said. "I can't wait to meet the fairy that was worth all this trouble. Also can you make me a new arm? The straw is going to start coming out of this hole soon."

She nudged the storage room door open and went inside, heading for her dog basket bed. Even this, a small bed meant for pets, was just another reason to make Filthy Henry suffer a thousand times over. What queen in the history of History had ever been reduced to so lowly a station?

It was not until she flopped down onto the basket that Medb noticed the newcomer in their little hidey-hole.

He was sitting on a wooden chair, one brought in from the offices Medb assumed, tucked into the corner of the room. A wineglass in his left hand, half filled with the darkest red wine she had ever seen, while he rested his right hand on his lap. His suit was immaculate, not a crease to be seen, and utterly black. Even his shoes were polished to reflective perfection. Medb guessed that Lauren had conjured up his attire, which would

631

explain why they appeared so perfect. The black was in direct contrast to the man's skin, a pasty white colour that bordered on dead-like pallor. This was somebody who rarely, if ever, ventured out into the sun.

What bothered Medb about him, aside from the fact he was in their little sanctuary, was how he stared at her. His eyes were like that of a predator looking at a meal.

The crone shuffled into the room, closing the door behind her.

"This him?" Medb asked, pointing with her one arm at the man. "This is what we spent centuries working towards?"

"Not exactly," Lauren said, shaking her head. "The half-breed did some damage during the ritual."

Medb looked back at their silent guest.

"So this guy is…?"

"I happened to be in the right place at the wrong time," he said, smiling before taking a sip from his drink.

The liquid slowly moved around the inside of the glass, more like molasses than wine. If she could have frowned, Medb would have.

"Do you have another glass of that?"

He slowly shook his head.

"I don't believe you'd enjoy this, it is a particular vintage."

"I've soaked in some pretty nice red wine," Medb said. "What's so particular about your vintage?"

"You've soaked in Type O before?" he asked, looking momentarily confused.

"Who the hell is this guy?" Medb demanded, staring at Lauren. "I thought your fella was meant to be big and powerful. I expected horns and things."

"He was on the other side of the gateway," the crone explained. "Turns out that after he died some pact he had made kicked in. He became the Emissary for The Elven King. When the gateway was forming he was waiting, watching until it was ready. Right before it collapsed he jumped through to our side. Turns out he has a grudge with the fairy detective as well."

"Who doesn't?" the rag doll asked. "Also, I've never heard of Type O wine before."

"That's because it isn't wine," the pale man said. "It's blood. Lauren was kind enough to stop off at a blood bank on our way here. It has simply been ages since I last tasted the delicious blood of mortals."

Medb was thankful she did not have a stomach at that moment. Drinking blood was the stuff of nightmares and horror stories. Stories like the ones she had heard growing up as a young girl. Stories about creatures that shunned daylight and lived forever on the blood of mortals. Stories about...

"You're a vampire?" the rag doll asked in a whisper.

"I am," he said. "A fairly popular one as it happens."

"He was turned into one after writing a little book about them," Lauren said. "He has gone by a few names."

"But the one that I use these days is Abe St. Toker," Abe said. "And I owe Filthy Henry a very hot and fiery death."

97015856R00348

Made in the USA
Columbia, SC
12 June 2018